FOLLOWING HER BLISS?

The old red farmhouse looked the same as it had when I was a girl. I'd been back for five weeks and had worked nonstop, converting the downstairs of the house into my own designer dressmaking shop, calling it Buttons & Bows. The name of the shop was in honor of my great-grandmother and her collection of buttons.

What had been the dining room was now my cutting and work space. My five-year-old state-of-the-art digital Pfaff sewing machine and Meemaw's old Singer sat side by side on their respective sewing tables. An eight-foot-long white-topped cutting table stood in the center of the room, unused as of yet. Meemaw had one old dress form, which I'd dragged down from the attic. I'd splurged and had bought two more, anticipating a brisk dressmaking business, which had yet to materialize.

I adjusted my square-framed glasses before pulling a needle through the pants leg. Gripping the thick synthetic fabric sent a shiver through me akin to fingernails scraping down a chalkboard. Bliss was not a mecca of fashion; so far I'd been asked to hem polyester pants, shorten the sleeves of polyester jackets, and repair countless other polyester garments. No one had hired me to design matching mother and daughter couture frocks, create a slinky dress for a night out on the town in Dallas, or anything else remotely challenging or interesting.

I kept the faith, though. Meemaw wouldn't have brought me back home just to watch me fail.

Pleating for Mercy

A MAGICAL DRESSMAKING MYSTERY

Melissa Bourbon

AN OBSIDIAN MYSTERY

OBSIDIAN
Published by New American Library, a division of
Penguin Group (USA) Inc., 375 Hudson Street,
New York, New York 10014, USA
Penguin Group (Canada), 90 Eglinton Avenue East, Suite 700, Toronto,
Ontario M4P 2Y3, Canada (a division of Pearson Penguin Canada Inc.)
Penguin Books Ltd., 80 Strand, London WC2R 0RL, England
Penguin Ireland, 25 St. Stephen's Green, Dublin 2,
Ireland (a division of Penguin Books Ltd.)
Penguin Group (Australia), 250 Camberwell Road, Camberwell, Victoria 3124,
Australia (a division of Pearson Australia Group Pty. Ltd.)
Penguin Books India Pvt. Ltd., 11 Community Centre, Panchsheel Park,
New Delhi - 110 017, India
Penguin Group (NZ), 67 Apollo Drive, Rosedale, Auckland 0632,
New Zealand (a division of Pearson New Zealand Ltd.)
Penguin Books (South Africa) (Pty.) Ltd., 24 Sturdee Avenue,
Rosebank, Johannesburg 2196, South Africa

Penguin Books Ltd., Registered Offices:
80 Strand, London WC2R 0RL, England

First published by Obsidian, an imprint of New American Library,
a division of Penguin Group (USA) Inc.

First Printing, August 2011
10 9 8 7 6 5 4 3 2 1

This book is dedicated to all the quilters and seamstresses in my life, past, present, and future, including, but not limited to:

My great-great-grandmothers, Susan Elizabeth Townsend Sears and Texana de Lavan Montgomery; my great-grandmothers, Coleta Frances Montgomery Sears and Bertha Archer Massie; my great-great-aunt May (Montgomery) McDaniel; my great-aunts Marjorie Sears Cranford Yowell and Lucy (Melba Lucille) Sears Miller; my aunt Judy Bourbon Dewey; my grandmothers, Laverne Valentine Massie Sears and Winifred Helen Conrath Bourbon; my sewing nieces, Georgina, Paskalina, and Liet Bourbon; my daughter, Sophia Tess Massie Ramirez, with all my love; and especially to my mother, Marilyn LaVerne Sears Bourbon for passing on to me all the wisdom of those who came before.

ACKNOWLEDGMENTS

When I was an elementary schoolgirl, my mother began teaching me to sew. By the time I was in sixth grade, I'd completed my first solo project: a dress with two different fabrics and buttons. I still remember the pride I felt showing it to her ... and how proud she was of me. Because she taught me to sew, something I continue to do today, I was able to create Harlow Cassidy's world ... and loved every minute of it. For that, Mom, I'll be forever grateful.

Writing a book is not a solo venture by any stretch of the imagination ... and as a writer, my imagination is great! Thanks to my mother and father, who are always my biggest supporters, and to my family for helping me make my writing dreams come true.

Thanks, also, to Holly Root for her continued support and belief in my career, to Kerry Donovan for her faith in Harlow Cassidy and her dressmaking world and for her fantastic editing, and to Jan McInroy for her careful eye and attention to detail. Also, a deep Southern curtsy to the NAL team, especially to the artists for bringing a corner of Buttons & Bows to life. Nana's goat absolutely speaks to me!

A big thanks goes to John Kelsey for his lawyerly advice and for planting the Godfather seed in my brain, and to Anne Jones at Latte Da Dairy for sharing her love of goats with me.

Finally, giants hugs to my blogging buddies, LA Lopez, Heather Webber, DD Scott, and Tonya Kappes—you make blogging so fun!—and to my critique partners, Beatriz Terrazas, Wendy Lyn Watson, Mary Malcolm, Marty Tidwell, Jill Wilson, Jessica Davidson, and Tracy Ward. This journey is so much better with all of you by my side.

Pleating for
Mercy

Chapter 1

Rumors about the Cassidy women and their magic had long swirled through Bliss, Texas, like a gathering tornado. For 150 years, my family had managed to dodge most of the rumors, brushing off the idea that magic infused their handwork, and chalking up any unusual goings-on to coincidence.

But *we* all knew that the magic started the very day Butch Cassidy, my great-great-great-grandfather, turned his back to an ancient Argentinean fountain, dropped a gold coin into it, and made a wish. The Cassidy family legend says he asked for his firstborn child, and all who came after, to live a charmed life, the threads of good fortune, talent, and history flowing like magic from their fingertips.

That magic spilled through the female descendants of the Cassidy line into their handmade tapestries and homespun wool, crewel embroidery and perfectly pieced and stitched quilts. And into my dressmaking. It connected us to our history, and to one another.

His wish also gifted some of his descendants with their own special charms. Whatever Meemaw, my great-grandmother, wanted, she got. My grandmother Nana was a goat-whisperer. Mama's green thumb could make anything grow.

Yet no matter how hard we tried to keep our magic on the down-low—so we wouldn't wind up in our own contemporary Texas version of the Salem Witch Trials—people noticed. And they talked.

The townsfolk came to Mama when their crops wouldn't grow. They came to Nana when their goats wouldn't behave. And they came to Meemaw when they wanted something so badly they couldn't see straight. I was seventeen when I finally realized that what Butch had really given the women in my family was a thread that connected them with others.

But Butch's wish had apparently exhausted itself before I was born. I had no special charm, and I'd always felt as if a part of me was missing because of it.

Moving back home to Bliss made the feeling stronger.

Meemaw had been gone five months now, but the old red farmhouse just off the square at 2112 Mockingbird Lane looked the same as it had when I was a girl. The steep pitch of the roof, the shuttered windows, the old pecan tree shading the left side of the house—it all sent me reeling back to my childhood and all the time I'd spent here with her.

I'd been back for five weeks and had worked nonstop, converting the downstairs of the house into my own designer dressmaking shop, calling it Buttons & Bows. The name of the shop was in honor of my great-grandmother and her collection of buttons.

What had been Loretta Mae's dining room was now my cutting and work space. My five-year-old state-of-the-art digital Pfaff sewing machine and Meemaw's old Singer sat side by side on their respective sewing tables. An eight-foot-long white-topped cutting table stood in the center of the room, unused as of yet. Meemaw had one old dress form, which I'd dragged down from the attic. I'd splurged and bought two more, anticipating a brisk dressmaking business, which had yet to materialize.

I'd taken to talking to her during the dull spots in my days. "Meemaw," I said now, sitting in my workroom, hemming a pair of pants, "it's lonesome without you. I sure wish you were here."

A breeze suddenly blew in through the screen, fluttering the butter yellow sheers that hung on either side of the window as if Meemaw could hear me from the spirit world. It was no secret that she'd wanted me back in Bliss. Was it so far-fetched to think she'd be hanging around now that she'd finally gotten what she'd wanted?

I adjusted my square-framed glasses before pulling a needle through the pants leg. Gripping the thick synthetic fabric sent a shiver through me akin to fingernails scraping down a chalkboard. Bliss was not a mecca of fashion; so far I'd been asked to hem polyester pants, shorten the sleeves of polyester jackets, and repair countless other polyester garments. No one had hired me to design matching mother and daughter couture frocks, create a slinky dress for a night out on the town in Dallas, or anything else remotely challenging or interesting.

I kept the faith, though. Meemaw wouldn't have brought me back home just to watch me fail.

As I finished the last stitch and tied off the thread, a flash of something outside caught my eye. I looked past the French doors that separated my work space from what had been Meemaw's gathering room and was now the boutique portion of Buttons & Bows. The window gave a clear view of the front yard, the wisteria climbing up the sturdy trellis archway, and the street beyond. Just as I was about to dismiss it as my imagination, the bells I'd hung from the doorknob on a ribbon danced in a jingling frenzy and the front door flew open. I jumped, startled, dropping the slacks but still clutching the needle.

A woman sidled into the boutique. Her dark hair was pulled up into a messy but trendy bun and I noticed that her eyes were red and tired-looking despite the heavy makeup she wore. She had on jean shorts, a snap-front top that she'd gathered and tied in a knot below her breastbone, and wedge-heeled shoes. With her thumbs crooked in her back pockets and the way she sashayed across the room, she reminded me of Daisy Duke—with a muffin top.

Except for the Gucci bag slung over her shoulder. That purse was the real deal and had cost more than two thousand dollars, or I wasn't Harlow Jane Cassidy.

A deep frown tugged at the corners of her shimmering

pink lips as she scanned the room. "Huh—this isn't at all what I pictured."

Not knowing what she'd pictured, I said, "Can I help you?"

"Just browsing," she said with a dismissive wave. She sauntered over to the opposite side of the room, where a matching olive green and gold paisley damask sofa and love seat snuggled in one corner. They'd been the nicest pieces of furniture Loretta Mae had owned and some of the few pieces I'd kept. I'd added a plush red velvet settee and a coffee table to the grouping. It was the consultation area of the boutique—though I'd yet to use it.

The woman bypassed the sitting area and went straight for the one-of-a-kind Harlow Cassidy creations that hung on a portable garment rack. She gave a low whistle as she ran her hand from one side to the other, fanning the sleeves of the pieces. "Did you make all of these?"

"I sure did," I said, preening just a tad. Buttons & Bows was a custom boutique, but I had a handful of items leftover from my time in L.A. and New York to display and I'd scrambled to create samples to showcase.

She turned, peering over her shoulder and giving me a once-over. "You don't *look* like a fashion designer."

I pushed my glasses onto the top of my head so I could peer back at her, which served to hold my curls away from my face. Well, *she* didn't look like she could afford a real Gucci, I thought, but I didn't say it. Meemaw had always taught me not to judge a book by its cover. If this woman dragged around an expensive designer purse in little ol' Bliss, she very well might need a fancy gown for something, *and* be able to pay for it.

I balled my fists, jerking when I accidentally pricked my palm with the needle I still held. My smile tightened—from her attitude as well as from the lingering sting on my hand—as I caught a quick glimpse of myself in the freestanding oval mirror next to the garment rack. I looked comfortable and stylish, not an easy accomplishment. Designer jeans. White blouse and color-blocked black-and-white jacket—made by me. Sandals with two-inch heels that probably cost more than this woman's entire wardrobe. Not that I'd had to pay for them, mind you. Even a bottom-of-the-ladder fashion designer employed by Maximilian got to shop at the company's end-of-season sales, which meant fabulous clothes and accessories at a steal. It was a perk I was going to sorely miss.

I kept my voice pleasant despite the bristling sensation I felt creep up inside me. "Sorry to disappoint. What does a fashion designer look like?"

She shrugged, a new strand of hair falling from the clip at the back of her head and framing her face. "Guess I thought you'd look all done up, ya know? Or be a gay man." She tittered.

Huh. She had a point about the gay man thing. "Are you looking for anything in particular? Buttons and Bows is a custom boutique. I design garments specifically for the customer. Other than those items," I said, gesturing to the dresses she was flipping through, "it's not an off-the-rack shop."

Before she could respond, the bells jingled again and the door banged open, hitting the wall. I made a mental note to get a spring or a doorstop. There were a million things to fix around the old farmhouse. The list was already as long as my arm.

A woman stood in the doorway, the bright light from outside sneaking in around her, creating her silhouette. "Harlow Cassidy!" she cried out. "I didn't believe it could really be true, but it is! Oh, thank God! I desperately need your help!"

Chapter 2

I *knew* that voice. Recollection tickled the edge of my brain. I forgot about Daisy Duke and walked toward the door. It took a second, and then it came to me. Josephine Sandoval. She'd been a year behind me in elementary school and had spent second grade following me around telling me that she wished she could be part of the Cassidy family. *"Josie?"*

She stepped inside and I could see that she was nodding, but before I could get a look at the woman Josie'd grown to be, two more women elbowed their way in behind her, shoving her forward. Her feet tangled and she lost her balance, crashing into me.

My arms flew up to block the impact, but she kept coming. I felt resistance as the needle I was still holding plunged into her arm.

She screeched. "Ow!"

"Oh! Oh!" I pried her grip from my arm, pushed her off of me, and pulled the tip of the needle out of her flesh. Her hand flew up and a cluster of beaded bracelets slid down her arm as her fingertips pressed against the microscopic wound.

A cacophony of high-pitched voices came all at once. "Are you all right?" one of the women asked, her voice rising above the others. They'd surrounded us like clucking hens.

"I'm fine, I'm fine," she said, backing away from me. "Are *you* okay, Harlow?"

I looked around for a place to ditch the needle. There was a puffy pink pincushion on top of the antique secretary desk just outside the workroom. I didn't remember setting it there, but I quickly stabbed my needle into it and turned back to the women. "I'm okay." I squinted at the bubble of blood on Josie's arm. "Do you need a bandage?"

She shook her head. "It's fine." Her face broke into a toothy smile. "I can't believe it's really true. I told Loretta Mae how great it would be if you came back. We talked about it just before she passed." She paused, quickly crossing herself, from forehead to breastbone, left shoulder to right. "God rest her soul." She hurried on. "She came into Seed-n-Bead—that's where I work— and I told her I wished you would come back to Bliss. And do you know what she told me? She said, "Josie, honey, don't fret. Harlow's on her way back.""

I stared. "Really? She said that?"

"Exactly that," Josie confirmed. "I'm not surprised she was right. She was always right."

More proof that Loretta Mae Cassidy really did have the gift of foresight and knew what would happen long before it ever did.

I'd listened intently to Josie's rapid narrative, all the while taking a better look at her. She was a little shorter than my five feet seven inches. Her coffee-colored hair hit just past her shoulders. She had full cheeks and was rounder than I remembered, and also prettier. She was very Jennifer Lopez, all womanly curves, and those curves were in all the right places.

The other two women looked vaguely familiar, but I couldn't place them. "This is Karen," Josie said, gesturing to the shorter woman on her right, "and this is Ruthann." Ruthann unwound the Grace Kelly scarf she had draped over her head and tucked it into her purse. She was tall, probably five feet eleven inches. Perfect bone structure and not an ounce of fat on her body. She could have made it as a model if she'd been twelve instead of thirtysomething. Karen, on the other hand, was the complete opposite. Five-five, round, but without the perfect curves that Josie was blessed with, and flyaway hair that hadn't been protected from the wind.

I kept *my* hair in two ponytails just below my ears most of the time so I didn't have to fuss with it. Like all the Cassidy women, I had thick chestnut ringlets with distinct streaks of blond woven throughout, one quite prominent strip right in front, like the stripe of a skunk. Not even a sophisticated Jackie O or Princess Grace scarf would keep it tamed.

"Nice to meet you—"

"We went to school together," Karen said with a little laugh. "Karen Lowe. Now Mitchell. Guess I wasn't too memorable."

Like all Cassidy women, I'd kept to myself in high school to stay under the radar, not that I had anything to hide or a secret to protect. I smiled as big as I could, waving away her comment. "Karen Lowe! Of course. It's been a long time." Almost fourteen years, to be exact. I'd left for college when I was almost twenty.

We chatted for a few minutes before Ruthann, who was perched on the edge of the settee and looked like she belonged in the swanky Preston Hollow neighborhood of Dallas, asked, "What brought you back here?"

I spread my arms wide. "Seems my great-grandmother deeded the house to me on the day I was born. I've owned this place all my life and I never knew it."

"Your mother didn't want to move in instead? So you could stay in New York?" Ruthann, with her perfectly coiffed hair and neat-as-a-pin summer dress, asked the question so innocently. Little did she know that life in New York was no picnic.

"No." I shook my head, remembering the conversation I'd had with my mother. "Harlow Jane," she'd said to me over the phone when I'd asked her that very question, "when you were born, Meemaw took one look at your face and she said she could see your whole life laid out. She put your name on the deed that very day. She said that that old house was your future. 'She might not understand it at first, Tessa Cassidy,' she told me, 'but one day she will.'"

"So you quit your job in New York and moved back here, huh?" The voice came from behind me.

"Nell!" Josie jumped up as the Daisy Duke look-alike joined the group around the coffee table. "You're here!" She turned to me. "So you've met?"

Daisy, who I now knew was Nell, had practically disappeared into the rack of clothes and I'd forgotten all about her. "Not officially," I said, and I thought to myself what a misfit group of friends Josie had.

"Nell Gellen, Harlow Cassidy," Josie said. We nodded at each other, and Josie went on. "Nell owns Seed-n-Bead."

I had to force my mouth not to drop open in surprise. This *really* did not compute. Josie, with her full white skirt and springlike yellow top, looked crisp and together. *She* looked like a store owner. Nell, on the other hand, looked like she'd ridden into town on the back of a hay truck. "I love beads," I said, trying to remember that things are not always as they seem.

Sitting back on the paisley couch, I crossed my legs. Hopefully they had some dressmaking need I could fulfill. "So, what can I do for you ladies?" I asked when the chattering had died down.

I might as well have opened the floodgates of a dam. They all began talking at once, each voice straining to be the loudest. My head jerked from one moving mouth to the next, trying to figure out which one I should be listening to.

A shrill whistle broke through the noise. Josie was next to me on the couch and had her thumb and index finger in her mouth. She let out another high-pitched sound. "Shut it!" she shouted and, amazingly, they did. "Harlow," she said turning to face me.

I leaned forward. "Yes?"

"I'm getting married."

From the way she'd blurted the news to the way her frenzied hands twisted around each other as she spoke, I didn't know whether to congratulate her or say I was sorry.

But Karen laughed, clapping her hands, and I noticed the nondescript wedding band on her left hand. *Mitchell*, I mused. I couldn't remember any Mitchells from school. I felt disconnected from my hometown. "So exciting!" she said.

Nell nodded. She'd tucked one heeled foot up under her on the love seat and her lips curved into a pleased, if subdued, little smile. Ruthann sat primly on the settee. Her ring finger was bare, but her smile looked genuine. As different as they were, they all seemed happy for Josie.

A little thrill went through me. A wedding! The idea of catering to brides hadn't occurred to me, but now the possibility circled in my head. Vera Wang hadn't started making wedding gowns until she was thirty-nine! I was only thirty-three. *And* I didn't need or want Vera's level of success. I'd be happy making a comfortable living doing what I loved to do. If I made a small, or maybe medium, mark on the fashion world, that would be the gravy on my biscuits.

Maybe Josie had some sort of family heirloom dress she needed altered. Or maybe it was just a small job. Sleeves she wanted removed or a train shortened. It didn't matter. Even a small job was better than no job. My foot started tapping on the floor. There were so many possibilities.

"Congratulations," I said calmly. I didn't want to scare them off with my eagerness. "When's the big day?"

"Assuming he doesn't break her heart, you mean," Nell said under her breath.

My chin snapped up and I met her steady gaze. Josie, Ruthann, and Karen didn't look like they'd heard her, but I had. It was as though she'd whispered the words right into my ear. But she went on, casually resting one arm across the back of the love seat and the other on the armrest, and I wondered if I'd imagined it. After all, why would a man break his fiancée's heart?

"It's on the twenty-fourth ... a little less than two weeks away," Josie deadpanned, and just like that, all the air was suddenly sucked out of the room.

"Less than two weeks?" I repeated when I'd found my voice again.

Josie nodded, frowning. "Have you heard of the Bridal Outlet?"

Her friends, as if on cue, all groaned.

The Bridal Outlet. It didn't ring a bell. "No," I said.

"*Hate* that place," Karen said, her freckled forehead crinkling.

Ruthann grimaced. "Highway robbery."

Nell had turned her attention to the knot on her blouse. She'd undone it, and was rolling up the excess fabric, tying it again. "Lying lowlifes," she muttered.

"It's a bridal shop in Fort Worth—"

"Was," Nell corrected, her eyes still cast downward.

"Right," Josie said. "Was."

I put one and one together and deduced that the Bridal Outlet had done a number on Josie. "Let me guess. It went out of business?"

Josie stared. "How'd you know?"

"Just a hunch," I said, not telling her that it was far more common than people realized. Small businesses started up and failed in less time than it took to stock up on supplies at the nearest warehouse store. Bridal shops were particularly vulnerable since the bridal industry was seasonal.

Karen snapped her fingers. "It happened just like that. One day they were there, and the next day they were gone. It's so unfair."

So Josie probably needed me to finish up the alterations on her wedding gown. A small job, after all.

"I'm getting married in twelve days," Josie said, her voice rising to near hysteria, "and I don't have a dress!"

My thoughts came to a screeching halt. "What do you mean you don't have a dress?"

"No bridal gown, no bridesmaid dresses, no nothing!" Josie clutched at the arm of the sofa. She breathed in and out through her nose. "See?" she said when she'd calmed down. "It's like I jinxed myself when I told Loretta Mae about the wedding and said I wished you were here, but now you *are* here, so it'll all be okay." She winked. "Not that I ever should have doubted Loretta Mae. You can do it, right?"

They all stared expectantly at me. It felt like we were playing connect the dots, it was my turn, and a number was missing from the picture. I leaned forward. "Do *what*?"

Josie grabbed my hand and angled her head toward her bridesmaids. "Make our dresses," she said. "I've been all over tarnation and there isn't a single gown that'll work. It all has to be just perfect." She took my hand in hers and met my eyes. "You know," she added, "I'm marrying Nate Kincaid. Of the Hood County Kincaids?"

A lightbulb went off in my head. "Ah," I said. And suddenly I understood perfectly.

Chapter 3

I never would have put Nate Kincaid and Josie Sandoval together as a couple. The Kincaids of Hood County were one of the oldest families in Bliss and Josie was from the wrong side of the tracks, an unfortunate fact I could relate to. I'd dated Derek Kincaid, Nate's older brother. The breakup had been ugly.

"Show her the ring," Ruthann said, nudging Josie's arm.

Josie's rosy cheeks brightened. She held her arm out, dangling her hand.

It was a platinum band with a single princess-cut diamond. Light seemed to bounce up through the cut, highlighting its brilliance. "It's perfect."

"Isn't it?" Karen gazed at it from over Josie's shoulder. "It was Nate's grandmother's."

"So much better than the first one," Nell said.

"The first one?"

Josie's blush deepened. "Nate was trying to impress me."

Nell tilted her head to the side. "He got this amazing diamond and had a ring made for her. Spectacular. Huge radiant-cut rock and a bunch of little diamonds in a channel setting. That ring was gorgeous—"

"But Josie didn't like it," Karen said, shaking her head like she still couldn't believe it. "That diamond . . . What was it, like three carats?"

Josie looked like she wanted to disappear. "It wasn't *me*. I'm not all highbrow—"

"You're just a small-town girl," Ruthann said with a laugh. "You sure you should marry a Kincaid?"

"Very funny," Josie said. "Of course I'm sure. Nate totally understood. His dad took it back and said not to worry."

"This one is absolutely you," Ruthann finished, holding up Josie's left hand. The ring was simple, but brilliant and sparkling. Size, it turned out, didn't matter.

The next hour passed in a blur. Three women who were out for a stroll around the town square and had heard about Buttons & Bows blew into the shop. I excused myself from Josie and her entourage to answer a slew of questions from them. *How would you describe your style? What actresses have you designed dresses for? Have you had a dress on the red carpet at the Oscars?*

I answered as best I could, listening to each group with one ear until Lori Kincaid, Josie's soon-to-be mother-in-law, waltzed in, another woman by her side. She turned and waved out the door, a signal to her driver that she'd be a little while, no doubt. Then she put her arm through Josie's. They chatted quietly, and I heard her say, "Are you sure about this?"

Josie's expression clouded. "Of course I'm sure. Harlow's all set—"

"There's a bridal show in Fort Worth this weekend," Mrs. Kincaid said, interrupting her. "It might be fun to go, don't you think? And you might find something you adore." She turned to the bridesmaids. "Nell, dear, are you available Saturday?"

Nell stared, lips parted. She seemed at a loss for words, but finally found her voice. "Um, no. Sorry. I have plans on Saturday."

Mrs. Kincaid gave an encouraging smile. "But we can make a day of it," she nudged. "We could have lunch at Reata in Sundance Square. Karen, Ruthann, have you been there?"

Ruthann piped up. "I have."

"Not me," Karen said, "but my husband's been plenty of times for work. He loves it."

"Nell?" Mrs. Kincaid asked.

Nell had started riffling through the rack of ready-to-wear separates. "Don't think so," she said over her shoulder. "Mrs. Abernathy, what do you think of this?" she called to Mrs. Kincaid's friend.

The woman wrinkled her nose. "Pardon me?" she said, as if she could hardly stand to utter two words to Nell.

Nell held out a dress I'd created using Escher as inspiration. It was an architectural design with an optical illusion effect. Black and white and a definite mixed bag of textiles and textures.

Mrs. Abernathy coughed, scoffed, and turned her back on Nell.

"Really, Nell," Mrs. Kincaid scolded. She looked her up and down and frowned. "It takes time and effort to maintain an image. It's like a house of cards. One bent corner, and the whole thing comes toppling down. Helen Abernathy is *not* going to throw away her reputation by wearing a dress like that."

Nell's nostrils flared like a bull facing a matador, but Josie stepped in before anybody charged. "We can go to lunch at Reata sometime, Lori," she said hurriedly, "but there just isn't time before the wedding. Harlow will need us all around for fittings—"

"Fine." Lori Kincaid's expression turned to stone. With a stiff spine, she glided over to study the pictures on the display wall. I'd used a rectangular sheet of galvanized steel and trimmed it with a length of spectacular black beaded cording I'd found in Meemaw's collection. Photographs of models wearing my designs, or ones I'd worked on, were held in place on the wall by tiny magnetic dots.

Mrs. Kincaid seemed to be taking in every last detail of my work, from my construction and technique to my creative flair, comparing it all to whatever high-priced Dallas designer she favored. I suddenly realized she needed to give her blessing before I could go forward with the dresses.

She turned to me a moment later, smiling. "These are quite lovely."

I released the breath I'd been holding and a wave of surprise flowed through me. Blessing given. And not a speck of worry on her face over some imaginary curse I might put on her. Maybe rumors about the Cassidy women had finally stopped. "Thank you."

A happy feeling settled over the shop as another handful of women—more of Josie's friends, her mother, and another woman I took to be an aunt or a family friend—popped into the shop. I explained to my captive audience that no, I'd never had one of my designs worn to the Oscars, and no, I had no plans to go on *Project Runway*, but yes, to see Heidi Klum in one of my designs would be like a dream come true.

The front door opened again, the faint jingling of the bells making me wonder what the fire code for occupancy was. The room suddenly went completely silent. I followed the gazes of the fifteen or so people in the shop, stopping for a second when I thought I recognized Miriam Kincaid, Josie's soon-to-be sister-in-law. A squeal broke the silence; then a blur passed in front of me, pulling my attention away from the crowd that had gathered. It was Josie racing toward the man now leaning in at the door. He hesitated, as if he was afraid of actually setting foot inside such a girlie shop, but she threw her arms around him and practically dragged him across the threshold.

I searched his face for signs of familiarity. His blond hair was short and spiky on top and neatly trimmed; he was clean shaven and his chin was solidly marked by a vertical cleft. It looked like the perfect spot to rest a thumb. If a thumb needed resting, that is. His complexion was slightly ruddy, but it worked for him. Not drop-dead gorgeous, but handsome enough. He looked an awful lot like I remembered Derek looking. This must be Nate Kincaid.

His look of discomfort threw me for a loop. Would the idea of being inside Buttons & Bows be that disconcerting to every man, or was it just Nate Kincaid? I glanced at the room, saw Lori Kincaid again, and realized that my eyes had played a trick on me. Miriam wasn't here, but the mother and daughter looked an awful lot alike ... at least from what I remembered of Miriam.

The disarray in the room stirred up a ball of anxiety in my gut. A small box was overturned on the coffee table, buttons spilling onto the floor. Rolls of trims and spools of ribbons that had been neatly lined up on a shelf against the wall were scattered around. Pillows had fallen off the couch and instead of picking them up, the excited wedding party stepped over them.

My head swirled. When had I lost control of my shop?

"I'm sorry. What?" I said, realizing that one of the women I'd been talking with was beckoning to me.

Mrs. Zinnia James was pointing to one of the pictures on the design board behind the love seat.

"This is just lovely," she said again.

It was a novelty dress that Maximilian had designed for an Earth Day fashion show the previous year. "That's made entirely of recycled mater—"

I stopped short as a loud bang shook the wall between the workroom and the boutique, quickly followed by the unmistakable sound of shattering glass.

Chapter 4

"No! Oh, crap!" someone yelled from the workroom. "No, no, no."

My heart stopped. Meemaw's old Singer was in there, as well as jar after jar of buttons, trims, and other notions. "Excuse me," I cried over my shoulder to Zinnia James and her friends as I rushed to the workroom. I stopped short at the French doors, barely managing to stifle the scream that climbed up my throat. It looked like the room had been the victim of an isolated earthquake. Buttons, mixed with the chunky glass pieces of the broken jars, splayed across the floor.

For just a moment the boutique was utterly silent. I could have heard an antique button drop. But like a funnel cloud slowly swirling and building strength, the silence transitioned into a low prattle that then grew into a frenzied chatter.

"Nell!" Josie's voice rose above the jabbering. "Are you okay?"

Nell stood like a wax statue in the middle of the mess, looking more than a little shell-shocked. The antique shelf now resembled the Leaning Tower of Pisa. Buttons and glass were fanned out on the pecan-planked floor around her, a lone mason jar of colorful buttons in one of her hands.

She nodded, her expression going from stunned to sheepish to indignant in the blink of an eye. "I was just looking at your collection," she said. "Then *bam!* It collapsed, just like that! Piece of crap," she muttered, setting the jar on the ground. "It's a hazard in here. No wonder people say to watch out for the Cassidys," she said under her breath.

I bristled, quickly glancing around to see if anyone was listening. The last thing I needed was rumors about Buttons & Bows being dangerous or run-down—or about magic happenings in the shop. I guessed the Cassidy legacy lived on after all.

The women in the front room must have been straining to overhear us, but they never broke from their conversations. I sighed. If there was going to be fallout, there was nothing I could do about it now.

The mess in my workroom danced before my eyes. I couldn't even begin to understand how it had happened, but the rickety piece of furniture had definitely gone rogue. It looked like the front right leg of the antique piece had been shot out of a cannon, landing on the opposite side of the room. I added the dent it had left in the wall and repairing the shelf to my list of work to be done.

But in business, the customer is always right. Not always easy to embrace, but I stuck to it. A lawsuit would put me out of business before I ever really started. "I'm so sorry!" I gushed, truly hoping she wasn't hurt.

Nell's shoulders relaxed, but her expression was still strained and she bit down on her bottom lip. "I'm fine. No harm, no foul." She looked like the Tin Man as she carefully moved one limb at a time, reached for her Gucci bag, and began crunching across the button, glass, and ribbon minefield. The smaller chunks of glass crackled under her feet. She glanced over her shoulder at the mess. At least three, maybe four, large mason jars were broken to bits. "If you have a broom, I'll—"

I waved the offer away. "Don't worry about it. I'll take care of it." While I spoke, I mentally subtracted the hours it would take to painstakingly separate the buttons from the glass debris and clean the room from the hours I had available to make the four dresses for Josie and Nate's wedding. The clock was ticking.

"I don't mind—"

"You're bleeding." A thin ribbon of red trailed down Nell's shin. "Let me get you a bandage for that."

"But—"

"I'll sweep up," Karen said, jumping into action.

"Are you sure? I can—"

"No, I got it." She asked for the broom.

"There's a little closet next to the refrigerator," I told her, and she scurried off in the direction I pointed.

"I have a bandage," Ruthann said, leading Nell to the settee. Her knockoff Prada bag sat on the coffee table. She grabbed it and started rummaging.

"This is ridiculous," Nell said. "I can help." She started to get up, but Ruthann gently pushed her back down. "You're bleeding! Let Karen take care of it."

Karen came back with the broom, dustpan, and plastic grocery bags and got straight to work sweeping up the mess of glass and buttons. The ladies in the shop had all gone back to whispering.

My nice little dressmaking boutique suddenly had an aura of mystery about it. All these people milled around, but only a few of them had business here. I wished they'd all leave so I could put the shop back to rights and get to work planning the bridal party's dresses.

Josie must have felt the same thing. Within a few minutes, Nate left, and she led her mother and another woman to the front door. "We can wait for you," her mom said in halting English. She and Josie were the same height, but where the younger Sandoval was curvy, the older one was more of an apple shape. Her rounded top half balanced on skinny legs and she looked like she might topple over at any moment. Her smile was cautious, like she wasn't sure what to make of the grand wedding her daughter was planning.

"It's okay, Mom," Josie said, tugging the front door open and sending the bells hanging from the knob into another jingling frenzy. "I'm going back to the store for a while, and then Nell and I are coming back here so Harlow can take our measurements. Nell said she'll drop me at home later."

"*Sí*, Nell? You bring Josie home?" Mrs. Sandoval called from the door.

Nell sat on the couch looking pensive, her hand on her bandage. "No problem."

Mrs. Sandoval nodded. "*Gracias,*" she said as she left.

Karen came out of the workroom frowning and wiping her brow. She held the broom and dustpan in one hand, a loaded plastic grocery bag in the other. Her frown vanished when she saw me. "I found this in the cupboard," she said, indicating the two-handled bag. "Wasn't sure what you wanted to do with it all. I can take it out to the garbage—"

"Oh, no. They're my grandmother's buttons. I'll sort through them. After the wedding," I added with a wink. I slipped my hand through the handle, taking the bag from her. Relief flowed through me. Karen was a pioneer woman. She'd dug in and had gotten to work, simply doing the job that needed to be done. "I can't thank you enough."

"No problem," she said. Watching her walk off to the kitchen to put the broom and dustpan away, I could envision how the dress I'd make for her would swish as she walked.

I quickly set the bag of buttons and glass in the corner behind the couch, then snapped up my sketchbook from the coffee table. Time slipped away as I drew with precise strokes of my fine-tipped pen. Karen's dress needed to soften the hard edges of her jaw and draw in the thickness of her middle, giving her more of a waist. If it hit just above the knee, it would give the illusion of height. A little flare at the hemline would make it flirty. I could see the completed picture in my head like a snapshot of a finished piece.

I paused at the details of the bodice. Pleats or tucks? Pleats, angled in a V, would work, but I hesitated. My pen hovered over the paper. No. Pleats weren't right for Karen. Tucks would bring the eye down, making her look slimmer and taller. I added the vertical lines to the sketch.

The back door slammed and Josie appeared right behind Ruthann, two bricks in her hands. I hadn't even realized they'd gone outside. How long had I been in my creative zone? "I found these on the side of the house," Josie said. "Maybe they can hold up the shelf? For now anyway."

"Brilliant!" I closed the sketchbook and went to help her. Ruthann joined us and together we lifted one side of the shelf while Josie slid the bricks under the corner. It wobbled slightly, but was stable enough to work until I could get it fixed properly.

We chatted for a while longer until I felt sure I knew enough about how Josie pictured her dream gown. Time was short. I'd be able to dig out swatches of sample fabrics to show Josie when she and Nell came back.

After they'd all gone, I went back to my sketches. I'd envisioned Ruthann's bridesmaid dress the moment Josie said she needed dresses for her bridal party. A simple, elegant sheath with darts to give shape to her thin body, cut above the knee, a V neck in the front and a lower V plunging halfway down her back. I'd seen the allure of the wraparound concept she favored, but I kept coming back to the sheath. I filed both away for now, unsure which direction to go.

The other mystery was Nell. Her Gucci purse, her jean shorts and plaid shirt, her diamond earrings and her haphazardly pulled-up hair all puzzled me. I couldn't put my finger on her style. I wondered if *she* knew her style.

Next to me on the couch was the pile of swatches she'd been looking at. They were all silks and taffetas. On top was a square of plaid cotton, the edges zigzagged with pinking shears. The colors—rust, blue, and off-white—were masculine. I picked it up, turning it over as if there'd be a message on the back telling me how it had gotten mixed up with the dress fabrics.

Of course there was no such message. Finally, I tossed it into the old embossed tin box sitting in the middle of the coffee table and went back to my designs. I still had time to think on Nell's dress. I had to start with Josie's gown anyway, making a pattern and a muslin sample before I could even consider beginning the others.

At first, Josie had said she wanted cap sleeves, but the wedding was in late April and the weather was already turning warm. My instincts told me that she would really prefer strapless, and I started a new sketch, this time with no sleeves. I drew in a very subtle sweetheart neckline and a dropped waist. I added side draping on the skirt. Beaded floral embellishments at the waist. It would have to be lined. Zipper in the back. I jotted notes down next to the final sketch.

On and on I went, replaying everything the four women had said until I felt completely confident that Josie would love what I'd come up with. Only Nell's comment about Nate breaking Josie's heart nagged at me. I couldn't help worrying about why she believed he might.

Chapter 5

All the Cassidy women have an affinity for fabrics and trims. It's in our blood, just as sure as Butch Cassidy's charm runs through our veins. The attic in the old farmhouse on Mockingbird Lane held stacks of neatly folded fabric that had belonged to the Cassidy women through the generations, dating back to my great-great-great-grandmother and Butch Cassidy's love, Texana Harlow. The hundred or so mason jars upstairs were filled with buttons, ribbons, and trims, a collection that had been added to by all the Cassidy women. Aside from spending time in the attic, surrounded by the things that bound me to them all, I felt closest to Meemaw when I was in her kitchen. The distressed pale yellow cabinets, the reused red brick on either side of the deep, white farmhouse sink, the large red-and-white checkerboard-patterned curtain on a pressure rod below the sink, and the copper pots and pans hanging from an exposed beam above the long pine farm table had been her vision. Even though it belonged to me now, it was still hers. It always would be. I stood at the old farm sink, scrubbing the grouted edges, thinking about Josie and the dress I couldn't wait to start making for her.

The sound of the front door crashing against the wall made me jump. With all the crazy noises, creaks, and moans, it felt like the house could very well be haunted. A feeling of melancholy settled over me. If only it were true and Meemaw really was still here with me.

I snatched one of the embroidered tea towels Nana

had given me as a housewarming gift. Happy little goats danced at the bottom of one end. Drying my hands, I hurried into the shop. The French door was wide open. I popped the screen door open and poked my head outside. The front yard with its patches of bluebonnets, lavender, and roses was dappled with pale moonlight. The air outside was still and quiet. It should have been comforting, but instead it felt like a tornado was coming. It made me wonder if I could pull off a wedding gown and three bridesmaid dresses in less than two weeks. I closed the door, breathing out the tension that had gathered inside me as I went back to the kitchen.

A short while later, Mama waltzed in carrying a vase bursting with lavender. For a split second, I thought it was a young Meemaw. Mama looked just like her mother, Coleta, who was a dead ringer for Loretta Mae. There was never a doubt that a Cassidy was a Cassidy—the auburn hair with the trademark blond streak was our genetic signature.

The teakettle whistled. I was bursting with news of my commission, and a thread of worry that I'd bitten off more than I could chew, but I held my tongue. "Where are those from?" I asked, gesturing to the flowers.

She set the vase in the middle of the pine table next to my sketchbook. Adjusting her Longhorns cap and tucking in a wayward strand of hair, she sat down. "I planted lavender, and you know how it goes. Start with one, grow a million and one."

That's not how it went for everybody, but that happened to be my mother's gift. Her thumb was greener than the Jolly Green Giant's, while mine was the color of an eggplant, more or less. I didn't have a bit of talent when it came to gardening.

"How'd your day go?" she asked as she arranged the flowers, fixing the few that had torqued during transit.

I beamed, determined to do whatever it took to make the dresses. "I talked to Josie Sandoval today. Do you remember her?"

"Does a ladybug have wings? Of course I remember her. I saw her a few days ago when I was leaving—" She suddenly stopped, regrouped, and finished with "—when I was, er, visiting a friend."

"Well, she's getting married and can you believe that the place she bought her dress from went out of business?"

Mama *tsk*ed. "That's awful."

"That's not the worst of it. Her gown and the bridesmaids' dresses are MIA."

My mother sucked in a breath. "Very bad luck."

Tessa Cassidy was a firm believer in superstition. She was forever tossing salt over her left shoulder and crossing herself, even though she wasn't Catholic. I didn't know if a missing wedding dress was universally bad luck, but sometimes it was better just to nod than to argue a superstition point.

"Their wedding's in a few weeks," she said. Her eyebrows pulled together as she eyed me. "What's she going to do?"

"Twelve days, actually. Her misfortune is my good luck." I felt a smidgeon of guilt over being happy about the Bridal Outlet going belly-up, and although Josie was out the deposit on the dresses she'd ordered from the store, I firmly believed it was her absolutely good fortune that I was on the job. "She hired me to make them. Her gown and all the bridesmaid dresses."

Mama placed her palms flat on the table, interlaced her fingers, and stared me down. "Oh, no, Harlow Jane, you can't do that."

"Of course I can. It's an unbelievable opportunity!" I slid into the ladder-back chair opposite her, pushing the vase of flowers out of the way so I could look her in the eye. "So far, everything I've designed and made has been for myself, an assignment, or based on someone else's vision. If I lay eyes on another Maximilian dress with the artsy collar and the structured shoulders, I'll scream. Bridal gowns. It's such a niche market. They may be just the thing to put me on the map."

But my mother was shaking her head. "Making someone else's wedding dress means bad luck for your own romance."

I sat back, folding my arms over my chest. "Mama, I'm not going to turn away this contract because you think it's bad luck."

"I don't want the Harlow and Cassidy names to die out," she said with a frown.

"So that's what this is about? Grandchildren?"

"I'm not getting any younger, and your grandmother would sure love some great-grandbabies from you."

Nana spent every waking moment in the company of her goats. I didn't think she was holding her breath over me producing great-grandbabies for her. "You both have Red's kids."

"You know I love those boys to pieces," she said, a smile ticking up one side of her mouth. My brother's kids were the apples of the Cassidy family's collective eye. Cullen was four and Clay was two. "But," Mama continued, "they don't have the Cassidy gift."

"*I* don't have the Cassidy gift!" I exclaimed. I'd held out hope throughout my childhood, into my teenage years, and even into my twenties that my charm would make itself known. It hadn't happened, and I was resigned to the fact that it never would. "Even if I have a daughter someday, she probably won't be charmed, either," I added wistfully. "Time to let it go, Mama. If there's romance out there for me, great, but I'm not going to stop living in the meantime."

"Your charm will materialize one of these days. It's in you," she countered, as if she knew it for a fact. "And your daughters will have it, too."

I was firmly into my thirties and hadn't had a serious boyfriend in more years than I cared to remember. And now she had me bearing multiple daughters. Enough was enough. I picked up my sketchbook and opened it to the designs I'd done earlier for Josie and her bridesmaids. "I took the job," I said, burying my lingering doubts and sliding the book in front of her. "The wedding's in a week and a half. I'm going to need another seamstress to get it all done in time." I batted my eyelashes at her. "Will you help me, Mama?"

Chapter 6

My love of sewing had started when I was nine years old and had spent an October weekend at Mockingbird Lane with Meemaw. She'd laid out a length of blue-and-white-checked gingham on her cardboard cutting board, pinned McCall's pattern pieces onto it, and cut it apart with shiny silver shears. I'd watch in awe as she sat at her Singer, telling me step by step what she was doing, and before I knew it, the day was gone and Meemaw had created a dress identical to Dorothy Gale's from *The Wizard of Oz*. I'd worn it for Halloween that year, and nearly every day after that until my mother had looked at me sideways and said, "Should we make another dress so you can give that one a rest every now and again?"

My eyes had gone wide and excitement bubbled inside me. "Will Meemaw make me another one?"

"I'm sure she will," Mama said, "but I think we should teach you how to do it. Give a man a fish, he eats for a day. Teach him how to fish, he eats for a lifetime."

I'd stared at her, not understanding what fish had to do with sewing, but I understood now. Meemaw had made me a dress and I felt like a princess when I wore it. Mama and Meemaw had taught me to sew and from that moment on I had been a queen. When I'd made a mistake and cried, Meemaw had said, "Darlin', there are no mistakes in sewing. Only opportunities for design."

Those were words I still lived by today.

"These are beautiful," Mama said, flipping through

the pages of sketches I'd done for Josie. She tapped the book with her index finger. "This is your gift, Harlow Jane."

It wasn't a Cassidy charm, but if I'd been a peacock right then, my feathers would have spread with pride. "Thanks to you."

"Pshaw!" She waved away the credit. "Meemaw and I gave you the foundation. What you've done with that is damn impressive."

A sound from the sink caught my attention. The faucet was suddenly dripping, slowly at first with a steady *plop, plop, plop*. It grew faster, changing until it sounded like *yep, yep, yep*. I jumped up and adjusted the rusty handle until it stopped dribbling. "This place needs a lot of work," I said. I penciled "leaky faucet" on my list of things to repair—right next to "doorstop" and "hole in workroom wall"—and sat back down at the table. "Meemaw wasn't great at maintenance, was she?"

"She was on past a hundred. No surprise that the old house needs some TLC. I'm sure she knew you'd take care of it. She did have someone come in to do odd jobs every now and again," she added. "He'll be by before too long, I'm sure."

Mama pointed to the lines angling up the bodice of Josie's dress. "Is this pleating?"

I nodded. "At first I thought I'd do inset seams or darts, but the more I looked at Josie and saw what she liked in my design books and the bridal magazine she brought, the more I thought the inset seams would be completely wrong. This is so her. I feel it in my bones."

"It's fine work," Mama said, "even if it is a weddin' gown." She ran her fingertips across the fabric swatches I'd stapled onto the page with the final design. I'd selected White French satin, Diamond French silk, Ivory organza, and Ivory Duchess taffeta. "Which one do you like?"

I leaned over and touched each one, feeling the differences in texture and weight and noticing the variations in sheen. "The silk," I said finally. It would drape beautifully, and the tone of the ivory would make Josie's skin glow. I glanced at the clock. 8:03. "Josie and her maid of honor are coming by again at eight thirty. If she likes the design and picks a fabric, I'll do a rush order on it while I work on the pattern and the mock-up."

She nodded with approval. "It's perfect for her. She'll look like a million bucks." She turned the page. "What about the bridesmaids?"

"They're so different. One's really tall and thin. One's shorter and a little round. And one—" I conjured up an image of Nell, trying to reconcile her incarnation as Daisy Duke, her pricey accessories, and the fact that she was Josie's boss and a business owner. "One I haven't quite figured out yet. I decided to go with different looks for each of them."

Mama flipped through the next few pages, commenting on the details of the designs.

"I just hope Josie likes the idea." We'd brainstormed styles, but left the bridesmaid dress designs undecided.

"She's easygoing," Mama said. "She's always mighty friendly. With the weddin' so near and no other options, she probably won't care all that much what it looks like."

My head snapped up. This was the third time she'd made a reference to Josie as if she knew her.

"Mama," I said, "how exactly did you say you know Josie?"

Her olive irises clouded and her eyes narrowed into what I could only describe as an expression of alarm. She snapped her gaze to the vase of flowers and started rearranging them, pulling stems out, then jamming them back into the same place. "I don't believe I said I *know* her, other than when she came around as a child."

"You said the wedding gown would be perfect for her, that she's so friendly and easygoing, and you said something about running into her . . . somewhere."

She poked another flower stem back into the vase, turning the thick-bottomed glass before plucking out yet another. "Bliss is a small town. People know one another's business," she said. "It's impossible to keep a secret, and impossible not to know the basics about a person."

That was the truth, but I didn't buy her answer.

As I was deciding how to respond, voices from outside drifted through the open window. The sink and the window above it faced Mockingbird Lane. I glanced at the oven clock. The predigital readout—white numbers on a black background—said 8:05. The motor made a faint scratching noise as the numbers rotated, changing to 8:06. The oven and clock might be archaic, but they worked. *If it ain't broke, don't fix it,* Meemaw always said.

Josie wasn't supposed to be back for another twenty-five minutes or so.

Mama said something about college kids and frozen yogurt.

I blinked. "Sorry. What?"

"I said it's probably just some kids. You're frowning. What's wrong?"

"It sounds like they're arguing, doesn't it?"

We both sat perfectly still, our ears cocked to the window. One of the voices belonged to a woman and seemed angry and agitated. Whoever she was talking to was much quieter. Men and women . . . their emotions were like oil and water.

I got up, flipped off the lights, and leaned over the sink to peer out the window. I cupped my hands above my eyes to cut the glare of the streetlights, but couldn't make out any figures on the sidewalk. The pecan tree to the left of the window blocked my view of the front flagstone walkway and the gated arbor leading from the sidewalk into my yard. The voice I could hear seemed to be coming from that direction.

I listened, picking out pieces of the angry woman's words: ". . . what's mine . . . owes it to me . . ." It went on for at least another thirty seconds. My heart beat faster the longer I listened. But then, just as quickly as the row had started, it was over.

"A lovers' spat," my mother said with a knowing nod. "Probably kissing and making up."

With her on my heels, I went to the front room and peered out the picture window. The street was partially blocked by the honeysuckle-covered fence. The bright pink miniature rosebushes lining the walkway also obscured my view of my own yard. I looked both ways, but from what I could see, which wasn't much, the street and sidewalk looked deserted. "I don't know . . ."

"You've always been too curious for your own good. I'm sure it's fine," Mama said.

We both collapsed onto the love seat, putting our feet up on the coffee table. "I know." When I hadn't been sewing with Meemaw as a child, I'd been reading Nancy Drew or spying on the townsfolk, even going so far as to hide under a table to watch Red getting a good what-for from Mama.

Ten minutes later, the door was flung open, sending the jingling bells flying off the doorknob once and for all. Startled, I sprang up from the couch like a gymnast. Josie collapsed in the doorway, tears streaming down her face, her breath coming in gasping sobs.

"C-call 911," she blurted.

I raced to her while Mama ran to the kitchen for the phone. "What is it?" I did a quick once-over, looking for an injury, but she looked fine. No blood. "Are you hurt?"

She slapped the tears off her face and gathered herself up. Grabbing my hand, she pulled me out the door, across the porch and down the steps. "It's N-Nell," she choked out. "I—I felt for a pulse. N-nothing. Oh, my God." She pointed to the arbor and gate welcoming people into the garden, and into Buttons & Bows. There, to the right and nestled amid a patch of bluebonnets, was Nell Gellen's motionless body. "Harlow," she said in a harsh whisper, "Nell's d-dead."

We didn't need 911. We needed a coroner.

Chapter 7

A slow shiver wound its way through my body and took hold of my senses. It started at my toes and worked all the way up to the hair on my head. It was hard to wrap my brain around the fact that someone I knew, even only slightly, had been murdered. I could only imagine how her friends and family would feel.

The mayhem that soon arose on Mockingbird Lane had me wondering if I'd brought New York City chaos back with me to Bliss. Leading the pack was Sheriff Hoss McClaine. He stood on the sidewalk just outside Meemaw's arbor, shouting orders, directing the powerful rigged lighting setup, and jotting things down on a little notepad. He kept one eye on Josie, who stood at the end of the porch talking on the phone to her soon-to-be mother-in-law. He also kept an eye on Mama and me, I noticed. Over the years, the Cassidy women had been blamed for plenty of things that had gone wrong in Bliss. When people didn't need something from us, they were quick to judge. I prayed Hoss McClaine didn't start a witch hunt.

The sheriff kept working as Mama and I sat on the front porch, moving back and forth in tandem on our wooden rockers watching the commotion. All I needed was to be chewing on a wheat stalk and the hillbilly look would be complete. It was dark out now, but it might as well have been broad daylight with the power of the artificial light gleaming down on the yard. For a small town, Bliss seemed to have some decent equipment.

A black woman marched through the arbor and straight over to the sheriff, clearly not intimidated by his deep growls and barks. He greeted her with a slight dip of his chin. She folded her arms across her ample chest and waited. After a short exchange, he let her pass through the rosebushes to the cordoned-off scene of the crime.

When she stood under the lights, I could see she was shorter than I was, full-figured, and had cropped hair that clung to her head. Something hung around her neck, but I couldn't quite see what it was. I leaned forward, stopping my chair from rocking. "What's she got?"

"A camera," Mama said just as the woman lifted it to her face and started snapping. She took pictures of the arbor, the ground, and everything but the dead body. Mama kept on rocking and I suspected her attention was glued to the sheriff.

"So who is she?" I asked.

"That's Madelyn Brighton," Mama said. "She's a transplant. Literally. She's from England. Met her Texan husband over there and came back with him. He's a professor at the University of North Texas and she works for Bliss."

I never would have guessed that Bliss could support any more staff than the sheriff, a handful of deputy sheriffs, a few office employees, and the mayor. We were a spit of a town. Growing, yes, but not anywhere near the size of a metropolitan city. "Doing what?"

"Any photography that needs doing, she does. I reckon she's taking pictures for the medical examiner, or whoever crime-scene photos go to." Mama kept her eyes on Sheriff McClaine as she rattled on. "I hear she's creating a tourist brochure for Bliss. There's a master plan for the community now. Bike trails, horseback riding trails, parks. Things like that. They have an architect and a civil engineer on staff so we don't sacrifice our historic, small-town feel."

I gaped at my mother. This was not the same Bliss I'd grown up in. "You're kidding, right? A tourist brochure? As in people coming here for vacation?"

Mama just shrugged. "A lot of people want small-town living. They like to see the old history. Plus we have the lake. You came back, didn't you?"

She had a point. I was back, and I had to admit there was a lot to like about small-town life.

If you could overlook having a murder take place in your front yard.

I sat back and started rocking again. Madelyn Brighton looked like a force to be reckoned with. She was crouched next to the dead body in my front yard at 10:20 on a weekday evening, which told me she had bigger aspirations than taking pretty pictures of Bliss. Medical examiner, maybe? But one body did not make for a career in criminal justice. Surely murder—and I was convinced it was murder; how else would a healthy young woman wind up dead in a stranger's yard?—couldn't be a common occurrence in Bliss.

"Why would anybody kill her?" Mama prattled on to herself as she creaked back and forth in her rocker. "She was a nice girl. Built the bead shop from the ground up. Not literally, of course; it's on the square. But she remodeled it, taught classes, hired your friend Josie. She put all her time and energy into Seed-n-Bead. Did I show you the bracelet I made?" She thrust her arm toward me, her fist nearly ramming my chest. "She helped me, you know. Dug out her special stash of premium beads just to find ones that matched my eyes," she said.

I turned my palm up and Mama rested her hand in mine. I knew less about beads than I did about Nell. I had worked long enough in the fashion industry to admire quality costume jewelry, though, and the double strands of silver and crystal beads with two spectacularly bright green ones strung on the center of each bracelet wire were spectacular.

She wriggled her wrist, letting the silver and glass jingle. "I'll always think of her when I wear it."

"It's lovely," I said, but what really caught my eye was the ring on her other hand. I hadn't noticed it before, but now it glinted in the moonlight. My heart skittered to a stop. "Mama, is that a diamond?"

Her gaze shot to her right hand, to the yard, then back to me. Not to the yard, I realized. To Sheriff Hoss McClaine. Holy cow, Mama and Hoss McClaine? Was there something going on there? Could he have given it to her? But a man didn't buy a diamond ring for a casual friend.

She tucked her hand by her side, the shimmering stone out of sight for the moment. Like that would make me forget about it. I dropped the subject . . . for now. Which was a good thing, because at that very moment a shrill voice carried into the garden. "She can't be dead! I was with her practically all day today. She was almost ready to—"

"Calm down. You need to calm down, now," a man said, drowning out her words, but the woman kept talking.

"Just. Today!" She didn't seem to realize that everyone who dies had been alive just moments before, so the fact that Nell had talked with the woman shrieking in the street earlier today wasn't anything unusual. In fact, I figured the sheriff would want to talk to everyone Nell had spoken with today in hopes of gathering some clues about what had happened.

A low voice countered the shrill one that was still ranting just beyond the entrance to the yard. As she calmed down, a flicker of recognition flitted through me.

"It's a mistake. It has to be. Josie's wedding . . ." The voice trailed off as a man and the woman stepped through the archway, framed in the moonlight. I recognized her immediately. She'd been with Nell practically all day today—right here at Buttons & Bows.

"Karen!" Josie stumbled across the gravel pathway toward the couple, tear streaks glistening on her face in the moonlight. They fell into each other's arms. She still had her cell phone pressed to her ear, and I couldn't tell if she was talking to the person on the other end of the line or to her bridesmaid.

Whether Karen was holding Josie up, or Josie was holding Karen up, I couldn't tell. I felt like an intruder on Meemaw's porch, watching Nell's friends grieve for her. "She was only thirty-five," I heard a muffled voice say. Mama and I looked at each other. Tears pricked behind my eyelids. It didn't matter how old Nell was. Her life was over far too soon. She was just a couple of years older than me, and I felt like I'd hardly even started living.

What was it that people said these days? Thirty was the new twenty, and forty was the new thirty. My whole life was ahead of me, just like Nell's had been just a few hours ago.

"Thirty-five," I muttered, shaking my head. Mama rested her hand on mine and squeezed, seeming to understand the thoughts circling through my head. Looking at Josie and Karen, and at Nell's body, still being photographed by Madelyn Brighton, seemed to put everything into perspective. Life, after all, was fragile.

The man with Karen looked a little like a young Robert Duvall, complete with balding head and watchful eyes. He had to be Karen's husband.

Josie's spine suddenly stiffened. "Oh!" She pulled away from Karen and quickly raised her cell phone back up to her ear. "Sorry, Mrs. Kincaid," she said, listening, then speaking, then listening some more. "Yes . . . I know, but . . . I can't." She wiped her eyes with the back of her hand. "But Nell's dead!"

She looked at the ground, cupping her hand over her eyes as she listened to Nate's mother on the other end of the phone. The tall man with Karen hunched his shoulders and whispered in her ear. I felt as if I was in the middle of a movie. The characters were bleeding with emotion and I was on the outside looking in.

"They should postpone the ceremony," my mother said under her breath. "A wedding on the heels of death is sure to bring bad luck."

I didn't always believe her superstitions, but this one actually made sense. Starting a new life as another one ended felt disrespectful, though it was the natural order of things.

"No . . . yes . . . you're right," Josie said into her phone, a new calm slipping into her voice. Karen grabbed her wrist in support.

I held my breath, thinking she might gather up her gumption to postpone, but she didn't. She kept her gaze down and nodded. "Okay," she finally said and disconnected the call.

Chapter 8

"Ms. Cassidy."

Mama and I both stiffened as Sheriff McClaine came up the walkway. Josie, Karen, and the Robert Duvall look-alike startled and stared up at us. They'd had no idea we were here, I realized.

Josie's eyes were wide and spooked. She raked one hand through her hair, staring at us, then at the sheriff. She shoved her phone into her pocket as Hoss McClaine walked up the porch steps.

Mama took her hand off mine and gave a barely perceptible nod.

"Ma'am."

"Sheriff." Mama looked out into the garden. "Quite a tragedy."

"Yes, ma'am, it is."

I looked from Mama to the sheriff and back, wishing I knew what each of them was thinking. Were they hiding a relationship?

After a long twenty seconds, he turned his lazy gaze to me. "Harlow."

"Sir." I felt like we were playing chicken, and if I blinked, I'd lose. "It's been a long time." Though not near long enough. I'd been back in town for less than two months, but when I'd been a resident here, that was probably the longest stretch of time I'd ever gone without seeing the sheriff—he'd hauled me into the station too many times to count on two hands. "Who do you think did this?"

The look he gave me sent me reeling back to when I was eighteen and he'd brought me home after catching my friends and me tipping cows or that time we'd been busted for climbing Bliss's water tower. Slipping back into adolescent roles was easy in a small town, especially when you've had a few brushes with local law enforcement. I had a momentary feeling of doubt about coming back to Bliss.

His gaze was steady and unyielding, but I couldn't figure out why he was staring so intently at me. "Can't say quite yet, ma'am," he said, finally answering my question.

Mama flicked her chin at the sheriff's notebook. "You have some questions for us, Hoss?" He barely had a chance to acknowledge her before she continued. "That girl's been murdered. Guess you'd best do your job and figure out who did it."

"Guess I should at that," he said. The side of his mouth quirked up, just a hint, and I got the distinct impression that he liked my mother's fiery personality. "Anybody see Ms. Gellen today?"

Mama shook her head no, but Josie nodded from the bottom step, breaking down with another sob. Karen's husband draped his arm over his wife's shoulder as she, too, nodded.

"We were all here. Except Mama," I said. "Josie, Nell, Karen, Ruthann, and me. I was going to make her bridesmaid dress."

He jotted something down in his little notebook, writing slow, just like he did everything else.

"Is that all?" Mama asked after he'd asked a few more questions.

"I do have some questions for you," he said, turning his gaze my way, but he stood there another few seconds doing nothing.

"Well, are ya waitin' for a written invitation?" Mama demanded, but there was a little gleam in her eye and I suspected she was playing up how aggravated she was for my benefit.

The sheriff flipped a page in his notebook and tapped

his pen against it. "Where were you earlier tonight?" He scanned the porch with lazy eyes, but I knew they were taking in every last detail, right down to the spool of azure thread sitting on the white-painted window frame and my sketchbook on the little table between Mama and me, opened to the drawing of Josie's wedding dress.

"I've been here all day. Mama's been here since, what . . ." I looked at her. "Seven forty-five?"

"Sounds about right," she said.

I'd put a little extra emphasis on the word "Mama," but he didn't react. Cool and collected—that was Hoss McClaine. Which just made me wonder what in tarnation Mama was doing sneaking around with him in the first place. She deserved somebody who'd take her out on the town—or at least on the town square. Hiding—whatever it was they were hiding—wasn't enough for Tessa Parker Cassidy. She deserved better.

He lifted his gaze to me. "What were you doing here with your mama, Harlow, while Nell Gellen was being strangled in your yard?"

From the tone of his voice he may as well have been commenting on the lovely weather we were having. It couldn't be more than seventy-five degrees, a beautiful, mild Texas night in April. But even though his voice was calm and he tipped his cowboy hat back all casual-like, I got the feeling he was suggesting something else, like maybe I had something to do with Nell Gellen being—

It took a few seconds, but I finally found my voice. "She was strangled?"

He gave one slow nod. "By the looks of it."

"She was waiting on me!" Josie blurted, stumbling up the porch steps and tripping on the last one. I lunged from my rocker and caught her, stopping her from landing on her knees on the splintered wood. "I'm getting married and Harlow's making my dress," she said as I pulled her up. "Only . . . only . . ." She sobbed. "Only not Nell's dress now . . ."

Time was on the sheriff's side. He waited while Josie dried her tears, and then he continued calmly as if there hadn't been a break in the conversation. "What time did y'all leave the shop here?"

"Nell drove me home around four o'clock," Josie said.

"Ruthann and I left together right around the same time," Karen added from the bottom of the steps.

"That's Ruthann McDaniels?"

A small-town sheriff tended to know everyone. Hoss McLaine was no exception.

Karen nodded. "That's right."

"And none of you saw Ms. Gellen after that?"

"She dropped me off at home," Josie said. "That's the last . . . the last . . . the last time I saw her." She broke down with another sob. "W-we were supposed to meet b-back h-here."

Karen held a clump of tissues to her face, quietly crying. With my peripheral vision, I saw that Madelyn Brighton had made her way around Nell and was now crouched on her other side. Every few seconds, a flash of light lit up the already artificially bright yard. All I could think of was that Madelyn was going to end up winnowing down seven hundred corpse shots of Nell.

We all turned as a car screeched to a stop just behind the sheriff's car. I couldn't see the make, but by the sound it made, even when coming to a quick stop, it had to be expensive. A woman hurried through the flower-covered arbor. "Josie?"

Mrs. Lori Kincaid, Nate's mother. She'd changed clothes since her visit to the shop this afternoon. Gone was the sophisticated cream-colored sleeveless summer frock she'd been wearing. It had been replaced by gray slacks, a white oxford blouse, and a prim cardigan. This was a rich woman's *It's nine o'clock at night and there's an emergency* outfit.

She put a comforting arm around Josie's shoulders. "Come on, now, pull yourself together." It was a gentle command, and it did the trick. Josie gave a final sniffle, wiped her eyes, and stood stoic.

Impressive. *That* was power.

"This here's a crime scene, folks." Sheriff McClaine's accent was thick, like gravy on biscuits.

"Not to mention a private property," Mama added stiffly. She didn't like all these people hovering around her childhood home.

From the corner of my eye, I saw the flower head on a weed waving in the yard, growing before my eyes. I flashed a quick look at my mother. "Stop it!" I hissed.

She frowned at me. "What?"

I jerked my head to the right. She stuck her chin out and narrowed her eyes like she was trying to figure me out. "You have a twitch, Harlow Jane. What's wrong with your neck?"

"Nothing's wrong with my neck!" I lifted my chin this time, trying to get her to look at the garden without alerting anyone else.

She finally looked in the direction of the two-foot-tall black sunflower and the cluster of weeds surrounding it. Her eyes grew round. None of that growth had been there moments before.

"Mama," I whispered, a good warning in my voice, "you pull it together."

"Ohhhh," she murmured. She fisted her hands and relaxed her face. I looked back at the weeds. They were still . . . and didn't seem any taller. She'd gotten it under control, but not before another flash of light from Madelyn Brighton's camera went off.

"Miss Sandoval," I heard the sheriff say, "would you step over here?"

Josie looked at Mrs. Kincaid for reassurance, her brown eyes rimmed with red. Nate's mother nodded. "Okay," Josie said, but she looked like a deer caught in the headlights of an oncoming car.

"Where's her fiancé?" Mama mused as Josie stumbled down the porch steps and over the flagstone path away from the little group gathered on and around the porch.

Good question.

The sheriff turned back to me. "We'll need statements from all of you," he announced to the group. To me, he drawled, "I'll need to ask you a few more questions, and we'll be searching the premises. A deputy'll be up here in a minute. The rest of you," he said with a wave of his hand, "go out the way you came and give your names and contact information to the deputy with your statement."

He flagged down a woman dressed in an identical beige uniform, minus the off-white cowboy hat, and gestured to her. She nodded at him, took out a small pad of paper, and intercepted Karen and her husband as they headed toward the sidewalk.

Mrs. Kincaid threw a look over her shoulder, her gaze seeking her future daughter-in-law. "She's had a terrible shock. It was her maid of honor. What's he asking her?" she demanded when she got to the deputy.

"It's routine, ma'am," the deputy said.

"Routine." She scoffed. "It's not like she had anything to do with this . . . this . . ." She waved her arm toward Nell's body. "With *this*," she finished.

"Like I said, it's routine," the deputy said. "Now, if I can get your name and address."

Mrs. Kincaid's voice turned curt. "Mrs. Keith Kincaid," she said, then rattled off her address.

The deputy didn't seem fazed by the fact that she was talking to a member of Bliss's founding family. She wrote the information in her notepad. "Thank you. Now, if you'll wait for your son's fiancée outside the gate, we'd certainly appreciate it."

"You'd best find out who did this," she challenged, wagging her finger at the deputy.

"We'll do everything we can."

The breeze kicked up as Mrs. Kincaid glided through the arbor, turned left on the cracked sidewalk, and waited at her car for Josie.

From where I stood, I could hear the gruff rumble of Hoss McClaine's voice, but couldn't make out the words.

"I was coming back to do measurements," Josie said, and I could picture her putting her hand on her heart as she spoke.

The sheriff's voice was muffled, but Josie's grew louder. My skin turned cold as she said, "She was dead when I got here!"

I perched on the edge of the rocking chair, my chin on my fist, trying to keep my worry at bay. Mama sat next to me. We both tried to ignore the commotion in the street with neighbors and passersby stopping to stare.

"She's the one who discovered the body. He's got to ask the questions," Mama said.

I stared at her. "How do you do that?"

"Do what?"

"How do you always know what I'm thinking? You're not a mind reader."

"Harlow Jane," she said, "I'm a mother, and that, sweetheart, comes with a whole 'nother set of abilities."

I sat back and rocked. All I could think about was the fact that Josie was in a mighty precarious position being questioned by Dirty Harry. "Josie couldn't have done it," I said.

"You don't know that. She discovered the body."

I amended my statement. "I don't believe she could have."

But we both knew that since no one had been with Josie when she discovered Nell's body, she had no alibi.

Chapter 9

The next morning I sat at the kitchen table, my arms folded and serving as a pillow for my head. *Now* sleep wanted to come? It figured.

The sheriff and his crew had stayed until nearly one in the morning. They'd searched the yard and then I'd let them into the shop. Big mistake. They'd riffled through every last drawer and cupboard, leaving things in worse disarray than they'd already been in.

I was up until three a.m. cleaning up the shop and trying to push away the thoughts running rampant through my mind. To say I was spooked was an understatement. A woman had been killed on my property, after being in Buttons & Bows, and the sheriff and his deputies had searched high and low for clues. What if Nell had been killed before seven forty-five when Mama got here? I would have no alibi. Would I become a suspect?

I'd tossed and turned the rest of the night. But the roosters at Mr. Higgins's place directly next door didn't care that I needed to sleep in. That was a peculiarity about Bliss. Zoning restrictions were basically nonexistent. We had tiny farms in the middle of town. You needed an acre for a horse, but a chicken coop was fair game on our quarter-acre lots. By six o'clock, I gave up trying to sleep through the cacophony and crawled out of bed. Not even coffee could perk me up.

A fervent knock on the door of Buttons & Bows made me jump. I rubbed my eyes and looked at the red-faced vintage wall clock hanging exactly where it had been, on the brick column next to the kitchen sink, for the last thirty years. For a moment I wondered if, just maybe, it had finally stopped working because according to the hands, it was six fifty in the morning, and that was *way* too early for someone to be needing designer clothes. But it sounded like I wasn't the only one who hadn't been able to sleep.

The pounding on the door repeated itself, followed by a voice. "Harlow! It's Josie."

I jumped up. If there was anyone I desperately wanted to see right now, it was Josie Sandoval. Mrs. Kincaid had whisked her away after the sheriff had interrogated her, so we hadn't had a chance to talk again. "Coming!" I called.

I'd brushed my teeth and pulled on a pair of cut-off jeans and a sleeveless plaid blouse before coming into the kitchen, none of which painted a picture of a fashion designer. Now I darted a glance around the farmhouse kitchen looking for a way to see my reflection. It might be early and the visit unexpected, but I still figured I should look presentable since Josie was a client.

I spun around. No mirrors. Meemaw had been a purist. A kitchen was for cooking and gathering, not primping. The white plantation shutters at the window above the farm sink suddenly rattled. A wave of panic flowed through me. The murder in my front yard had put me on edge. I'd checked all the window latches before going to bed, hadn't I? Or maybe I'd just imagined I had.

I pushed the slats open wide enough to reach my hand through to shut the window—"Odd." I bit my lip. It was closed and locked tight. So what had disturbed the shutters?

Josie pounded on the door again. As I turned away, I caught a distorted glimpse of my reflection in the window. Oh! I was *not* a pretty sight at the moment. Two hours of fitful sleep had that effect on a person. I combed my fingers through the tangles in my hair trying to get it to lie a little flatter. Finally I just gave up. What I looked like at the moment had no bearing on my design and sewing abilities. Josie wouldn't even notice anyway.

I yanked open the front door and caught Josie with her fist raised, ready to pound on the door again. "I didn't expect you," I said.

She dropped her arm to her side. "I know. I'm sorry."

I brushed her apology away, closing the door after she stepped inside. "Did you get any sleep?" I asked, though from her disheveled hair and red-rimmed, bloodshot eyes, I already knew the answer was no.

She shook her head and collapsed on the sofa, in the exact spot where she'd sat the day before. She buried her face in her hands and her shoulders heaved. I reached for a box of tissues, thinking she was going to break into sobs, but her body stilled and she suddenly sat up straight and looked me in the eye. "How could this have happened?"

My hackles went up. It almost felt like an accusation, and I'd had enough of *that* from the sheriff and the deputy. I didn't even *know* Nell, for pity's sake. "I, um . . . Josie . . . don't know. I hope you don't think—"

She looked at me, horrified. "Oh, God, no!" She wedged herself into the corner of the sofa, pulling her knees up. "It's just . . . I mean . . . I can't believe she's dead."

That made two of us. The deputy's questions the night before had focused on why Nell would have been killed on *my* property. I had no answers to any of her questions. "I only met her today," I'd told the officer, to which she'd replied, "Interesting."

"You know, just when things were going really well for her. It's not fair," Josie said.

"I don't think murder is ever fair."

Josie ran her index fingers under her eyes, wiping away the tears pooling there. "But she had a tough childhood, you know? She was a foster kid. God, the things she told me." She sniffed, dabbing her red-tipped nose with a tissue. "I had it pretty rough as a kid. No dad. My mom worked two jobs. That's why I glommed on to you, you know? I felt like we were the same. Neither one of us had a dad around, but you had your mom, your grandmother, and, of course, Loretta Mae. I used to wish I was part of your family. There was something so special about all of you."

Guilt wound through me. I hadn't known then what Josie had needed from me. I'd just seen her as a shadow, a constant presence, and had never paid her any mind. "I'm sorry I wasn't—"

She flung up her hand. "Don't. There's nothing to be sorry for, Harlow. You were there for me, even if you didn't know it. I remember thinking to myself: *She made it without her father. So can I.* And now look." She spread her arms wide. "I'm marrying into a good family and I'm in love. I've been lucky." Her smile faded. "Nell wasn't."

"What do you mean?"

"Is it wrong to talk about her now?" The look she gave me sent me reeling back to when we were kids. Her big brown eyes would gaze up at me like I was her big sister. She'd thought I had all the answers back then, which I didn't. And I sure didn't have them now. I made it up as I went along, pulling pieces of wisdom from Mama, Nana, and Meemaw—my holy trinity. "Of course not. She died, but we aren't going to forget her."

She dropped her chin, shaking her head as if she was disappointed with herself. "I just . . . I wish I could have stopped her from making mistakes."

I got up and moved in front of her, sitting on the edge of the coffee table. "It's not your fault."

"I was running late last night, counting the RSVPs for the wedding. If I'd been on time . . ."

"We don't know why she was killed. If you'd been on time, you might have been a victim, too."

"She was hooking up with guys she met on the Internet. Exaggerdating, she called it. Not a single one of the guys she went out with was honest in his profile."

"Why'd she keep doing it?"

Josie stared into space for a minute. "She never thought she was good enough, like being on her own for so long meant no one could really love her. It was a self-fulfilling prophecy, you know?"

Oh, yeah, I knew. I'd met dozens of people in the fashion world who were on collision courses of self-destruction and they all had their warped, twisted reasons. Not enough love. Too much love. Power. Money. Jealousy. Binging and purging. Drugs instead of food. All the dirt comes out in the wash, as Meemaw would say.

"She said she found Mr. Right, but I think he was just using her," Josie continued.

"What makes you think that?" I asked.

"He just came and went as he pleased. She'd meet him every day for a few weeks, then nothing for a month. He couldn't commit, but didn't want to give up the fun."

I'd met plenty of that kind of man. "Why buy the cow when you're getting the milk for free?" Meemaw said when I complained to her about the guys I was dating.

"I'm not giving anybody any milk!" I'd been indignant, and also untruthful. I'm sure she knew I'd poured a glass or two over the years, but I'd learned my lesson. I was past the point of settling for someone who wasn't in it for the long haul.

"What if he's the one that . . . that . . ." Josie looked at me and said, "What if he did this to her?"

I was asking myself the very same question. "Did you tell the sheriff all of this?"

She nodded. "He said they'd look into it. They'd search her apartment. Look through her computer."

"If they took her computer, I'm sure they'll be able to find out who she dated and see if there's a connection. Can I get you something?" Josie looked like she could use a stiff drink, but I offered tea or coffee.

"Coffee," she said.

I went into the kitchen, grabbed a couple of black-and-gold Maximilian mugs from the cupboard, and opened my coffee drawer to contemplate the selections. Emeril's Vanilla Bean, Extra Bold Dark Magic, Mudslide, and Southern Pecan were my favorites. I took a wild guess as to which Josie would prefer and went with Southern Pecan. I popped the sealed pod of flavored coffee into the machine, pressed a button, the coffeemaker purred to life, and thirty seconds later a steaming cup of brewed coffee was ready. I didn't know if the wedding was on or off, but right now, it seemed Josie just needed a friend.

I brewed the Dark Magic for myself, added cream, and carried both cups back to the sitting area. "Here you go," I said, sounding much more chipper than I felt. Josie had painted a picture of Nell as a damaged woman. She'd never found the happiness she'd been searching for. This realization felt like a cold fist closing around my heart.

We sipped in silence for a few minutes. Finally Josie set her mug down on the coffee table and reached for her purse. Hers was not designer like Nell's had been, which made me curious. "Where did Nell get her Gucci purse? One of her boyfriends, maybe?"

"From Mr. Right."

Even though Josie was marrying one of the richest bachelors in town, she carried an ordinary inexpensive cloth handbag. It had tiny little colorful flowers on a cream background—and it fit her, just like everything else she wore. Maybe it was like the engagement ring. Josie knew who she was and what she liked. It was all comfortable, casual, and understated. No pretense.

Nell had not embodied the same philosophy with her accessories.

Josie pulled out her checkbook and the next second she was tearing out a check and handing it to me. "We didn't talk price," she said, "but I hope this'll be enough to get started on the dresses."

I faltered, recoiling as if the check was one of the hundred-plus varieties of snakes in Texas. "The wedding's on?" I hated to look a gift horse in the mouth, but I was not an opportunist, either. One more reason I wasn't a good fit in the cutthroat world of New York fashion.

Her olive skin was sallow. "We can't postpone it," she said. "Nate's brother and father have been gone for almost three months, on and off. His dad's flying in from Angola to be here. Too many out-of-town guests coming, arrangements that can't be canceled ..." She sounded like she was repeating verbatim what had been drilled into her. "No, I talked to Nate this morning. We're going ahead with the wedding."

I glanced at the check—a thousand dollars—and lost my breath. That, combined with the final bill for the gown and three—er, two—dresses, would be enough to keep Buttons & Bows afloat for a while. But the slip of paper felt like a lead weight in my hand.

I handed it back to her, suddenly remembering what Nell had said about hoping Nate didn't break Josie's heart. Things happened for a reason. If Nell's death was a way for Josie to have more time, she needed to take it. And if Nate loved her, he'd understand. "Josie, you don't have to rush it."

She paled even more. Her lips quivered. "How can I smile and celebrate when she's gone? She was going to be my maid of honor."

Right. Would Ruthann or Karen fill that role now?

A rogue thought occurred to me. I remembered overhearing something about a shotgun wedding yesterday. If we were in the 1950s, I'd be wondering if Josie was pregnant and the hurried wedding was to save the family's reputation.

Of course we were in small-town Texas, so it was sort of the same thing. "You're not . . . um . . . Are you . . ." I couldn't figure out how to ask her tactfully.

She leaned forward with each of my starts and stops like she could pull the words out of me.

I cupped my hands over my belly. "You know—"

She flung herself back on the couch. "God, no! We don't want kids right away. We want to be a family, him and me, before we add that to the mix."

I breathed out a sigh of relief. "So there's no hurry. If you don't feel right about it . . ." This time I trailed off. Who was I to tell her to postpone her fairy-tale nuptials?

She laid the check on the coffee table. "Harlow," she said, "I need you to make my bridal gown, and Karen and Ruthann's bridesmaid dresses. The wedding is on."

As I hesitated, a gentle puff of air, nothing stronger

than an afternoon breeze, swept under the check Josie had written. The paper fluttered off the coffee table and landed in my lap.

A shiver stole through me. The windows in here were definitely closed. I had the sudden feeling that Josie and I weren't alone in the house, that the check had been picked up and placed on my lap by some ghostly presence.

Meemaw.

Josie put her hand on mine. "Please, Harlow. I want to marry Nate."

I took her hand and nodded, hoping it was sincerity I felt emanating from her and not desperation. The dress I made for her would have to be beyond perfect. Every seam I stitched would hold together her dreams. Every bead I sewed would bring sparkle back into her life. And every pleat I added would help her fold her grief into manageable pieces.

I went into the workroom, grabbed a package from a cardboard box I hadn't had the chance to unload yet, and handed it to her. "Go put this on."

She flipped it over. "Spanx?"

I'd become a shapewear convert when Maximilian gave a sampler pack to his employees for Christmas one year. I'd witnessed the before and after with my own eyes. My "now you see them" jiggles had been transformed into a sleek silhouette.

She opened the envelope and pulled out the Hide & Sleek Hi-Rise Body Smoother, the perfect thing for her to wear under her strapless Empire dress. I'd be giving her the illusion of a longer, leaner line with the high waist. No regular hose or shaper would do.

"Um, are you sure?" she asked skeptically.

"One hundred percent." I steered her to the distressed red wooden privacy screen off to the right of the room. The screen looked like old oversized window shutters hung together with antique hinges. Lengths of fabric draped over one side. Clothes hangers were hooked onto the slats, displaying samples of some of my favorite designs. "Even Jessica Simpson wears Spanx."

Her eyes popped wide. "Really?"

Jessica was a Texan. That gave her extra credibility with other Texans.

I winked. "It's gonna be great. Trust me."

A minute later she came out from behind the screen practically glowing. "It works!"

"Of course it does." She went on, raving about how comfortable she was, that she'd still be able to dance, how much better it was than the girdle her mom had bought from Walmart, and how Karen and Ruthann, but especially Karen, were going to flip when they discovered these. "They're always talking about their tummies. Karen's got her husband, but Ruthann says she better find herself a man quick before her looks go. And Nell . . ."

Her gaze darkened, but she pulled herself together. "Nell would have loved this," she finally said. "She was forever complaining about her muffin top. Said there was no stopping it."

I'd noticed Nell's midsection. She would have been a Spanx convert for sure. I'd decided long ago that every woman needed to feel good about her body, and if it took shapewear to accomplish that, then so be it.

I spent the next hour measuring Josie's beautifully compressed curves and going over the final design when she was dressed again. She peered at the sketch I'd done. "I don't really get the pleating," she said.

I'd played with our original design and had come up with the perfect dress for her. The pleats ran horizontally. I'd changed the sweetheart neckline to a slightly scalloped cut. It would fit her beautifully, accenting her in all the right places. "The pleats give it structure," I said. "The sketch is rough, I know, but it's going to be fantastic, Josie. You'll look like a princess. Trust me."

"But strapless?" Her shoulders hunched slightly, as if she was imagining herself in it right this minute, and she couldn't quite picture it. "Are you sure? I'll never do it justice."

I turned her around to face the full-length oval mirror in the corner. "Look at you! You're beautiful." One of Meemaw's maxims came to me, another bit of wisdom I lived by. "This dress is going to complement you perfectly, Josie. It's not meant to steal the show."

Her spine straightened and she threw her shoulders back. Bless her heart, she was trying her best to envision it and feel confident. After all, I was a designer. I could see the dress in my mind. It wouldn't be so easy for someone who didn't live and breathe fashion, clothing, and design. "So it'll have beads?" she asked.

"Plenty of sparkle," I confirmed.

She smiled—an honest-to-goodness grin—for the first time since she'd arrived here this morning. "I trust you, Harlow."

"Good," I said just as a knock sounded on the front door.

My ragtag appearance hadn't improved over the last hour and a half. As I padded toward the door, I made a new rule for myself. Be presentable before I came downstairs, just in case this trend of early visitors continued.

I peeked through the glass of the front door and gasped. Sheriff Hoss McClaine stood there, cowboy hat in hand, toothpick between his teeth, looking like he was ready to hang someone with a brand-new rope.

Chapter 10

I held the door open as Sheriff McClaine stepped inside. He greeted me, raising his bushy eyebrows when he noticed Josie. He nodded to her, a polite Southern gentleman to the core. "Ma'am," he said, though he stretched the word out until it had an extra syllable and sounded like *MAY-um.*

She jumped up, nearly crashing into the rustic coffee table. "Did you figure out who did it, Sheriff? Do you know who killed Nell?"

"No, ma'am."

As he turned those slow roaming eyes of his to the main room of Buttons & Bows, I once again got the feeling that underneath the indifferent gaze, he was a sharp-eyed officer of the law. What I couldn't imagine was what he was looking for.

The front door jerked under my hand, slamming shut, almost of its own volition. I spun around, half expecting to see Meemaw, her iron gray hair piled on top of her head in a loose bun. But of course she wasn't there. My imagination—or simply the deep-seated wish that my great-grandmother was still with me—was getting the better of me.

His gaze settled on me for a beat before landing back on Josie. "I need ya to come on down to my office, Miss Sandoval."

She rested her palm against her chest. "M-me?"

"Yes, ma'am. I got a few more questions for ya."

There it was again, that Southern charm that concealed a razor-sharp knife.

Josie's left eye twitched and she looked as if she'd been sucker punched and pushed into a hole that she would never manage to claw her way out of. "Do . . . do I have to?"

The sheriff lowered his chin, his jaw working. "No, ma'am, 'course you don't, but I'd be obliged if you would."

She reached for her purse and pulled out her phone. "I . . . uh . . . can I c-call Nate?" She tried to punch the numbers, but her hands trembled. Her cell dropped with a dull thud onto the pecan planks of the hardwood floor.

I could feel her panic like it was rising up in me, and I stooped to pick up the phone. If she couldn't form a coherent sentence in this house, there was no way she'd be able to manage under the manipulative charm of Sheriff McClaine on his home turf.

A sudden pocket of cold air surrounded me, instantly growing warmer as it enveloped my body. I knew what I had to do. I couldn't let Sheriff McClaine drag Josie out of here, scared half to death. I put my arm around her shoulder, hoping the warmth enveloping me would seep into her. "Why do you need her?"

Hoss McClaine gave me a beady-eyed look. "Like I said, I got a few questions for her, is all."

I channeled all the gumption I'd had to muster up every day when I lived in New York and leveled my gaze at him. "Can't you ask your questions here?" I asked, hearing the South creep back into my voice.

His dark brown hair was particularly dull this morning, and his thick mustache and soul patch gave him a weathered cowboy look. He didn't waver, blast him. "No, ma'am, I don't believe I can. I'd rather Miss Sandoval come on with me."

I felt all my Southern roots spread through me as if they were stretching through the soil, searching for water from a long-past thunderstorm. "Well, then, I guess I'll come along. If it's all the same to you, Sheriff." My mama might well be dating the man, but *I* wasn't. And at this moment I wasn't too fond of him.

Josie squeezed my hand. "Would you?"

Wild horses couldn't have stopped me. Josie needed a friend and here I was. "I was fixin' to go out for a morning walk, anyway." The lines on her forehead smoothed and her grip on my hand loosened.

"Thank you," she whispered.

"Anytime."

The Sheriff's Department, which used to be the old Baptist church, is within spittin' distance of Buttons & Bows. Once the church had finished its new, modern building just off the main thoroughfare, the city bought the old building, gave it a minor facelift, and moved the city offices into it.

I ran upstairs and changed out of my cutoffs. In record time, I slipped on the first thing I could get my hands on—a prairie dress, belting it on my hips—tethered my hair in two low ponytails, stuck on a cadet hat that I'd made years ago, and pulled on my favorite Frye burnt red harness cowboy boots. "Ready, Sheriff," I called, hurrying back downstairs. Although what I was ready for I didn't know.

The sheriff looked me up and down, but whatever he thought, he kept it to himself. Smart man.

Josie was facing the wall that held my display board, her cell phone pressed against her ear.

"Miss Sandoval," McClaine said, gesturing to the door.

Josie held up one trembling finger as she frantically whispered something into her phone. A moment later she was being ushered out the door, followed by the sheriff. I brought up the rear. I'd barely made it out when the door slammed behind me. All by itself. I threw the house a backward glance, puzzled, but the mysterious happenings were just one more thing I'd have to think about later.

Chapter 11

The Sheriff's Department still looked like a church with its faded brick siding and peaked roofline. The building had been around since the late 1800s. A fresh coat of paint, some stain, and a few nails couldn't shake the worship out of the old building.

We walked into the vestibule. To the left was the old sanctuary, which still looked like a . . . sanctuary. Even the pews were still there, though they were pushed up against one wall. The whole place retained a solemn air and I got the sense that the town officials didn't know what to do with it or how to make it feel like government offices. I wondered if they had much leeway. It seemed likely that the building was part of the historic registry.

Josie and I stayed a step behind Sheriff McClaine. Even his walk was lazy, his bowed legs making him look like he belonged on a horse rather than in a police car. Josie clutched my arm, slowing me down. "What do you think he wants to ask me?" she said in a feathery voice that still seemed too loud for the former church.

I couldn't even speculate. Miss Marple's St. Mary Mead and *The Murder at the Vicarage* had not prepared me for a real murder. "Routine questioning?" I said, hoping I was right and that McClaine just wanted to fill in whatever gaps his deputy might have left from the night before.

"He's not going to arrest me, is he?"

"I'm sure he's not," I said, praying that I was right.

"So I'll just answer his questions and he'll let me go. Not cooperating would be bad, right?"

She seemed to need reassurance. I offered what little I could. I nodded.

It seemed enough to bolster her. As she shuffled to catch up to the sheriff, I glanced over my shoulder. Still no sign of Nate screeching to a halt just outside the door, ready to barrel in, Josie's knight in shining armor.

It was quieter outside than a field of cotton.

We walked up the ramp across from the sanctuary, turned right, and made our way down a hallway that used to lead to the church classrooms but now seemed to house all the actual city offices. Brown placards engraved in gold identified the occupants of each space. We passed the mayor's office, the council members' offices—one for each of them—animal control, business services, public works, personnel, and finally, at the end of the hallway, law enforcement.

There was a separate entrance with a counter and a clerk who probably dealt with traffic violations and such. Poor Josie. By the look on her face, the scenic route through the building had done a number on her.

We stopped in front of McClaine's office. He took the toothpick from his mouth and used it to point to a hollow aluminum-framed chair. "You can have a seat there," he said to me.

Humph. I'd naively thought I would be able to stay by Josie's side when he questioned her, for moral support as much as to stay in the loop. The murder happened on my property, after all. "Tell Nate where I am when . . . when—" She broke off, her voice trembling. "If he comes," she finished.

I squeezed her arm. "He'll come," I said to reassure her. Then they disappeared into the office and I sank down onto the uncomfortable chair, wishing I had been blessed with the ability to hear through walls. That was a Cassidy gift that would come in handy right about now.

No matter how close I pressed my ear to the wall, I couldn't hear a thing.

"Ms. Cassidy?"

I jumped, knocking my cadet hat askew. Madelyn Brighton stood in front of me. I noticed she was shorter than she'd seemed the night before. Up close, her skin was the color of sable, the black of her short hair several shades darker. It didn't look as perfectly coiffed, more like she'd poked her finger in an electrical outlet, sending stray strands on end. It reminded me a little of Alfalfa from *The Little Rascals*, only instead of one wild hair, she had them all over. Oddly, it worked for her.

"I'm Madelyn Brighton. I work for the department."

"The photographer, right," I said. "My mother said you're working on a town brochure?" I was still trying to connect the dots between a Madelyn Brighton, crime photographer and Madelyn Brighton—

"Freelance," she said, answering my unasked question. "I contract out with the city, do weddings and graduations." Her British accent landed somewhere between Eliza Doolittle and Dame Judi Dench. "You name it," she said, "I photograph it."

I took her extended hand. She pumped up and down exactly three times before dropping mine. "I saw you last night . . . taking pictures of . . . of Nell Gellen."

"It's a bit of a coincidence seeing you here." She smiled. "I was going to phone you today, actually."

A knot formed in the pit of my stomach. Our town pseudo medical examiner or crime photographer or whatever she was phoning me up about something didn't sound good. "Oh?"

"Do you have a minute, by chance?"

I glanced at Sheriff McClaine's closed door. I hadn't been able to hear a thing through the wall and there was no way to tell how long he'd keep Josie in there. "I guess so," I said, reluctant to leave my post but curious about why Madelyn Brighton had planned to call me.

She led me along the hallway to a little conference room. Her wide-legged pants flopped around her calves as she walked and her square jacket hid any shape she had. She was like a blank canvas. Too bad she wasn't asking me for a fashion consult.

I sat down at the little circular table and waited while

she pulled a black laptop out of the computer bag slung over her shoulder. "I have to tell you," she began, "I'm something of an American crime buff. I've watched every episode of *Law and Order*, *The Closer*, *Cagney and Lacey*, and *Supernatural*. You name it, I've seen it."

Her accent was thick and I had to concentrate a touch more than normal as I listened to her. She probably felt the same way about Texans. "I'm more a *Project Runway*, *Dancing with the Stars*, and *Iron Chef* kind of girl," I said. The photographer and I didn't have much in common. Too bad. There was an inherently likable quality about her.

"I wanted to show you something in the photographs from last evening," she said, sitting across from me. Her laptop sat between us.

I was immediately apprehensive, but I'd faced worse than Madelyn Brighton flashing pictures in front of me. Even photos of Nell's body. My immediate supervisor at Maximilian, for example, had dressed like Tim Gunn, but had acted like Attila the Hun. All bite, no bark. I could handle whatever Madelyn threw at me.

But then I noticed that Madelyn's pudgy cheeks had a rosy sheen and she looked more like a kid in a candy store than a warrior out for blood. Whatever it was she wanted to talk about was giving her a giddy little thrill.

Be noncommittal and give nothing away. Those were the rules I'd learned to live by in New York. *Let others lead the conversation.* They'd either tell you what they wanted, or they'd tell you what they hadn't intended to just to fill up the dead air.

"I noticed flowers," she said.

"Flowers," I repeated.

"Specifically the flowers around the body."

"And . . . ?" I asked, but of course I knew just what she'd seen. My mother's emotions at work.

"At first I thought my eyes were playing tricks on me, but after a while I was quite sure they weren't. When I started taking pictures, the flowers were small. But—"

Was that a smile tickling her lips?

"—by the time I was done," she continued, "they looked like this."

She ran her index finger over the touch pad of her computer and tapped it with her fingers a few times. Bringing her gaze back up, she spun the computer around to face me.

My breath caught in my throat and for an instant I lost track of my surroundings. My mother's green thumb had gotten the better of her—and Madelyn Brighton had caught the evidence on film. I thought I'd stopped her from making the weeds and flowers sprout before anyone could notice, but I'd thought wrong. Now I understood Madelyn's emphasis when she'd said "supernatural."

But it wasn't the flowers that struck me about the picture. It was the swirl of white, like a wispy cloud, at the edge of the frame. It reminded me of . . .

"I've never seen anything like it," she said, tapping the screen with the pad of her finger. "The rumors are true, aren't they?"

Just like that, I was back in the room. I sat a little straighter in my chair. Rumors were never good. Ever. "I don't know what you mean, Mrs. Brighton."

She ran her hand over her head, but instead of helping her hair to lie flatter, her touch seemed to make the strands respond. Static electricity. The woman was charged.

"Madelyn," she said. "And I'm sure you do know what I mean." She tapped the computer screen again. "It's right there in full color. Small, then large."

Footsteps and male voices came from the hallway. I glanced over my shoulder, wondering if this was some sort of good cop, bad cop—with the bad cop hidden somewhere. Except that Madelyn Brighton wasn't a cop. Was she?

"Are you a police officer?"

She laughed, an infectious, bubbly laugh. "No. Could have been. Maybe *should have* been. I'm a photographer, Harlow. Can I call you Harlow? And no, I'm not in training to be a police officer, either. I'm not asking questions for the police. This is for my own personal interest only." She leaned closer and her voice dropped to a whisper. "Truth be told, I'm sort of a magic junkie. *Lord of the Rings*, *Harry Potter*, all that."

I leaned closer, too. "I thought you were into crime."

"I am. I'm a photographer. A writer. A photojournalist. But it's tough to make a living doing any of that. Which is why I do a bit of all of it. Truly, I love to photograph the unexplained. And this . . ." She clicked the arrow on the computer screen and the next picture appeared. In this one Nell's body could hardly be seen through the two-foot-tall zinnias and lavender. "This is unexplained."

She glanced over her shoulder, her white blouse gaping between the buttons. When she turned back to me, she lowered her voice even more. "I've heard about the Cassidy women."

My jaw dropped, my glasses slipped, and everything went blurry. "Wh-what have you heard?"

She sat back, leaving the laptop facing me, the evidence of the bionic flowers staring back at me. She didn't look menacing, like she was ready to lead a witch hunt, but people were not always what they seemed.

"I've heard that your grandmother talks to goats. And that your great-grandmother—you live in her house, right?—I hear she could just make things *happen*. If she wanted it, she basically got it. And your mother, well . . ." There was that bubbly giggle again. It made Madelyn Brighton endearing and not nearly so threatening as she could be, considering the topic of our conversation and how highbrow her accent made her seem. She nodded at the computer. "It's clear what *her* charm is." She cocked her head, her brow furrowing, her smile turning contemplative. "Everyone says you don't have a gift, though. Why is that?"

A wave of dizziness crashed through me. I'd never had to explain the charmed ways of the Cassidy women before. It was private. And a gift. A gift I didn't share, but still . . . To talk about it made me feel like I was betraying all the Cassidy women, past and present.

But Madelyn Brighton was not going to let it drop. I shrugged helplessly, wishing I knew the answer for my own sake. "I don't know."

She bolted up and spun around. "Aha! So I was right!" she bellowed, then quickly slapped her hand over her mouth and sat back down. "I was right," she said again in a whisper. "The Cassidy women, minus you, are charmed."

I stared at her. All proper and British, my foot. She had completely tricked me. I cringed at how artfully she'd slipped the question in and how easily I'd replied to it, corroborating her suspicions. Damn. I'd been away from Bliss too long. I was out of practice with the secret-keeping. I'd have to be careful about that. Or try it myself when I needed information.

"Did you get some good pictures of Nell?" I asked, and then immediately cringed. That had not come out right. "I mean, do they show anything, like who killed her?"

"I know what you mean. They revealed plenty. I probably shouldn't show you this, but—" She gave a furtive look around, whipped the computer back to face her, tapped a few times, and whirled it back to face me. "Strangulation, plain and simple."

My stomach roiled. It was a close-up of Nell. The skin around her eyes and mouth was swollen, tiny pinpricks dotting the surface, making her look like a used pincushion. Her neck was marked with an uneven zigzag pattern. I pointed to the markings. "Why does it look like that?"

"Uneven pressure during strangulation," she answered. "I'm no expert, but it looks like the markings from a braided rope, or something." She indicated the larger markings of the zigzag pattern on Nell's neck. "See these? One strand of the braid was bigger than the others. That's my guess, anyway."

The realization of just why the sheriff had searched

Buttons & Bows knocked the wind out of me like I'd been thrown off a mechanical bull. The search hadn't been routine.

He'd been looking for something very specific amid all the trims and cording in the shop. He'd been looking for the murder weapon.

Chapter 12

Out of nowhere, Nate Kincaid careened down the hallway, past the table where I sat with Madelyn Brighton. I could barely find my voice—Madelyn and her photographs were having that effect on me—but when I did, I muttered, "I gotta go." I scraped the chair back and hurried after Nate. He'd stopped in the middle of the hall, arms spread, spinning around like a lost child.

I reached out, touching the sleeve of his gold-colored polo shirt with the tips of my fingers. "Nate."

He whipped around, handsome as ever, looking more like a crazed prom king than a buttoned-up Kincaid son. "Where is she?" He looked up and down the hallway. "Where does that dim-witted sheriff have her?"

"He's not dim-witted," I said, for the life of me not knowing why I was defending Hoss McClaine. "He's just doing his job."

"By interrogating my fiancée?"

"No, by investigating the murder of her maid of honor."

"She had nothing to do with it." He spoke with such conviction, but I had to wonder how well he really knew her. She'd admitted they hadn't been dating all that long. Was his faith in his fiancée misplaced, or— My suspicious mind took over. Could he be protecting her?

What motive could the police think Josie had? Nell's words about Nate possibly breaking Josie's heart came back to me. What if Nell had warned Josie she didn't trust her fiancé, and Josie had flown into a rage? It could have been a crime of passion.

Or what if Nate wasn't really Josie's one and only true love? Could the improved lifestyle she would gain by marrying a Kincaid have had anything to do with Nell's death?

Really, what did *I* know about Josie other than what I remembered of her when we were kids and what she'd said about having a rough childhood? Nothing. How far would she be willing to go to ensure a different future for herself? If Nell had known something about Josie's true motives, would she have revealed it? And would Josie have killed to keep her silent?

My head swam. It was all a big pile of what ifs.

"Where were you last night?" I asked Nate. That was another one. What if he'd killed Nell for some reason? The problem, of course, was what reason?

"I was working."

"Well, Josie's a wreck," I said, trying not to sound accusatory. I don't think I pulled it off. But seriously, unless he had reason to stay away—like he was guilty and was destroying the murder weapon—where had he been when he should have been comforting Josie?

"I got here as soon as I could," he snapped. His eyes blazed with a vaguely familiar anger.

I stumbled back, my limbs suddenly weak. Up close, Nate looked even more like his brother, Derek. It sent me reeling into the past. I never thought I'd have anything to do with the Kincaids again, yet here I was. "I'm—I'm sure she'll be glad you're here," I said.

"Where is she?" he asked again, his emotions dropping down to a powerful simmer.

I pointed at the door Sheriff McClaine had taken Josie through. "They're in there."

Without another word, he burst through the door.

"What the devil do you think you're doing?" Sheriff McClaine bellowed.

The door slammed and I was alone in the hall. I listened to see if I could gauge how Josie was holding up, but the voices were muffled. Nothing to do but go and open the shop. Not that anyone would be there waiting for custom couture.

Footsteps sounded behind me, then stopped. I looked over my shoulder. Madelyn Brighton stood halfway down the hallway, staring at me as if she could read my every thought. From out of nowhere, a vision appeared in my head. She was wearing a skirt that hit just at the knee, made in a bold print, a light-weight denim jacket, and a homespun scarf.

Behind her was a misty form—just like the one on the edge of the photo she'd shown me.

The vision disappeared with a pop.

Something was definitely amiss in Bliss.

Chapter 13

The town square in Bliss, listed on the National Register of Historic Places, looks like it came straight out of a movie set. With its hundred-plus-year-old limestone courthouse smack in the center and quaint restaurants and shops circling the perimeter, it was easy to see why people might come back home to roost. Or land here later in life and decide to stay.

It took me just eight minutes to walk from the Sheriff's Department to the square. One more block and I'd be home. First order of business? Scour Meemaw's boxes and jars of trims looking for anything that might create the odd pattern left on Nell's neck. I prayed I wouldn't find a thing, which would mean whoever killed Nell used cording or trim from somewhere else, not from Buttons & Bows.

My shoulders drooped. So many people had been in the shop the day Nell had died. The place had been chaos. It would have been easy for someone to pocket a random piece of trim with no one the wiser.

My pace slowed as I passed the ice cream parlor, a throwback to the early twentieth century, before Baskin-Robbins and Cold Stone Creamery existed. The red-and-white awning and matching interior of Two Scoops was enough to make a girl feel like she was five years old and clamoring for a double-dip cone.

Bliss was waking up. When I'd left the shop with Sheriff McClaine and Josie, only the birds and insects had rubbed the sleep out of their eyes. Now cars were parked, angled in, at Villa Farina. People spilled out onto the sidewalk as they sipped their coffee and tea and wallowed in carb heaven.

In the short time I'd been back in Bliss, the Italian Pasticceria had become one of my favorite places on the square. Villa Farina, owned and operated by pastry chef Bobby Farina, a third-generation baker who'd moved to Bliss with his wife, Colleen, carried on the family tradition of mini Italian pastries just like the original bakery in New York. I'd never been to the New York store, but I could live happily in the Bliss establishment. From cannoli to *sfogliatelle*, superthin layered dough with light orange-ricotta filling, everything chef Bobby made could bring a grown man to tears.

Like a fish being caught on a line, I caught a whiff of roasted coffee beans and I was hooked. A shot of caffeine. Just what I needed. I followed the ribbon of scent, hurried across the street, cut in front of the courthouse, crossed the opposite street, and shambled into Villa Farina.

Once inside, I sucked in the deepest breath I could muster. It was April, warmer today than it had been all week, but the weather didn't make a lick of difference to me. I could drink a hot cup of joe on a sweltering day just as easily as I could in forty-degree weather. Ground beans and warm pastries soothed my soul.

I waited in line. Gina, a college student who worked for Farina's and looked like a tough Jersey girl with her two-toned black-and-red hair, was all country on the inside. "Morning, Harlow," she greeted when it was my turn, her voice pleasantly husky like Taylor Swift's. "I'd ask if you want the usual, but y'all always get something different."

Gina used "y'all" to refer to one person or a group of people. Still, I glanced over my shoulder to see if this time someone else was behind me.

No. I was at the end of the line. One of these days I'd stop looking.

"I have to try one of everything before I can decide what I like best," I said.

"What'll it be today?"

I took it all in, finally deciding on a pasticciotti. She put the cream puff on a thick white plate, added a fork, and went to work making my cinnamon dolce latte.

My name is Harlow Jane Cassidy and I'm a carb addict.

"Sad about Nell," Gina said over her shoulder. "I heard they brought Josie Sandoval in for questioning."

Bad news traveled fast in a small town. "Sheriff McClaine had a few questions for her. Since she discovered the body and all." I threw in the last part to give some context to Josie's questioning. Villa Farina was the gossip hub of the square. Hopefully Gina would spread my explanation and suspicion about why Josie was questioned would be defused.

She finished foaming my milk and poured it into the espresso she'd brewed. "Is she, gonna, like, inherit Seed-n-Bead?"

I stared at Gina's back, speechless for a second. First, because to inherit something required that there be a will, and I hadn't marked Nell as a planner. Second, it hadn't occurred to me that Nell and Josie were *that* close. Friends, yes. Coworkers, also yes. But businesses were passed from generation to generation within a family.

"Why on earth would Nell leave her business to Josie?" I asked when she came back to the counter with my coffee.

Gina shrugged. "Way I heard it, Nell didn't have anyone else. Might as well leave it to Josie. They were close, far as I could tell."

I laid six dollars and some change on the counter to pay for my morning calories. "Yes, but do you think Nell had actually made a will?" That took a lot of forethought. "I only met her once, but she didn't strike me as the type."

Through the small windows of the swinging doors, I could see Bobby rolling out some pastry dough. A new confection to add to the day's offerings. Colleen came through the doors carrying a tray loaded down with a fresh batch of éclairs. A line had started to form behind me. Gina leaned over the counter, all cloak-and-dagger-like, and whispered, "I *know* she did. She's been in here with her lawyer."

"So?"

"Just last week," she said conspiratorially.

That was interesting, but . . . "Okay, but they could have been discussing anything," I said, scooting over so the man behind me could place his order.

"Uh-uh." Gina rang him up and grabbed him a fresh éclair. "They were definitely talking about her will. I didn't hear the details, though. Whatever she decided, he didn't think it was a good idea."

Gina took the man's money and handed him his plate, going straight to work on his coffee order. "They went back and forth for a while." She talked louder over the whir of the machine as she heated the milk. "She seemed pretty determined to do what she wanted from where I was standing. Which was right here," she added over her shoulder.

I scanned the café portion of the bakery. Three small round tables sat in the center and either side wall had three square tops. There was no way Gina would have heard a conversation that took place at one of the front left tables. "Where did they sit?"

She pointed at the table closest to the counter, right next to us.

Huh. So Gina *had* heard their conversation. I didn't know what it might mean, but the fact that Nell had drafted a will just a week before her murder seemed suspicious.

I had Gina put my lemon cream puff in a bag and left, realizing I should have asked who Nell's lawyer was. I peeked back in the bakery, but the line was already out the door. I was not Nancy Drew, I reminded myself. I'd just pass the information on to the sheriff and let him deal with it.

I started to turn left so I could take Mockingbird Lane all the way home, but stopped in my tracks. Seed-n-Bead was right next door on the right. I did an abrupt change of direction and stood in front of the bead shop. I'd intended to stop by many times since I'd been back in Bliss, and now I was kicking myself for not making the time. I would have liked to have known Nell better, if only because she died on my property.

The CLOSED sign hung on the door and the inside lights were off. With Josie and Nate still presumably with the sheriff and Nell probably on a cold slab in some morgue in Fort Worth, there was no one to open the store.

Would Josie try to keep it going? She hadn't said anything about it and I hadn't asked. If Nell had left the store to her, did she know?

When I'd first opened up the dressmaking shop, I'd planned to collaborate with the bead shop to bring in trendy accessories to complement my designs. Things like cuffs, double-stranded necklaces with chunky flowers and pendants, and simple bracelets to match my casual creations.

I needed a bead source, too, especially if my wedding gowns ever really took off.

Cupping my hands on either side of my face, I peered in the window. It was a long, narrow space. Tables lined the perimeter, stacked with square containers holding beads. Sample jewelry and strands of beads hung from pegs and display boards.

The question that had continually run through my mind since last night was, Who had something to gain by Nell being dead? A while ago, I'd thought that any motive Josie might have had was flimsy at best. But if she was the benefactor of Nell's will—well, that changed things.

I walked home, sipping my coffee, swinging my pastry bag, and thinking. I didn't like that line of thinking, though. Josie was marrying Nate, after all, and Nate came from one of the wealthiest families in the county. Josie wouldn't *need* to work if she didn't want to. No, I felt sure there was someone with a stronger motive for killing Nell. If I wanted to help clear Josie's name, then I had to search for a different answer. Someone else who had something to gain by Nell's death.

Chapter 14

I studied the facade of Meemaw's redbrick farmhouse as I approached. The garden was green and colorful with too many varieties of flowers to count. The arbor was like a welcome mat, telling people to step right through into the magical land of Buttons & Bows.

The only thing missing was a sign. And a group of customers clamoring to get into the shop. A sign wouldn't bring instant business, but if I wanted people to stop by and commission couture fashion, they needed to know I was here. I added signage to my mental list of things to take care of.

I walked through the arbor and up the flagstone path. Like a magnet to steel, my gaze was drawn to the depression in the bluebonnets left by Nell's body. I slowed down, pondering the woman who'd died there, but I was propelled up the porch steps as if pushed by two invisible hands. I barely managed to flip the wooden CLOSED sign to OPEN and unlock the door before I stumbled inside, muttering, "Who could have killed her?"

I realized that I half expected Meemaw to materialize and answer me. I thought I felt her presence more and more in the old house, but it was quite possible that I was simply losing my mind. "And why kill Nell here?" I asked, my voice louder this time.

"If not here, it would have happened somewhere else."

My hands flew up, knocking my glasses clear off my face as I screamed. My heart thudded in my ears. I flung my pastry bag halfway across the room and my nearly empty coffee cup went flying.

Behind me, the door slammed shut.

That had not been Meemaw's voice, which would have been freaky enough. But no, it was a man. Here, inside my shop. Inside my *house*.

I forced my heart out of my throat, mustered all my courage, and whirled around, brandishing my purse as a weapon. It made contact with someone. Without my glasses, and high on adrenaline, I saw the man only as a blur in my line of vision. Tall. Swarthy. Baseball cap turned backward. Wielding a hammer.

I held one arm out like I was Diana Ross singing "Stop in the Name of Love." "Who are you?" I said in my best Sigourney Weaver kick-ass voice.

"Take it easy, Cassidy."

Oh my . . . Meemaw was the only one who called me Cassidy instead of Harlow. Was this a home invasion? Had he already riffled through my personal journals to get to know his victim?

"Who are you?" I repeated, swinging my purse again at his fuzzy form. I wasn't going down without a fight.

He took a step back, waving a hand in front of him. "Whoa, what's in there? Bricks?"

"Ha, very original," I scoffed. "The usual. Wallet. A paperback. Pepper spray." I was lying about the pepper spray. I had some in a drawer upstairs. Never left home in New York without it, but I hadn't thought it was necessary in Bliss.

I advanced on him, swinging my purse with intention this time, back and forth, back and forth. "Now," I said, sounding much more confident than I felt considering this could well be Nell's killer, "for the last time, who the hell are you?"

Chapter 15

"I'm Will Flores." When I stared at him blankly, he continued. "I came by to fix a few things?"

The surprise of finding him in the house had me in a New York state of mind. By that, I mean hyperwary. "By breaking and entering?"

A look of indignation formed on his face. "Uh, no."

My eyes narrowed. "Then how'd you get in here? I know I locked the door."

My body tensed, my grip tightening on the strap of my purse, as he reached into his jeans pocket. His hand reappeared a second later holding up a key.

I darted forward to snatch it out of his hand, but he palmed it. "How'd you get a key to my house?"

"Loretta Mae gave it to me."

"No, she didn't."

"Uh, yes, she did."

I peered at him, trying to focus my vision. Who did he think he was? "She would *not* have given some stranger a key," I said slowly. He could not pull the wool over my eyes.

He raised one irritated eyebrow. "First of all," he said, "I wasn't a stranger."

I could feel the dark, scorching look he had trained on me and it sent a chill up my spine.

"And second of all, it's not like you've been around here the last"—he made a show of counting on his fingers—"fifteen years to know whether or not your great-grandmother gave me a key."

The words slashed the air between us, carving a hole right through my heart. How did he know how long I'd been gone, or that Loretta Mae was my great-grandmother? My temperature skyrocketed. I sputtered, speechless.

But he went on, cool as a cucumber. "She would be horrified to see you've lost every ounce of whatever Southern grace you once possessed."

I gasped, recoiling like I'd been slapped across the face. How dare he stand in my house and hurl ... The truth dawned on me. Oh. My. God. This guy was one of those scammers who duped the elderly. "Get out."

He spun around, muttering something under his breath that sounded an awful lot like, "There you go, right there, damn Yankee."

"I am *not* a Yankee," I said, shooting daggers at him. Like my long-departed Uncle Jimmy used to say, "Once a Texan, always a Texan."

Will Flores, whoever he was, had planted a seed, though. A fissure of doubt opened up inside me. Could I have lost some of my Southernness? And why did the mere idea of it fill me with such sadness?

He threw up his hands, the hammer still gripped in one. "Let's start again, shall we?"

I shook my head. "We're not starting anything until you drop your weapon."

He glanced at the tool, then at me, one side of his mouth curving up. *"Por supuesto,"* he said, then quickly added, "Sure."

As he turned to set it down on the antique desk next to the workroom, I scrounged for my glasses, finding them on the seat of the settee.

When he turned, I got a clearer look at him. Still tall, maybe six feet one. Still wearing a rear-facing ball cap. A Longhorns cap, which meant he couldn't be *all* bad. Still swarthy. Puerto Rican, maybe? No, Mexican. And a goatee.

One thing was for sure. He was handsome as all getout, but in an arrogant, Rhett Butler kind of way.

"I'm Will Flores," he said again. "Your great-grandmother arranged a standing handyman appointment with me. Every Tuesday, I come by to do whatever repairs are needed."

Right. Like I was going to buy *that*. I kept my purse at the ready. "I've been here for almost two months. That's eight Tuesdays. So, where've you been?"

Before he could answer, I continued. "You're pretty unreliable. Loretta Mae wouldn't have tolerated that."

"I've been out of town on business. Happens every now and then. Loretta Mae didn't have a problem with it."

"Handyman business? Uh-uh. Loretta Mae expected people to be dependable."

"No, not handyman business, and I am dependable."

"When it suits you."

"All the time."

We went back and forth until steam was ready to come out my ears. Why would Meemaw have agreed to some half-cocked arrangement with this guy—

And then it hit me. I smacked my forehead with the heel of my hand. "Oh, no, Meemaw. No, no, no."

The sheers on either side of the front window fluttered. God almighty, this was a fix-up from the great beyond. Meemaw wanted me back home and here *I* was. She wanted this handyman to come around weekly and here *he* was. Now, lo and behold, here *we* were, together.

Somewhere, Loretta Mae was nodding her head in complete satisfaction.

Will gave the windows a quick examination. He shook his head. "There's no place a draft could be coming from. I sealed those windows myself." He turned back to me, the right side of his mouth quirking up. "Looks like you have a ghost in the house, Cassidy."

With those ten words, my world came to a staggering halt. My mind raced. The gathering room had been Loretta Mae's favorite spot. I spun, taking a careful look around, absorbing every detail and comparing them to the details of the past. Even with the addition of my things, the room maintained the same feeling it had when Meemaw was right here.

Dappled sunlight shone through the front window. The warm mustard color of the walls and the antique furniture made it cozy. The magazines were neatly stacked on the coffee table and two pairs of flip-flops, one black, one brown, sat side by side right next to the front door. The pictures hanging on the display board were perfectly aligned. Everything was just as it should be. As it always had been.

Will said something and I registered him going from window to window, but I was too distracted now to pay attention. Loretta Mae always said she'd wanted me home in Bliss so she could spend more time with me. Recently I'd felt drafts of air and heard doors slam when all the windows were closed. Could it be . . . could she really still be here in the house?

It was an impossible idea. Goat-whispering and a bionic green thumb were a far cry from haunting. Even for a Cassidy woman. And yet . . .

I could test the theory, couldn't I? If she was really here, would she materialize if I asked her to?

The idea stuck with me. I dug in my purse until I found my little portable sewing kit, something I carried at all times. Inside was a mini pincushion with a needle, a tape measure, and spools of white and black thread, all for emergency clothing repair. Grabbing the black thread, I set it next to Will's hammer on the antique desk.

"Meemaw," I whispered, feeling more than a little ridiculous. "If you can hear me, move the thread."

I held my breath and waited, my eyes glued on the spool. It didn't budge. I forced a little laugh, but tears pricked behind my eyelids. I'd *wanted* it to move. I wanted Loretta Mae to be here with me.

There was a slight disturbance in the air behind me. "Meemaw?" I whirled around and saw . . . Will.

My shoulders sagged and my hopes deflated.

"Who are you talking to?" he asked.

"Nobody."

His left eyebrow angled down as he peered at me. He

looked like he thought I belonged in the loony bin. Maybe I did. I eyed the thread again. It was exactly where I'd placed it. I had to face that Meemaw was gone.

I blinked away the tears that threatened and re-grouped, directing my emotions at Will. This stranger was still in my house, and was apparently accustomed to coming and going as he pleased. *That* was a habit that needed to be broken. "About whatever deal you had with Meemaw—I don't need a handyman."

Which was a complete lie. I needed a handyman, bad, but not one Meemaw picked out for me.

"I'm not—"

He stopped when I held my hand out. Then, as under-standing dawned, he dug the house key out of his pocket and set it on my palm.

As I wrapped my hand around the key, what he'd started to say sunk in. "You're not what?"

He turned his hat around. "A handyman."

Not what I'd expected. "You're not a . . . Then why did Loretta Mae hire you to come repair things?"

His eyes had darkened and his smile faded. "I got the impression you and she were close."

I bristled. Who *was* he to pass some sort of judgment on my relationship with Meemaw? I could almost hear her laughing, but it was just the sheers fluttering again.

My heart stopped. The sheers . . . again. And it *did* sound like laughter. "We *were* close," I said as I moved stealthily toward the window.

"If you say so."

"I do."

"Then I'm surprised you don't know about our ar-rangement, since it involves you."

I whipped around. "It involves me how?"

"Loretta Mae didn't *hire* me, Cassidy. We negoti-ated."

The sheers had fallen still again. The room was full of anticipation, as if it were holding its breath, waiting to hear the bomb he was about to drop.

He folded his arms over his chest and rocked back on his heels, looking like he was enjoying this showdown a little too much. "We agreed that I'd do repair work around here in return for you giving my daughter sewing lessons."

I stumbled back, not because Will Flores had a daughter, which meant he also had a wife, which was good. I had other things to think about. And not because he'd told me about the sneaky deal he and Meemaw had made behind my back.

No, my knees buckled because the shoes that had been neatly lined up next to the front door were now staggered in a footprint pattern.

Oh, my God. Meemaw hadn't moved the thread. She'd moved the shoes.

Chapter 16

Will ran his hands around the window frame one last time. "No draft," he pronounced with finality.

"That's a relief."

"She's itching to get back at it," he said over his shoulder.

I'd lost the thread of the conversation. "Who's itching to get back at what?"

"Gracie. My daughter?" He felt my forehead with the back of his hand. "You doin' okay there, Cassidy?"

I batted his hand away. "Right. Of course. I'm fine."

He picked up his hammer and went up the three steps to the kitchen. "She started with an apron. She's made a couple skirts and a vest. I've been holding her back, giving you time to get settled, but she's itching to get started. She's coming by this after—"

A shrill holler came from the workroom. No! My heart seized and I ran toward the noise. I knew that sound all too well. Thelma Louise.

The Geena Davis/Susan Sarandon movie was Nana's favorite. When naming the grand dam of her goat herd she hadn't been able to decide: Thelma or Louise? In true Texas tradition, she settled on both.

The doe whacked her flat, Romanesque nose against the window in the workroom between her ear-piercing bleats. I charged forward. "Stop it, Thelma Louise!" I scolded, wagging my finger at her. "Shoo!"

The ornery Nubian dairy goat ignored me. Her floppy white ears swung back and forth on either side of her black-and-brown face as she shook her head. I stared her down. She never blinked, but just as suddenly as she'd started banging on the window, she stopped, ducked her head, and vanished.

There was plenty of grass for the goats to graze on Nana's farm, especially after Mama paid a visit and her charm made it grow extra lush, but *my* yard, which Meemaw had tended to so carefully, was full of flowers. And now Thelma Louise had scampered off to wreak havoc.

"Oh, no, you don't," I said, dodging the cutting table and a dress form as I raced out of the workroom.

Will leaned against the back of the couch, watching the scene unfold as if it were dinner theater and he wasn't sure what his part was or when to step in. "You need help, Cassidy?" he asked as I zoomed to the kitchen door to cut Thelma off at the pass.

He'd already helped me enough by bargaining with Meemaw. I flung my hand up in a dismissive wave. "Nope, I'm good."

First order of business: Stop Thelma from destroying the flowers.

Second order of business: Figure out how to postpone sewing lessons for Gracie Flores.

Third order of business: Make Josie's wedding gown, and the bridesmaids' dresses.

The screen door banged behind me as I ran across the back porch and took the steps in a single bound. Nana and Granddaddy had five acres behind my lot and their land stretched the entire block behind the square. I had a little less than a third of an acre, which was more than plenty. I caught a glimpse of the gate between my property and my grandparents' farm. Wide open. Easy to see how Thelma Louise had escaped.

Maybe Will would fix *that*. We could renegotiate and I could pay him cash for the repair work. And then he could find a different sewing teacher for his little girl.

Scratch that. I didn't have any money to spare.

I scanned the yard. "Here, Thelma Louise," I called, clucking my tongue. I followed the flagstone steps to the front. As I rounded the corner, my stomach dropped. The doe stood, nose to the ground, just a few feet from where Nell had died. "Thelma Louise!"

I dashed over to her, grabbed her by the pale green collar Nana put on all her goats, and yanked her away from the scene of the crime and the leftover crime scene tape. It all felt very ominous in my yard. Any evidence had already been taken, but what if they'd missed something? Goats were notorious for eating anything and everything. I didn't want Thelma to digest something that could lead to Nell's killer.

"Come on," I said to her.

She dug her hooves into the ground, rooting herself there. "Ornery" was an understatement. She was downright defiant.

"Thelma, come on. Let's go." I stroked her neck and side, trying to coax her forward, but she wouldn't budge. Instead she let out a long, mournful sound that settled over the yard like a light dusting of snowflakes.

Nana's Nubians, as well as her LaManchas, couldn't bear to be away from her. She was like their mother. They connected on some deep, inexplicable level. The goat-whisperer. All she had to do was touch them, or coo, and they calmed and obeyed.

I was definitely not a goat-whisperer.

"Let's go home," I cooed, but Thelma wagged her head.

I tried a few more times, finally giving up and backing away. I couldn't leave her here. She'd destroy the flowers for sure. But I couldn't get her to move.

The front door creaked open, the faint jingling bells dinging as it banged shut. Will sauntered across the porch, a length of rope swinging from his right hand. He didn't even bother hiding his amusement. "Need a rope, darlin'?"

Darlin'? My blood boiled. I was not his darlin'. I was *nobody's* darlin'. "No, thanks, cowboy," I said, regretting my pride. That rope would come in handy.

I stroked Thelma's neck again, scratching at the Fu Manchu beard under her chin. "Come on, girl. Let's go."

She cocked her head and looked up at me. I couldn't see the rectangular pupil, but her usually soulful black eyes looked like she was plotting something. She suddenly kicked her hind legs and took off, scooting across the front yard, past the archway, to the street. I sped after her, snatching the rope from Will's hand as I passed him.

He didn't say a word, just released it to me as I kept on the chase, my skirt slapping around my legs as I ran after the ornery goat.

Thelma turned around, darted past me, and trotted back to where she'd been a minute before. She stopped, cocked her head, and gave me a penetrating look that seemed to go straight into my soul. With a start I realized she was standing in the exact spot where Nell's body had lain. Before I could grab her, she bolted again, charging through the yard, slowing to scratch her body against the low, jasmine-covered fence.

I tiptoed up to her and before she could dodge me again, I slipped the rope through her collar, grabbed both ends, and tugged at it. "Come on, Thelma, move," I said. She followed, but I'd made it only a few steps when something reflected in the sunlight.

Holding tight to the rope, I bent down.

"What's that?" Will's voice was directly behind me now.

He was not going to leave, was he? Mentally, I shook a fist in the air at Meemaw, wherever she was, but in reality, I lifted the object for him to see. It was a small handheld mirror. And it had definitely seen better days. The glass was scratched like someone had taken a knife to it, the plastic handle worn and smudged.

How long had it been buried under the foliage of Meemaw's yard?

"Thelma Louise! You naughty girl." Nana barreled toward us, her straw cowboy hat tipped back on her head. Her outfit, from her Wrangler jeans to her pink-and-gray plaid shirt, looked like it had come straight out of a Drysdales catalog.

Thelma Louise gave Nana a contrite look. The jig was up. "Someone took the bungee cord off the gate," Nana said. "Without it, Thelma Louise can open the latch, no problem. She's the smartest of the bunch," she added, a touch of pride in her voice.

I handed her the rope. Wagging my finger at Thelma Louise, I chided, "Don't do that again, you hear me? I have some dresses to make. No time for your shenanigans."

The doe ignored the scolding, instead giving me that penetrating gaze again. As I watched Nana lead her back to her farm, I wondered how smart goats really were.

Chapter 17

By two o'clock, I'd placed a rush order on fifteen yards of Diamond French silk and the other fabrics needed for the bridal dresses, *and* I'd searched every corner of Buttons & Bows, including the attic, looking for any piece of trim, cording, or braiding that might have left the odd strangulation markings on Nell's neck.

Nothing came even remotely close.

Despite leaving a message for Josie, I hadn't heard from her since I'd left her with Nate at the Sheriff's Department. I directed all my restless energy on the muslin mock-up of her gown.

Then I finalized my sketch for Karen's dress—a flirty black number with just enough flare to be fun. She seemed buttoned up, not the fun-loving type. If I made her the right dress, maybe she'd let loose at the wedding a little bit and really enjoy herself.

Will Flores gathered up his things after patching the gouge in the wall left by the rogue shelf leg. He pointed to the shelf itself. "Nice fix-it with the bricks."

I thanked him and he left.

We hadn't gotten off on the right foot and now he was trying to make nice. Yes, I'd freaked walking in to find a strange man in the house, but maybe I'd overreacted.

Though there'd been no more conversation about me teaching his little girl how to sew, I felt a fissure of guilt opening up over it. Loretta Mae had made a promise. There was no way I could not honor it. I just had to get through sewing the wedding gown and the bridesmaid dresses first.

My little dressmaking shop felt suddenly quiet without him rattling about. I was left thinking about Loretta Mae, the shoes by the front door, and how Will had remarked that I had a ghost hanging around. I was pretty sure he was right. "You're here, aren't you, Meemaw?"

The wind seemed to moan, and it almost sounded like someone said, "Yes," only there wasn't any wind today. The air outside was still.

I stepped back from the dress form, setting my pincushion down on the cutting table. Slowly, I turned around, looking for a sign. "Meemaw?"

The air outside seemed to sigh and murmur in response, the green spring leaves on the tree branches brightening. Every creak of the old house was magnified. Even the silence was deafening to my ears.

My imagination was definitely getting the better of me.

I turned back to Josie's muslin sample, but a movement by the front door, followed by a shuffle, made my breath catch. I'd left the shoes in the odd footstep pattern I'd found them in earlier, but now the two pairs of flip-flops were side by side, in another pattern. One black, one brown, one black, one brown.

My heart skittered. It had to be her! Meemaw was forever wearing two colors of socks, two different shoes, mismatched gloves. "All to go with my eyes," she'd say. She had one blue eye and one brown eye, something, thankfully, I hadn't inherited.

"Meemaw! Is that you?"

From the coffee table, the cover of my lookbook flipped open. The pages snapped back and forth, like someone was frantically searching through them. I lost my breath as I watched. Would this be happening if Mama were here, or Will Flores, or anyone else? Or was this haunting encounter for my eyes only?

Finally, the fanning pages settled down. The book lay open on the table next to the embossed box I'd brought back from Chinatown in New York.

I slowly walked toward the couch, glancing over my

shoulder, half expecting to see a ghost hovering behind me.

"How . . . ?"

No answer.

I caught sight of my reflection in the antique oval floor mirror. My shoulders were hunched and my face was pale. "It's Loretta Mae," I muttered, trying to stay calm, "not Freddy Krueger," but my heart still thundered like it was ready to beat right out of my chest.

"Meemaw?" I whispered, but there was no response. Perching on the edge of the couch, I gingerly pulled the lookbook toward me.

It was open to the beginning of my Southern Industrial collection, a look I'd envisioned while working on Maximilian's urban chic line a few years back. The Southern Industrial collection was a combination of feminine fabric and edgy details: a ruffle thrown in to balance the hard lines or a custom-designed floral fabric with an angular black belt. My small-town sensibility always crept in.

I read the introduction text.

> The Southern Industrial collection bridges my Texas roots with a modern style. It is a tribute to the women in my life: Coleta Cassidy, my grandmother, Tessa Cassidy, my mother, and most of all to Loretta Mae Cassidy, the woman who taught me to sew, my inspiration, and the original Southern Industrial woman.
> This is for you, Meemaw.

I didn't need any more proof that Meemaw was right here by my side.

For an hour, Meemaw and I did a little get-to-know-you dance. Of course we already knew each other, probably better than anyone else ever could, but with her being an invisible ghost and me, well, *not*, it seemed a good idea to learn how to communicate more effectively.

I moved an object and she moved it back. "I miss you,

Meemaw. Why'd you have to go?" I said aloud, though my thoughts were more self-chastising. *Why hadn't I come back sooner? Why had I been so foolish?* I was full of whys and why nots, but none of them really mattered at the moment.

The pages of several magazines on the table flipped back and forth on their own. It took me a minute, but I'd finally realized she was trying to communicate with me. It took a while longer to piece together her response. *I'm here with you now, sugar.*

Yes, she was, and it was as though a weight I hadn't even known I'd been carrying was suddenly lifted off my shoulders. I felt lighter. Freer. Like running my dress-making shop and boutique in this house on Mockingbird Lane really was what I was supposed to be doing. It felt as though a sun-soaked cotton sheet, pulled straight off the clothesline outside, had been carried in by a breeze until it floated down over me, warming me to the bone.

We went back and forth, with me posing questions and her flipping the magazine pages until I could puzzle out her responses.

I finally asked her the question that had been on my mind since I'd learned I'd inherited her house. "Why'd you leave this place to me?"

Everything was quiet. The window sheers hung limply. The leaves on the trees and the flowers outside were motionless. Every cell in my body constricted. I'd had her back in my life for less than an hour. She couldn't be gone already.

Finally, the corner of a magazine page fluttered. Slowly, as if it were made of lead instead of paper, it turned. I exhaled and the tension I'd built up in the last sixty seconds released with a burst. She was still here.

The pages gained momentum, flipping back and forth until Meemaw apparently found the word she was looking for. I didn't know which word on the page she wanted me to read, but a drop of water suddenly fell on the glossy paper. Moisture spread, encircling the word "wanted."

There was no rain. I didn't have a leak. So where had the tiny drop of water come from?

Page by page, she communicated the answer to my question. *Wanted you home where you belong.* Another drop fell, the moisture spreading across the page, and in that moment, I realized it wasn't water or rain or anything else making the droplets. They were Meemaw's tears.

She spelled out the rest of her message. *And you know I always get what I want.*

Chapter 18

"I'm here," Mama said as she burst through the front door of the shop. Her hair was pulled into a loose ponytail, her sunglasses perched on top of her head, and her cheeks were flushed. This time she carried a terra-cotta pot. A sad-looking orchid drooped despite the stake holding it up. "I brought this, just in case," she said when she caught me frowning at it.

I swallowed the last bit of the smashed lemon cream puff I'd finally remembered and rescued from the bakery bag. "In case what?"

She held the pot tighter. "When you called, I could tell somethin' big's goin' on. Better that my energy go to this plant than to the weeds outside."

My mother had never been a planner, least of all where her charm was concerned. Carrying a plant with her so she could direct her energy was real progress. Particularly in light of Madelyn Brighton's photographic proof that something was fishy with the foliage in my yard.

"Now, where's the fire?" she said, setting the pot down on the coffee table.

Before I could respond, Nana crashed through the kitchen door and barreled into the shop. "I came as fast as I could. It's a full moon tonight and Thelma Louise and Junebug are downright rascally. I've had to give 'em both a good what-for." Even her rushed words sounded slow-paced with her drawl. She looked at me, then at Mama and her droopy orchid. "What's goin' on?"

I sat them down and filled them in on Josie being taken in for questioning, Madelyn's pictures, the strange pattern on Nell's neck, and the sheriff's people searching Buttons & Bows. I wanted to keep Meemaw to myself a little longer, even just a few hours.

A clatter came from the workroom. Maybe she had other ideas. I spun around and started to say, "Meemaw?" but stopped myself just in time.

The noise vanished.

Mama and my grandmother hadn't heard a thing. "Ladybug," Nana was saying, "they can't possibly think you had anything to do with that poor girl dying. Why, you didn't even know her. It'll be fine."

I sank back against the sofa, pushing my glasses to the top of my head and pinching the bridge of my nose. The dress form with the muslin sample of Josie's dress beckoned me and Nell's murder weighed heavy on my mind. I still hadn't heard from Josie. I wondered what else could happen to turn this day topsy-turvy.

A light swishing sound came from the workroom, like there was a tornado slowly tunneling right inside the house. "Thelma Louise?" Nana shrilled. She jumped up, making the terra-cotta pot with the orchid teeter as she raced through the French doors.

I grabbed the pot to stop it from falling. "It's coming from outside," I hollered.

She stopped short, turned on her sock feet, and hurried past me, straight into the kitchen. Mama was on her heels. It wasn't Thelma Louise, or Junebug, or any of Nana's goats. I knew that, but I wanted at least one more minute alone with Meemaw before I had to share her. I held open the door to the back porch and the two of them skipped down the steps and into the backyard, spinning around, looking for a goat that wasn't there.

I stayed inside.

For a second I thought I'd imagined the ruckus, but

then a movement next to the stove caught my eye. "Meemaw?" I whispered, afraid that if I spoke too loud the nebulous glow in the corner would spook and vanish.

I stared at the hazy shape, but I couldn't make out any details. There was no definition to the form, no structure or facial features visible, no limbs, and no color. It was like a curvy cloud. I couldn't say it was a human form, but I was still sure it was Loretta Mae.

All the possible words to describe what I was seeing flew through my mind. *Wraith, specter, spirit, ghost, spook, apparition, phantom.* I didn't know what to call her. I took a gingerly step forward. "Meemaw?"

In true Loretta Mae form, the apparition spun around, turning into a funnel cloud, skirting across the floor, passing right through the cutting table in the center of the room. I gasped.

"Is it really you?" I whispered, but quickly clamped my mouth shut as Mama and Nana plowed back into the kitchen. I held tight to Mama's flowerpot, my fingers trembling and cold. The orchid shivered. The white of the petals had become brighter and the soft pink streaks had turned to a hot, vibrant color.

I stood there, shaking, as the wispy form shimmied in front of me.

"Did the goat come in here?" Nana searched the room, even crouching and looking under the table, but Mama stared at me. Stared at the flower. "Harlow, what's wrong? You look like you've seen a ghost."

My jaw dropped. She didn't see the apparition. Before I could answer, the front door to the shop flew open and Josie stumbled in.

"Harlow." She collapsed onto the floor, leaning back against the wall as if she couldn't hold herself upright, her sobs scattering away the spookiness.

With a furtive glance at Meemaw, I hurried to Josie, kneeling by her side. "What happened? Are you okay?"

Mama and Nana followed me back to the shop.

Tears streamed down Josie's face. A dark trail of mascara stained her pale cheeks. "I-It's N-Nate."

Oh, God, was he hurt? Had there been an accident? "Tell me," I said, my hand stroking her back.

"The sheriff—" She broke off, hiccuping and gasping for breath. "He . . . he . . . he's saying Nate's a person of interest . . ." She choked the rest of the words out. "They think he might be involved in Nell's murder."

Chapter 19

"Please, Harlow," Josie begged, "you have to help me. He didn't kill Nell."

My mind spun in circles. I wasn't a police officer or a detective. I was a dressmaker. My expertise was in fabrics and design. Not to mention that given the way the sheriff's people had combed through Buttons & Bows, I also might be a person of interest.

I didn't know how to help Josie. But she was a friend—or at least she might become one as we got reacquainted. And her future was skittering down the drain.

Nana had skipped out to do the second daily milking of her does. I had gathered Josie and my mother around the kitchen table, where we sat sipping coffee.

"What exactly did the sheriff say?" I asked.

Josie wrapped her hands around her coral-colored mug and twisted it back and forth. "He asked me about Nell. He wanted to know about our friendship, how long I'd worked for her, plans for the store, if she had any enemies."

Okay. Those all seemed like good questions. "What did you tell him?"

Her face was drawn. "I've worked at the bead shop for three years. I love it. Nell was a pretty good boss. We became friends."

"What about enemies?" I asked. That seemed like the most pertinent question.

She looked at me with red-rimmed eyes. The morning

at the sheriff's office had taken its toll on her. "Not that I know of. She wasn't real close to a lot of people, but I didn't know anyone who didn't like her."

"And Nate ... ?"

She hung her head, her bangs falling over her eyes in bedraggled clumps. "Apparently they went on a few dates once."

"They ... you mean Nate and Nell?"

"But it was a long time ago!"

All the breath left my body as Nell's words came back to me like a sucker punch to the gut. "I hope he doesn't break her heart." She'd sounded like she cared about Josie, but what if she'd been speaking from her own experience with Nate? Had he broken Nell's heart? Had she threatened to tell?

"How long ago?" Mama asked.

"Before I knew Nell," she said, "so more than three years ago. Nate has no reason to k-kill Nell."

Mama's face was pensive as she listened to every word Josie uttered. She lowered her chin and I knew just what she was thinking. Hoss McClaine must have good reason to be watching Nate Kincaid, and a previous relationship with the victim fit the bill. I didn't love it that the sheriff appeared to be sneaking around with my mother, but he'd always been as honest as the day is long.

If Nate had an alibi, he'd be in the clear. Had he offered one up to the sheriff? "Where was he last night?"

Josie spun her untouched coffee mug around. "Working."

"With other people?" I asked.

She kept her eyes downcast. "I don't know. He said he couldn't talk about it."

Josie had spent quite a while on her cell phone the night before after discovering Nell's body in the bluebonnet patch. She'd spent a lot of that time talking to Nate's mother, but had she talked to him? "Did you call him last night?"

A little spasm crossed her pale face, there and gone so quickly I thought I imagined it. "He wasn't able to take any calls."

So Josie didn't know where he'd been, hadn't talked to him, and he wasn't offering up an alibi. That didn't bode well for Nate. But if Nate had killed Nell, why would he step one foot in the sheriff's office? Wouldn't the murderer steer clear of the authorities?

Either he wasn't guilty . . . or he was playing a dangerous game.

"He burst in on the sheriff and me this morning and demanded to know what was going on, why I was being interrogated again. He was like my knight in shining armor, you know?"

What I knew was that Josie sounded like she was trying to convince herself that he was her white knight.

"It'll sort itself out," Mama said, laying her hand on Josie's shoulder.

One way or another.

Josie's face clouded as she looked at Mama. "I don't know. The sheriff asked me to step out so he could talk to Nate alone. They were in there for a good hour. And when they came out of the room—" Her mouth pulled down on either side and her eyes welled with tears. "When they came out of the room," she said around her sobs, "he warned Nate to stick around and said he'd be seeing him real soon."

My sketchbook was propped up on the kitchen counter, still open to the final sketch of Josie's wedding gown. It was like a beacon, drawing my eye. I'd wanted so much for it to be the perfect dress for her, to weave in her wishes and dreams so they'd come true. But everything in Bliss was suddenly unraveling and I was completely at a loss. "I don't know what I can do," I said, circling back to her asking me for help.

Clutching my hands, she looked at me with her doe eyes. "He had nothing to do with Nell's death." She pulled one hand free and wiped away a stray tear. "I shouldn't have brought up the investigation. The wedding's in eleven days. All you need to do is make the dresses."

Mama and I both started, flashing each other another look.

"Josie," Mama said, "maybe you'd best sleep on things. See how you feel in the morning."

She scraped her chair back and stood up, pulling herself together. "Uh-uh. I don't need to sleep on anything." She angled her head to the side, looking calm and in control again. "He's innocent."

She knelt in front of me, taking my hands. "He's the one, Harlow. I know Nell never believed he loved me. I don't know, maybe she still had feelings for him. Maybe she saw everyone else in relationships and was jealous. But he loves me. I *know* he does. Just like I know he's innocent."

Suddenly Josie was eleven years old and trailing behind me, telling me she wished she was a Cassidy and had a family like I did. I blinked, and the image slipped away. Slowly, I nodded. "If I have anything to do with it, there will be a wedding. I'll make the dresses, Josie, and I'll keep my ears open, too."

"Harlow!" Mama hissed under her breath, but I ignored her.

I'd do whatever I could to either prove Nate's innocence or prove his guilt. Either way, Josie would have an answer, and hopefully the security of the family she'd always wanted. And I'd be able to live with myself.

Josie stood up and flipped her bangs out of her eyes. "Thank you," she said, breathing out as if the weight of the world had been lifted off her shoulders. "Should we do a fitting or something?"

The muslin mock-up was far enough along for her to try on. I started to follow her to the workroom, but Mama grabbed hold of my sleeve, pulling me to a stop. "Harlow Jane Cassidy, what do you think you're doin'?"

I gingerly unwrapped her fingers from my arm. "I'm helping a friend."

"You've known that girl for twenty-four hours."

I tapped my thumb against the tips of my fingers like I was counting. "Plus about twenty-five years, give or take."

"Goin' to school together doesn't mean you know her. Or Nate Kincaid." She gave me a slow, appraising look. "You and I both know that family will do anything they can to get out of a prickly situation."

"Maybe Nate really *has* changed."

She shook her head, not willing to give an inch.

No matter what Mama thought, Josie had asked me for help. She wanted to believe in her fiancé. How could I turn my back on her?

But he's a Kincaid, I thought, *and being a Kincaid means looking out for no one but yourself.*

I slammed the door on the little voice in my head. I'd made my mind up and nothing would change it. "If he *is* guilty, she's going to need a friend. And if he's not, then someone else killed Nell on *my* property. Maybe even after being in *my* shop." None of that sat well with me. In fact, it pretty much had my head swirling in a frenzy of disbelief.

I'd always gauged a lot of my decisions by Loretta Mae's standards, just like all the Cassidy women did. She was like our moral compass. "What would Meemaw do?" I asked, shooting a lightning-quick glance around the kitchen in case Meemaw's nebulous form suddenly reappeared, but there were no disturbances to the air.

"She'd help out a friend, no question," Mama said with a sigh.

And that was that.

Chapter 20

By the time I ushered Mama out the back door and got to the workroom, Josie was in her body shaper and the muslin dress sample, such as it was, holding it closed at the side.

My stomach was still twisted over the revelation that Nell and Nate had dated. Did that mean dated, as in chaste and innocent, or *dated*, as in a passionate relationship? I doubted Josie knew the details, so despite her brave front, her gut was probably in complete knots.

She climbed onto the old milk crate I'd found in the backyard as I looked for my pincushion. It was not where I'd left it. I finally spotted it on the shelf that had attacked Nell, sitting in front of a row of button-filled mason jars.

"*Meemaw,* you trickster," I said under my breath, but inside I smiled. It comforted me to know that she was present in the house. I studied the sample dress on Josie, thinking about the cut and the fit. Meemaw had taught me to "check twice, sew once." No pattern—ready-made or custom—ever fit a person perfectly. This was no exception.

I got right to work, using a red, fine-tipped marker and pin-basting the new seams on the muslin so I'd get the perfect fit on the actual garment. Making a muslin sample took extra time, but it was worth the effort. It would serve as my pattern when I was done, and it would guarantee the wedding dress would fit properly. Better to tweak and manipulate inexpensive muslin than the expensive silk.

My hopes for Josie—that Nate was innocent and that their marriage would be filled with love and family— flowed through my fingers and into the fabric as I pricked it with the sharp points of the dressmaker pins. But if I was going to help them, I had to ask the hard questions. "So Nate never mentioned he and Nell had . . . dated?"

There was a heavy pause before she answered.

"No. Neither did she." She swallowed before continuing and I knew she was working hard to hold herself together. "He . . . he told me after he talked to the sheriff. He said he didn't want me to hear it from someone else."

I couldn't help the grimace that immediately crinkled my lips. It sounded to me like Nate had 'fessed up because the sheriff had found out and called him on it.

Mama's voice in my head kept repeating, *He's a Kincaid.*

Nate worked for the family oil business, but from what Josie said, his passion was the charity organization his grandparents had started: The Justin and Vanetta Kincaid Family Foundation. Grabbing my sketchbook, I flipped to the back page and scribbled down a few quick questions as they popped into my head.

- Did Nate tell the truth about when he had a fling with Nell, or was it more recent?
- Could Nell have been blackmailing Nate about their past?
- What business was Nate doing when Nell was killed?

I closed the book and moved to Josie's other side, sliding a pin in to tighten the seam along her torso. "And you never suspected they'd dated?"

"No, never."

She fell silent and when I looked up at her, she was frowning.

I stopped pinning. "What?"

"It's just . . . she always said things like, 'The Kincaids are all charmers, Josie. Don't get involved' or 'Hope you know what you're doing.' Stuff like that. Now I'm wondering if she said all that because she was still . . ."

She broke off, but I finished the sentence in my head: . . . *in love with him.*

"Do you think she wanted you to break it off?"

"I never thought so, not really, but now . . ."

I moved in front of her, adjusting the horizontal pleats. "How long have you and Nate been together?"

"Eight months."

The three pins I'd stuck between my lips fell when my jaw dropped. "That's not very long."

She allowed herself a small smile. "When you know, you know," she said.

But *did* she know? I wondered as I picked up the sharp pins.

She stared out the window toward Nana's goat dairy, lost in thought. Finally she said, "Do you know Miriam?"

"I used to know her." Once upon a time.

"She comes into the bead shop all the time."

"Really?" Miriam Kincaid hanging out in a bead shop made about as much sense as her mother cleaning her own windows. The Kincaids' only daughter had always seemed pretty levelheaded, but she also didn't strike me as a do-it-yourself costume-jewelry kind of woman. "I thought they were more into diamonds and rubies, not plastic."

"Nate's mom is, definitely, but not Miriam. She's more like Nate, pretty down-to-earth."

"And she makes her own jewelry? With beads?"

"She tries. She's taken a few classes with her daughter, Holly."

I remembered hearing that Miriam had married and divorced right after college. Guess I'd forgotten she'd had a baby, too. "How old is her daughter?"

Josie pulled her hair back, holding it away from her face, fanning herself with her other hand. "Fifteen. She's a nice girl. I asked them both to be in the wedding. I thought Miriam should be the maid of honor."

I'd wondered about that. It had seemed odd to me that Nate's sister wasn't a bridesmaid. As we chatted, I made a mental note to adjust the vertical darts underneath the pleating. They shot up like arrows from the waist, ending just under the breasts, giving shape to the bodice.

The fabric slipped. Josie dropped her hair and pressed her palm against the muslin to hold it in place, answering my question before I could even ask it. "She was going to be in it, but then she came into the shop about a week ago and something happened. I remember it so clearly. She was fine, you know? Chatting with everyone and laughing. She picked out beads to make Holly a key chain. The next day she came by again and told me she couldn't be maid of honor. Couldn't be in the wedding at all."

I'd stopped pinning. "Did you ask her why?"

Her forehead crinkled, like it was a strain to remember. "She said she just couldn't do it. That was it." Her voice cracked. "I don't know what happened. She stopped coming to the bead shop after that. It's like she doesn't even want to talk to me. Derek's the same way. He's never given me the time of day."

"That's not surprising," I said with a grimace. "From what I heard, he pretty much fell off the face of the planet."

"Off the planet and right into the oil business. He travels a lot, but he comes back pretty regularly. I'd hate it if Nate traveled like that. Why even be married?"

I completely agreed, but not everyone saw it that way. "Works for Nate's mom."

Josie smiled, the first genuine smile all day. "Money, money, money," she sang. "Must be funny, in a rich man's world."

"Abba is so wise," I said with a laugh, but decided to add the question, Why did Miriam drop out of the wedding? to the list in my sketchbook.

I finished the darts and moved on to the back of the bodice. "Does Nate get along with his siblings?" I asked.

She thought about it, taking her time answering. "They're all different, you know, but Nate and Miriam get along pretty well. Not lately, since the bridesmaid thing," she said, "but usually. Derek's different. More like his dad, I guess."

"How so?"

She hesitated. "They're going to be my family."

I'd wanted to hear her take on the Kincaids, but their reputation painted a pretty clear picture of them. "I think I know what you mean. It's all image and who has the most money and the biggest diamond and the fastest car—"

"Which he does, in case you were wondering. A GranCabrio."

I raised my eyebrows in question.

"A Maserati." She dropped her voice as low as it would go, mimicking a man's voice. "Canvas hood. V8. Aerodynamic."

"A little fancier than Loretta Mae's pickup."

She laughed. "It's like the gene pool was divided and the everything's-about-image genes got concentrated in Derek."

All the money talk reminded me of the conversation I'd had with Gina at the bakery. She'd said Nell met with a lawyer. I slid another pin into the fabric. "Did Nell have a will?"

Josie shifted on the milk crate and the pin met the resistance of her hip, pricking her. "I . . . Oh!" She jerked, tottering on the makeshift platform, nearly losing her balance. "I don't know," she said, righting herself.

We were distracted by the jingling of the bell on the front door of the shop. A girl stepped in. Her owlish brown eyes lit up as they zeroed in on Josie and me in the workroom. She looked like a typical teenager: jean shorts, flat-soled flip-flops, tank top, dewy and fresh-faced like the girl-next-door image, but she could barely contain the excitement oozing from her pores. She waved, her arm making a back-and-forth half-circle motion like she was on a parade float. "Are you Harlow?" she cooed.

She left the door open slightly, practically skipping across the room until she was by my side.

I waved back at her. "That's me. Would you—" Before I could finish asking her to shut the door, the bell jingled again and it closed. I peered around her.

Will Flores was back, swagger and all. Nobody could pull off a goatee, black V-neck T-shirt, jeans, and black cowboy boots like a true country boy, and Will had the look down solid. He probably slept in those boots. "Don't be shy," he told the girl, propelling her into the workroom.

I looked from him to the girl and ... Oh, my God. In my mind, I'd imagined his daughter to be ten years old or so. This girl was practically grown up—give or take a few years. I straightened up from my crouched position, momentarily tongue-tied. I'd already mentally mapped out basic sewing instructions for a little girl. I quickly regrouped, shifting my ideas to something easy but more grown-up.

I found my voice again and extended my arm. "You must be Gracie."

She looked at my hand like she wasn't quite sure what to do with it. Okay, maybe not *quite* grown up. Finally she shook it. "Yes, ma'am," she said. "I'm Gracie Flores. Nice to meet you."

She had her father's coloring, a beautiful olive skin tone, high cheekbones, and shimmering highlights in her hair. But whereas his eyes were dark and sparkled with mischief, hers were bigger and ... I looked closer. Oh, I'd thought they were brown, but seeing them close up, I realized they were jade green with golden brown flecks. Or were they golden brown with jade green flecks?

Either way, she was ethereal, shining from the inside out. This, I thought, is what a fairy looks like.

A ray of light from the window bathed the room in a warm glow. Gracie smiled and it hit me. I'd been tossing around the idea of an autumn fashion show. If she could work an outfit and stay upright in high heels, she'd rock the runway. *If* her mom and dad would let her be a model for a day.

"Any more unexplained drafts, Cassidy?" Will settled back on the heels of his boots as Josie scurried behind the privacy screen.

I peered at him. Why was he averse to using my first name? "No, no more unexplained drafts," I said. I knew exactly what was causing them now—her name was Meemaw—but I kept this tidbit to myself.

He stayed on the shop's side of the French doors—chivalrous through and through—and adjusted the cowboy hat perched on his head, flashing a grin that said *I told you I'd be back*. "Gracie," he said, "this is Harlow Cassidy."

I was distracted by his hat. Most Texans had at least two: a straw hat for everyday wear and a leather or felt one for fancier occasions. Will's was black straw. He was a cross between Tim McGraw and Toby Keith, with those intense eyes, a swarthy complexion, and the swagger to pull it all together.

I'd seen him twice now and I couldn't help but wonder how much hair he had under the hats he wore. A full head, or was he a thirtysomething balding man trying to hide the evidence?

"So you're making a wedding dress?" Gracie rubbed her hands together in front of her, then clasped them. "That's so awesome!"

I felt I could almost see into her soul through her wide, glowing eyes. She looked like I felt being back in Bliss—all enthusiasm and spirit and energy. If I were to make her an outfit, it would be a lovely sheath dress beneath a whimsical, flirty sheer top layer embossed with tiny hearts. She had a touch of the romantic in her personality and I wondered what she wished for when she was alone.

"She's making the most beautiful dress in the world," Josie said, stepping out from behind the screen. Her eyes were still puffy from her earlier tears, but she looked better than she had this morning. It was as if the wedding gown was already bolstering her spirits.

"I can't wait to get started."

I froze, only my gaze flying from Gracie to her father. "Get started . . . on what?"

Chapter 21

"Loretta Mae said I'd be helping you."

My brain suddenly turned slushy. How did we get from sewing lessons to collaborating on a wedding dress? "She did?"

Gracie's hair swept over her shoulders as she gave an enthusiastic nod. "Kind of like your assistant! Isn't that so cool? I just can't believe my first project gets to be a wedding dress."

"Whoa, m'ija." Will wrapped his hand around his daughter's arm and pulled her back toward him. "Lessons, remember? That's what the deal was. I do a little work on the side here, and you get to hone your craft."

Gracie nodded. "I know, but Loretta Mae said I was born to be a—"

The pipes above us groaned with a loud clanking sound that drowned out Gracie's words.

"Sorry—I couldn't hear," I said. "What did Loretta Mae say?"

"She said I was—"

The pipes rumbled, louder this time, and it sounded like an angry foghorn.

I stared at the ceiling. *Meemaw.* I had a feeling my great-grandmother wasn't going to let me hear just what, exactly, she had told Gracie. "You're diabolical," I muttered under my breath so Josie, Will, and Gracie couldn't hear me. But I knew Meemaw did when the pipes gave a final rolling boom before settling back into silence.

Will tilted his head back, studying the ceiling. "Hiring a plumber might not be a bad idea."

I started to wave away the suggestion, but remembered the kitchen sink and changed my mind. "Are you offering—"

He threw his hands up. "Whoa. I'm not a plumber, I'm a—"

The pipes moaned again, louder this time.

Gracie leaned back against her dad, a spasm of concern crossing her face. She looked up at the ceiling like she was afraid the pipes might burst any second and shower us all with rusty water. "That sounded bad."

"This old house just has . . . spirit," I said. To myself I added, *And her name is Loretta Mae.* A rattling, like heavy chains being dragged across a sheet of metal, came from the kitchen.

Gracie's face turned pale. "Dad . . ." she implored.

"I'm not a plumber—"

"But you can still fix it, right?" She arched her neck back to look at him. "Please?"

The adoration of his daughter and her faith that he could fix anything wore him down. Plus she snuggled up under his arm when the pipes howled again. "I'll put it on the list," he said.

She wrapped her arms around him and gave him a hug, exhaling her relief. "Thanks, Dad." She looked at me. "Doesn't that freak you out?"

Another clank came from the kitchen and the fine hairs on the back of my neck stirred. Meemaw's spirit was as feisty as she had been in life. "They're just harmless pipes," I said loudly enough so she'd hear me, wherever she was.

Josie appeared from behind the privacy screen, looking a little bewildered. She was fully dressed and had her purse slung over her shoulder.

How in the world had she gotten out of the muslin? The only way was to . . . "Oh, no. Josie. You didn't undo all the pins, did you?"

"I didn't touch them."

"Then how—"

She handed me the mock-up. "It just sort of . . . opened up and let me out," she said, as if it was completely normal for pins to undo and then repin themselves, which we both knew wasn't possible.

I stared at the muslin. I hadn't finished marking the left side with my dressmaker's marker, but it was done now, the line continuing from under the arm to the waist. Even the darts were marked.

Josie looked spooked and ready to hightail it out of here, but she stopped to chat with Gracie. "I didn't know you sewed."

"Oh, I love it," she said. "I plan on being a designer, just like Harlow."

Their conversation floated around me. I vaguely registered Will giving Gracie a peck on the cheek, then waving as he headed out the door, but everything else had faded as I considered a new idea. The sheriff thought the murder weapon might have come from my shop. If it had been taken by someone who'd been in Buttons & Bows that day, had Meemaw seen it happen?

Did she know who the murderer was?

Chapter 22

Karen and Ruthann were due to arrive for their fittings any second. I couldn't delve into a project with Gracie until later, so I brought in the bag of buttons and trims Karen had swept up after Nell's run-in with the shelf. I gave her three clean mason jars: one for buttons, one for trims and bows, and the third for whatever else she found that didn't fit in the other jars. "Watch out for any chunks of glass," I warned, "and put those straight into the trash."

She didn't seem to mind the menial task. She sat cross-legged in the corner, spilling the contents of the plastic grocery bag onto the floor in front of her, clearly just happy to be in the workroom. We chatted about school, sports, boys, *Project Runway*, and whatever else crossed her mind.

I pulled out another bolt of muslin and flipped the page of my sketchbook to the bridesmaids' designs.

"I go to school with Holly Kincaid," she said.

I slipped my glasses off and gave the lenses a quick wipe. "Who?"

"Holly Kincaid. Your friend who was here, Josie, who's marrying Nate Kincaid? That's my friend Holly's uncle."

"Ah, Miriam's daughter."

She nodded.

"And Miriam is Nate's sister, and Nate's marrying Josie, so Josie will be your friend's aunt." Small town equaled small world. Six degrees—or fewer—of separation worked for more than just Kevin Bacon.

"Yeah."

"You and Holly are good friends?" I asked.

"BFFs."

I absently loaded spools of thread onto a thread rack I'd hung on the wall as we chatted, wondering if Gracie had any insight into why Miriam had dropped out of the wedding. "I heard that Miriam was supposed to be in the wedding, but now she isn't."

Her smooth brow furrowed. "Yeah, that was weird. First she was the maid of honor. Then she wasn't. She went a little cuckoo."

"Cuckoo how?"

She dropped a few buttons into the mason jar. "Like now she wants to know exactly where Holly is *all* the time. Holly lost her cell phone and has to pay for a replacement, but Ms. Kincaid got her a new one and said she can work it off, but Holly has to take pictures of where she's at and send them to her mom. She won't let her stay out past ten o'clock anymore. Stuff like that."

That all sounded like fairly reasonable mom behavior to me, but if it was out of the ordinary for Miriam, then I wondered what had caused it. Something must have happened to set her off.

Maybe Josie hadn't really *wanted* Miriam in the wedding. She'd said they got along, but did they really?

If they didn't get along, had Josie forced Miriam out, opening it up for Nell to step in? If Miriam was as prideful as the other Kincaids, maybe she harbored some bitterness over being forced out of the wedding.

Could she have taken her anger out on Nell?

My imagination was getting the better of me. Miriam hadn't been in Buttons & Bows—or had she? I remembered thinking for a second that I'd seen her before I'd realized it was Mrs. Kincaid. What if it had been Miriam after all? Could she have darted in, hoping to blend in with the crowd, just to find a murder weapon to use on Nell later?

"Holly doesn't know why her mom dropped out?"

She shrugged. "She might."

Two things I'd learned about Gracie already: she

wasn't shy and she definitely had opinions. "Do *you* have a theory?"

She nodded. "I think maybe she's jealous."

Interesting. Jealousy was a spin-off of the motive I'd already thought of. My reasoning was sketchy since I didn't really know them, but Gracie would have more insight. "Jealous of Josie?"

"Yeah, totally," she said. "You know Mrs. Kincaid? The grandmother, I mean?"

"I think everybody in town knows Lori Kincaid."

"Yeah, well, when Miss Miriam left her husband, Mrs. Kincaid sided with *him* in the divorce." She huffed indignantly. "Shouldn't she have sided with her own daughter? I mean, that's just wrong."

It did sound wrong, but there were always two sides to a story, and this particular version was twice removed, so it definitely needed to be taken with a grain of salt.

"A mother should be there for her daughter, right?" I nodded, but it was clear she'd already answered that question for herself when she said wistfully, "I think she totally should be. Always. Why have a baby if you're not going to be there for her? Period and the end."

"Mrs. Kincaid wasn't there for Miriam?"

Gracie plucked a few more buttons from the floor and dropped them into the jar. "Nope. Not even close."

"Or for Holly?"

She shook her head. "Nope. Holly's dad wouldn't move out of their house, so Miss Miriam left instead. Took Holly and moved into"—she made air quotes—"'the castle.' That's what we call it because of the moat and bridge and everything."

"You nailed it. The Kincaids' mansion looks like a big ol' stone castle. Or a fortress." I perched on the edge of the stool, leaning my elbows on the cutting table, completely sucked in by Gracie's story. "So what happened?"

"Well, Mrs. Kincaid, the grandmother, I mean, wouldn't let them stay at the castle. She actually kicked them out. Can you believe that? Holly said she heard Mrs. Kincaid tell her mom that she couldn't put her head in the sand

and hide. She had to face things head-on. 'Go back to your husband,' she told her."

I'd kept up with a lot of the town gossip during my years away, but I'd somehow missed the story of Miriam's messy divorce. "But she must have had a good reason for wanting out of the marriage, right?"

"Oh, yeah. Holly's dad's a jerk. Doesn't come around, never goes to her soccer games, calls her mom names. Miss Miriam couldn't get to any of her money. That's why Miss Miriam asked my dad for help. They stayed with us till he helped them get into an apartment."

"It's a good thing you were there to help," I said. Glimpsing behind a family's closed door was like reality television: you couldn't predict what would happen and there was always a surprise around the corner. The Kincaids were no exception.

Neither were the Cassidys.

I couldn't imagine what Miriam must have felt, but I'd lost the connection to what this story had to do with Miriam's being jealous. If there was one. "So what's your theory about the wedding?"

"Oh! Right." She dropped a few more buttons into the first jar, added a length of ribbon to the second jar, and a hunk of glass to the bag. "When Mrs. Kincaid found out Holly and her mom moved in with us, she totally wigged out."

"But why?"

"I don't know, but *I* think Miss Miriam dropped out of the wedding because she's jealous that her brother and your friend are in love and that Mrs. Kincaid is so happy about it when she wouldn't even help her get divorced from Holly's dad."

I had to admit it was a good theory, but it seemed too thin. I came back to *why?* Questions and answers funneled through my mind.

Why would Lori Kincaid refuse to help her daughter during her divorce?

One: Gracie's understanding of the marriage was simplistic, one-sided, and painted Miriam as the victim, but if the husband had been betrayed by Miriam, Mrs. Kincaid's allegiance might make sense.

Or two: Appearances were big to the Kincaids and divorce would be a big ol' black spot. Bullying worked with schoolkids, but it also worked with adults. Mrs. Kincaid may have sided with Miriam's husband in order to try to coerce Miriam back into the marriage.

Why wouldn't Miriam be glad for Nate and Josie? Their happiness had nothing to do with her. But I knew from the fashion world and the cutthroat modeling business that jealousy was ugly and had more to do with a person's insecurities than anything else. Did the thought of her brother's picture-perfect wedding highlight her own failed marriage and divorce?

And three: Why would Lori Kincaid have been so upset about Will Flores stepping in to help his daughter's friend and her mother?

Miriam moving in, even briefly, with someone else made it pretty clear to anyone who cared—which meant all of the gossipmongers in Bliss—that there was definitely trouble in Kincaid paradise. And that she'd turned to outsiders instead of her own family.

Another idea popped into my head. Oh, no. I fiddled with the pincushion, lining the pins up in neat rows, hoping the thought might disappear.

It didn't.

What if the problem was that Will Flores and Miriam weren't just friends? What if there was something going on between them . . . and it was happening right under poor Mrs. Flores's nose?

That would have been bad. A double black spot on the Kincaids' reputation.

I suddenly had the unmistakable feeling I was being watched. Gracie was focused on fishing out chunks of glass from the pile in front of her, steadily dropping buttons into the mason jar. There was no sign of Meemaw.

So why—?

A loose floorboard creaked in the front room.

I whipped around, caught a glimpse of a woman, and nearly fell off the stool.

Chapter 23

Zinnia James, one of the women who'd come into Buttons & Bows the day Nell had died, stood on the threshold of the French doors.

"I didn't mean to startle you," she said.

I looked past her, wondering why the bells on the door hadn't chimed.

She followed my gaze. "It was open."

Gracie hopped up. "I'll get it." She scurried past Mrs. James and pushed the door closed.

Mrs. James spread her arms, palms up. "You *are* open?"

I shook off the chill that had crept up my neck, hurrying to her and taking one of her hands in both of mine so she wouldn't leave. "Oh, yes, of course!"

The cool, papery feel of her skin made me take a closer look at her. She had a heavy hand with her makeup and her silver hair was styled in a big Texas 'do. I could see that she was actively working to stave off aging. The indentation of fine lines curved around both sides of her mouth and her eyes, but her skin pulled tight over her bones and her forehead was smoother than mine.

A face-lift *and* Botox. I'd seen women far younger than Mrs. James have that frozen-in-time look, the skin so taut it looked unnatural. I didn't know what Mrs. James had looked like before cosmetic surgery and treatment, but it felt like I was looking at a cloned version of her true self.

"I couldn't help but overhear you discussing Miriam Kincaid's divorce. The first in the family, I believe," she said.

"Gracie was telling me about it. She's friends with Holly Kincaid," I said, wondering just how long Mrs. James had been standing there. "I was just curious why Miriam isn't in her brother's wedding and—"

"That's easy enough to answer," she interrupted. "Keith Kincaid always had political aspirations, but he's been too indiscreet over the years to run for office."

She came closer, lowering her voice to a conspiratorial whisper. "I'm going to let you both in on a little secret—as a senator's wife, you know."

I did a mental head slap of realization. Of course. Her husband was longtime Republican Texas senator Jeb James. I *knew* she seemed familiar. I'd forgotten they lived in Bliss.

Gracie stood wide-eyed, stock-still, and expectant, as if the secrets of the world were about to be revealed.

"Squeaky clean before you get into office, that's the golden rule. After you're elected, you can do whatever you want. People are more reluctant to admit they were wrong once they've voted someone into office. They're more willing to forgive, shall we say, indiscretions."

Mrs. James rattled on. "Lori hung her hopes on her children, but that was a losing proposition. Nate had no interest in politics. Derek's a wild card—too unpredictable. And Miriam? Well, she was always the black sheep of the family. She tried to fit in by marrying that new-money Dallas boy, Jim Dexter, which, as you know, didn't work.

"I suspect that Miriam's walkout has nothing to do with Nate or his bride, and everything to do with retribution. Lori never hid how she felt about the divorce. In her world, if there are problems in a marriage, you turn a blind eye or deal with it behind closed doors. Addressing it in public isn't an option. Nor is the dissolution of a marriage."

Her explanation left Nate and Josie as unintended casualties of passive-aggressive payback. It also made complete sense. Another thread I could mull over as I sewed through the night.

"There is something else," she said, turning to Gracie. "You're Will Flores's girl?"

Gracie nodded. Mrs. James's observations of her friend's family had her looking a little unsteady.

"I mean no offense by this, my dear, and believe me, the irony of what I'm about to say isn't lost on me, but the same people who are willing to turn a blind eye to a public figure's . . . extracurricular activities, shall we say?— and who are good, churchgoing folks—are often the first to deem another's actions immoral."

Oh, boy, I didn't like the sound of this. I was quickly learning that the senator's wife was brutally honest— and blunt—not typical Southern attributes. Personally, I liked that about her, but the stab of anxiety in my gut had me wary. "Mrs. James—"

"That you were born out of wedlock doesn't bother some folks—"

My brain hiccupped on Gracie's birth, but it stopped working altogether when I saw the color drain from Gracie's face.

"—and while a political candidate can speak out for the homeless and stand up for health insurance, close personal relationships with reprobates are less than desirable."

Reprobates like Will Flores. From Gracie's stare, I guessed she didn't understand what Mrs. James was saying. Thankfully.

But the hairs on the back of my neck stood on end as the senator's wife kept on. "An illicit affair resulting in a—"

"Mrs. James," I snapped.

"—resulting in such a lovely girl as you, but nonetheless, outside of marriage vows, would not look good for the Kincaid family."

"*Miriam* isn't Gracie's mother," I said.

"Makes no difference in the eyes of the righteous. Miriam Kincaid involved with someone like William Flores—"

Gracie sprang off the stool. "My dad's not reprobative or . . . or whatever you said!"

"Simmer down, child," Mrs. James said, waving her hand as if she were fanning a flame. "Of course he's not. I'm merely alerting you of how some people think." She shot a pointed look my way. "You know what I mean, Harlow, dear, don't you? Being related to Butch Cassidy and all. Talk about reprobates."

I blinked, my tongue frozen in my mouth. Not many people were direct about the less than reputable side of Butch Cassidy and his Hole-in-the-Wall Gang—and my family's connection to them. I had to give Mrs. James credit. She didn't play games or beat around the bush like so many Southerners did. "We like to focus on the good in my great-great-great-granddaddy."

She gave a solemn nod. "He did leave quite a legacy with the Cassidy women, didn't he?"

This time I felt the color drain from my face. If people didn't often talk about Butch Cassidy, they talked less about the charms his descendants were rumored to possess. First Madelyn Brighton had confronted me on the family magic, and now Mrs. James alluded to it. Was there no more subtle pretending in Bliss?

Mrs. James turned back to Gracie. "Knowledge is power. Your daddy is a fine man, and he's done right by you. It's not every man who would sacrifice everything to raise his child by himself."

Any thought about my family's charms flew out of my head. What had Mrs. James said about Will? Sacrifice everything and raise his child . . . *alone*?

My heart went out to Gracie. Her insistence that a mother should be there for her daughter hadn't been indignation over Mrs. Kincaid and Miriam. It must have stemmed from her deepest desire to have her own mother with *her*, something Meemaw had known wasn't likely to happen.

This is why Meemaw had bargained with Will. She wanted me to have a relationship with this girl, to be that woman she could talk to, just as Mama and Nana and Meemaw had always been there for me. She wanted her safe in the cocoon of 2112 Mockingbird Lane.

Gracie didn't blink, didn't move, hardly breathed. "My dad says my mom blew right out of Bliss like a hurricane. She only came back so she could hand me over to him."

Mrs. James considered Gracie thoughtfully. "Her loss," she said.

I'd been in Gracie's shoes. My father had left my mother when she was six months pregnant with me, when he discovered her gift. His first and only thought was that she was a witch and from that moment on, he'd wanted nothing to do with her—or me. He'd run straight for the hills and had never looked back.

Mama maintained I was all Harlow and Cassidy and had no part of my father's lineage. Tristan Walker had left Bliss behind. I was well adjusted, but even at thirty-three I thought about him, wondered if I had even a sliver of him left in me. Sometimes I longed for the wisdom a father might give his daughter, but if I let myself think about it for too long, an ache began to grow within me until I could taste the hole.

My hand brushed against Gracie's and I could almost feel the barriers she had in place to protect her heart.

"My father left before I was born," I said quietly. "I've never met him."

She linked her fingers with mine and whether she knew it or not, we were initiated into a secret sisterhood all our own at that moment. Mrs. James noticed, and nodded.

"My mom hasn't been back in a while, but she's due for a visit real soon," Gracie said.

The words were colored with hope.

Mrs. James cleared her throat. "I should leave. I don't want to interrupt the two of you any more than I have."

Gracie grabbed Mrs. James's hand. "No. Please stay."

"But you're working ..."

I waved away her concern. "It's fine. We're getting ready to do the bridesmaid fittings."

"Of course. I was here the day you were meeting with

the bridal party." She glanced at the dress form that held the very beginnings of Josie's gown. "I can't imagine who could have done such a horrible thing to that poor girl."

"Did you know Nell?"

"Oh, no. I'd seen her around, of course, but no, I didn't *know* her." Her perfectly preserved, immobile face clouded. "But there is something . . ."

My ears perked up. My impression of Mrs. James was that she was a smart senator's wife who knew what she wanted and was rarely at a loss for words. Not so at this moment. She trailed off, patting her silvery hair, sighing in frustration.

"About Nell?"

"Mmm-hmm. I came here to see . . . That is, something she said that day . . ."

"Something Nell said?"

"Yes, yes. Something she said that day . . . well, quite frankly, it's been bothering me. Though," she added, "it may be nothing." She hemmed and hawed another few seconds before fluttering her hand. "Sometimes my mind doesn't work the way I expect it to, you know." She gave a self-conscious laugh. "An unhappy consequence of growing older."

"If it's about Nell, maybe you should go to the sheriff—"

"No, no. He might just laugh me out of the office."

"Oh." My hope deflated. I glanced at the clock. Karen and Ruthann were late, which meant they really would be here any second. "What *is* it, Mrs. James?"

Her nervous fluttering tapered off as she drew in a bolstering breath. "Nell Gellen lied, my dear," she stated very matter-of-factly. "She stood right here in this room and lied. I'd bet my life on it."

Chapter 24

"Nell lied—" she said again. "And now she's dead."

"Okay," I said, "people lie. But whatever she lied *about*, it's bothering you. You can't ignore *that*. It's like my grandmother always says. You can't ignore the girls in the attic."

Her mouth twitched into a small grin. "Does she still say that?"

I nodded. "Which means, don't ignore your intuition."

She shuffled a low-heeled foot against the floor, then sighed, making up her mind to speak. "Yesterday, when the bridal party was here, Lori Kincaid talked to Miss Sandoval and the bridesmaids about shopping in Fort Worth. Do you recall?"

It was imprinted in my memory. Mrs. Kincaid had tried to pull the rug right out from under my feet. "I remember."

"She asked if they'd been to a restaurant called Reata—"

"Right." It felt like Gracie and I had breathed in every bit of air and were holding it in our lungs as we waited.

"Nell said she'd never been," Mrs. James continued, "but the thing is, I saw her there not too long ago."

I exhaled. Loudly. "She probably thought Mrs. Kincaid was talking about someplace else."

She wagged her finger. "I don't think so. The name of the restaurant was repeated several times. Someone said it was at Sundance Square. She knew. In fact, I swear I could see it in her eyes."

I decided to play devil's advocate, even though I was beginning to wonder if Mrs. James was a little bit dotty in the head. "Okay, so you saw Nell at Reata at Sundance Square," I repeated, "but she'd said she hadn't been there. Why does that bother you?"

"Think about it a moment, Harlow Jane."

And *bam!*, the lightbulb went off over my head. I also saw Gracie out of the corner of my eye. Oh, God. Was it even okay for her to be hearing all of this? "How old are you, Gracie?"

"Fifteen. And I'm old enough to know what's going on," she said, hands on her hips. "My dad says knowledge is power."

"He's not the only one, so he's in good company, then," Mrs. James said.

"Well?" she demanded. "Why does it bother you? Did you see who she was with?"

Mrs. James shook her head, tapping her temple with the pad of her index finger. "I have glasses but prefer not to wear them. Pride and beauty trump age, you know."

Not for me. Like a Pavlovian response, my finger immediately pushed my glasses up the bridge of my nose.

"I was close enough to be fairly certain it was her. When I heard her say she'd never been to Reata, I started doubting myself, but the more thought I've given it, the more I'm sure it was her. Unfortunately, whoever she was meeting was already seated and too far away for me to see. But now . . ."

Gracie gasped. "But now what?"

"But now," I said, finishing Mrs. James's sentence, "it's pretty clear she was with someone she shouldn't have been with."

Mrs. James touched a finger to her nose. "Exactly."

The sound of Gracie sliding buttons across the hardwood floor was like steady rain on the roof. One by one, she plucked them off the floor and dropped them with a *ping* into the jar.

"I'll be right back," I told her, following the senator's wife into the front room.

Instead of going to the front door, Zinnia James headed straight to the display wall of my designs. "You're quite talented."

She wasn't a celebrity, but I'd take it. A politician's wife, especially a fashion-conscious one, was a close second. "Thank you."

"Your great-grandmother talked about you all the time, you know. She missed you something fierce. She was convinced you belonged here. No—that you were *needed* here."

Instinctively, I looked around the room, hoping for a sign that Meemaw was around, but all was still. "She said that? That I was needed?"

Zinnia James nodded solemnly. "She said New York wasn't a good fit for you."

I hadn't ever admitted it out loud—possibly I hadn't ever admitted it even to myself—but with every minute I spent back in Bliss, I knew this was where I belonged. I wasn't wired for the high stress and fast pace of Manhattan. "She was right."

"She usually was," Mrs. James said with a chuckle.

"I didn't realize you knew my great-grandmother that well."

She gave me an affectionate smile. "Oh, goodness, yes, everyone knew Loretta Mae. But I was actually friends with your grandmother in school. And of course there was the Margaret Festival. We were in it together."

I gaped. "Really? Nana was a Margaret?" Bliss was famous—or infamous, depending on the source—for its annual Margaret Moffette Lea Pageant and Ball. The debutantes were called Margarets after Margaret Moffette Lea herself. She'd been the third wife to Texas's favorite son, Sam Houston, former president of the Republic of Texas, back when Texas tried to be its own country. She'd become a respected first lady of the state when he'd been governor, though being shy, she'd probably roll over in her grave at the celebration we'd created in her name.

"Reluctantly," she said, "but yes, she was. You should have seen her gown. Spectacular. I spent my fair share of time right here in this house."

I'd spent my whole childhood here, but I'd never seen hide nor hair of Zinnia James visiting Nana when I was growing up. Or a pageant gown fit for a Margaret.

She continued, as if she'd read my mind. "We had a little . . . falling-out. I remember it to the very hour of the very day it happened." Her voice took on a hint of regret. "We both had a crush on the same young man. We said we'd never let it break up our friendship, and I think we both meant it, but then he asked *her* to homecoming instead of me. I'm ashamed to admit it now, but jealousy reared its ugly head."

"You and Nana liked the same boy?"

She laughed, nodding. "Hard to believe, looking at us now."

Yes, it was. She'd ended up with a good-ol'-boy politician and my grandmother had married a cowboy and talked to goats. I couldn't imagine the type of man who would attract them both.

"When he asked her to marry him, well, that was it. We haven't spoken since."

I stared and poked my finger in my ear. Had I heard her right? "*You* were in love with my grandfather?"

She nodded sheepishly. "I got over him, of course. Jeb and I are quite happy. But, yes, Wood Jenkins was my first love."

"And you and Nana never made up?"

"It was one of those touchy situations. When Coleta tried, I wasn't ready. When I tried, she wasn't ready. Loretta Mae acted as a go-between once or twice, but it just never quite worked."

I couldn't believe I'd never heard this story. Did Mama know her father had had two women fighting over him? "Wow. Meemaw was right."

"About what?"

"Every day, you learn something you never knew before. The day you don't is the day you die."

"Things happen for a reason," Mrs. James said. "I do

believe that. And I think Coleta and I will reconnect one day. Loretta Mae believed it would happen."

"If Meemaw wanted you and Nana to be friends again, it *will* happen. Trust me on that."

"Oh, believe me, I do," she said with a little laugh. "Now, I did come here for a reason." She pointed to the display board. "I want to commission a gown. The senator and I are hosting a fund-raising event. It's not until late summer, but I wanted to make sure I'm on your calendar."

Months away. That was good because I couldn't possibly add another dress to my current schedule. "You're the *only* one on my agenda."

"Also, I have a few other events up my sleeve," she said, a glint in her soft gray eyes. "An event at Christmas, but before that, the festival and pageant."

"The Margarets?" If I remembered correctly, it was held around the Fourth of July, when Texas was nearing the top of the heat index.

"I'd like to commission you to make my granddaughter's gown."

I sputtered. "Um ... aren't the Margarets' dresses period pieces?" Straight from the mid-1800s, if memory served. I had nothing like *that* in my portfolio.

She nodded, her lips thinning as she smiled. "Indeed, and Libby will look lovely in one. I'll give you more details soon, but put that on your books, too."

She didn't give me a chance to argue. "You're a delight, Harlow Jane," she told me as she walked down the steps. "Loretta Mae would be proud."

Those two sentences filled me with equal parts joy and sadness, but knowing Meemaw would be proud of me—and that she was here, somewhere—edged away a little of the grief.

I pushed the festival and pageant out of my mind and went back to the workroom. The subtle scent of vanilla floated in the air. Everything Zinnia James had said about Miriam, Will, Gracie, Nana, Nell, and Reata bounced around in my head. Was there something in the jumble that would point me toward Nell's killer?

Gracie watched my every move as I laid pieces of fabric over the dress form, trying to get a sense of the garment I was going to make for Karen.

"Your dad keeps pretty busy," I said, making conversation. Gracie had gone too quiet. "I wouldn't have thought that many people would need handyman work done."

"Handyman?"

"I have a pretty good list of things for him to tackle."

She cocked her head to the side and looked at me. "My dad's not a handyman."

The pin I'd been poking through the muslin slipped and pricked my thumb. I stuck it between my lips to soothe the sharp pain. "He's not a handyman?"

She shook her head, her hair falling in front of her shoulders. "*N-o-o-o.* He just did that stuff for Loretta Mae."

I jumped, my heart leaping to my throat, as my Pfaff powered up out of nowhere, the needle slowly moving up and down, up and down, in a steady rhythm that sounded suspiciously like Meemaw guffawing. I marched over and pressed the power button, turning the machine off. "Funny," I muttered.

Gracie froze. "Is the machine, like, programmed?"

"Just has a funny glitch, sometimes," I said, glossing over it. "Remember what I said—this old house has spirit."

"It's like it's haunted," she said. Her cheeks had paled and her arms were folded over her chest.

I waved away the very idea. "Gracie, you've been watching too many movies," I said. "The house is not haunted—"

I drew in a sharp breath as the lights flickered on and off. The sewing machine needle moved up and down again.

"Are you sure?" she asked shrilly.

"It's just a cranky old house," I said, reassuringly. Then, to distract her, I asked, "What *does* your dad do?"

Another creak came from the ceiling and her nostrils

flared, but she said, "He works for the city. Plus he's on the Bliss Historical Society."

"What does he do for the city?"

"He's the architect."

I stared, speechless. From handyman to architect in the blink of an eye. I had whiplash.

With impeccable timing, the bells on the front door jingled. Karen and Ruthann had arrived for their fittings.

Chapter 25

Karen stood on the milk crate with me on one side of her and Gracie on the other. I wrapped a lavender measuring tape around her waist, noted the number, then repeated it aloud.

Karen covered her ears with her hands. "Don't tell me the number. I don't want to know."

"It's just a number," I said.

"But I want it to be a smaller number," she complained.

I stifled the reprimand that had started sliding up my throat. I'd spent years working with models who were borderline anorexic and obsessed with numbers. Weight, waist, hips, thighs. You name it, they were trying to make it smaller. "Smaller numbers won't change who you are." I gestured up and down her body. "*This* is you. You have to rock what you've got, Karen Mitchell."

"But I've got too much of this." She pouted, patting her hips. One hand slid to her belly. "And this."

Gracie was taking in every last detail of the conversation, listening with undivided attention. "You're beautiful," I told Karen, knowing it would sink into Gracie, too.

Karen frowned. "Josie's beautiful. You're beautiful." She pointed to the front room, where Ruthann was browsing, her measurements done. "*Ruthann*'s beautiful. Me? I'm frumpy."

"Sugar, half that frump you're feeling is coming straight from inside," I said, sounding more like Loretta

Mae than I ever had before. The right design and styling could transform her figure, emphasizing the best things while downplaying the problem areas. "It's attitude. What you feel in here," I said, hand to my heart, "shines through in everything you do."

Ruthann popped her head around the French door and said, "That's right, Karen. It's all attitude. You can get whatever you want if you act like you deserve it."

"Right. Think it and you'll start to believe it," I said, piggybacking on Ruthann's encouragement. The Cassidy women—Nana, in particular—had always been strong believers in the power of affirmations.

Karen didn't look convinced, but she straightened her posture and held her chin a trifle higher. It was a start.

I reached around her hips. "Measure twice, cut once," I said, rattling off the number for Gracie to jot down in my sketchbook.

Gracie stared at me like I suddenly had a nose piercing and lip rings. "You, too?"

"Me, too, what?"

"Measure twice, cut once. That's what my dad says whenever he builds anything. Oh, my God, he has all these models around the house. You should see them. They're crazy." She gave a little roll of her eyes. "Took him forever to build them because he does everything two or three times to make sure it's perfect."

"Guess it works for sewing and building. Loretta Mae taught me it's better to be safe than sorry." She was a trickster, but where quilting and sewing were concerned, she'd mapped everything out. "That way, there's never a surprise," she'd say.

I'd wondered, more than once, if things always turned out the way she wanted them to not because she was charmed, but because she dotted her i's and crossed her t's. Twice.

When we finished, Karen stepped down from the crate and took a closer look at the small rack of shapewear in the corner. "Is this what Josie was talking about?" she asked.

"It's like magic," I said, nodding. It would hold Karen's jigglies in place. I took a package off the shelf and handed it to her as Ruthann came back into the workroom.

"My husband might not like this," Karen said, scratching the back of her head with her fingertips.

Ruthann scoffed. "He's not going to be the one wearing it, is he?"

Karen had opened the package and pulled out the lingerie slip. She tugged at the fabric, stretching it across her splayed fingers. "No, but will he know it's there?"

Ruthann arched an eyebrow. "Does it matter?"

"He won't know it's there," I said, "but Ruthann's right. It doesn't matter. It just firms everything up so you'll feel a little more—"

"Poised," Ruthann finished. Perched on a stool next to the shelf of buttons and trims, absently poking her fingers into a mason jar, she was the epitome of composure. I couldn't help but think that when she was a kid, she should have responded to those open-audition radio spots calling for child actors or auditioned for *America's Next Top Model*. Appearance and self-possession could open doors. Being smart enough to walk through them could take a woman far in life. Either the doors hadn't opened for Ruthann or she'd chosen not to walk through them.

"Trust me, Karen," I said. I didn't design clothes for other people to oooh and ahhh over and steal the show. I designed clothes that complemented the person wearing them, that made her glow and shine, and made her ready to walk through any door, head held high.

From the corner of my eye, I could see Gracie scribbling in a miniature notebook. A funny zing—like I was a sensei and she was my karate kid—shot through my core and a feeling of responsibility blossomed.

"What do you think of this?" I slid my open sketchbook over so Ruthann could see the design I'd come up with in the middle of the night. "I know you said wraparound, but I had this idea." It was a strapless dress, still cut at the knee, but with a full skirt made of a pale green chiffon. The torso and waist were accentuated by a wide fitted sash starting just under the bustline and ending at the waist. The bodice itself had vertical pleats, complementing Josie's dress, and it would add a little *va-va-voom* volume to Ruthann's toothpick body.

She took one look at it, pressed her hand to her heart, and nodded enthusiastically. "That's the one. I want you to make me that dress!"

I hadn't realized I'd been holding my breath until I exhaled. *I'd* known it was perfect for her, but often women chose clothes that didn't complement their figures. Thankfully, Ruthann wasn't one of those women.

She slipped behind the privacy screen to try on something she'd pulled from the ready-to-wear rack up front—a sleek army green jumper with an abundance of zippers and hardware. I pulled out a bolt of muslin, plopping it on the cutting table and unwinding the fabric until I had a good length of it to drape with.

"It just doesn't feel right without Nell here," Karen said glumly.

We all murmured in agreement. It wasn't hard to pretend for a just a little while that things were normal, but the pretense couldn't last long. Someone had killed Nell.

"I heard the sheriff questioned Nate," Ruthann called.

"For three hours," Karen said, her expression dubious. She absently played with a scattering of buttons.

I frowned. Already the story had grown. By tomorrow, the rumors would have him in lockup, perched on the edge of an electric chair.

Ruthann's voice drifted to us through the angled slats of the screen. "A little birdie told me that Nate told Josie about him and Nell."

A few buttons scattered from Karen's lap to the hardwood floor. "Sorry," she muttered. The stool scraped against the floor as she slid off it. She crouched and scooped the buttons up. "What birdie?"

Ruthann popped her head out from her changing room. "George Taylor."

"Who's George Taylor?" Gracie asked. I was taking in every word, adding it to what I already knew about Nell in order to help Josie, but Gracie—she was in high hog heaven. She'd leaned two bolts of fabric in front of her buttons and glass cleanup project to help me measure, and now she pinned and listened, pinned and listened, and all I could think was that this probably wasn't what Will had had in mind when he'd arranged for her to take sewing lessons with me.

Ruthann sauntered into view. The jumper fit her like a glove, like I'd made it just for her. It hugged her body, transforming the hard lines of her hips into hourglass curves, no small feat for such a thin woman. She glided straight over to Gracie, placed a hand on her shoulder, winked, and said, "George Taylor is only the most eligible bachelor in Bliss next to Derek and—"

"Nate," Karen finished with a little laugh.

"Right, but Derek's in the Middle East and Josie took Nate off the market, so that leaves George." Ruthann moved in front of the full-length mirror, slowly spinning around, taking in every inch of her figure in the jumper. The angles of her face transformed as she broke into a giddy smile. "*This* is magical, Harlow." She spun around, peering at her backside over her shoulder. "It's for sale, right?"

"I don't think another soul could wear that," I said, "and I can't let you leave without buying it."

Karen let the buttons she played with fall through her fingers. "What else did George say?"

Ruthann turned away from the mirror. "Well, apparently he told Louie Flapman, who told Janine Crandle, who told *me* that it looked like he and Nate had—" She grimaced and made quote marks in the air with her fingers as she said, "fished in the same pond."

I cleared away the indignant lump in my throat. "For the record, George Taylor does *not* sound like the most charming bachelor in town." I'd almost be tempted to choose Derek Kincaid over a man who told people where he'd fished at all. Almost, but not quite.

"Ah, he's harmless," Ruthann said. "And he's a hottie.

The point is, I'd forgotten that Nell and Nate had dated. I know it never meant anything—"

"Didn't mean anything to *him*," Karen snapped, "but it sure did to her."

A little spasm flitted through me. Nate had told Josie he and Nell had barely dated, but Karen certainly had a different impression.

Ruthann whirled around, her hands on her bony hips. "She never told me anything like that, and we told each other everything."

Karen's face turned ashen. "She didn't want Josie to find out and you . . ."

"I what?" Ruthann demanded, her lower lip quivering.

"She didn't think you'd understand."

Ruthann balked. "Not understand?"

"You . . . you've never been in love—"

"Oh, yes, I have. I'm—"

"And Lester Kramer from high school doesn't count, Ruthie."

Ruthann blinked away her daze. "I was her best friend, too."

I butted in, wanting to stop the catfight I was afraid would materialize. "People can have more than one best friend," I said. "I'm sure you were both very important to her."

Ruthann pressed her palm against her chest. "I was with her when she almost lost her shop."

I looked at Karen. "And I bet you were with her at some other important time—"

Karen blinked back her tears, half nodding, half shaking her head. "You weren't there for her when she was puking her guts out. I was."

Nell's words about Nate breaking Josie's heart rattled around in my brain. What if Nell had decided Josie couldn't have with Nate what she herself had been denied? She had seemed on edge when I met her yesterday. I imagined a confrontation. The argument Mama and I heard from inside the house—could it have been Josie and Nell? Was it a coincidence that Josie had discovered Nell's body, or could she have been the one to kill her, conveniently making the discovery when the time was right?

Or could it have been Nate and Nell arguing? He'd been conspicuously absent last night. Overwrought with guilt because he'd resorted to murder to stop Nell from ruining his wedding?

A chill spread through me. I didn't want it to be either of them. These were people I'd hoped to be friends with now that I was home in Bliss.

Ruthann's shoulders hunched as she retreated behind the screen to change. "Guess I should cancel my date with George," she said.

Karen gaped. "I thought you said you weren't seeing him anymore."

Gracie had finished pinning the pattern pieces I'd drawn to the muslin. I handed her a pair of dressmaking shears, Ginghers with red chrysanthemums and petite blossoms on the handles. "Go ahead and cut it out," I whispered, not wanting to interrupt Karen and Ruthann.

"I wasn't, but he asked again," Ruthann said over the rustling of her clothes as she changed.

"Do you know what he told Ted?"

"Who's Ted?" Gracie whispered to me.

"I don't know," I whispered, getting lost in their rapid-fire discussion.

Karen flicked a glance at us. "Ted's my husband," she said.

"What did George tell him?" Ruthann asked with a dejected sigh.

As Karen hesitated, looking like she was having second thoughts, I imagined a similar conversation between Nell and Josie, only with Nell not holding back at all, instead revealing to Josie the relationship she'd had with Nate.

I rubbed my temples, trying to loosen the suspicions taking root there. I was supposed to be helping Josie prove Nate was innocent, not redirecting suspicion toward her.

"George told Ted that Nell always looked like

she'd ..." Her voice cracked. Another button dropped. The sound of sharp metal sliding across metal as Gracie opened and closed the scissors magnified in my brain.

"Just spit it out," Ruthann said.

She cleared her throat, and said, "George told Ted that Nell had been rode hard and put up wet. He's slimy, Ruthie. You can do better than him."

Gracie stopped in midcut, scissors open wide. "Rode hard ... you mean like a horse?"

Oh, boy. "Yeah, you know horses need to be groomed. Brushed and stuff after they've been ridden. George was just saying that, uh ..." God, I had no idea how to explain such a crude remark to a fifteen-year-old girl. "He was just saying—"

"He was saying that Nell got around," Ruthann blurted from behind the screen, "which is more a statement about *her* than about George."

Unless he was the one doing the riding, I thought.

"He's a user, Ruthie."

"Why does your husband hang out with him, then?" Ruthann shot back.

"He doesn't."

"Oh, right, he's not with the city anymore. He's a big shot now."

They went on and on, but I couldn't get Nell out of my mind. It sounded to me like her self-esteem had been crushed over and over again and she'd ended up with a reputation that was going to live on.

Long after Ruthann and Karen left, I was left wondering if George Taylor could be the man Nell had been dating.

Chapter 26

The next morning, Madelyn Brighton blew through the door of Buttons & Bows like a mini tornado on a tear through Bliss. She knocked into the little antique table as she entered. The door banged behind her against the wall. As she spun around, clutching a camera strap in her hand, the lens swung wide and hit the back of the sofa.

No, not a tornado. A bull in a china shop. A petite, squat British bull, but a bull nonetheless. Her hair still looked electrified, and she still seemed a tad disheveled. I was beginning to think it was how she always looked.

"Hi," I said, dropping my pin box on the cutting table and hurrying toward her.

"Oh, good, you're here," she said. "I was afraid I'd miss you."

Something about her accent made me stand a little straighter and smile. "This is where I always am during business hours."

"Right. Okay, down to it. I have a thought."

"Just one?" I said with a chuckle.

She stared at me, unblinking, for a few seconds; then, like someone flipped a switch, she laughed. "Ha! No, not just one. You don't want to know *all* my thoughts, Harlow. Trust me on that. But this one, you just might."

I'd lowered myself halfway to the couch when she said, "It's about the Cassidy *magic*." My glutes seized, panic rushing through me. And to think she'd almost won me over with her fun British accent and charm.

For a while, I'd been able to forget about the fact that I'd accidentally confirmed her suspicions about the Cassidy women, but with her here, in Buttons & Bows, there was no more avoiding it.

My throat constricted. I tried to say, "What about the Cassidy magic?" but it came out a prolonged groan.

She held up a hand. "Relax, mate. I'm not going to turn you in to the Ministry of Magic." She winked. "Though wouldn't it be absolutely fabulous if there were such a thing?"

I stared blankly.

"Harry Potter?" she said. "Ministry of Magic?"

"Right!" I forced myself to laugh with her. I had stayed up late and made progress on all three muslin mock-ups, but time was still marching on. Talking magic wasn't on my agenda. "So, about that thought you had?" I prompted.

"I've been thinking about your family lineage. I'm sort of a history buff, too," she said as an aside. "Was your great-great-grandmother Cressida gifted? And what about her mother, Texana?"

I felt my eyelids strain as they opened wide. What if Madelyn was a stalker? It just wasn't normal to know so much about someone else's life, was it? All I knew about her was that she was from England, took pictures, and was married to a professor. That was a whole lot different than knowing about a family's magical charms. "*How* do you know about my family?"

"Writer, remember?" she said, though when she said "writer," it sounded more like "writ-a."

Even through my wariness, I felt there was something likable about Madelyn Brighton. But was she diabolical under the unassuming exterior? "Let me rephrase that. *Why* do you know so much about my family?"

"Like I said before, Harlow, I'm a bit of a magic junkie. I've studied the Salem Witch Trials. My husband is a leader in the North Texas Paranormal Society. Your family, Harlow, is renowned in those circles."

The pipes upstairs creaked. We both glanced at the ceiling. I hoped Meemaw wouldn't choose now to materialize. I hadn't seen her since last night when her wraith-like form had appeared before me and I'd asked if she knew who'd killed Nell.

I gulped, trying to wrap my mind around what she was saying. All these years, I'd thought the Cassidy women flew under the radar, but according to Madelyn, that was not the case. "What, exactly, do you mean by 'renowned'?"

She fiddled with her camera, taking the lens cover off. "Maybe renowned is overstating it a bit. Nobody seems to know that it's *your* family, specifically, but just that there is a family in Texas whose women have some sort of magic in them."

"But how would anyone know that?"

"People talk, Harlow, and if the right person is listening—and the Paranormal Society is *always* listening—then stories get around."

Madelyn pressed buttons on her camera, finally lifting it and aiming at me. "Do you mind if I take a photo? I'm actually doing an article for the *Fort Worth Business Review* on women entrepreneurs. I'd love to interview you for the piece."

My mind reeled. She had a hundred irons in the fire, including her hunt for the paranormal. What else did she have up her sleeve?

I nodded, and she set to work, snapping a series of pictures of both me and the shop. "My deadline's day after tomorrow, but I'm also photographing a fund-raising gala for the Kincaid Family Foundation and writing a piece for the *Bliss Record-Chronicle* on Nell Gellen's funeral. Quite busy at the moment, but I do want to include your dressmaking shop in the *Business Review* piece. If I could just shadow you for a while today and ask a few questions . . ."

I went over my plan for the day. The silk for Josie's dress had arrived, as well as the other fabrics I'd ordered. I'd be diving into the actual dressmaking, which meant Madelyn would probably be bored out of her mind. Sewing wasn't an action-packed activity. Gracie was coming back for another visit. There should be no harm in allowing Madelyn to stay.

"Sure," I said, but I had a niggling feeling in the pit of my stomach that things were going to get curiouser and curiouser.

Madelyn asked me question after question, going back and forth from my life in New York, to my return to Bliss, the opening of Buttons & Bows, and the Cassidy charms.

"Your great-grandmother bequeathed you this house?" she asked.

"Actually, she deeded it to me the day I was born."

"She knew then that what she wanted was for you to live here. Hmm, interesting. So you always knew you'd come back."

I looked up from the cutting table where I had yards and yards of Diamond French silk laid out for Josie's dress. "No. I hadn't planned on coming back until I found out about the house, but it was definitely the right thing to do."

Like a magnet, my gaze was drawn to a pile of quilts I'd brought down from the attic. All the Cassidy women, starting with Butch Cassidy's daughter, Cressida, had pieced together bits of clothing and fabric to tell the stories of their lives in quilts they made, sometimes together, sometimes alone. From hand-tied creations to painstakingly pieced patterns, the threads of the quilts bound us together.

"This is where I belong," I said.

She jotted something down in her fabric-covered notebook. I went back to my silk, a warm comfort settling around me. She looked up from her writing. "Is someone baking?"

I breathed in the scent of fresh-baked banana bread, one of Meemaw's favorites. Every day, the house seemed to be coming more and more alive with her presence. "The window's open," I said, gesturing toward Nana's farm. "My grandmother must be baking."

She looked skeptical, even sneaking a peek out the French doors toward the kitchen to be sure. Finally, she walked over to the cutting table and sat down on the stool I'd pulled up next to it. "Tell me how it works, Harlow."

I took the pins from between my lips, glancing up from the paper pattern I'd created for the wedding gown's bodice. "How does what work?"

Her hazel eyes sparkled. "The *magic*."

The pipes groaned again, first in a high-pitched tone, then deeper, like a foghorn. It reminded me of the guitar players in the seventies like Peter Frampton who'd hooked their instruments up to talk boxes and made their guitars speak. *Tell. Her. Tell. Her.*

The creaking grew louder, more persistent. Madelyn's shoulders curved in. A nervous tint colored her face. *Tell. Her. Tell. Her.*

"What's that?"

"Just old pipes," I said, sending a surreptitious scowl around the room, hoping Meemaw would see and get the message.

She must have, because the creaking stopped as suddenly as it had started. Madelyn visibly relaxed, but I felt like I'd absorbed her tension. We'd kept the family gifts under our hats for so long, it didn't seem right to share details with a complete stranger. I'd already said too much.

Madelyn closed her notebook, but her finger held the page she'd been taking notes on. "Were Texana and Cressida charmed?" she asked.

"Is this off the record?" I asked, even though the question seemed silly. It was right up there with a lawyer purposely saying something during court that he knew would be stricken, but once the jury heard it, could it really be erased from their minds?

She let her finger slide out from between the pages. "Absolutely. Look, Harlow, I can see you don't trust me, but I promise to keep your secrets. I'm simply fascinated by your history and I'd love to learn more."

I didn't trust Madelyn, but I trusted Meemaw and she seemed to *want* this woman to know our story. I didn't understand, but I knew if I started to say something I wasn't supposed to, Meemaw would rattle a chain or do something to interrupt me. I'd seen it happen when Will and Gracie were here. I had no doubt I would see it again.

I sucked in a bolstering breath—I'd never uttered these words to anyone outside the Cassidy family—and said, "We all think Texana and Cressida were charmed, but I don't know what their gifts were. For me, it started with Meemaw."

Her eyes danced with excitement. "So Loretta Mae started getting what she wanted, but when did she realize it was more than just luck?"

"I don't know. That's the only way I ever knew her. She never talked about it."

"Hmm. How did it work? Was there some ritual? Some incantation, or something?"

"We're not witches, Madelyn."

"No, no, of course not," she said, watching as I absently picked up my happy red scissors, the blades sliding open and closed with a smooth, slick sound.

"And to be honest, I don't know how it works—"

"Works?"

"Worked," I corrected, darting a glance at her, hoping I hadn't clued her in that Meemaw was still up to her old tricks. "She could never explain it. It's the same with my mother and grandmother. It's like they have some emotional connection to the world. Their thoughts and emotions float off into the universe and connect with something. For Meemaw, what she wanted came true. My mother's emotions are tied in to things that grow. Could be weeds, flowers—could be anything. For my grandmother, it's the goats."

"Then it skipped a generation with you?"

I started cutting, carefully slicing through the two layers of silk. Since I was old enough to understand about the charms of the Cassidy women, I'd felt I'd missed out on something big, had done something wrong that prevented me from having a gift, or worse, was just not worthy of the charm.

But now that I knew Meemaw was with me, and apparently I was the only one she could communicate with, I felt revitalized. I was a Cassidy woman, through and through. "I guess so," I said, but I smiled inwardly. She sighed, disappointed. She asked a few more questions before we fell silent.

After a few minutes, I said, "Let me ask *you* a question, Madelyn."

"Anything."

I held my scissors. "You've been in Bliss for a few years now, right?"

"Three and a half. Bill grew up here. After Oxford, he wanted to come back home."

Bill Brighton. That name did not ring a bell.

"And you seem to be in the thick of things, what with your photography and journalism and work with the sheriff's department and the city." I set the scissors on the table and turned to face her. "Who do *you* think would have wanted Nell Gellen dead?"

Chapter 27

"That woman turned heads," Madelyn said after she took a minute to ponder my question.

Between Josie, Karen, Ruthann, and Zinnia James, I'd heard plenty about Nell, but I was curious what Madelyn thought.

"Turned heads? What do you mean?" I'd moved to the dress form I'd adjusted to reflect Josie's measurements. Piece by piece, I began pinning the bodice together, mentally fast-forwarding through the darts for her bustline and pleats for shape and structure.

"I took a bead-making class from her a few months ago," Madelyn said.

"I think everyone in town took bead-making from her."

"It's something to do."

"That's true. I used to climb the water tower. Might have stayed out of trouble if I'd had beads."

Madelyn laughed. "I can't picture you in trouble, Harlow."

"That's why I got away with it," I said with a wink.

"Nell couldn't get away with much. I could always tell when something was on her mind."

"How?"

Madelyn drew her bottom lip into her mouth and clamped her upper teeth down. "She'd chew her bottom lip, like this," she mumbled. "Like it was a good hunk of Turkish Delight."

I wasn't sure what Turkish Delight was, but I got the picture. I knew Madelyn must have some insight on

Nell. Being a writer and photographer made you a student of human nature, just like fashion design did.

It was my job to create the perfect garment for a person, to see beyond what she imagined an outfit could be, to bring out her inner beauty through what she wore. In order to do that, I had to study human nature, too.

"Do you think she had a man on her mind?" I asked her.

The house creaked, like it was settling after an earthquake. Except Texas doesn't have earthquakes and I figured that any settling the old farmhouse was going to do had happened decades ago.

Madelyn didn't pay the sounds any mind. "Could be. I didn't know her well enough to say. But I bet if we nosed around," she said, then pointed her finger back and forth between us, "we could figure out who killed her."

The lights flickered and one of the dress forms lurched forward. Madelyn gasped. "Bloody hell, what the devil's going on?"

I was getting tired of explaining that it was an ornery old house, but what choice did I have? Better than explaining it was an ornery old ghost, I suppose.

Did Meemaw's ruckus mean she wanted me to work with Madelyn? I edged a tentative toe forward. "We might could at that," I said, gasping the moment the words left my mouth.

I giggled. I hadn't combined "might" and "could" in a sentence since before I'd lived in New York, but it felt good, like coming home. Like skinny-dipping in the lake. Or standing on top of a water tower, arms spread wide, yelling, "Yeehaw!"

Madelyn grinned. "What's so funny?"

I gave a final gleeful hoot. "I was just thinking that it's good to be home."

Her smile waned. "I bet."

"Do you miss the UK?"

"Sometimes," she said. "I miss my mum and dad. My sister had a baby. I haven't met him yet."

With sudden clarity, I realized that her clothes reflected her loneliness. Maybe she filled her time with so many different things so she wouldn't think about being homesick. She needed color. Something a little more fun that would add a touch of sparkle to her life here. "Do you think you'll ever move back?"

She cupped one hand behind her head, scratching her scalp. "It's hard to say. Bill's quite happy at the college. It's not easy finding a position. One day at a time, we always say."

"Well, maybe your family will come here for a visit."

She waved away the idea. "It's so bloody expensive, overseas travel. Not likely to happen anytime soon."

A few minutes later, we were back to the original subject. I filled her in on the theories I'd formulated so far. "So it could have been Josie, or Nate. They both have possible motives. And then there's the possibility that the murder weapon was taken from my shop, but so far I haven't seen anything that could leave those strange marks on Nell's neck."

"You're assuming her murder is directly related to whatever relationship she may have had with Nate, past or present, but what if it's not? What if that was long over and is now serving as a distraction—a sort of organic red herring?"

"Then who would have wanted to kill her?"

Madelyn shifted uneasily. "And why?"

It was clear we had our investigative work cut out for us.

Chapter 28

That night, sleep completely escaped me. Mama and Gracie had both stopped by in the afternoon. I'd worked for hours on the bridal gown while they worked on the linings for all the dresses. Long after they left, I kept going. By one in the morning, my fingers felt numb and swollen, incapable of holding a tiny needle anymore.

In bed, I mulled over the list of people who'd been in Buttons & Bows the day Nell died. Anything to point the finger at someone other than Nate or Josie.

Josie and her bridesmaids had been there, of course. And Mrs. Zinnia James and her friends. Josie's mother had stopped by with Josie's aunt. And Lori Kincaid had come in with Nate. Had Miriam been there, or not?

Questions floated in and out of my mind, but the one that kept surfacing circled in my brain like a hawk. Who had hated Nell enough to want her dead?

By ten o'clock the next morning, I'd shaken off my grogginess and had found my groove with Josie's dress. Mama waltzed in just as the clock struck twelve—she always had impeccable timing like that. The smoky scent of barbecue wafted over to me. I dropped the pincushion, turned my back on the dress form, and walked like a zombie to the kitchen. Another of Mama's gifts was knowing just what I needed, though this was magic that most mothers seemed to possess.

"Bet they don't make barbecue like this in New York," she said as she set down the picnic basket she'd filled to the brim.

"No, ma'am, they don't." Not even remotely close.

"Brisket, slow-cooked all night long," she said as she unpacked the earthenware container she'd brought it in. Next came a metal bowl with a snap-on lid. "My secret sauce. Bet you missed this, didn't you, Harlow Jane?"

"Yes, ma'am." I could almost taste it, the memories were so strong. Once a month the Cassidy women, and my poor outnumbered brother, would have barbecue right here at Loretta Mae's house. If the weather was nice, we'd sit out on her back porch. If a thunderstorm hit, we'd huddle under the eaves until it passed. If a real storm brewed, we'd sit around the kitchen table.

"Corn on the cob," Mama said, the crinkle of tinfoil snapping me out of the past. "Macaroni salad." She put another bowl on the table. "Now, it's too early in the season for watermelon, so I made a dump cake. Blackberry."

I stared at the spread on the table. "There's enough food here to feed all Nana's goats, Mama, and then some."

"Leftovers. I expect you'll be needing them. Lord knows you won't be cutting any corners with the detail you put into them dresses," she said. "You best keep your strength up, and not spend your time cooking."

I just grinned at her. No matter how old I got, it was always sweet to be mothered. "Yes, ma'am."

"Now, let's get started before it all turns cold."

The diamond on the ring of her right hand flashed and sparkled as she scooped brisket onto a roll, ladled barbecue sauce over it, and handed me the plate. I forced myself to keep quiet. She'd tell me when she was ready.

We talked about the dresses, moving on to Nell as we finished eating. "What else do you know about Nell Gellen?" There was no need to be subtle with her. Other than hiding our gifts, we Cassidy women were a what-you-see-is-what-you-get family. The roundabout way of the South was lost on us, just as it was lost on Zinnia James.

"Why?" Mama asked, though from the way she

snapped her head and peered at me, I got the feeling she knew exactly why I was asking.

I met her gaze. "I just want to know more about the woman who died on my property. It's a little unnerving to think there's a murderer waltzing around town like nobody's business."

She lowered her chin slightly, peering up at me. "You don't think your gift is being a detective, do you?"

"No, I don't fancy myself a detective, Mama, and I definitely don't think that's my gift." Although I *had* solved the mystery behind the haunting of Buttons & Bows. Ever since then, I was more and more confident that my Cassidy charm was communicating with spirits. After all, I was the only one who had sensed Meemaw's presence.

"Good, because you have dresses to make. You don't have time to get distracted by amateur sleuthing."

She had a point there, but I said, "I'm just curious. You knew her from the bead shop, right? Was she nice? Did she have a boyfriend? Was she happy?"

"Most of the time. On and off. No," she answered as she pushed her chair back from the table, carried her plate to the sink, and rinsed it off.

I started packing up the leftovers, stooping to close the lid of the flip-top picnic basket. Inside there were stacks of Tupperware containers holding duplicates of everything we'd just eaten. So this was her first stop—and I knew precisely where stop number two would be.

Curiosity nearly oozed out of me. I bit my tongue as I tucked container after container of *my* leftovers into Meemaw's relatively new, yet retro-style refrigerator. Freezer on top, fridge on the bottom. The refrigerator, the stove, and the dishwasher were some of the upgrades Meemaw had done. She'd always known exactly what she'd wanted: to preserve the historic look of the house. All three appliances had stamped metal bodies and were vintage buttercup yellow.

And I loved them.

They were complete functionality under subtle style, just like the clothes I designed. Just like the way I lived my life. But apparently not how Mama was living hers. Hoss McClaine might be as comfortable as a tattered old quilt, but as long as he hid his relationship with my mother, in my opinion he was seriously lacking in style, comfort, and functionality.

But I knew she didn't want to talk about it, so I pushed the thoughts aside and tried to stay focused on Nell. "Why don't you think she was happy?"

Mama turned and leaned against the farmhouse sink. "Because she said as much."

"Mama, how could you not tell me that before? What do you mean?"

"When did you take over the investigation?" she asked.

I lowered my chin, giving her a look. "Oh, just after you got that there ring," I said.

She slapped her left hand on top of her right hand. Her cheeks turned a blotchy red. "She didn't say it to me, in particular. She was talking to the whole bead class."

I felt like stomping my foot, which had the domino effect of sending me spiraling back to childhood and my exasperation with not having a gift. Mama hadn't been able to explain it. No one had, and it had driven me to the edge a few times. Which is right where I found myself now. "Mama," I said. "Come on. I know you've thought about it. Why do *you* think she wasn't happy?"

She folded her arms over her plaid shirt, the fabric gapping slightly between the snap closures. I'd have to fix that for her one of these days. "All I know for sure is that it *usually* had to do with a man."

The way she said it made me think that something had changed and Nell's most recent bout of unhappiness *wasn't* because of a man. "You're holding out on me," I said, wagging my finger at her like I was scolding a child.

Her eyes widened for a fraction of a second and I knew she caught my double meaning, but they narrowed again just as quickly. She pushed away from the counter and scooped her arm through the picnic basket's handle.

"I'd gotten the impression things were looking up for her, like she had herself a man again. She had a tendency to get a little hyped up sometimes, I guess is the best way to put it. When she simmered down, though, I could always catch glimpses of that broken girl scrounging around for scraps. But you listen here—whatever made Nell happy or unhappy was her business, not mine. Some things are just private."

The line of what we were talking about turned blurry, but I stayed firmly on the Nell side. "Not if she was killed over it."

"I've already told the deputies everything I know about Nell Gellen. The rest is up to them. What happened to her is tragic. She was a lost woman, but you can't lay your happiness on the shoulders of the people around you. I don't think she ever learned that. You've got to make your own happiness." She pointed at me. "You, missy, need to understand that." She came over and kissed me on the cheek. "Don't you worry about me, Harlow Jane. I'm just fine."

As she left, carrying the picnic she'd packed for the sheriff, I wondered when Mama had crossed over to Hoss McClaine's side of the blurry line.

Chapter 29

Nell might have lost her struggle for happiness, but I wasn't going to let her memory slip away without trying to win her some justice. I was struggling with concerns that Josie might somehow be involved, but it was easy to push that aside for the time being and stay focused on Nell. She'd been found dead on my property. As a result, the responsibility I felt toward her grew with every passing day.

Luckily I could practically sew in my sleep, and I nearly did, once again working into the wee hours of the morning, this time on Ruthann's bridesmaid dress. I thought the finished product was absolutely stunning.

I hoped she would think so, too.

At ten o'clock, she showed up for her final fitting. She was wearing her golden hair in a bun. She had the well-defined cheekbones to pull off such a severe look. "I thought you were finishing Josie's gown first," she said as she glided in.

"That *was* the plan, but I needed a break." I'd realized over the years that people told you what they wanted you to know, which was rarely all of the story. I was no exception. I did want a break from the yards and yards of ivory silk and the endless hand pleating of Josie's bodice, but I also wanted an excuse to talk to Ruthann alone.

Within minutes, Ruthann was behind the screen, shimmying into her body shaper, a style that hit just below her breasts. The result would be the illusion that there was a bit more in the bust than there actually was. Ruthann was gazelle-like, all limbs and very graceful, but she didn't have any extra padding. Anywhere.

The dress I'd designed was a perfect match for her. The full skirt would hint at curves. The vertically pleated tube bodice with the fitted sash just under the breasts would substitute for cleavage. I helped her slip into the dress, checking the fit and the length, then finally marking the back closure so I'd know exactly where to place the zipper.

When I released her, she glided over to the full-length mirror, did a one-eighty, and froze as if she'd looked into Medusa's eyes.

Oh, God, she hated it. I'd stayed up most of the night and had felt my energy flow right into the fabric as I'd sewed. I didn't know Ruthann, but I'd been sure this dress would make her feel more feminine and powerful than she'd ever felt before.

"Ruthann?" I moved closer until I stood behind her, slightly to one side. I looked like I'd stayed up all night. My hair, pulled into my usual two low ponytails, looked dull and lackluster. Even the blond streak had lost its shimmer. The bags under my eyes were smoky gray and my skin looked sallow.

Ruthann, on the other hand, looked like she'd been lit up from the inside by a firefly. The strong olive green chiffon made her skin sparkle with life. Effervescent. There was no other way to describe how she appeared.

"How?"

This was my first made-to-order dress. It was almost completed. A simple bridesmaid's dress and I'd botched it. "How what? You don't like it?" I hurried on, hoping to convince her this was better than what we'd originally discussed. "I know we talked about a sheath. And you wanted that wraparound dress, but Ruthann, this . . . *this* is *you*."

I held my breath, waiting for her to say something. *Anything*. Then the corners of her mouth lifted and her lips parted. She plucked the fabric on either side, holding it out like she was ready to curtsy. And her face lit up further. "How did you do this? It's . . . it's . . ." She trailed off, and spun around, gazing over her shoulder at the unfinished back of the dress. "It's absolutely perfect."

My skin pricked with excitement and my knees buckled with relief. I stepped back, letting her absorb her reflection. I didn't cry easily, but when I saw how thrilled she was, my eyes blurred and I came awful close to tears.

After a moment, I turned a critical eye to my construction and design. I jotted a few notes in my sketchbook, reminders to check the measurement from waist to hem all the way around the full chiffon skirt and the silk skirt underneath. They needed to be exactly the same so that one wasn't longer or shorter than the other.

"How did you do it?" she asked again.

"I've had a lot of training," I said after I was satisfied that I knew exactly how I would finish Ruthann's dress. "I worked with Maximilian for a long time. Graduated with a degree in fashion design—"

"No."

I glanced up from my sketchbook.

"That's not what I mean," she said, brushing a tear from her cheek. "Do they train you to make a person feel different?"

"What do you mean?"

A few strands of her hair had slipped from her bun, softening the hard lines of her face. She shook her head, glanced up at the ceiling. "I don't know how to explain it. It's like you always see yourself one way. The tall girl sitting home alone instead of going to prom. I never even had a homecoming mum." She spun around again and for a second I thought she was picturing the oversized Texas version of a corsage. Then I saw her face and realized she was gazing at her reflection as if it was the first time she was seeing herself.

To say I was flabbergasted would be an understatement. Shocked. How could someone as stunning as Ruthann have grown up thinking she was an ugly duckling?

If I reached out, I felt sure I'd be able to touch the emotion pouring out of her. I suddenly realized why I hadn't liked the wraparound dress design for her. The idea of crisscrossing two pieces of fabric over her body felt like I'd be constricting her. All the feelings she was experiencing at this very moment had been bottled up inside her forever. A wraparound dress would have kept them sewn up tight. But this dress freed them instead.

"But now?" she said, looking at me in the mirror. "Who cares about a silly mum? All those people who thought I was stuck up won't believe it. It's like you knew just what I needed."

I knew it now, but it had been pure instinct—and the fabric had led me. "I guess it's like women's intuition," I said with a smile. To make people feel the way Ruthann felt at this very moment. *This* was what Meemaw had taught me and *this* was why I'd wanted to design clothes.

"I wish Nell could have felt this way," Ruthann said, her voice simmering with regret.

"You don't think she did?"

Another strand of hair fell from her bun. "I know she didn't. If she just could have . . . maybe it would have been different for her." She turned her back to the mirror. "What kind of dress would you have made her?" she asked.

She'd died before I'd had a single idea that seemed to fit. "I honestly don't know. I couldn't get an image of her. It's almost like I—" I broke off, a cold chill sweeping over me. It was almost like I'd known she wouldn't be alive long enough to wear a dress I designed.

"She was such a wild child, you know. So much fun. She liked things that were colorful and vibrant." Ruthann's voice drifted into remembrance. "She always wore things that made people do a double take, but she wasn't really like that on the inside."

I knew people often projected one thing while inside

they were something entirely different. I'd only seen Nell in her cutoffs and knotted plaid shirt, but she was a businesswoman. She had to have been smart, committed, and savvy to make her shop stay afloat. There had definitely been more to her than met the eye. "How long did she own the shop?"

"She only bought it about six months ago. She was really frugal. Always saving, you know? She rented, and the landlord finally made a deal with her." She shook her head. "It's so unfair. Just when everything was starting to go really well ..."

I unpinned the back of her dress and she slipped out of it with a fond glance at the garment.

I hung her dress on the second dress form in the workroom. "I heard she had a will," I said as Ruthann disappeared behind the privacy screen.

Like a jack-in-the-box, her head popped out from behind the screen. "No, she couldn't have."

"Why not?"

A look of hurt came over her. "I guess I just thought she would have told me something like that. We shared everything."

"That's right—you two were close."

She smiled. "Yes, we were."

"Ah, well, who knows if it's true," I said.

"Oh, it probably is," she said quickly. "Nell was very shrewd. She knew exactly what she wanted and she worked hard to get it. I can see her not wanting to leave anything to chance, especially considering her upbringing."

I stayed busy at the dress form, needle and thread in hand, finishing the slip stitch on the sash. I slid the needle through the fabric, gliding it along the inside fold and sliding it back out. "Did she have a boyfriend?"

Josie had filled me in on Nell's self-destructive love life, but Mama's take on it was that things had been looking up. But by all accounts, she had a good business mind. Surely the two sides of Nell could be knitted together somehow.

"Oh, she was in love."

I jerked and the needle pricked my thumb. "She

was?" I said, pressing my thumb between my lips to soothe the biting pain.

"She wasn't telling people yet. Afraid she might jinx it, I think," Ruthann said from behind the privacy screen. "I only found out by accident."

"But I thought you two were best friends."

She reemerged, back in her white capris and floral top, the strands of hair framing her face giving her an ethereal look. "We *were* good friends, but Nell didn't get real close to anyone. I think I felt closer to her than she felt to me or to Karen, or even Josie. It was like she always had on battle armor, you know? Like she had to protect herself from being hurt."

From what little I knew of Nell, that made perfect sense. "How'd you *accidentally* find out she was in love?"

She looked through the French doors at the empty front room. No one had come into the shop all morning. "Can you keep a secret?" she asked.

I nodded. "Of course." Unless it was about Nell's murder, but surely that was understood?

"She was pregnant." She breathed out a heavy sigh of relief and her shoulders relaxed. "There, I said it."

Blood surged through my veins, my heart suddenly constricting. "Pregnant?"

"Pregnant."

"How far along?" I asked, remembering the slight pooch I'd noticed in Nell's belly. And I had overheard Ruthann and Karen talking about Nell getting sick. It all fit.

"Around fourteen weeks, I think." She shrugged her shoulders. "But honestly, I'm not sure. She wouldn't give me any details. Just said she was in love and this time it was going to work out."

"This time?"

"She's had a lot of near misses. And some not so near misses. But she said this guy was the one."

Before I let my imagination run wild, I went ahead with another question. "But why was it a secret?" I asked.

"It wasn't, I guess. Not exactly. She just wanted to tell

everyone in her own way. She'd been planning to make the big announcement at Josie and Nate's rehearsal dinner."

"Wouldn't Josie have minded her stealing the spotlight? I mean, someone else's wedding festivities doesn't seem like a very good time to make a personal announcement."

"Yeah, I thought so, too, but she said Josie wouldn't mind at all. She was the maid of honor, right? I guess she'd know."

Ruthann left the shop a few minutes later, but my conversation with her stayed with me long after she'd gone. I didn't know if the sheriff knew about Nell's pregnancy, but somehow he'd zeroed in on the two people I kept coming back to as I talked to Nell's acquaintances. Nate Kincaid and Josie Sandoval.

The scenarios clouded my mind and distracted me from my work. Nate had confessed to a past relationship with Nell. What if it had been more present than past, and what if *he* was the father of the baby? If he'd gotten wind that Nell was going to make the announcement at the rehearsal dinner, not only about their clandestine affair but about the pregnancy, how far would he have gone to try to stop her?

On the other hand, what if Josie had discovered the affair and the pregnancy? Would she have killed Nell in order to preserve the happily-ever-after she wanted so badly?

I knew that anyone who had been in Buttons & Bows the day Nell had died could have taken some random piece of trim and later strangled Nell with it. Nate and Josie had both been there.

I sank onto the couch. My temples throbbed from thinking about the murder investigation. "What am I supposed to do now?" I moaned, dropping my head to my hands.

"Do about what?"

My gaze snapped up.

Three inexplicable things hit me at once. One: Will Flores stood just outside the door, which was slightly ajar. Baffling, since I could have sworn I'd closed it. Two: The bells hadn't jingled, yet there it was, open, and there *he* was, looking at me like I'd lost my marbles. Three: And sitting right in front of me on the coffee table was a container of ibuprofen.

Chapter 30

As Will Flores tackled the pipes under the kitchen sink, I finished the zipper on Ruthann's dress and started doing the final measurements from waist to hem. One dress down wasn't quite one-third done with the bridal dresses. Josie's gown counted as double. At least. But it was progress, and with Nell's funeral tomorrow and the wedding just a week and a half away now, the clock was ticking.

Unless, of course, the bride—or the groom—was guilty of murder. That could seriously thwart Josie's plans to move forward with the wedding.

I'd opened the windows that morning, hoping the spring breeze would clear my head. But it still felt weighted down, like the thick humidity of summer had already descended and was especially concentrated around 2112 Mockingbird Lane in general, and me in particular. "I should just go talk to the sheriff," I muttered.

"You make a habit of talking to yourself?"

I jumped, whirling around. Will stood at the threshold of the French doors, carrying his toolbox with one hand, scratching his head under his cowboy hat with the other. "I'm just wondering if that's what I can expect from Gracie after she's been here with you for a while. People's peculiar little quirks tend to rub off on one another when they spend time together."

I bristled, dropping the measuring tape I'd been holding. It looked like a pale lavender snake slithering across the hardwood floor. Heat rose from my core until I was sure my neck was splotched red. I mustered up my best Southern affect, threw my hand on my hip, and drawled, "Well, I am Loretta Mae's kin, and you know the apple don't fall far from the tree."

He let his cowboy hat drop back onto his head. "That a fact? In all the times I've been here, I don't think I ever heard Miss Loretta Mae talking to herself."

That's because she didn't, actually, but I couldn't tell *him* that. "Your daughter will be just fine," I said. Then changing the subject, I said, "She's a fast learner. Who taught her to sew, anyway?"

"A friend," he said, but the way his eyes darkened and the sharpness of his answer made it clear this was not a subject to pursue.

Maybe I'd have the chance to ask Gracie more about it sometime. "So what's the verdict on the pipes?" I asked as I wound up the measuring tape.

"I couldn't find anything wrong under the sink, but like I told you, I'm not a plumber."

No, he was an architect and a historical society guy.

"You'll have to hire yourself a real plumber for that problem," he said.

"Okay, then," I said, but I suspected there was nothing wrong with the pipes except Meemaw's spirit hammering around with them. "What else is on the list?"

He reached one hand into his shirt pocket and pulled out a folded sheet of paper, handing it to me.

I got a mouthful of grief when I recognized Meemaw's spindly handwriting. The list was at least fifteen items long, from sealing the window casements to refinishing the kitchen table. Looked like I'd be spending a lot of time with Gracie Flores as payment. "You can cross number ten off the list," I said, handing the paper back to him.

His eyes scanned the list. "You don't want help organizing the attic?" One eyebrow arched up. "I've been up there."

I would honor as many of Meemaw's wishes as possible, but the attic was personal. It was filled with family memories, heirlooms, and Cassidy history. I didn't want to share that with a stranger. "It'll be work, I know, but I'll do it."

He didn't mention it again, just folded the paper back into a square and tucked it away in his shirt pocket. "The application to make this house part of the historical society is almost processed," he said, turning to go.

I blinked with surprise. "What?"

He stopped at the front door. "You didn't know?"

Slowly, I shook my head. Good Lord, what other land mines had Meemaw set?

"Loretta Mae showed up at the Bliss Historical Society about a month before she passed. Not only is this house one of the original dwellings off the square and one of the oldest homes in town, but when Bonnie and Clyde went on their rampage through the county, they hung out in Bliss, robbed the bank on the square, and hid out in your backyard."

I gawked in disbelief. "I've never heard that story." I folded my arms over my chest and tapped my foot. "Is that really true? They hid out *here*?"

"It's true, Cassidy. This house is going on the registry. The society sent your great-grandmother letters for years, but she never answered them. Then one day, she just showed up and asked what in tarnation we'd been waiting for," he said with a chuckle.

"Well, I'll be. Do I need to do anything?"

"I'll bring the final documents by when they're done. At some point, we'll have our photographer come out. The society's making plans for a calendar and a book of Bliss history and unforgettable characters. This house will be in both."

Out back, the *slap slap slap* of the gate banging in the breeze sounded like raucous clapping. *Meemaw—she was up to her usual tricks*. Once again, she'd gotten what she'd wanted. "Do you have that gate latch on your list?" I asked. If Meemaw kept messing with it, Thelma Louise, or one of Nana's other feisty goats, was sure to find the way back into my yard.

"Yep."

"Good. Maybe it can move to the top?"

He nodded. "Gracie's going to stop by this afternoon," he said as he headed out.

So I had a few hours. I needed a break from my workroom. And I needed to talk to Hoss McClaine. I grabbed my purse, stepped onto the porch, and locked up. On a little hook to the right of the door, I hung up a little custom chalkboard sign I'd had made.

> The Dressmaker's on a fashion errand.
> Back at _____ .

I filled in the blank with "3:00 p.m.," then hightailed it down the steps to the sidewalk. I turned left on Mockingbird Lane and started walking toward the Sheriff's Department.

Before I'd accompanied Josie, the last time I had been in the sheriff's office was when I was eighteen. I'd been accepted at UT-Austin. I'd packed my bags and I'd been itching to shake the dust of Bliss off my boot heels and strike out on my own, but my brother, Red, had persuaded me to go joyriding through a field of Longhorns out on Old Hickory Road one last time. Too bad the rancher who owned that land and those cattle hadn't thought our riding through was a joy. He'd called the sheriff, then come out to play chicken with us. Red drove Nana's beat-up old pickup, and Old Man Poindexter manned a brand-spanking-new Ford 4x4. "There's no way he can win," Red yelled. He revved the engine, then gunned it, dirt spewing from beneath the back tires as they spun.

But he'd underestimated the rancher's gumption. He didn't want teenagers messing around on his ranch, troubling his cattle. "He's not turning!" I shrieked, squeezing my eyes shut and ducking my head.

"Shit!" Red cranked the steering wheel to the left, round and round and round. I braced myself, waiting for the impact of the crash, but instead, we spun out, and then finally jerked to a stop.

Poindexter was already out of his truck, bearing down on us, the barrel of his rifle steady. We stayed like that till Deputy Sheriff Hoss McClaine came to haul us away.

It took everything I had not to slip back into the memory of being read the riot act by McClaine before he'd been sheriff. That was then, this was now. I was years wiser than my eighteen-year-old self. Hopefully, he realized that.

We sat opposite each other, his monstrous oak desk like a battlefield between us. I had the sudden feeling that *he* knew that *I* knew about him and Mama, though how he'd know, I didn't know, and it was a big ol' white elephant in the room. But Mama's words had stuck with me. She was making her own happiness. I might not like that Hoss McClaine was keeping their relationship on the down-low, but it wasn't my business.

"What can I do for ya, Harlow?" His gravelly voice was like sand under my bare feet. It was warm and soothing, despite the roughness.

"I have some information about Nell Gellen that I think you should know." The weight of the promise I'd made to Ruthann pressed on my heart, but I'd deal with that later. If it helped bring Nell justice, surely Ruthann would understand.

McClaine listened, his hands laced together on the desk, while I told him about Nell's reckless love life, the fact that she thought she'd finally found love, and her pregnancy. "If Nate is the killer, Josie can't go through with the wedding. And if Josie's the killer, then . . . then . . ." Then my faith in old friendships, my judgment of character, and maybe of humanity, would be totally shattered.

McClaine waved one of his weathered hands around in front of him. "It'll be okay. You always did go straight for the drama."

My hands gripped the arms of the chair. "What?"

"This is good information, Harlow," he rumbled.

I breathed slowly, letting his comment slide away. "So you'll look into it?"

I half expected him to respond by saying something

like "Is a gopher happy in soft dirt?" Instead, he nodded solemnly. "Oh, I'll be lookin' into it, don't you worry."

I thanked him and started to leave, but stopped at the door. "Sheriff?"

He leaned back, the front legs of his chair lifting from the ground. "Yes, ma'am?"

"I'm making Josie's wedding dress."

"I heard tell about that. Heard it's bad luck to make another woman's marriage gown."

Ah, he'd been talking to Mama. "That's silly, and I don't believe it. I was just wondering, do I keep working on it? If she or Nate did—"

The front legs of his chair dropped to the ground. "You keep working on it, Harlow. We don't know yet what happened to that woman. As of now, the Sandoval-Kincaid wedding is on, which means that girl needs a dress. You stop working on it, they'll wonder why, and that won't help my investigation none."

Hoss McClaine was a straight shooter. Had to appreciate *that* about him. I thanked him again and stepped back into the hallway . . . and bumped right into Madelyn Brighton.

"Harlow!" Her eyes darted to McClaine's door. "Everything okay?"

I grabbed her sleeve, pulling her down the hallway with me. "It's nothing. He's, uh, seeing my mother, but *shhh.*" I held my finger to my lips. "It's a secret."

She pressed her lips together, turned an imaginary key with her fingers, and smiled. "Got it." We walked together down the hall toward the exit. "I was just about to ring you up," she said.

I lifted my shoulders and smiled. "You were?"

"Yes." She bounced slightly as she walked, like she was bubbling over with excitement. "The Kincaid family's having a big gala for their foundation."

"Uh-huh."

"My husband can't make it. He's got a committee meeting at the college. Scholarships, you know. There's so much administrative work to be done. Anyway, I have an extra ticket if you want to come along."

My stomach instantly knotted. I was more a behind-the-scenes kind of person. I made garments for other people to shine in while I steered clear of the limelight. Being front and center at a Kincaid event wasn't my style. "I have a lot to do, what with the wedding—"

She dropped her voice to a whisper. "It might give you an opportunity to snoop around a little bit. Talk to people. Do a little of that sleuthing we talked about. What do you say?"

I wavered. I could dress up like Cinderella and snoop like Jessica Fletcher or Miss Marple. "On second thought, it sounds great, Madelyn. Thank you."

"Excellent! Pick you up at six thirty. See you then. Ta-ta!" She pivoted on her practical, flat-heeled shoes and headed back down the hall, skipping every third step. Nell's pregnancy, and her plan to announce it at the rehearsal dinner, had changed everything for me. Madelyn was right. Going to the gala would be a great opportunity to talk to people, but I no longer thought I was helping Josie by proving Nate innocent.

Chapter 31

What I found as I searched my closet was that I had plenty of classic pieces, the foundation of any wardrobe, but not much that was really gala-worthy. I'd never had a need, so I'd never created a gown for myself. My best option was the little black dress I'd designed for my roommate and fellow Maximilian minion back in New York, Orphie Cates. I'd almost finished the dress, but before the final fitting, the pressure of Maximilian had gotten to her. She'd up and quit one day, packed her belongings, and left Manhattan. I hadn't heard from her since.

To leave the dress undone was the equivalent of starting a book and not finishing it. I couldn't leave characters hanging in my mind with no conclusion to their story. By the same token, I couldn't leave an article of clothing I was working on incomplete, unable to realize its potential for the wearer, whoever that might be. I'd adjusted the sizing and finished the dress so it would fit me, but I'd never had an occasion to wear it.

Until now.

I'd kept Meemaw's full-length mirror when I'd moved my things into her room. The buttercup walls and dormer windows made the room bright and warm, but that didn't banish the feeling that this wasn't really my room. And even though Orphie had never worn the little black dress, I still felt like it belonged to her, not me.

I looked at my reflection, remembering the hours and hours I'd spent on the beadwork tracing the deep V neck-

line. The inch-wide strip of black, silver, and gold irides-
cent beads caught the light as I turned. I'd used ruching on
the bodice, a technique that brought the eye inward, slim-
ming the body. Of course, the Spanx I wore underneath
didn't hurt in that department, either. When I paired the
dress with transparent black tights patterned with tiny
dots, I had to admit I was pleased as punch with it.

"It needs something, though," I mumbled as I pulled
my corkscrew hair up in back, securing it with a few
bobby pins in an artfully messy bun.

The closet door slid open with a bang. I gasped.
"Meemaw! You're going to give me a heart attack!" I had
accepted that she was still here with me, but dang if it
didn't still catch me by surprise every time she made her
presence known. I padded toward the crammed closet
and peered into the depths. I waited, but nothing happened. Maybe Meemaw was just bored.

But as I took a step back, my foot landed on something hard. I looked down. Lying on the floor, where it
hadn't been a few seconds ago, was a beaded cuff. The
perfect accessory for my little black dress.

As I bent to pick it up, a warm pocket of lavender-
scented air moved around me. My head snapped up.
"Meemaw?" I held up the bracelet. "Thank you." Who
knew where it had come from, but I didn't care. I just
wanted to see her. To hear her voice. To hug her.

The closet door slowly slid closed behind me. I turned,
my gaze drawn to a pair of black suede pumps I'd bought
more than a year ago at one of Maximilian's accessory
sales. Even with the employee discount, they'd been pricey,
but the edgy zipper detailing at the toe and heel had been
such an unexpected twist that I'd splurged. "I forgot about
these," I murmured, slipping them on.

I suddenly knew just how Cinderella had felt after
her fairy godmother had chanted, "Bibbity bobbity boo"
and done her magic. I felt bathed in love and warmth.

The lingering floral scent was fading. "Are you still
here?" I spun around, hoping to see the swirling air or
her ghostly form, but I was alone.

Meemaw's rocking chair sat in the corner next to the

oval mirror. My dresser held photos of Orphie and me during Fashion Week in front of the fountain at Lincoln Center's Damrosch Park, Nana surrounded by goats nipping at her pockets, and Mama and Meemaw, the spitting image of each other right down to the blond streak in their hair, on the front porch of this house. I picked up the frame. Mama's smile didn't quite reach her eyes. I'd never noticed that before. Meemaw gazed right at the camera, her head tilted toward Mama, her smile genuine and complete as she stood there with her granddaughter. It was all about family for Meemaw. It always had been. I suddenly understood how broken-hearted she must have been when I'd left Bliss.

My gaze went back to my mother, and I felt a little piece of my own heart fold in on itself. I'd been well into my twenties when it finally hit me that not only had my father left my brother and me, but Mama's husband had walked out on her. The sadness was right there in plain sight. I'd have seen it if I'd only been looking.

A knock on the door downstairs snapped me back to reality. The clock read six thirty on the dot. Madelyn was punctual.

I headed down the stairs, my heels clicking against the hardwood.

"The OPEN sign was still out and the door was unlocked," she called, "so I came in."

"Of course—" I broke off, stopping short as she came into view. She was covered from head to toe in beige. Beige skirt. Beige blouse. Nude stockings. Even a beige clutch. My left eye twitched and my pulse skittered. Beige, beige, beige. She was too young to look so matronly. She was like a flavorless biscuit, plain and bland. Where was the style? The personality? The sparkle I'd seen when she talked about magic and ghosts and that wacky paranormal society?

It was all buried under clothes the color of oatmeal.

I snapped my jaw closed, hoping she couldn't read my expression. Then I noticed *her* staring at *me* with a wondrous look on her face. "No wonder you're a designer," she said, utter reverence in her voice. "If I looked like *that*, Bill would never pass up another gala event in favor of a department meeting."

"Pshaw. That has nothing to do with it. He loves you." At least I assumed he did.

"Well, of course he does. But he's not here, is he?"

"And you wish he were."

She pursed her lips in true British style. "Oh, I'm sorry. I didn't mean . . . That came out wrong—"

I waved away her apology. "Stop! I know what you meant. If I had a husband, I'd want him by my side, too."

She looked me up and down, heaving a deep, sorrowful sigh; then she slowly fluttered her hand in front of her body as if she could shoo the dreariness away. "This is just horrifically drab."

That was all the encouragement I needed to propel me into action. I was going to help her find her effervescence again or I had no right to call myself a fashion designer. I hurried down the last few steps, grabbed her arm, and yanked her into the workroom. "It's your lucky day, Mrs. Brighton. We're going to vanquish the drab. You game?"

Her lips quivered nervously, but she nodded. Already there was color in her cheeks and a glint of excitement in her eyes. "Work your magic, Ms. Cassidy," she said.

And I did.

Chapter 32

As Madelyn and I started across the arched stone bridge, we passed a gorgeous pond and waterway directly below us. The castle. Gracie Flores was right on the money about this place. I'd forgotten how ostentatious it was.

With each step, I felt like Alice in Wonderland slipping further through the rabbit hole, slowly growing smaller and smaller, landing in a place where I just didn't belong. The Kincaids were out of my league. I'd come from goat farmers and bandits, not oil and . . . oil. The last time I'd been here, they'd made it perfectly clear that the two did not mix.

And to top it off, a dressmaker did not a detective make. My chest felt heavy, like one of the Kincaids' oil derricks sat right on top of it, a drill bit steadily boring a hole straight through to my pounding heart. What was I thinking? Miss Marple. Ha.

Madelyn stopped at the summit of the bridge. "Are you okay?"

A couple sauntered up one side of the bridge. I waited until they passed, then whispered, "I . . . I don't know if I can go in there." Somebody had killed Nell. This was no game. I certainly didn't want to be the next victim. And I was having flashbacks to my brief, and less than pleasant, stint as Derek Kincaid's girlfriend. "I shouldn't be here."

Back at Buttons & Bows, I'd taken control and reoutfitted Madelyn. I'd had no choice but to stick with her camel-colored skirt, but I'd paired it with a sheer black blouse from the rack of clothes in the front room. Two rows of white-trimmed vertical ruffles ran up the center of the blouse and around the neck, the same ruffles mirrored on the edges of the extralong sleeves. It was a little snug on Madelyn, but with the right body shaper underneath, she pulled it off.

The practical pumps were another story. "What size shoe do you wear?" I'd asked.

"Six," she said.

"I'm an eight and a half." She'd walk right out of my shoes. I'd tapped my finger against my cheek, thinking. There had to be something.

The floorboards had creaked right next to us. We both whipped our heads around. No one was there. When I leaned against the cutting table, thinking and gripping the edge with my hands, the scent of lavender wafted past. A pocket of warm air suddenly hovered around us.

Madelyn's brows pulled together like she thought something was off, but she couldn't put her finger on what it was. When the heel of my right hand brushed against something soft and plush, I knew without looking that Meemaw had come to the rescue. Bows. Of course!

"Give me your shoes," I said after I'd heated up the glue gun. A minute later, lovely velvet bows had transformed her pumps from plain Jane to chic. I pulled back one lock of her hair, securing it with a subtle bow. "Voilà!"

But that was then, and this was now.

"What you're doing," she said, her confidence bolstered, "is helping your friend clear her name."

She was right, of course, but I didn't want to hear it. "I don't even know where to start."

"Let's just go in and check things out. Maybe you'll find something helpful or maybe you won't. You'll figure it out as you go." This time she grabbed my arm, pulling me over the bridge and through the front door.

The second I crossed the threshold, someone thrust a drink in my hand. Heavy crystal stemware filled with red wine. I closed my eyes and took a sip, letting the warmth of the alcohol ease my mind. A few seconds later, I looked up. "Holy mother of . . ." We'd been transported to a fancy Fashion Week reception in New York, Texas style. The men wore blazers, dark jeans, big silver belt buckles, and boots, and the women had bling on their fingers, wrists, necks, and anywhere else they could get away with it.

Madelyn whipped her camera out and started snapping pictures. One minute she was by my side, the next minute she'd been swallowed by the crowd. And I was left to ... to see if I could learn anything at all about Nell and Nate and Josie and the whole sordid mess.

I took another bolstering sip of my drink and moved through the crowd. After ten minutes, I was clear about one thing. I had no idea where, or how, to begin.

"My future daughter-in-law's dress must be done if you're here," a voice said from behind me.

I turned and smiled at Lori Kincaid. She was perfectly coiffed, from her hair—expertly ratted, molded, and sprayed into place—to her halter-topped shimmery dress. I was pretty sure the word "understated" was not in her vocabulary. "Not quite," I said, "but I'm getting there."

"I'm glad to hear that," she said. "It is a surprise to see you here."

She hadn't actually asked a question, but it was implied. Why, exactly, *was* I here?

"A friend asked if I'd like to come with her." I had no intention of getting said friend in trouble for bringing an uninvited guest, so I zipped my lips, not giving Madelyn's name.

I felt Mrs. Kincaid's scrutiny as she took in every detail of my attire. I must have passed because finally her lips curved up. If she was worried about Nate and Josie having been questioned by the sheriff that morning, I sure couldn't tell. Her smile seemed as genuine as could be. She didn't seem to be harboring any ill will toward me from my past with her elder son, either. I breathed a little easier.

"I'm sure Josie will be glad to see you. We're so blessed to have someone with your talent right here in Bliss. And the timing was perfect," she said.

I bristled. Yes, Meemaw's death had come at the right

time, allowing me to move back home and set up shop just in time to make Josie's dress. I forced a smile, managing not to point out that I'd rather never sew another stitch in my life if I could only have Meemaw back.

"Keith, dear," she said to the man by her side, "do you remember Harlow Cassidy? Harlow, my husband." She waved her hand between us with the introduction, the sparkle on her ring finger almost blinding me. That was no artificial bling. Just another perk of the oil business. Whereas I had rhinestones—not even cubic zirconia— Lori Kincaid had the real thing.

Keith Kincaid, who couldn't have been more than five feet ten inches, pushed six feet with his taupe suede cowboy hat on. He had his own bling on the ring finger of his right hand—a two-pound Texas A&M ring. Even his turquoise inlaid belt buckle screamed money.

Minus the bling, he and Nate were clearly cut from the same cloth. Same dirty blond hair. Same chin dimple. Same height. The only difference was the good-ol'-boy attitude Keith exuded, from his biscuits-and-gravy accent to the pat on the behind I caught him giving Lori. Her flinch was barely noticeable, but enough to show she didn't relish the public show of affection. I didn't blame her.

"Pleasure to meetcha," he said, shaking my hand with a firm, double-handed grip, his beefy palm dwarfing mine. A sudden look of understanding crossed his weathered face. "Ah, wait just a sec. Harlow Cassidy. Derek's old . . ."

"The dressmaker, dear," his wife interrupted.

He gave a slow nod, releasing me from his clammy grip. "Where Josie's friend was . . ." He trailed off, scratching his head like he didn't quite know how to put it.

I nodded, shifting uncomfortably. Nell was going to be the maid of honor in their son's wedding. Did the Kincaids even know her name?

He found his way. "Quite a sad story. Poor girl. Does the sheriff have any suspects?"

I wanted to say, *You mean aside from your son and future daughter-in-law, who I'm sure, by the way, is innocent, but I'm not so sure about the fruit of your loins?*

I'd been uncomfortable since Madelyn's car had rolled onto the property, but now my head swam. If I had any hand in proving Nate guilty, I'd be betraying the oldest friend I had in Bliss.

Not that I *would have* a hand in it. I was a dressmaker, not a detective. I gave a small shrug of my shoulders. "They don't keep me updated."

"No, no, I guess they wouldn't," he said thoughtfully.

"Keith, dear," Mrs. Kincaid said, "now's not the—"

"Right," he said with a curt nod. "But the details have been sketchy. Did she have money? Assets? Enemies?"

Lori's jaw clenched as she gritted her teeth. Keith reminded me of Meemaw. It seemed that whatever he wanted, he got, even if his wife put her foot down. "I only met her for the first time the day she died," I said.

Lori Kincaid glanced around, then lowered her voice to a gossipy whisper. If you can't beat 'em, join 'em. "I heard that she bought that little bead shop a few months ago. What I'm curious about is where she got the capital."

I dove in with both feet. If Mrs. Kincaid could gossip, so could I. "I heard she made a will."

Mrs. Kincaid nodded her head approvingly. "Good for her. So her heirs will get her money, not the government."

"Oh, yes, but I got the feeling she didn't have any family." Unless you counted the baby she was carrying.

I experienced another wave of profound gratitude that I was back in Bliss, near Mama and my grandparents, and Red and his family. I'd moved away, pretended like it was what I wanted, but when a door opened to come back, I'd run through it. Nell hadn't had that choice. She'd had no one and no place to go home to. There'd been no open door for her.

"Such a tragedy," Mrs. Kincaid continued a moment later, "and so close to the wedding."

"Maybe it should be postponed," I suggested. That was one surefire way to ensure that Josie wouldn't marry a killer.

Mrs. Kincaid set her lips in a thin, unwavering line. "Impossible. With Keith's travel schedule and all the guests coming in, we have to make the best of it and go forward."

Make the best of having a member of the wedding party murdered. How exactly did you do that?

"Don't you agree, dear?" she asked her husband.

Mr. Kincaid, looking a little jet-lagged, with dark, puffy circles under his eyes, had been surveying his guests. "'Course. Right," he said absently, but Lori had moved ahead to another conversation, answering a question nobody had asked.

"Miriam is going to step in as maid of honor," she said.

"Really?" So maybe Gracie's theory about why Miriam wasn't in the wedding was all wrong. "Does Josie know?"

"Of course she knows. Goodness, it's her wedding. She's quite an agreeable girl—"

Like a Stepford daughter-in-law?

"—and Miriam couldn't be more pleased."

All I could think about was poor Nell, followed by a fleeting thought of how easily we could all be replaced. I raised my glass to take a sip.

"Miriam will be by your shop in the morning for her fitting," Mrs. Kincaid said.

My hand jerked and I gasped. All the wine left in my glass poured into my mouth. My throat spasmed and I choked. Stifling a cough only forced the wine down my windpipe. I slapped my hand over my mouth and nose, using every bit of gumption I possessed to swallow so I wouldn't spew it all over Mrs. Kincaid's fancy silk gown.

When I could breathe again, I said, "She'll be by where? For her what?"

"Buttons and Bows for her fitting, of course. Shall we say ten o'clock?"

She reached up and patted her husband's shoulder. He started, bringing his distant gaze back to her. He'd been far more interested in the goings-on in the room than in the rotating maid-of-honor situation. "Yes, yes. Do what you like," he said to her, giving her another thump on her rump.

She lurched forward from it, her neck straining. "Keith," she warned, but her admonishment fell on deaf ears.

"Unfortunate about Josie's friend," he twanged, "but I'm glad not to miss the nuptials."

I smiled stiffly and nodded, but my mind whirled. Now I needed to add a dress for Miriam Kincaid to my already packed sewing schedule. A completely crazy thought shot through my mind. Could Mrs. Kincaid have killed Nell just to open up a spot for her daughter in the wedding?

Everything was about appearances to them, right? I gave her a good once-over. Tasteful hyacinth blue gown skimming over a well-maintained figure, diamond choker to match the rock on her finger, perfectly applied makeup, immobile hair.

Lori Kincaid could win a Mrs. Texas pageant any day of the week. *That* part of Gracie's theory was definitely true.

Was it possible that Mrs. Kincaid's brain was so soft that she would choose murder over the public slight of having her daughter absent from the wedding party?

God, I hoped not.

If there was a bright side to making a bridesmaid dress for Miriam, it was that I'd get a chance to find out what she, and maybe Nate, knew about Nell's pregnancy. "I'm sure Nate's glad you're here," I said.

Mrs. Kincaid threaded a possessive arm through her husband's as she spoke to me. "You'll be able to do it all on time?"

Nice of her to ask.

I nodded, maybe a tad more confidently than I actually felt, but I was already planning how to tackle the additional dress. Aside from Nell's funeral tomorrow, I didn't have to leave Buttons & Bows at all. If Mama could do the muslin mock-up and the slip . . . "Definitely," I said, but I sensed the beginnings of a headache coming on—the tension in my neck, the pressure at my temples.

Mrs. Kincaid looked me up and down again like she was taking mental snapshots of the beading, ruching, and pleating of Orphie's dress. "That's a lovely ensemble." she said.

My hands instinctively ran down my sides. I started to

say, "Thank you," but an appreciative male voice from behind me cut me off. "Very lovely . . ."

I turned to see Will Flores wearing a hint of a smile and looking spiffy in his Sunday best—black jeans, white dress shirt, and black leather cowboy hat. Men's formal wear, Texas style. He pulled it off expertly.

Keith Kincaid untangled himself from his wife's arm and thrust his hand out. "Will, appreciate the help with the bags earlier," he said, giving him an enthusiastic handshake. "Jet-lagged and gin. Could be worse. Lemme get you a Coke."

Will laughed. "Sure."

"What kind do you want?" Keith asked.

"Dr Pepper," Will said with a wink.

That had to be a joke only a Texan could appreciate. I smiled as Mr. Kincaid let out a belly laugh and slapped Will on the back. "Good to see you, young man," he bellowed. "You clean up real good. Glad to see those old houses aren't breaking your spirit."

He took Will by the elbow with a firm grip. "How's that girl of yours?"

"Doing real well, sir," Will said, showing his good manners. Yes, sir. No, ma'am. Yes, ma'am. No, sir. We'd all been raised with manners like our mamas taught us.

"Good, good, glad to hear it. Got a minute?" he asked, leading Will a few steps away from us. "Got something to talk to ya about."

The phrase triggered something in my brain. A surreal image of Mr. Kincaid leading me by the elbow and steering me out the door and over the bridge played in my mind. It was like watching myself in a dream. "Thank you, sir," I heard myself say, though I didn't know why I was thanking him. He looked over his shoulder, hollered for Nate, then snarled, "Got something to talk to ya about." My legs buckled under me. He did? But like a flash, I was in the backseat of a car, driving, driving, driving . . . until the whole scene disappeared into a cloud of smoke.

My breath caught in my throat as the conversations and people around me came back into focus. "Historical society business, or something else?" Will was saying.

"Little of both," he said with a wink. "Miriam's got some cockamamy idea about a bookstore." He back-handed Will's shoulder. "Don't know why we need that. Digital, I told her. E-books, now, that's the wave of the future, but she wore me down. She found a site off the square. I happen to have a little extra capital to play with, so . . ."

Interesting. Mr. Kincaid was so buddy-buddy with Will Flores, yet according to what Gracie had said, Miriam had been shunned when Will had tried to help her. And if he and Miriam had been involved, it shouldn't have mattered since there was no Mrs. Flores.

Another knot in Bliss's tangled social web.

I looked up to find Will back and studying me. It wasn't what I'd call a slow, steamy look, but it came darn close and had the same effect. I shifted my weight un-easily, raising my glass to my lips before I remembered how I'd so ungracefully finished my wine.

He took the crystal stemware right out of my hand. "Let me get you a refill, Cassidy. Anyone else?" The Kincaids both shook their heads no and Will sauntered off. Mere seconds later, he was back with a fresh glass of ruby red wine.

I thanked him, scrunching my nose to edge my glasses back into place. Then my stomach rumbled and all I could think was that I should have stayed home because I was much better *behind* the scenes, dressing people for their parties, than being one of the partygoers myself. Another reason it had been so easy to leave New York.

Keith Kincaid had launched back into talking about the new project he was cooking up with Miriam, shifting Will's attention again. Which was fine with me. I wanted to find Josie. My stomach growled again, but I ignored it, taking another sip of wine as I looked around. I hardly knew anybody at this shindig. I'd been born and raised in Bliss, but at this moment I felt like a stranger in a strange land.

I scanned the room looking for Karen or Ruthann, or even Zinnia James, the only other people I *did* sort of know, but I couldn't spot any of them.

Will's voice snaked into my consciousness again. "Better slow down there, Cassidy. From the sound of it, your stomach isn't gonna like all wine and no food."

I'd hoped no one could hear my complaining tummy, but no such luck. Instead of food, I swallowed my embarrassment. There was something about the sound of his voice that wound right through me and gripped my insides in a bear hug. I couldn't put my finger on it. I'd heard slow Southern drawls all my life, so I didn't think it was that. Maybe it was the gritty undertone of his tenor, or the way he somehow infused his words with a smile. Or maybe it was all three converging in a perfect storm.

Whatever it was, I kind of liked the feeling it created inside me.

"Will, my boy, you're the man for the job." Keith Kincaid's John Wayne voice snapped everything back in place, including my fuzzy head. "Let's talk details."

He led Will away just as a waiter approached with a tray of appetizers. "Flatiron steak martini, miss?" he asked. I traded my wineglass for a martini glass as he rattled off the ingredients. Toasted juniper berries, Spanish olives, pickled onions, crumbled blue cheese, and thinly sliced grilled flatiron steak.

It could have been Froot Loops, for all I cared. Anything to stop the ruckus in my belly. One bite of the vermouth-marinated steak and my stomach quieted, my head cleared, and I knew I could make it through the rest of the evening.

Will threw me a glance over his shoulder, followed by an apologetic shrug of his shoulders. I responded by fluttering my fingers in a way that said he didn't owe me a thing. I never expected anything from any man, and I was never disappointed. Early lesson from my father.

"There's Josie," Mrs. Kincaid said, pointing to a cluster of people next to the bar.

Josie stood slightly apart from the others, looking drawn and sallow, and like she was carrying the weight of the world on her shoulders. Worry . . . or guilt? "I'm going to go—"

A familiar-looking woman edged between Mrs. Kincaid and me, cutting me off. "Lori, you look stunning, as always," she said in a syrupy voice.

"Me?" Mrs. Kincaid pressed her diamond-bejeweled hand to her chest and batted her eyelashes. "Look at *you*, Helen. You look simply divine."

I couldn't place her after a minute or two, so I gave up. Twice I tried to interject, but twice I was cut off. I stood there, half listening, feeling like a third wheel while they chatted, waiting for an opening so I could break away. It was harder than it should have been.

"Such a tragedy," Mrs. Kincaid was saying.

"I couldn't believe it when I heard," the woman said. "I can only imagine what you and Keith must have felt. Buddy said ..."

I tried to catch Josie's eye, which was impossible since her back was to me.

"... paying for the funeral ..."

That caught my attention. I had figured that without next of kin, Nell would be cremated without a service, which had struck me as so ... so ... sad. When I'd heard there would be a funeral, I'd wondered who was footing the bill.

"... least we could do for Josie," Mrs. Kincaid was saying. "She's broken up over it."

As the conversation shifted to the church rummage sale, I turned my attention to the details of the room. There was an emphasis on flowers everywhere I looked. Floral upholstery on the overstuffed sofas. Both print and solid-colored pillows with elaborate trim and tassels artfully accented the room.

The women droned on.

"... or Nate will bring them by ..."

"... too many dishes and books ..."

"... whatever's left to the 4-H for the girls to practice with ..."

Mrs. Kincaid had a thing for dried flowers. Arrangements decorated the fireplace mantel, the center of the glossy mahogany coffee table, and a matching side table in the corner of the room. *She should donate one of those to the rummage sale*, I thought. *Or all of them.*

". . . nice to have the Lincoln," the woman was saying. "Buddy won't let me buy a new . . ."

Cars? I had to escape. Now. "Excu—" I started, but Lori Kincaid tittered. "You know Keith's rules. No exceptions. The Lexus comes home to mama tomorrow."

Lincoln and Lexus. Those were two car makes I would never own. I had Meemaw's beat-up old Ford pickup, but with a dead battery, it didn't do me any good. In a pinch, I had a bicycle, but I'd spent enough time in New York that I preferred walking anyway.

I debated my options: stay put or slowly walk away. Finally, I realized I might never find a pause in their conversation. "Ahem." Clearing my throat seemed like a cliché, but it worked. Mrs. Kincaid stopped talking about who could drive which car and they both focused on me. A lightbulb seemed to go off in Mrs. Kincaid's head. "Oh, my stars, I do apologize, Harlow," she exclaimed a little overzealously. "Helen, you were asking about the dressmaker."

"I was," she said in true East Texas form. "Was" became *waaa-uz*. She tilted her chin down, eyeing me through her lashes. Just like everyone else in town, Helen gave me a good once-over, from the streak in my curly Cassidy hair to my zipper-adorned heels. "Is this . . . ?" "This" sounded like *the-is*.

Mrs. Kincaid beamed, looking like she'd discovered her own personal diamond in the rough. "Yes, it is. This," she said, sweeping her arm toward me, "is Harlow Cassidy. Harlow," she said, "meet Helen Abernathy."

Of Abernathy Home Builders. Another high-powered Bliss woman. So why did they both come off as mere seconds to their husbands? "Nice to meet you," I said, holding my hand out.

"I hear you're making all the dresses for the wedding of the year," Mrs. Abernathy said, leaving my hand dangling.

"Yes, ma'am," I said, lowering my arm. "I—"

She cut me off, saying, "I seem to recollect Miriam taking sewing lessons once upon a time."

Mrs. Kincaid scoffed. "Once upon a long time ago.

That machine hasn't seen the light of day in years. She thinks Holly might take it up one day. I'll believe it when I see it."

"A bit of good fortune for you that there's a dressmaker in town now." Mrs. Abernathy turned back to me with a thin smile. "Coleta Cassidy's granddaughter, come back home to roost. Your grandmother and I go way back, you know. We were in school together."

A lot of people went way back with Nana, I was discovering. Mrs. Abernathy. Mrs. James, the senator's wife. Nana had some highfalutin friends once upon a time.

I gave a polite response, sneaking a glance at the bar. The spot where Josie had been standing was filled with a new group of people. Drat.

"Harlow?" Mrs. Kincaid snapped.

"I'm sorry. What?"

Helen Abernathy pinched her lips, but repeated the question she'd apparently asked me. "Maybe you can get your grandmother to sell that land? It's prime location."

I caught a glimpse of Josie heading upstairs. "She, um . . ." I inched away from them.

"You know the city wants to build a park there."

"Over her dead body, she always says." Mrs. Kincaid and Mrs. Abernathy didn't get the joke. I wiped the smile off my face. "She's not selling."

"All those goats," one of them said.

"It's a crazy hobby," the other responded.

"It's not a hobby," I said, keeping one eye on the stairs, but Josie wasn't in sight anymore. "I'm sorry. If you'll excuse me," I said, backing away.

I left them muttering about Nana's goats and the value of land off the square. Weaving through the mess of people, I dashed up the stairs as fast as my three-and-a-half-inch heels would take me.

It wasn't until I was at the top that I remembered where I'd seen Mrs. Abernathy before.

In Buttons & Bows, alongside Zinnia James, balking when Nell had held up my Escher-inspired black-and-white textile dress.

Chapter 33

I didn't find Josie, but I did find Karen. She was leaning against the banister overlooking the gathering room, watching the people below with the focus of a master artist committing a scene to memory so he could interpret it on canvas later. She wore navy slacks and a conservative powder blue blouse and looked more business casual than glitzy. Not the right choice for an evening with the first family of Bliss.

My little pep talk hadn't worked.

She jumped when I greeted her, clutching her hand to her heart. "Oh, God, you scared me, Harlow."

Even though she'd said my name, she looked at me like she was walking down the cereal aisle at Walmart and had suddenly seen a celebrity. Clearly she couldn't quite adjust to seeing me out of Buttons & Bows and in the Kincaids' house.

"Yep, it's me. I spend most of my waking hours at the dress shop, but every once in a while, I escape."

"I didn't know you were invited to this," she said, redirecting her gaze to the people below us. Either she didn't want to miss a second of the festivities—which seemed unlikely, since she was hiding up here—or she was a stalker whose prey was on the move.

I took advantage of the bird's-eye view and did a quick search for Derek. There was no sign of him. I couldn't imagine he'd miss his brother's wedding, but the gala? It didn't surprise me that he hadn't made an appearance.

"Yeah, well . . ." I stuck an olive from my martini glass in my mouth. Seemed easier than explaining my fast friendship with Madelyn, her husband's prior commitment, and her last-minute invitation for me to join her. I smiled, pushing my slipping glasses back into place.

"Whatcha doing up here?" I asked, peering over the balcony. From here, it looked like everyone in Bliss was crammed into the Kincaids' mansion. I couldn't keep my suspicious mind from wandering. Who among the party guests might have wanted Nell dead?

"I just came up here to get a few minutes of quiet," she said.

I gave her a sidelong look. What if Karen had killed Nell? I created a quick list in my head of reasons why she might be guilty, wondering at the same time if this was how Sheriff McClaine worked.

Why did people kill? Every TV show and movie focused on one of three motives. Revenge. Greed. Jealousy. Had Karen wanted to get back at Nell for something? From what I'd gathered, they'd been good friends. Greed? Nell owned her shop, but other than that, did she have any assets to speak of? Nobody had mentioned anything, so I doubted it. From what Ruthann had said, Nell's upbringing wasn't wrought with riches so she didn't have anything much to steal. Greed seemed unlikely.

Jealousy, then?

Oh! My heartbeat ratcheted up a notch. What if—

A horn blared from down below, a collective hush falling over the crowd. Keith Kincaid's voice, projected and tinny, greeted his guests. "I wanna thank all y'all for comin' out tonight," he began, slow and lighthearted, just like John Wayne. "I'm gonna cut the bull crap and get right down to it. The Kincaid Family Foundation is in honor of my folks, Justin and Vanetta. They wanted to bring our family together for a common goal, making Bliss, Texas, a town to be reckoned with, and they did just that."

A raucous cheer went up, drowning out whatever Keith said next. I searched the crowd, looking for the man to go with the voice, finally spotting him in the far corner, a Texas A&M megaphone pressed to his lips. He pushed a button and the horn sounded again, instantly quieting the crowd.

"We know y'all share our values and we thank you for continuing to honor the memory of my folks by donatin' to the foundation. We couldn't do what we do without y'all."

I bristled. If there was one thing I was sure of, it was that *my* concerns weren't the same as the Kincaids' concerns. Their disapproval of me when I'd dated Derek had driven that point home.

I caught a glimpse of Will Flores. The scowl on his face indicated he might not share the same values as Keith Kincaid, either.

Mr. Kincaid set the megaphone on the built-in bookshelf behind him, interestingly absent of actual books—guess he wasn't kidding when he scoffed at Miriam's plans for a bookshop in town—snagged a drink from the portable bar, and was sucked into the crowd.

Karen had zeroed in on someone down below. I followed her gaze and spotted a tall man standing next to Nate. I recognized him from the night Nell died. Ted, Karen's husband. For a second, I thought I saw Zinnia James as well, but the woman was instantly swallowed up by the crowd so I couldn't be sure.

As my thoughts circled back to a possible motive for Karen, I automatically went to the lowest common denominator. What if Nell's secret lover had been Karen's husband? Or, better yet, what if he was the person she'd met at Reata? Karen had even said that Ted frequented that restaurant.

He hadn't struck me as the cheating type, but Meemaw had taught me long ago never to judge by appearances. "Look through the eyes," she'd always said. "Windows to the soul."

I made small talk with Karen, leaning against the banister, trying to craft a question without being too blunt.

Turned out I didn't have to make the effort. After a

minute of awkward starts and stops, she ripped her attention away from the crowd downstairs and looked at me. "I . . . I don't know what to do, Harlow."

"About what?"

She looked over her shoulder at the deserted landing and hallway, then back over the banister. We were completely alone. "The sheriff questioned Ted today about Nell."

"Your husband." I kept my voice steady and my face still, but maybe my rogue thought wasn't so far off.

She nodded. "This is Bliss. Nothing stays quiet for long. People are going to find out. What if they think he had something to do with it? It could ruin him."

At least now I knew why Karen was dressed to disappear and was hiding upstairs. She was already afraid the gossipmongers of Bliss had turned their forked tongues her way. "Why would they think that, Karen?" I replied. "It was probably routine. I mean, when was the last murder in Bliss? Probably eons ago. So this is a big deal. They're probably questioning everyone who knew Nell."

"No," she blurted. Her eyes welled with tears, her lower lip trembled, and her whole body seemed to quiver. "He . . . he saw her. Just . . . just before she died."

Whoa. "He did?" I flashed back to the night of the murder, when Josie, Mama, Karen, and I had all been questioned by the sheriff. He'd asked if any of us had seen Nell after she'd left Buttons & Bows. All of us had said no. Karen's husband hadn't been with her at my shop—the reason, I guess, the sheriff hadn't even asked him if he'd seen Nell. The question, then, was why hadn't he offered up the information?

"Nell wanted to revise her w-will—"

"Wait. So you knew she had a will?" But Ruthann hadn't.

She nodded. "Ted did it for her."

"Your husband's a lawyer?" Now I was up to speed. It looked like Nell had used her friends for very specific things. Ted must have been the lawyer Gina had seen Nell with at Villa Farina.

She nodded. "He doesn't even do wills and trusts. Strictly oil and gas. But she asked me for his help. He . . . he only did it as a favor. He met her that night at Seed-n-Bead so they could go over the final document, but . . . but . . ."

I put my hand on her shoulder. Her body stopped shuddering, her tears subsiding. "But what?"

"There was no one to witness it," she said, looking completely devastated.

"Who was supposed to?"

"I have no idea. She wanted me to convince Ted to help her, but she didn't tell me any more than that. But, see, he's a lawyer. He should have made sure there was a witness, right? So why didn't he?"

It wasn't hard to read between the lines. What she *really* wanted to know was if her husband and Nell were working on the will at all, or had their *meetings* turned personal? She looked at me like I might be able to help her make sense of things, but I couldn't.

"Have you asked him?"

"I tried." She lowered her voice, darting another furtive glance over her shoulder. We were still alone. A hint of anger crept into her tone. "He turned it all around, like I was trying to tell him how to do his job, and how dare I doubt him. I want to trust him, but why wouldn't there be a witness when they were meeting to sign the will so she could leave everything to her bab—?"

She broke off before finishing the word, but too late for me not to fill in the blank. To her *baby*. So Karen knew about Nell's pregnancy.

"I presume the will's not valid."

"Not if she never signed it." She spoke sharply now, unloading everything she'd been keeping bottled up inside. "They met a bunch of times to work on it, but when I asked him about *that*, he said I was being selfish, that he was just doing his job and helping *my* friend."

What if Ted was the father of Nell's child and she'd turned to *blackmail*? That was something I hadn't considered. If Nell had threatened to spill the beans about their illicit affair, would Ted have killed her to silence

her? A sullied reputation in a small town would be hard
to live down.

I mentally penciled Ted—and Karen—onto my list as
suspects. Of course, all I had was a bunch of meaningless
theories. With no proof, none of them would hold water.

Oh, how I wished I'd known Nell. Even one close
glimpse into her life could have told me so much about
who she was and what she was up to.

One thing was clear. If both Karen and Ruthann
knew about the pregnancy, chances were others did, too.

"If there's anything I can do . . ."

But Karen had her eyes squeezed shut and her hands
clenched around the banister. Her anger was melding
with fear that her husband had betrayed her. Tears were
threatening and she was doing everything she could to
ward them off.

It took a good couple of minutes for her lips to turn
pink again and for her face to relax.

"So what'll happen to the store now?" I asked.

She sighed, that lower lip starting to twitch again.
"We . . . we were partners," she said, her voice so low I
almost didn't hear.

"You and Nell? In the bead shop?"

She nodded. "She'd been saving forever, but wasn't
making much headway. She asked me if Ted and I would
help her. She promised she'd be able to pay us back in
just a few months."

"But she didn't?"

"She kept saying she wasn't quite ready, that she
needed a little more time. I think Ted realized she didn't
really have the money. He was furious."

I took this all in, mulling it over. From what I knew,
murder was usually an act of passion brought on unex-
pectedly. Karen and Ted each had another possible motive. Either one of them could have snapped.

"How was Nell planning to get enough money to pay
you back? Was business really good?"

"She was always in the middle of some scheme or
plan. All she'd tell me was that she was getting her
happily-ever-after. Said I'd find out the rest soon enough,

along with everyone else. Whatever she was up to back-fired this time."

The announcement at the rehearsal dinner. "Guess it did."

She let out a biting little laugh. "Some happily-ever-after."

I wasn't quite sure if she was talking about Nell's happily-ever-after or her own. Neither one had ended as planned. Nell was gone and Karen's marriage had some big ol' red flags flying over it. She was back to staring over the banister at the party scene below. I left her alone with her complicated grief and went off in search of Josie.

Chapter 34

I'd started at the far end of the hall and had almost finished looking in each and every bedroom, but the bride-to-be seemed to have vanished. This soiree was a far cry from the high school parties I remembered, where hormonally charged teens looked for any available room to get, er, rowdy in.

A sewing machine sat on top of two clear plastic bins in the corner of one room. I couldn't resist sneaking in to take a peek. It was a midrange Pfaff with enough bells and whistles to keep a girl happy for a long time. The bins were full of notions and trims, patterns and fabrics. A few pillow forms were compressed inside. If this was Miriam's and she never used it, I wondered if she'd sell the whole kit and caboodle to Will so Gracie could sew at home.

I made a mental note to ask her about it, shut the door, and whirled around ... plowing right into a pair of strong arms, my hands pressed firmly against—

"Cassidy, what are you doing?"

Will.

"Will Flores," I said, surprised by the warmth he sent swirling through my body. "Are you following me?"

"I'm not, Harlow," he said, quirking a smile, "but I am curious to know what you're doing up here."

I barely knew Will, and to hear him using my first name seemed ... intimate and unfamiliar. I pushed away from him, a little whopper-jawed by how I felt. "I was looking for Josie," I said. "I saw her come up here. I wanted to see if she's okay. Since Nate's ..."

I hesitated. For all I knew, Will and Nate were old friends. And since one of the scenarios for Nell's murder put Nate as the killer, talking to one of his friends about it probably wasn't a good idea.

"Nate's what?"

"I was just wondering how long you've known the Kincaids."

He folded his arms over his chest, studying me. "Uh-uh. You're not getting off that easy, darlin'. Answer me this: Do the ghosts follow you everywhere you go?"

I started. Did he know that Meemaw's ghost seemed to be hanging around my house? Had Gracie told him something? "Well, of course not," I said, waving away the very idea with an idle laugh. "I'm just looking for Josie."

I started back down the hallway to where I had last seen Karen. Will stayed right beside me. It hadn't escaped my notice that he hadn't answered my question. "So, are you friends with Nate?" I asked.

"I know him."

The hallway and landing were empty. Maybe Karen had gone back downstairs. We stood side by side at the banister. Down below, people spilled out the French doors onto the stone-and-brick patio. There was no sign of a distraught brunette in polyester pants. Maybe she and Josie were comforting each other.

A willowy blonde glided through the room, stopping to chat with a few people before moving on to the next group. Ruthann. It wasn't her party, but it might as well have been. She looked like the quintessential hostess, ready to meet and greet her guests, throwing out her naked left hand to be kissed, the only adornment sparkling from her right hand. She was clearly available, and every man's gaze was instantly drawn to her. I pushed my glasses up the bridge of my nose. Did she know she was the most beautiful woman in the room?

Will leaned against the banister, his attention firmly on me. He had to have seen Ruthann below—she was impossible to miss—but he didn't seem fazed by her ethereal beauty.

I tucked a wayward strand of hair behind my ear. A wish that contact lenses didn't feel like boulders in my eyes came and went. There was no point in worrying over things you can't change. Glasses, contacts, or twenty-twenty vision, I was no Ruthann.

"Why'd you ask about Nate?" Will said.

"Just curious," I answered him, and left it at that.

A few minutes later, I made my escape from the event, rounding up Madelyn and hightailing it back home to the familiarity of my butter yellow appliances, hand-stitched quilts, Meemaw's settee, and my sewing machines. This was my cocoon. The scent of lavender enveloped me as soon as I walked in the door. This was home.

Chapter 35

Calling in the cavalry was nothing short of essential if I was going to finish the bridal dresses. I'd called Miriam to make sure that she was really going to be in the wedding, confirmed her appointment, then stayed up past two in the morning sketching designs for her dress. With no time to shop, I'd dragged bins of Meemaw's fabric down from the attic, riffled through them, and resketched so the design and the fabric would work together. To keep myself going, whenever I grew tired I flipped to the last page of my sketchbook and worked on a list of suspects and scenarios for Nell's murder. Josie, Nate, Karen, and Ted each had possible motives for wanting Nell out of their lives.

I'd slept on it, but in the morning I was no closer to any answers. I had to figure out a way to find out who Nell had been seeing and who had put the bun in her oven. Otherwise I was going to be too distracted to complete these dresses for the wedding.

With the wedding just days away, Nell's funeral at two o'clock, and Miriam already fifteen minutes late, I was running on pure adrenaline. There were a million and one tasks that needed to be done on the garments, but thankfully, the troops had been deployed.

Mama hunched over Meemaw's old Singer, finishing the French seams on the skirt of Josie's gown. Gracie bounded into the shop. "We're here!"

I'd been expecting her, but not her father. Will came

in after her, a soft black tool bag in one hand, a little white paper bag and a disposable coffee cup in the other.

"Morning," he said.

Mama whipped her head around the second she heard a man's voice. "Will Flores," she cooed. "It's been a coon's age."

A coon's age? Had Mama gone hillbilly?

Will set his tool bag down next to the shelves, smiling. "Yes, ma'am, it sure has."

"I guess introductions aren't necessary," I said.

"Will and I go way back. Now when was that problem you had with, what was her name, Maggie Sue?" Mama looked to the ceiling like she was trying to remember.

"Mama!"

She looked at me like I was off my rocker. "What?"

Will chuckled, a smooth, silky sound. "Maggie Sue is my neighbor's goat. She got through the fence onto my property and was harassing my horses."

He had horses. So he wasn't all hat and no cattle.

"That rascally doe wouldn't budge," Mama said. "Was that a year ago already?"

He nodded. "I tried everything, but she just laid down and stayed put. I'd heard stories about your grandmother. Cesar Millan is to dogs what Coleta Cassidy is to goats."

Mama flapped her hand at him. "Stop," she said, as if the praise was hers and not her mother's.

"I didn't believe it, but it's true," he said, admiration in his voice.

"Never doubt a Cassidy," I said. "Have you seen Nana with her herd? They follow her everywhere."

"Does she bewitch them?" Gracie asked.

Mama looked aghast. "Good heavens, no! She just happens to have a connection with them."

"That's an understatement," Will said. "She came right over, sat down next to Maggie Sue and had a conversation about God knows what, and would you believe that goat just popped right up and toddled back through the fence to her own yard."

"Goats are funny animals," Mama remarked. "My mama says most of us just don't appreciate them, but they've got so much personality and spunk, if they could speak English, we'd all be rolling with laughter. She says they respond to her because she listens to them, that's all."

Gracie's brow pulled into a V. I could tell she didn't understand how you listened to a goat. Honestly, I didn't either.

"Don't worry about it," I said, patting her on the shoulder. "It's like the creaky pipes. You'll get used to it."

Will leaned against the doorjamb, watching as I set his daughter up with a needle and thread in front of a dress form. His scrutiny unnerved me and brought up the same anxiety I used to feel before a test. If I handled Gracie the wrong way, I'd fail and he would abruptly yank her from my presence. My hands shook. The story of her mother leaving her had gotten to me. Loretta Mae might get what she wanted, but that didn't mean Will couldn't change his mind and call off the sewing lessons. Gracie had started to work her way into my heart and I didn't want to let go.

After a mini lesson on invisible stitching, she set to work hemming the skirt of Karen's flirty little dress and I turned to her father. "I'm going to Nell Gellen's funeral. If you want to come back for Gracie in a few hours—"

He shook his head. "I have some time. Thought I'd tackle a few more things on your repair list."

Now was not the best time, but I couldn't turn him away. The number one reason was Gracie, but the repair list was getting longer and longer. I'd added "fix loose floorboard in bedroom" and "leaky faucet in upstairs bathroom" to it, and I knew there would be more. A turn-of-the-century house was kind of like the Golden Gate Bridge. By the time the bridge was painted, it was time to go back to the beginning and start over. There'd always be something to fix in Meemaw's house.

"Those bricks have been bugging me," he said, angling his head at the short stack holding up the corner of the shelves in the workroom. "I'm going to fix that leg."

Great. Not only was he going to stick around the house, he was going to be right here where we were working.

It had taken me a while to identify another layer of emotions I'd been experiencing around him. Pinging nerves. Flirtatious urges. Anger mixed with excitement. All that good conflict.

Attraction, pure and simple. All things I hadn't felt since I was eighteen. It was like a light switch that had been turned off and no matter who I dated, it couldn't be switched back on. But Will had flipped it on without even trying and now I didn't know how to handle the flurry of emotions inside me.

And I certainly didn't have time to think about it.

So I did nothing but nod and help him take the jars off the shelves. "Why does one woman need so many buttons?" he asked after we'd carried the last of the thirty or so jars to the coffee table.

We walked back to the workroom. "This isn't even all of them. Meemaw has old tins full of buttons up in the attic. When I was little, she'd pull out a tin and dump it out so I could sort them by color or size. They'd keep me busy for hours and hours. Every now and then, I'd find a treasure and hold it up for her to see. She'd instantly remember where that particular button had come from and tell me the story."

"She has the buttons of one of your great-great-great-granddaddy's shirts somewhere," Mama called from her sewing table. "Those are worth some money, let me tell you."

Will looked skeptical. "Buttons can be worth money?"

"No—" I started to say.

"Yes!" The steady sound of the Singer stopped as Mama turned her head. "Because they belonged to Butch Cassidy."

"Mama, that's crazy. They're just buttons."

"Who's Butch Cassidy?" Gracie asked from her stool.

Mama gasped. "You don't know who Butch Cassidy is? Butch Cassidy and the Sundance Kid?"

"N-no."

"They lived a long time ago, Mama—"

"They were famous bank robbers," she said.

"Infamous," I corrected. Their lives were glamorized by Paul Newman and Robert Redford, but they'd been thieves and the Hole-in-the-Wall Gang had killed plenty of people in their day.

Mama rolled her eyes. "Butch Cassidy is legendary, and he's my great-great-granddaddy, which makes him Harlow's great-great-great-granddaddy."

"Wow," Gracie said, looking mightily impressed.

"It's our family's claim to fame," I said, leaving out the part about Butch's wish at the ancient Argentinean fountain and the charms bestowed on his descendants. Will and Gracie didn't seem to know about the Cassidy magic, though I wasn't sure how that was possible. It seemed to be the talk of the town.

"Now, if only we could find where Meemaw hid the treasure Butch sent Cressida," Mama muttered so only I could hear.

I shushed her with a finger to my lips and turned to help Will with the shelf. I held one end of the broken piece of furniture, helping lower it to its side.

It suddenly dawned on me that having Miriam and Will in the same room might not be a good thing, but there was nothing to be done about it now. I sat at my machine, working on the pleating on Josie's bodice. Sewing the bodice to the skirt would feel like a victory, one I hoped to reach by tonight.

Just as we all settled into a groove, the kitchen door banged against the wall as someone flung it open. "Just me and the chickens!"

Nana, come to join the fun.

Gracie looked up from her hemming, leaning to the right to see beyond the French doors. "The chickens?"

I laughed. "We only have to worry if she says, 'It's me and the goats'!"

Nana had ditched her boots at the kitchen door and padded into the workroom in her blindingly white socks. Her ability to keep them looking brand-new was one of her many mysterious talents. "I put some cheese in the fridge. Crackers are out on the table," she said.

"What'd you bring?" Mama asked. "Not more of that papaya chèvre, I hope."

Nana sniffed indignantly. "That papaya chèvre won an award at the Festival of Cheese in Austin last year."

Mama draped one arm over the back of her chair. "Yes, I'm aware of that, but you know I'd rather eat dirt than that particular cheese."

Nana blew a raspberry through her lips. "You're not the only one here, Tessa Cassidy, and not everyone likes the cayenne and nuts in the spicy pecan—"

She noticed Will crouched in front of the sideways shelf and jabbed her finger at him. "You. I helped you with a stubborn doe." It sounded like an accusation.

I could see him working hard not to laugh. "Yes, ma'am, you did."

"Good. Right. I never forget a goat. Maggie Sue."

"Yes, ma'am. She's my neighbor's goat."

"Maggie Sue took a vacation from her life that day. We humans like to go on vacation. A nice trip to Corpus Christi or Padre Island? You bet. For a goat? A little R and R and some nibbling on someone else's grass is all they need."

"Wow," Gracie whispered, gazing at Nana like she was a rock star.

My mother leveled a stare at Nana, still harboring some vexation over the goat cheese selection. "You don't have to bring spicy pecan. The sesame thyme or the fresh herb is fine. Anything but that papaya chèvre," she said.

Nana wagged her finger. "Tessa Cassidy, if you don't want the cheese I brought, don't eat it, girl."

I swallowed a laugh. For a split second, I could see Mama, fifty years younger, a skinny little girl, being scolded by a twenty-five-year-old Coleta Cassidy. Some things never changed. Bickering was sport to them.

Mama huffed, turning back to her seams. "Don't you fret. I won't eat it," she muttered under her breath.

"What kind did you bring, Nana?" I whispered.

She winked, a wicked little smile playing on her lips. "Spicy pecan," she said so only I could hear, "but I'm gonna let her stew there for a spell. She wouldn't know exceptional cheese if she sat on it."

As she poked around the room, looking at the dresses, a wisp of a warm breeze blew over me. I felt Meemaw's familiar presence. It rustled the skirt of Josie's gown, then swirled around me, ruffling my hair, wrapping me up like a blanket. Meemaw, Mama, Nana, and I were all here together in the yellow house off the square. It was comforting to be surrounded by family. There was no place I'd rather be, I realized.

The weight of someone's stare made me look around the workroom. The Singer purred along as Mama finished the seams, her attention utterly focused. Nana stood at the cutting table flipping through my sketchbook, absently oohing and ahhing. Will had a screwdriver plunged into a hole in the bottom of the shelf, wiggling it around like he was digging something out.

That left Gracie . . . I turned and saw her looking around the room, as if she was searching for something, her needle between her thumb and index finger, frozen in midair.

"Gracie?"

She didn't budge.

I moved toward her, snapping my fingers. "Gracie."

This time she blinked, back to reality like she'd come out of a trance.

Instantly, Will was by her side.

"Are you okay?"

"Yeah," she said, but her body twitched with a slight shiver. She looked at the heating vent in the wall. "Did the heater go on?"

My heart stopped, all the breath leaving my body. Had she felt the warmth of Meemaw's presence? Slowly, I shook my head. "N-no."

"Huh. I must have imagined it . . ." she said, trailing

off. She turned back to the dress form, lifted the hem of the dress, and slid the needle into the fabric.

I watched Gracie, baffled, wondering exactly what she'd felt—and why.

The bells on the front door jingled. I tucked my bewilderment away to think about later as Miriam Kincaid finally walked in, a teenage girl on her heels.

Chapter 36

"I don't have much time," Miriam announced before they'd even closed the front door. "This is my daughter. My mother said you're making her a dress—"

I gaped at the two of them darkening my doorway, stunned into silence. *Another* one? Did nobody understand what went into designing and making a dress? I couldn't spout some incantation, wave my magic wand around, and voilà!, someone was suddenly clothed in the most spectacular dress she'd ever seen.

Before I found my voice and said exactly what I was thinking, Gracie catapulted off the stool, leaving her needle hanging from the hem of Karen's dress. "Really?" she exclaimed as she hugged Holly. "You're in the wedding, too?"

Holly Kincaid didn't look nearly as excited as Gracie. "My grandmother just decided there needed to be a flower girl. Guess who they chose," she said glumly, flinging her arms wide.

Gracie's lower lip slipped out in a pout. "But flower girls are little kids."

Holly slouched against the front door looking like she wished she could just disappear. "Exactly my point."

"That's enough," Miriam said. "We both just have to hush up and make the best of it." She tossed her coral cashmere cardigan onto the chaise in the seating area, grabbed her daughter by the wrist, and dragged her forward, stopping short when she noticed Will bent over the shelf.

It felt like a junior high moment, full of angst and emotional despair, only I didn't know if the feelings were Miriam's . . . or mine.

"Miriam, good to see you," Will said, nodding at her, then going straight back to work.

"You, too, Will." No emotion, which was odd considering the history.

So I guess the feelings were mine.

Gracie whirled around, falling into step beside Holly. "Harlow Cassidy," she said when they passed the French doors, "this is Holly Kincaid. Holly, *this* is Harlow. She's, like, totally amazing."

I thought I heard Will mutter something, but he was intent on the bottom of the shelf, still working with the screwdriver. Good thing. I didn't want to know what he was thinking—probably that I was one step away from crazy, a so-called descendant of an old-time train robber with a goat-whisperer grandmother.

Holly had been bred with good manners. "Nice to meet you," she said.

I shook her hand. "Nice to meet you, too."

Gracie dragged Holly to the dress form. "Just look at this," she said. "It's for one of the bridesmaids. Isn't it gorgeous? I'm hemming it right now. Then it'll be done."

They whispered as Gracie showed Holly Josie's gown and Ruthann's dress. Miriam shifted from one foot to the other, as though she couldn't quite find a comfortable position. I glanced at the clock. It was nearly eleven. Miriam had arrived but was almost an hour late, there was a funeral to go to, and now I had *another* dress to design.

Nana slid my sketchbook across the cutting table. "You're biting off a lot, girl," she said, nodding at the book. She held my gaze. Had she seen the list of murder suspects in the back of the book, or was she talking about the flower girl dress that had been added to my workload?

"Don't start something you can't finish."

"I won't, Nana." I'd planned to go to the funeral, but

with my nearly doubled workload, I was reconsidering that idea.

"Gotta get back to my goats now," she said, padding out of the workroom. She threw me a look over her shoulder. "Don't you hold back, child. Ask for help. You're going to need it."

Oh, yeah. She'd seen the list.

"She has me," Mama said from her spot at the Singer.

Gracie's arm shot into the air. "And me, don't forget!"

Will's arm stayed conspicuously down. He wasn't part of my cavalry.

Nana gave me a wink. "Don't forget about the cheese," she called. "Spicy pecan, Tessa. Your favorite."

Mama whipped her head around, but Nana had already disappeared into the kitchen. The door slammed shut and a moment later we saw her mosey through the gate leading to her property.

Mama shook her head, an exasperated smile tickling her lips. "That woman is full of—" She broke off, darting a glance at Gracie and Holly. "Vinegar," she finished, amending one of her favorite expressions to the PG version. She bent back over her pleats, but I saw her shoulders still shaking with laughter.

"I only have a few minutes. What do we do now?" Miriam asked. Her skin was sallow and black circles ringed her eyes. It looked like something had interrupted her sleep. I'd avoided the mirror that morning when I'd caught a glimpse of myself and my own drawn face. Whenever these dresses were done, whether there was a wedding or not, I was going to sleep for twenty-four hours straight. It looked like Miriam needed some extra shut-eye, too.

"But you just got here."

"I know. I have to help set up the reception, though. Sorry."

I swallowed a sigh as I flipped open my sketchbook and showed her the designs I'd drawn. The one I kept coming back to for her was a simple drawstring halter A-line dress. The shape of the cut, narrower on top and gently flaring out at the bottom, would be perfect for her figure. The mint green linen I'd found in Meemaw's fabrics had a subtle sheen and would complement the rusty highlights in her hair. With any luck, it might even eradicate her sour disposition.

She barely glanced at it. "Looks good."

Not the reaction I'd hoped for. I'd thought long and hard about the style. It had to complement the other bridesmaid dresses and Josie's gown, but it also had to fit Miriam. I'd always seen her as the artsy type and a little bit of a misfit in her own family.

I took a deep breath, reminding myself that this had been a last-minute addition to my workload. All I could do was my best. Hopefully that would be good enough.

I pulled out a tape measure. "I need to take your measurements."

We went behind the privacy screen. She held out her arms and I got to work. She was thinner than Karen, but healthier than Ruthann. Really, she looked almost like an exact replica of her mother. One by one, I took the measurements I needed, jotting the number down after each one. Waist. Hips. Bust. "Are you going to the funeral?" I asked as I let the tape drop from her waist to her knee.

She nodded, glancing at the clock. "I'm sure the whole town'll be there, just itching to get any gossip going around."

I changed position and measured from her waist up to her underarm. "Did you know Nell very well?"

She shifted her weight. "We were ... friends," she said.

I peered up at her, not knowing what to make of her hesitation. She stared out the window, a pained expression on her face. "Are you okay, Miriam?"

Her lips quivered, but she quickly jammed them together as if that would stop the emotions from spilling out. "Ye—" She broke off, her lips parting as she prepared to say more. Then her whole body convulsed, as if a spirit had jumped in and taken possession. "No," she said with a hiss. "Not even close."

I knew death often brought out people's fears of their

own mortality, but I wasn't sure if that was what Miriam was feeling. "Do you want to talk about it?" I asked.

Her eyes went a little wild and she grabbed me by the sleeve, pulling me into the front room. "I don't know what to do," she confided in a panic.

"Do about what?" I asked, wondering why people kept saying that to me.

She dropped her head into her hands and her shoulders shook. The emotions she'd been trying to block were coming out in full force. She looked up at me, her eyes glassy but clear, her lips trembling but resolute. "I think I know why Nell died," she said.

Black dots danced before my eyes. I wanted to poke a finger in my ear. Had I heard right? "Wh-what?"

She glanced into the workroom. The girls sat on the floor, gushing over a bridal magazine. Will was still fiddling with the shelf.

"Nell's dead," she said, turning back to me. "It's too late to protect her, so . . . so what do I do? Go to the sheriff and tell him who I suspect killed her? But . . . but, no, I can't." She notched her head toward Holly. "I won't let anything happen to her."

As we spoke, a vision of a dress I wanted to create for her daughter appeared in my head, as strong and clear as ever. I'd begun to wonder if being able to see the perfect outfit for a person was my family gift. I hadn't been able to conjure up an image of anything for Nell, though. Why not? My pulse raced as the answer slammed into my mind. As long as I could see a design for someone, maybe that meant they were safe.

"Nothing's going to happen to her," I said, hoping I was right. "The sheriff—"

"No. Nell is dead. A person who kills once will kill again—isn't that what they say?"

As she uttered the words, Miriam's dress in my mind's eye suddenly stretched and twisted, the green and off-white hues of the fabric distorting as if someone had dragged a paintbrush through the colors. "Does . . . whoever it is . . . does he know you know?"

She shook her head slowly. "Not yet."

"You have to tell someone, Miriam. Don't you see, if you keep this to yourself and the killer finds out you know, you'll be the one in danger." I suddenly couldn't picture the dress for Holly, either, and my breath hitched. "You *and* Holly."

Chapter 37

The Buttons & Bows atmosphere I'd imagined as I prepared to open my shop never included people coming in and announcing that they knew the identity of a murderer. But now that I found myself in that situation, there was nothing to do but forge ahead.

"Tell me, Miriam," I said, my palm flat against my chest. "I'll go to the sheriff so you don't have anything to do with it."

She hesitated and I could tell she was thinking about it. Her lips parted, her tongue pressed against her front teeth as she deliberated. I was on the edge of my seat, holding my breath, praying she wouldn't say a name I didn't want to hear. Finally, a sound came from her throat. The beginnings of a name. I leaned forward, wishing I could grab hold of the letters and pull them out of her mouth.

Before she could form a single complete syllable, Gracie and Holly bounded into the front room. Holly plopped down next to her mom. "I'm hungry."

Miriam snapped her mouth shut and just like that, the moment was gone. "You can eat at the bead shop after the funeral," she said.

"But—"

Miriam leveled a look at her daughter—one eerily similar to her mother's—that stopped Holly cold but propelled me into action.

"I'll get them something." Practically catapulting off the couch, I ran into the kitchen, feeling like a rodeo cowboy wrestling a steer. I was scrambling to rope and tie Miriam so she'd cough up the name of a killer. I spilled crackers onto a plate next to a couple spoonfuls of Nana's spicy pecan goat cheese, and threw a bowl of red grapes on the table. "Something to tide you over," I called to the girls, but it was dead quiet.

I peeked into the front room.

No Miriam. No Holly.

Leaving the plate on the table, I dashed down the three steps leading from the kitchen to the front room. "Where'd they—"

Gracie pointed to the open front door. "They just up and left."

No! I skidded across the hardwood floor, grabbing the door before it slammed shut. Holly was already at the sidewalk, walking in the direction of the square. "Wait!" I bounded down the porch steps two at a time, flying over the flagstone walkway, almost colliding with Miriam at the arbor. White flower petals showered over us in a frenzy.

"I didn't . . . measure . . . Holly," I said as I tried to catch my breath. Years of walking everywhere in Manhattan had kept me in shape. But a few short months of chicken-fried steak and queso had already reversed the effects and I was exhausted by the effort of chasing after her. "I can't make her a dress for the wedding if—"

She shot a quick glance at her daughter before looking me square in the eye. A spark of determination flickered. "Forget I said anything, Harlow. I'll take care of everything."

Before I could react, she ran down the sidewalk. Within seconds, she and Holly had turned the corner and disappeared.

When I got back inside the shop, the things she'd said, as well as the things she hadn't said, came together in my mind. She knew who the killer was, but believed she would be endangering her daughter if she said anything. She wouldn't go to the sheriff.

Who had Miriam been about to call out as the killer? I parted my lips, pressing my tongue to the roof of my mouth just like she'd done. "N-N-N-N." I made the sound over and over again. And then I uttered a name.

My skin pricked with the sensation of a thousand needle jabs. One of the names I didn't want to hear. "Nate," I said under my breath just as the click of footsteps sounded on the hardwood floor behind me.

Chapter 38

"What got her all riled up?" Will asked as he sidled up next to me.

"Nell's"—*Murder*, I thought grimly—"funeral. She had to go help set up for afterward."

"That woman's gotta get her own life," he said under his breath.

I shot him a look. "What do you mean?"

"I mean she's too worried about that damn family of hers and what they'll think to live her own life."

He sounded a little bitter. I flicked my finger at him, then toward the window. "Did you and Miriam ever ... Were you, you know, together?"

He gave me a long, searching look. "Now why would you ask that?"

"Just curious." I hooked my thumbs in the belt loops of my jeans. "Gracie mentioned that Miriam and Holly stayed with you for a while after her divorce, so I thought—"

"So you thought there was something between us."

I nodded. "Was there?"

"I'm curious why you're curious," he said, a hint of a grin pulling up the corner of his mouth.

"Gracie and Holly are best friends and they stayed with you, but you hardly said two sentences to Miriam when she came in. I was just wondering why."

He didn't answer right away, and when he did, his voice had dropped so Gracie and my mother wouldn't overhear. "Let's just say that the Kincaids are not my biggest fans. Miriam can't ever decide if she should listen to her parents about her friends or make up her own mind. When her mother threw a fit that they'd stayed with us, she took Holly and left and Gracie didn't see her for a long time. I managed to make her see that the girls' friendship had nothing to do with her parents, but now I just try to make it easy on her. If she doesn't get into it with her parents, Gracie and Holly can be friends and everything's good."

"But Mr. Kincaid acted like you and he were thick as thieves last night."

"'Acted' is the key word. They can put on a good show, Cassidy, and they do—when they want or need to."

"But why wouldn't they want you helping their daughter when she needed it?"

"Their married daughter staying with a single man who already had one child outside of marriage? Not good for the Kincaid reputation."

Exactly what Zinnia James had said.

"So you and Miriam were—"

"Friends, Cassidy. I do what I have to do to stay on good terms with people I do business with. Don't get me wrong. I'm not saying I haven't made mistakes, but I'll always do an honest day's work and I'll never betray the people I love."

I could feel his hackles rising with every word he spoke, but he kept his voice calm, steady, and matter-of-fact.

"I don't work with people I don't trust and respect. Will I help Keith Kincaid with this bookstore idea? Of course. I work for Bliss, and his business is with the historical society, not me personally. But will I travel to Timbuktu, or wherever, and import God knows what for God knows who, just to pad my stock portfolio? Hell, no. I do some work with Nate at the foundation. Him, I trust."

I was at an impasse. Will trusted Nate Kincaid, but Miriam had been about to name him as Nell's murderer—hadn't she? Their contrasting opinions tumbled around in my mind and I didn't know what to think.

He held out a wrinkled sheet of yellowed paper. "I found this," he said.

As I took it from him, the paper curled up on itself, crackling as I unrolled it and held it open.

The writing was spidery and looked rushed, and a few of the letters had been dropped from the words. Clearly a man's handwriting. As I read it, Meemaw's voice echoed in my head alongside mine.

3 April, 1898

T~

H and me are meeting up with Etta at Fannie's. New Mexico or Wyoming next, then to you and, God willing, the babe.

It was signed "RP."

The small hairs on the back of my neck stirred. It couldn't be. "Wh-where—"

"Did I find it?" he finished.

I nodded, shoving my glasses up the bridge of my nose before I unrolled the paper and read it again.

He pointed to the workroom. "There should have been a dowel on the leg that came off of that shelf. There wasn't. That whole thing's just been sitting on that loose ball of wood, no dowel, because that paper"—he tapped the top of the sheet—"was shoved inside the hole."

Every bit of breath left my lungs. The round leg had flown off when Nell was in the workroom, right before the jars of buttons fell. The whole scene had Meemaw written all over it. She had *wanted* me to find this paper. Maybe that's why she'd arranged for Will Flores to be around, so he could help. "You rascal," I muttered, my gaze darting around, searching for her misty form.

"Come again?"

"No. Nothing," I said, but my mind was racing. I bent over, trying to catch my breath, hands on my knees, elbows locked. If this was authentic, then Butch Cassidy really had sent something to Texana and it was probably here somewhere . . . God almighty, the stories were really true. And Meemaw had known the truth all along.

Will put his hand on my back and, like magic, breath filled my lungs again. "You okay, Cassidy?"

I managed a nod as I straightened up. "There's some family legend, but there was never any proof, but now . . . now . . ." I stopped and regrouped. "But this . . ." I'd let the paper roll into a tight scroll again and clutched it in my hand, afraid it might evaporate if I let go.

He felt my forehead with the back of his hand, then both of my cheeks. "You sure you're okay? You need to sit down?"

"I'm fine," I said, batting his hand away. "Look. Look at the date on this."

"I saw it. 1898."

"Right. My great-great-grandmother was born in October of 1898."

The shadow of confusion on his face cleared. "So you think the baby mentioned in the note was your great-great-grandmother?"

The Singer still purred from the workroom. I caught a glimpse of Gracie's foot. She was back to sorting the buttons from the jars Nell had dropped. I looked up at Will, keeping my voice low, my skin pricking with excitement. "It has to be. It's addressed to T. That's got to be Texana Harlow, my great-great-great-grandmother. H was Harry Longabaugh. Etta was *his* girlfriend."

"And Frannie?"

I laughed. After a high school research project, I knew almost everything there was to know about Robert LeRoy Parker. "Frannie Porter was a madame in San Antonio. They used her brothel as a rendezvous."

Will stared at me, riveted. "Family legend. Wait a second. You mean the old outlaw stories about Butch Cassidy and the Sundance Kid?"

A chill of excitement swept through me. "Butch's real name was Robert LeRoy Parker and Sundance was Harry Longabaugh."

Will tapped the rolled-up paper with his finger. "And

you think this note was written to your . . . great-great . . . however many greats . . . grandmother, from Butch Cassidy?"

"Yes!" I grabbed his hand, my excited whisper ringing in my ears. "I grew up hearing the stories. Butch Cassidy sent a letter and something else—a trinket—to Texana before he escaped to South America. She never saw him again . . . No one ever found the letter. We never had proof of our family lineage. But this"—I waved the note—"this verifies that it's all true. He and Texana really did have a baby together."

"Um, Harlow?" Gracie stood just inside the workroom. She held out her hand, palm up. "I think you should see this."

"Show-and-tell today," Will said as we went to see what she held.

It was a ring, the band made out of lustrous platinum. The biggest diamond I'd ever seen sat smack in the center of two rows of smaller diamonds.

Butch Cassidy and Texana were still on my mind. "Butch sent Texana something . . ."

"Hate to burst your bubble, Cassidy," Will said, holding the ring up to the light, "but this isn't a hundred and ten, or however many, years old."

He handed it to me so I could take a closer look. All my wishful thinking didn't make me right. This ring was shiny and brand-spanking new. "This was in that bag of buttons?" I asked Gracie.

"Yep."

Why would a brand-new ring be mixed in with Meemaw's buttons? My mind shot back to the day Nell died, yanking out buried images, rearranging them, and shoving them right back into my consciousness.

Nell had been in the workroom. I'd been too busy telling myself that the customer is always right to worry much about why she'd been back there. What had she been doing that could have unsettled the shelves and broken the button jars? Was she searching for something? But how would she have known there was something hidden there? And of all the jars, would she have picked the right one?

Then, for the second time in a few minutes, I lost my breath. She wasn't searching for it. "Oh my God, she was hiding the ring!"

The Singer had stopped its steady rhythm. "Who was hiding what?" Mama asked, coming over to us.

Instead of answering, I handed her the note. She scanned it, met my gaze, and just like that, all the color drained from her face. "This is proof," she whispered.

My eyes welled as I nodded. It was a monumental moment for the Cassidy family, but we were also in the thick of a murder investigation. Mama and I wrapped our arms around each other, savoring the moment for as long as we could, whispering about the discovery, Butch and Texana, and our family history.

Mama wandered off a few moments later, still in a daze about the note. Eventually, my mind drifted back to Meemaw and the ring. She'd never done things the easy way when she was alive. Now that she'd passed, everything was more puzzling.

I thought back to that day in the shop. She must have seen Nell trying to hide the ring. She'd made the leg of the shelf shoot across the room like a bullet, causing the button jars to crash to the ground. By her own orchestration, Will was at the ready to do repairs for me, and now I had a shelf that needed repairing. Meemaw had seen an opportunity to help me find the note from Butch, and she'd taken it.

"The first day Josie and the bridesmaids all came in here, Nell was in the workroom but we were all out here. She paced around, always going off on her own to look at swatches or the lookbook."

"Lookbook?" Will sounded like we were speaking a foreign language.

"My design book." I waved the whole train of thought away. "It's not important. The point is, maybe she was trying to get away from all of us so she could hide this." I held up the ring like a prize.

Gracie raised her hand like she was in class at school. "Um, I have a question."

We waited.

"It's just . . ." She bit one side of her lower lip. "Why would Nell have had your friend Josie's engagement ring?"

"Wh-what?" Will and I stared at Gracie, slack-jawed. "This isn't Josie's—"

I stopped short, caught off guard by her wagging head. "Not now it's not, but it *was*. I saw it after your friend got engaged to Holly's uncle."

And just like that, I suddenly remembered the day Josie and her bridesmaids had first come into Buttons & Bows and the story about her two rings. The first had been too flashy for her and they'd exchanged it for a simpler setting.

I stared at the sparkling diamond. This was *that* ring? "But why did Nell have it?" I asked aloud. Two other questions quickly followed in my head. Why had she been trying to hide it? And why, oh why, had she picked my shop to hide it in?

Chapter 39

I'd never fancied myself an amateur sleuth, but a desperate phone call from Josie changed my mind. She said she needed to know what had happened to Nell—for her own peace of mind. Part of me wondered if she was beginning to doubt Nate. With her first engagement ring tucked safely in a little navy velvet jewelry bag sitting in the middle of the cutting table, I was certainly doubtful of his innocence.

"Will you help? Just come to the funeral and . . ." Her voice faded away.

"And see what I can see," I finished for her.

"Yes."

"Whoever killed Nell isn't going to be wearing a sign announcing the fact," I said, but I was already scanning the notes I'd written in the back of my sketchbook. If I was right and Miriam had been about to name Nate as the killer, I couldn't let Josie go through with the wedding. The truth needed to come out before she married a murderer.

A number of clues seemed to point to Nate as the killer. Was he guilty of murder, or did the fact that Will trusted him mean I was barking up the wrong tree?

Mama and I had spent another hour reading, rereading, and discussing the note. Excitement at the discovery of a letter from Butch Cassidy to Texana Harlow raced through me. Mama finally left to share the note with Nana, and I tried to get back to work. Each time I sat down to sew, picked up a needle and thread, or handled my rotary cutter or shears, the pipes began creaking, cupboard doors flung open and then abruptly banged shut, or the shelves in the workroom shook, rattling the jars of buttons. It was as if Meemaw was trying to send me a message.

Finally, I realized that I wasn't going to accomplish any real work. As soon as I put down the needle I had been holding, a wall of air practically lifted me from the stool, pushing me toward the French doors. "Wait!" There was no way I was letting Josie's ring out of my sight. I broke away and snatched the velvet bag from my cutting table. Immediately, the unexpected strength of Meemaw's invisible hands propelled me all the way upstairs.

In my room, I opened my closet and grabbed the first thing I saw—a cream-colored blouse and a brown cardigan with a pink-and-cream argyle pattern down either side of the buttoned front. My mind had drifted from Nate and Josie to Butch Cassidy, the ring, and Loretta Mae. Meemaw had answers. I knew she couldn't hold a real conversation with me, but I asked the questions that came to my mind anyway. "Do you think Nate's guilty? Will there really be a wedding?" I searched the room for a response.

No ghostlike figures or wraiths appeared. Whatever had propelled me upstairs was gone.

But as I started dressing, a stack of magazines on the bedside table shook. The thick one on top, the spring issue of *Vogue*, fell with a loud *splat*. The cover of the most recent *Threads* flew open. Pages fanned back and forth. Just like the first time Meemaw had communicated with me, tiny drops of water spread on the words she was highlighting. One by one she spelled *Miriam*; then the pages opened to a jewelry ad, a diamond ring front and center.

Questions skittered through my brain. "But Gracie already said it's Josie's ring. She was at the Kincaids' house with Holly right after Nate proposed. She *saw* it. I don't need Miriam to verify that, and she doesn't want to talk to me anyway. I already tried."

The pages flapped spastically in response, and then, as if Meemaw were squeezing her hand around my fist, I felt my fingers tighten on the little jewelry bag holding the ring. My head suddenly felt filled with cotton, my heartbeat dull and muffled. It was as if she wanted me to remember something, but what?

I summoned up what I knew. Josie had returned the first custom engagement ring to Nate and he'd had a second one made with another custom-cut diamond. He wouldn't have been able to simply return the first ring to a store for credit, right? Did Nell steal it from him, or could he have given it to her as a bribe to keep quiet about the baby—if it was his?

I thought of one little glitch. If Nate *did* give the ring to Nell, she wouldn't have needed to hide it, and he wouldn't have needed to kill her to get it back—if that was the motive.

It was more likely that Nell had stolen it. "So if sweet Daisy Duke was a thief," I said aloud, "she may have been killed over that forty-thousand-dollar ring."

A soft breeze swept through the room, gathering speed. I thought it was Meemaw agreeing with me.

Will trusted Nate, but did I trust Will? For that matter, did I trust Miriam? I wasn't sure, but I was willing to take my chances. I wanted to share my theory with her and see if we'd come to the same conclusion.

I no longer needed my great-grandmother's encouragement to get me to the funeral.

Chapter 40

One phone call and thirty minutes later, Mama and I were on our way, the ring tucked safely in my gray-and-white Burberry handbag. Miriam's prediction had been right on the money. From the looks of it, the whole community had come out for Nell's funeral. The service was at the old Methodist church one block off the square, catty-córner to Mockingbird Lane. We cut a diagonal, crossing at the corner of Mockingbird and Elm, skirting the courthouse, crossing Dallas Street at the opposite corner, to join the parade of people filing into the old stone building.

The hushed whispers of the mourners all blended together into white noise. From the back of the sanctuary, I spotted Keith and Lori Kincaid sitting three rows from the front, both with their heads slightly bowed. Miriam sat next to her mother, her back ramrod straight, while Holly slouched next to her.

Josie was in the front row with Nate, her shoulders shaking as she tried to control her grief. Whether she was crying over losing Nell, or over her latent fears that her fiancé may have betrayed her, was anybody's guess. Ruthann and Karen sat on the other side of her, hip to hip. If Nate or either of the bridesmaids moved, I was afraid Josie would topple right over. Her mother and grandmother were at the end of the pew, tissues pressed to their noses.

Strains of a melancholy violin song sounded through the speakers while images of Nell flashed on a screen hanging behind the altar. Nell snuggling a long-haired gray cat. Nell behind the counter of Seed-n-Bead. A group of women with Nell in the center, all holding up their completed bead projects. Miriam and Nell, side by side, smiling into a mirror. Nell looked happy, like everything was right with the world.

My gaze was drawn straight to Nate. His head was bent, his lips close to Josie's ear. How much effort was it taking him to ignore the slide show? Probably not nearly as much as it was taking him to ignore the intense stare Miriam had trained on him.

I felt the weight of someone else's stare, but couldn't identify who was behind it.

Ruthann watched the pictures, dabbing her eyes with a tissue, but Karen stared at the screen, emotionless. She'd said her husband would be here with her, but he wasn't by her side. She'd set her heart up to be trampled, and I felt sorry for her.

I twisted around to look at the rest of the mourners. The deputy sheriff who'd been first on the scene after we'd discovered Nell's body sat in the last row, as far to the right as possible. She wasn't in uniform, but something about her posture and the jerky way she moved her head as she watched the slide show told me she was still here on official business. I looked at the altar just as another bead shop photo flashed on the screen. The deputy, in off-duty clothes, was in the photo, smiling and holding her wrist out to show off a bracelet.

Small-town living—there was nothing like it. You'd never get to know the law enforcement in a big city. New York cops didn't go to local beading classes. Not so in Bliss.

I spotted Sheriff McClaine standing in the back of the sanctuary. He caught my eye and gave a polite nod. He wasn't watching the slide show, either. Was he observing, as I was, who else was *not* watching, wondering if there was guilt behind the uninterest?

By now, almost everyone was riveted by Nell's life in pictures, except Josie, who was crying, and Nate, who continued to whisper in her ear.

I kept searching the crowd, my gaze flitting over people I didn't recognize, zeroing in on those I did. Just in case Miriam was wrong and I spotted the real killer diabolically gloating at getting away with murder.

No one gloated.

One man had his head down, as if he was texting or reading e-mail on a phone. He looked familiar, but from the back I couldn't place him. Then it hit me. It was Ted, Karen's husband, sitting on his own instead of sitting by his wife. That signified major marital trouble, which directed my theories away from Nate and back to Ted Mitchell as Nell's secret love.

Thank God I wasn't a detective. I think it would make me crazy. All those suspects and possible motives. Give me patterns and fabric any day of the week.

Mama and I forged through the throng of people and down the center aisle, looking for a place to sit. Gossip flew from one person to another, echoing in my head as if it were being hollered instead of whispered. "Poor girl." "I heard she was *pregnant*." "Had to keep our husbands locked up." "Too young to die." The sentiments were pretty evenly divided. Half the town was genuinely sad that Nell had died, but the other half seemed to think she got what she deserved.

"Pregnant?" Mama grabbed my wrist and whispered, raising an eyebrow at me. "Did you hear that?"

There hadn't been a chance yet to tell her about Nell's pregnancy. I nodded, prying her fingers off my arm. Her ring sparkled. I'd assumed Hoss McClaine would have already filled her in, and frankly, I was surprised he hadn't. My respect for him rose a notch for his professionalism—and another notch for the tasteful bling he'd bestowed on my mother.

"I told you, she never went for the right sort of man. Wonder if that's what was eating at her," she was saying.

Someone waved to me from a center pew. I grabbed Mama's hand and we picked our way past knobby knees and feet, finally squeezing in next to a cluster of women. Zinnia James, and her husband, the senator, scooted over to make room for us. I recognized the other women as the ladies Mrs. James had come to Buttons & Bows with the day Nell had died, including Mrs. Abernathy. We all nodded at one another.

The music ended, though the slide show kept playing, and the pastor stepped to the pew and began the service.

Mrs. James leaned toward me. "Very sad," she said quietly.

I watched the images on the screen. "It sure is," I whispered. I could feel tears welling at the corners of my eyes. You didn't have to know a person to be sad at his or her passing, particularly when it was a life cut short, like Nell's. If there was a lesson to be learned, it was that things could change in an instant.

The pastor spoke about Nell's contribution to Bliss, the energy and vitality she brought when she'd come here, and the friends who would sorely miss her. By the time he finished, there was hardly a dry eye in the church. She may have been a troubled girl, but she'd grown into a woman who'd touched a lot of people's lives. More than she probably ever realized.

As we filed out of the church, I lost Mama in the crowd, but stuck close to Mrs. James and her husband, making small talk and trying to chase away the lingering sadness by mentioning chartreuse as a color I'd like to explore for the gown I'd be making for her. Many people gathered in clusters on the sidewalk, while some headed straight to their cars and still others were strolling to the square and Seed-n-Bead, where the reception would be.

The Kincaids passed us, followed by a group of people I didn't recognize. Josie and her family shuffled past. I blinked and for a second I could see her in her wedding gown, gliding down the aisle toward her groom. I closed my eyes again and the vision was gone. When I looked up, Nate's arm was at the small of her back, gently guiding her.

"They're a lovely couple," Mrs. James said to her husband. Or to me. Or maybe to both of us.

The senator mumbled a noncommittal reply. I nodded, a sinking feeling in the pit of my stomach that the loveliness might be short-lived.

Ted Mitchell came next, his smartphone in his hand, his thumb working furiously as he tapped the keyboard. I leaned close to Mrs. James and pointed at him. "Do you know him?" I asked in a low voice.

"Who, the Kincaids' lawyer?"

My mind screeched to a halt. *The Kincaids' what?* "He's their lawyer?"

"Yes. His name's Ted Mitchell. Oh!" She snapped her fingers. "His wife was at your shop that day. One of the bridesmaids, in fact. Can't say I trust him—he's a lawyer, after all—but he's friendly enough."

"Zinnia," the senator said in a quiet voice. "Gossip."

The warning in those two words was clear, but Mrs. James just shrugged. "You feel the same way," she said to him.

He dug his hand into his suit pocket, pulling out his vibrating cell phone. "Prying eyes and ears," he replied, adding, "Excuse me," as he wandered away from us to take a call.

She dismissed him *and* his warning with a wave of her hand. "Punctilious to a fault."

That word wasn't part of my Southern vernacular, but I connected the dots. "I guess senators need to be careful what they say."

"Oh, yes, perfect decorum and behavior at all times," she said, wagging her finger like she was scolding me. Luckily she smiled. She and her husband seemed to understand each other, all the more reason she and Nana should let bygones be bygones, I thought.

She took my elbow, guiding me down the steps of the church. We turned and walked along the sidewalk toward the bead shop.

"So why don't you trust him? Ted Mitchell, I mean."

She took a moment to consider her words before responding. "Besides his career choice? Did you ever see *The Godfather*?"

I smirked. "Oh, yeah. My brother's all-time favorite movie. I've probably seen it a hundred times. *I'm gonna make him an offer he can't refuse*," I said, barely moving my lips, doing my best mumbled Marlon Brando.

"Nicely done." She chuckled. "It's a classic." We walked half a block in silence before she said, "Jeb was right. I don't really know him, so I shouldn't say a word."

I felt a *but* coming.

"But . . ."

Ha!

". . . with the Kincaids being an oil and gas family, I can't help but think of Tom Hagen. Remember him?"

Remember him? I could hear Don Corleone's adopted son, played by Robert Duvall, in my head as he said, *"Sonny . . . ?"*

We crossed the street at the corner. Mrs. James's high heels slowed her down. I filed away the observation so I'd remember to recommend a low heel to go with the gown I designed for her. "Ted's a bit taller, and has more hair than Tom Hagen," she said, "but he has the same blind loyalty."

I never figured the Kincaids as a Mob-type family but it would explain why Ted Mitchell was on duty at the funeral instead of comforting his wife. The lawyer knew who buttered his cornbread.

Seed-n-Bead was already crowded when we arrived. Josie waved to me from inside. Even from this distance I could see how drawn her face was. It looked like she'd lost ten pounds since she'd first set foot in Buttons & Bows. Her dress was going to need altering and I wasn't even finished with it yet. "Best be fixin' to work on it to the very last second," Mama had said after she'd caught a glimpse of Josie in the church. *If* there ended up being a wedding.

A group of people walked around Mrs. James and me, filing into the shop. The senator brought up the rear. Mrs. James said good-bye to me, took his arm as he approached, and they went in together.

Ted Mitchell strode up the sidewalk, Karen scurrying along after him, taking twice the number of steps that he did. "The same loyalty," Zinnia James had said, comparing Don Corleone's lawyer, Tom Hagen, to Ted Mitchell.

The image stuck in my mind. What else did I know about him? So Ted worked for the Kincaid family. At Karen's insistence, he'd helped Nell write a will. If his loyalty to Keith Kincaid extended to Keith's sons, then maybe meeting with Nell about a will was just an excuse. If the family had gotten wind of the pregnancy, maybe he'd really been trying to intimidate Nell to stop her from revealing it.

On the evidence of how'd they treated Miriam during her divorce and what Will had said about the Kincaids, it was a safe bet that they would not want Nell's secret coming out.

Just a few yards shy of reaching the door to Seed-n-Bead, Ted answered his cell phone and abruptly changed course. With a quick, dismissive wave to Karen, he darted into the street, dodged a truck, and cut across to the grass in front of the courthouse, phone still pressed to his ear.

I made a split-second decision and dashed across the street after him.

Chapter 41

Ted Mitchell disappeared around the north side of the courthouse. I slowed. Barreling around the corner in funeral attire might be a little obvious. Surely not how a private eye would do it. Of course I was just a dressmaker, but being the great-great-great-granddaughter of Butch Cassidy and Texana Harlow meant adventure was in my genes.

I was doing a fast walk now, jabbing my glasses back into place and blowing upward to get the spirals of hair out of my face.

I turned the corner and stopped short. Whirling around, I scanned the courthouse green. Where in tarnation did he go?

"There you are," a man said loudly just as a hand clasped my elbow. "I thought you weren't coming."

I tried to shrug free, but the grip tightened. Shielding my eyes from the sun, I looked up into Will Flores's face. "What are you talking—"

"*Shhh!*" he interrupted, never breaking his stiff smile. He lowered his voice. "Are you crazy, following Ted Mitchell like that?"

"How did you—"

"Darlin', you're about as inconspicuous as a copperhead at the beach."

My confidence deflated. Being a descendant of Butch Cassidy didn't mean my reconnaissance skills rivaled his during his primo train- and bank-robbing years. "What's going—"

He pulled me to him until not a puff of air could have slipped between our bodies. "Pretend like you're happy to see me," he whispered.

The short, staccato squeeze of his arms zapped the air from my lungs and cut me off. His warm breath through my hair tickled my ear. "I'm saving your ass, that's what's going on," he murmured. "You don't want to mess with Ted Mitchell. He works for the Kincaid family, and if he thinks you're snooping into their business ... Let's just say it wouldn't be good."

He released me and I pushed away from him. From the corner of my eye, I saw the flash of Ted Mitchell's eyes looking at Will and me as he crossed the street. "What's over there?" I asked after he disappeared behind a closed door.

I started to point at the space next to a vacant space on the square, but he gently pushed my hand back down to my side. "Not pointing at his office would be a good idea. I'll lay money down that he'll be watching us from his window."

I started to turn my head to look, but he caught my chin with his fingers, tilting it up until I looked in his eyes instead.

"Don't quit your day job," he said.

I'd been married to my sewing machine and the fashion world for so long that there wasn't a chance in hell I'd quit designing. But it also meant I hadn't remembered what it felt like to be this close to a man, and it was throwing me for a loop. My fluttering heartbeat turned my thinking upside down. In a movie, this would be the moment when the hero lowered his head until his lips lightly brushed the heroine's in a long-awaited kiss.

This wasn't a movie. There was no kiss.

Will dropped his fingers from my chin, put his hand at my lower back, and started guiding me back to Seed-n-Bead. When we were out of Ted Mitchell's potential line of vision, he stopped walking suddenly. Facing me, his black suede cowboy hat blocking the sun from my eyes, he demanded, "Cassidy, just what the hell do you think you're doing?"

Chapter 42

"It's possible it was a married man," Mama whispered. "She was awfully secretive about it."

"You mean an engaged man."

"Someone who was already taken," she amended.

I'd avoided Will's question and he'd escorted me back to the reception, leaving me at the door. He headed to the hardware store to buy some wood glue so he could finish repairing Meemaw's antique shelf while I went in search of my mother. Now we huddled in the corner of Seed-n-Bead, talking under our breath.

I showed her the ring and told her my theory that Nate might well be Nell's killer. One by one, I ticked the facts off on the fingers of my left hand. "First, he was in Buttons and Bows that day, so he could have taken something to use as the murder weapon. Second, Nell's mirror. I found it in my yard, all scratched up. She must have had it with her the night she died. Maybe she was hiding that, too."

"Or wanted to break it and give whoever she met that night seven years of bad luck," Mama said.

I went on. "Third, Nell told me she hoped Nate wouldn't break Josie's heart, but she said it like she'd experienced that particular heartbreak firsthand. Fourth, she was pregnant and told her friends she was going to announce something big at the rehearsal dinner. What better place to ruin the man who'd wronged her? Fifth, there's Miriam. She's worried Holly will get hurt, so she won't come forward about whoever she thinks the killer is, which means it has to be someone close to her . . . like her brother. Sixth, Nell tried to hide the ring in my shop. She must have thought the diamond was her insurance policy. Nate wouldn't dare hurt her unless or until he had that ring back. Seventh . . ." Was there a seventh? "Oh! The lawyer. He met with Nell to write her will. How creepy is that? And it doesn't quite compute, since he doesn't do wills and trusts. Karen told me so herself. I think he might have been trying to intimidate her into giving the ring back. Maybe even threatening her."

They were seven suspicious facts, but they were all circumstantial. I'd watched enough television crime shows to know it took more than circumstantial evidence to bring a murderer to justice. I dropped my hands, no more facts to tick off on my fingers. Perfect timing, since Josie immediately walked up to us. "What are you two whispering about?"

"Sweetheart, we were just wondering if you're really sure about holding the wedding so soon," Mama said. "Are you up to it?"

I snuck a surprised look at Mama. She'd never been good at fibbing, even with all the practice she'd had trying to hide her magical green thumb. All that sneaking around with Hoss McClaine had made her smooth as Texas honey.

"I wasn't, not at first," Josie said, "but now I am. Nell wouldn't have wanted me to cancel."

Yes, well, I was afraid Josie didn't know Nell nearly as well as she thought she did.

The funeral guests had all gone. Just Josie, Ruthann, Karen, Mrs. Sandoval, and I were left. A pearl white SUV pulled up to the curb in front of the shop. Nate got out and popped the back hatch. We loaded the car with the leftover food. "What are you going to do with it all?" I asked Josie.

"Nate's taking it to the women's shelter in Granbury."

I carried the last rectangular foil tray out to the car. Nate slid it into the back and pressed a button on his key ring. The hatch clicked, automatically closing. "Thanks," he said.

"Sure." I looked at him, wondering how a person could look so innocent, yet be so diabolical. What if he figured out where Nell had hidden the ring? Was I safe in my house? I looked at him, suddenly horribly afraid he'd be able to read every one of my thoughts.

"I meant what I said at the sheriff's," he said quietly.

I thought back. He'd said Josie wouldn't know how to hurt anyone, let alone kill Nell. And that he loved her. All the more reason for him to protect Josie from Nell's big announcement and his own betrayal of the woman he loved.

"I can see it in your eyes. After everything, you think I killed her, don't you?" He moved closer.

Criminy. My whole body trembled. *Yes*. "N-no."

"I didn't. Nell and I went out on a few dates. It was a long time ago. She was Josie's friend, that's it. I had no reason to kill her."

I clutched the strap of my purse. *Except the forty-thousand-dollar engagement ring she stole. Oh, yeah, and the pregnancy*. "Where were you that night? Why weren't you with Josie?" All he had to do was give his alibi and he'd be in the clear.

His expression hardened, the cleft in his chin growing more pronounced. "I was helping someone."

I threw my hands up, exasperated. "Do you know how much Josie loves you? How much she wants to believe you? She asked me to help prove you're innocent, Nate. You can't just say you were helping someone. Where *were* you?"

I didn't really think he would just cough up his alibi, but he never had a chance. Josie, Karen, and Ruthann came outside, and a second later Mr. and Mrs. Kincaid turned the corner and walked briskly toward us. Miriam was next to her mother, and next to her was . . . *Derek*?

Taking a step back, I tripped on an uneven piece of cement. My foot twisted under me. I fell, dropping my purse, my knee scraping against the edge of the curb. A sharp stab of pain shot from my knee to my gut, but I swallowed the angry sting the second I saw the contents of my purse scattered all around me.

All at once, everyone rushed forward.

Seven people were suddenly crouched around, gathering up my belongings. From the corner of my eye, I saw the little blue velvet bag in the street. Still on my knees, I lunged, snatching up the jewelry bag just as Mr. Kincaid and Derek both reached for it. The side of my face collided with Derek's shoulder, knocking my glasses out of place.

Derek mumbled, "You okay, Harlow?"

Some sleuth I was. If an encounter with an old boyfriend, which was really overstating what Derek and I had had, sent me reeling, what would a confrontation with a killer do to me? "Yup. Fine," I said. With the bag enclosed in my fist, I braced my knuckles against the cement to push myself up. A hand clasped my elbow, finishing the job. "This is becoming a habit."

Will. He always seemed to be right there when I needed him. Coincidence? I straightened my glasses and tried not to look at the blood I could feel dripping down my shin.

Mrs. Kincaid's hand fluttered to her neck. "Bless your heart, Harlow. What in heaven's name got into you?"

I couldn't say it was the shock of seeing all the Kincaid children together again for the first time in seventeen years, or that they'd almost discovered Josie's first engagement ring in my possession. I wanted to kick myself for bringing it with me to the funeral. In hindsight, it probably would have been safer tucked away at home.

I went for distraction, blurting out the first thing that popped into my head. "I guess I was just lost in my own thoughts. I was just talking to Will, and then I saw you, and I suddenly remembered you mentioning Miriam's old sewing machine." I rambled on. "Will's daughter is working for me now and I thought it would be perfect for her."

"Oh, dear," she said, frowning. "Miriam took it to the church for the rummage sale—"

"Not yet, I didn't. It's still in my car," Miriam said.

"You haven't . . . It is?" Mrs. Kincaid looked like she couldn't believe her daughter's irresponsibility. How dare she not deliver the used goods to the rummage sale in a timely manner. Mrs. Abernathy would be so disappointed.

"Of course Gracie can have it," Miriam said to Will. "I'll drop it off when I have a chance."

Will smiled. "That's great. Gracie'll love it. Really, thank you."

Mrs. Kincaid forced a smile, then looked at my leg. "That's a nasty cut," she said to me. "You'd best go on inside and get that fixed up."

"Good idea." I took a step, wincing as I tried to straighten my knee. "Mmmm," I moaned, my eyes stinging.

"There's bandages in the bathroom," Josie said. "I'll help you—"

"It's okay." Will slid his arm around me and I leaned against him. "I got her."

I looked at Derek. A little smile played on his lips, his attention moving from my leg to the people gathered around me. I quickly looked away, trying to ignore the anxiety gathering inside me.

I noticed Josie leaning into Nate before Will propelled me toward the bead shop and I lost sight of them. Their bodies seemed perfectly molded to each other. Doubt slithered through me. What if all the facts I'd ticked off were just coincidence? What if Nate had had nothing to do with Nell's death, just as he claimed? I wanted so much for him to be telling the truth. I closed my eyes for a split second and conjured up an image of Josie's wedding gown—I could still picture it clearly. Surely that was a good sign.

Karen handed Will my purse, and he guided me as I hobbled back into Seed-n-Bead. Mama dropped the broom she'd been using when she saw us. "What happened?"

I waved her away with my free hand. "I just tripped. It's n-nothing."

"Josie said there's first-aid stuff in the bathroom. I got it," he said over his shoulder.

I heard Mama pick up the broom and start sweeping again, but louder than that was the heat of her gaze on my back and the pressure of Will's hand on my side, both of which seemed to say, *You're in over your head, Harlow Jane.*

I wondered if she was right.

Chapter 43

Fifteen years of being a single dad to Gracie had given Will an unexpected bedside manner. He ran the water until it was warm, squeezed a dollop of amber liquid soap on a paper towel, and gently cleansed my wounds. "You did a pretty good number on this shin," he commented.

"When I do something, I do it all the way."

His lips quirked into a smile, little crinkles appearing around his eyes. "Is that right?"

I could feel the heat of embarrassment creep up my neck. I didn't dare look in the mirror to see how rosy my cheeks were. "Which is why," I continued boldly, "I'm trying to figure out who killed Nell. I promised Josie—"

"Josie shouldn't have asked you to get involved, Harlow."

My breath hiccuped. He hadn't used my first name very often and it sounded foreign coming from his lips.

"But she did," I said.

He was broodingly silent for a long minute. Finally he said, "Nell was murdered. This isn't a game."

He didn't have to remind me of that.

After another minute of him dabbing and me wincing, he rooted through the one cupboard in the small bathroom until he found a brown bottle of hydrogen peroxide.

"Here." I grabbed a cocktail napkin from a little pile on the counter and held it out to him, but he waved it away, his hand emerging from the cupboard with an old plastic bag filled with white fluff.

He doused a cluster of cottonballs with the liquid, pausing before he touched it to my skin. "This might sting a little."

"No more than it already does." I was all talk. The second the medicine hit my raw skin, I yelped, grabbing his shoulder, crumpling the napkin in my hand, keeping it at the ready in case I burst out in tears.

He grimaced as he pried my fingers loose. "Maybe just a *little* more."

"Maybe," I admitted.

He blew on it, cooling the pain, then crisscrossed five bandages from a small box he found, strategically placing them to keep as much of the abrasions covered as possible. "We should change these to some gauze squares when you get home."

He rolled up the bag of cottonballs and tucked it back into the cupboard. After another weighty pause, he broke the silence. "You didn't *just* trip out there. What spooked you?"

Taking off my glasses, I cleaned the lenses, then tossed the napkin in the trash. Peering up at him through my lashes, I said softly, "My past."

His eyes narrowed, but he seemed to understand that it was better left alone.

"How do I know if I can trust you?" I asked.

He cupped his chin, rubbing his fingers over the goatee trimmed close to his jawline. "How do you know you can't?" he asked, looking back at me.

"Because I don't really know you."

"I trust you with my daughter." He looked dead serious.

"And I trust *you* with Meemaw's old furniture and pipes."

He gave a dismissive, one-note laugh. "Not quite the same thing, Cassidy."

I gave a relieved sigh. He was back to calling me Cassidy. "No, I guess it isn't," I conceded.

A flurry of thoughts cascaded through my mind. I had

no reason *not* to trust Will Flores. I definitely felt a kindred spirit in Gracie, and I was back in Bliss to stay, so I might as well start trying to connect with people.

This wasn't Lower Manhattan where people looked straight ahead as they plowed through the crowded city, avoiding contact with strangers. This was small-town Texas where men tipped their cowboy hats, said, "Howdy do," and met at Johnny Joe's for coffee and doughnuts every Wednesday. Women moved in groups, spending mornings at their kids' schools adorned in their sequined spirit wear, hightailing it to a Carol Anderson by Invitation fashion show at a local coffeehouse, then heading off to Bible study. I was straddling a line between two worlds, but I needed to edge my way back over to the Bliss side.

Meemaw's voice sounded loud and clear in my head. *I wouldn't mislead you, Harlow. Leap fearlessly.*

Leap fearlessly. It was one of her favorite sayings. "If you don't take a risk, you'll never realize the potential reward," she explained when I was little. I'd used the same line on her when she questioned why I was leaving Bliss.

"You're not leaping," she said. "You're running." I still didn't understand how she knew the difference when I couldn't even comprehend it myself.

"Harlow?" He crouched down in front of me and took my fisted hands in his. "Are you okay?"

His dark eyes weren't quite as dark close up, or maybe he'd just let his guard down for a moment and let the light shine through. They glowed with little flecks of amber like they were lit from behind. *The eyes are the window to the soul*, Meemaw always said. Looking at Will, I knew it was true. My great-grandmother had already discovered what I was just now seeing—he was a man so locked up and protective of himself and his daughter that he didn't let anyone inside. But there were cracks in the surface if only someone could work her way into them.

I had a sudden vision of myself hunched over my sewing machine, working on some mysterious garment.

I couldn't see what it was, but I knew it was for Will and that making it for him would somehow allow him to let me in.

"Harlow." He snapped his fingers in front of my face.

I blinked, jerking out of my thoughts. "Sorry."

"Where were you?"

"Do you wear plaid?" I asked in response, though I had no idea where the question came from.

"Do I wear plaid?" he repeated, like he had to really think about it.

"Because I think you'd look good in plaid." Actually I *knew* he would.

He shook his head, looking baffled. "Hmm. I'll give that some thought." He held my wrist, running his thumb over the bump in the velvet bag in my hand. "You're walking around with a diamond that's probably worth more than Keith's Lincoln. That's not a particularly good decision."

"Yeah, I figured that out, but I didn't want to leave it alone."

He nodded like maybe he understood my thinking. "What's going on? Spill it, Cassidy."

Leap fearlessly. And so I did.

Chapter 44

Will leaned against the bathroom wall, never taking his eyes off me. "So you really think Nate Kincaid might have killed her?"

I couldn't answer that directly. With a mobster lawyer in the mix, I wondered if Nate would get his hands dirty, or if he'd have someone else do his dirty work. "What if she stole something of his—could he have, you know, taken care of it? Of her?"

He nodded toward the bag in my hand. "You're talking about the ring?"

"Like you said, it's worth a lot of money. Did you see the size of that diamond?"

"If it's even real," he said. "Fakes look pretty good these days."

Mirror, mirror, on the wall . . . The slide show image of Miriam and Nell holding a mirror flashed behind my eyes. A chill crawled up my spine. "The mirror."

"What mirror?"

"The day after the murder, Thelma Louise got loose, remember?"

"The goat."

"I found that little hand mirror and it was all scratched up. Were you at the funeral?"

He nodded, and I suddenly knew the stare I'd felt in the church had been his.

"That mirror was in one of the slide show pictures."

He didn't look convinced. "You sure it was the same?"

"Beaded edging and ribbons? Absolutely. Nell would

have needed to know if that diamond was real before she tried to sell it, right? Diamonds cut glass. She used a mirror to test it."

"She could have damaged the diamond," he said, as if that shot down my theory.

"Maybe, but she was probably willing to risk it. She had to know what she was dealing with, a thousand-dollar cubic zirconia or a forty-thousand-dollar diamond."

"So she tested it a hundred times? That mirror was completely scratched up."

Once would have been enough, so I didn't have an answer to that.

"So you think Nate killed her because she stole the ring?"

"I think it's a pretty good motive, only she hid the ring so he never got it back."

"You're assuming they were having an affair," he said. "That would be the only way she'd have had opportunity."

Yep. That was the one major unknown in my theory. If Nate and Nell weren't seeing each other, then I was back to square one.

An hour later, the ring was back inside the navy velvet bag, the bag was wrapped in a napkin, and Will and I were sitting across from the sheriff. Sitting there with him, I could see why Mama might fall for him, but it still rankled me that he was keeping their relationship under wraps.

He rested his elbows on the arms of his chair, steepling his fingers under his chin. "You givin' up dressmakin' in favor of detectin'?" he asked me when I'd finished ticking off what I'd discovered about Nell and her death.

"No," I said. "You giving up bachelorhood to make an honest woman of my mother?" I had to clench my fingers over the edge of the chair arms to stop myself from slapping a hand over my mouth. I couldn't believe I'd said that aloud.

I knew I'd crossed a line, but now it was out there,

good or bad, and I was on the edge of my seat wondering how the sheriff would respond.

"Remind me never to get on your bad side," Will murmured under his breath to me.

The sheriff's leathery face was usually hard to read, but not this time. He looked shaken up, like he'd fallen off the bull, but he recovered soon enough. "Young lady," he chastised, "you best get your facts straight before you go sayin' stuff like that. I'd climb to the top of the water tower—you know a little somethin' about that, don'tcha?—and tell the whole county how I feel about your mama, but she won't have none of it." He leaned forward, looking me square in the eyes. "I mean to marry that woman, Harlow, mark my words. Hell, I gave her a ring. Asked her a hundred times already. What does she do? Wears it on her right hand and says she needs time. I'll give Tessa all the time in the world, but it's not me keepin' a lid on things."

You could have knocked me over with a feather. *Mama* was the one keeping their relationship under wraps? "That's an *engagement* ring you gave her?" How could she have made light of it? She'd been holding out for true love ever since my father left her alone with Red and me. Why would she hold back with the sheriff?

He nodded, giving a wan smile. "You go on and ask her when she's gonna make an honest man outta me, why don'tcha."

That conversation would take some planning, but I said, "Yes, sir, I'll do that," all the while holding my breath, worried he'd kick me out of his office.

"Since I have you here," he said, "I wanna show you somethin'." He slid a sheet of paper across the desk to me. "Take a look."

He sat back, bending his leg to rest his right ankle on his left knee. Hoss McClaine wasn't just any old cowboy. He was the sheriff, and he had a job to do. He'd let my rash judgment of him slide and had gotten back to the murder at hand. Just like that, I switched sides. What in the world was Mama doing holding out on a good man like this? I knew it would take some work, but one way or another, I'd get her to see the light.

I picked up the paper and quickly scanned the hand-written list, going through it more slowly the second time around.

> *Nell Gellen*
> *Josie Sandoval*
> *Ruthann McDaniels*
> *Karen Mitchell*
> *Lori Kincaid*
> *Miriam Kincaid*
> *Nate Kincaid*
> *Keith Kincaid*
> *Zinnia James*
> *Wanita Lemure*
> *Helen Abernathy*
> *Dulce Sandoval*
> *Maria Garcia*

I slid the list back to him. "Assuming Wanita Lemure and Helen Abernathy were the ladies with Zinnia James, it's everyone who was in Buttons and Bows the day Nell was killed. Except for Miriam and Keith Kincaid."

"Keith Kincaid didn't come in the shop?"

"He was still out of the country, as far as I know."

"He got in right before the foundation gala," Will said. "I was just getting there myself when he pulled up. Helped him carry a suitcase in."

The sheriff steepled his fingers again, the creases on his forehead deepening as he thought. "That's what he said, but he took a private plane and I can't get verification that he was on the flight he says he was on."

The scene from my shop played like a movie in my head. Lori Kincaid had stopped in the doorway as she came in, waving at someone in the Lincoln Town Car. What had Mrs. Kincaid said about their cars? No one could drive the Lincoln except . . . ?

Why hadn't I listened more closely?

"What about Derek?" the sheriff asked.

"Until today, I hadn't seen him in years," I said, adding a silent *Thank God*. "Of course, I've been gone most of that time."

"Haven't seen him lately. Six months, at least," Will said.

"And what about George Taylor?"

"I see him every now and then," Will said.

The name was familiar. I racked my brain, miraculously pulling the information from somewhere in my memory bank. Ruthann had mentioned a George Taylor. "I've heard the name, but I don't know him."

"You've heard the name where?"

"It's all secondhand information, Sheriff." I didn't want to spread rumors about a man I'd never met.

"I'll keep that in mind," he said.

"The bridesmaids were talking about him," I said, when it was clear I had no choice. "One of them said she heard through the grapevine that he'd said he and Nate had"—I made the same air quotes Ruthann had—"fished in the same pond. With Nell," I added.

Will scooted his chair closer to the desk. "Do you think George has something to do with this?"

The sheriff shrugged. "Nell Gellen was pregnant by some mysterious boyfriend. You say she was gonna make an announcement at the rehearsal dinner. The thing is, Nate Kincaid admits he dated Nell in the past. He sat right in that chair," he said, pointing to Will, "and swore up and down that they'd never had . . ." He looked away for a split second while he said, ". . . *relations*." Then he said gruffly, "I don't have proof one way or another, but I believed him."

"But Josie told me you were gunning for Nate. You should have seen her. She was on the verge of a nervous breakdown."

The sheriff cocked his head and gave a mocking laugh. "I'm not a fool, Harlow. I didn't *tell* them I believed his story."

Right. "No, sir, I guess you wouldn't. What about Nell's will?"

"What about it?"

"I heard she had one. Did you find it?" And if it was never signed, then what?

"She had one, dated a few months back. No family to speak of," the sheriff said, "so it should hold up. She bequeathed her fifty percent interest in Seed-n-Bead to Josefina Sandoval."

Mixed emotions swirled through me. The inheritance meant another motive for Josie, or a stable future in case things didn't work out with Nate. "Does she know?"

He flipped his wrist to look at his watch. "She will in about half an hour."

"What about the murder, Sheriff?" Will asked.

"Nate Kincaid," he said flatly, "has an alibi."

Everything screeched to a halt. "He does?"

The sheriff nodded. "He was on a flight out of DFW at six thirty that night and got back just before nine the next morning. He couldn't have killed Nell. He was in the middle of something big the day she was killed." He puckered his thin lips and whistled, low and prolonged, giving Will and me both pointed looks.

Will leaned forward. "No kidding. He's a whistle-blower?"

"Made a few phone calls," McClaine said. "Definitely looks that way."

I followed the unraveling thread of what they were saying. "How can he be an informant for something? Wait—you mean he's blowing the whistle on his own family's company? About what?"

"Don't know, don't care," the sheriff said. "It'll come out. Eventually. But it means he's no longer a suspect."

My mind reeled. So someone in the Kincaid family was doing something illegal and didn't know Nate was about to blow the whistle. It meant the wedding could go on, but Josie was walking into a mess of trouble with that family. Not to mention that someone was still getting away with murder.

Chapter 45

I'd spent the remaining days before the wedding putting the final touches on the wedding party's dresses. I attached another hundred pearls to Josie's gown. Double-checked the stitching on Ruthann's zipper. Measured and remeasured from the waistline of Karen's dress to the hem. Slip-stitched the hem of Miriam's frock. Pressed Holly's dress.

There was nothing left to do beside the final fittings. At last the day before the wedding had arrived. This was it. The bridal party would be here in minutes. I couldn't believe I had gotten all the dresses done in time. My hands trembled from exhaustion; would I even be able to hold a needle?

I closed my eyes and let my mind wander. One by one, images of the bridal party popped into my head, all perfectly turned out in the garments I'd created. I heaved a relieved sigh. I was becoming more and more sure that being able to imagine and design the perfect dress for someone was my charm. Seeing each of them in my head released the kinks in my nerves.

But one thought zinged in and out of my mind. If I couldn't envision a person's perfect clothing—like I hadn't been able to with Nell—did that mean that person was destined to die? I squeezed my eyes shut to force the idea into a back compartment of my mind. I didn't want that kind of information about people.

I fielded a few phone calls while waiting for the wedding party to arrive, jotting down the names of people who wanted to come in for custom garment fittings, another bride in search of the perfect wedding dress, and a few folks who needed alterations to their polyester clothing. I feared the alterations might remain the bread and butter of my business for a while, although things were picking up. I'd noted all the dates and times in my lavender, button-adorned, fabric-covered appointment book. I wasn't booked solid by any stretch of the imagination, but I wouldn't be pleading for mercy with the creditors, either.

The phone rang again just as the bells on the front door jingled. Gracie came in, followed by Mama. Even Nana came to help, though she bounded through the kitchen door, as usual. The troops were here.

"Harlow?"

Mrs. Zinnia James's voice echoed in my ear. "Oh, yes, ma'am, I'm here!" I pointed, directing Mama, Nana, and Gracie to the three bridesmaid dresses. My chest swelled with pride. If Maximilian could see me now . . .

"Harlow," Mrs. James snapped.

"Yes, ma'am. Here." I turned my back on the workroom. "What can I do for you?"

"Two things, my dear. First, I want to make appointments for a new dress for that event I mentioned to you and for my granddaughter's fitting for her pageant dress."

We set a date for the following week and I jotted it down in my book. "What else, Mrs. James?"

"A fashion show."

"A fashion show?"

"A fashion show. At Christmas."

It felt like we were playing an obscure guessing game, but I kept at it. "A fashion show for teenagers, then?"

"Possibly. For women, too. A big event. Your designs. A fund-raiser for the library. Don't say anything yet. Just let the idea percolate for a while. We can talk more about it after the Sandoval-Kincaid wedding is over. Of course there's the pageant in July. That will be first. *Then* the fashion show during the holidays. I'll be keeping you busy, Harlow."

And then she was gone and I was left holding the

phone, visions of black and white and pink dresses floating in my mind. Mrs. Zinnia James, it seemed, was my personal event coordinator, which, as far as I could tell, would be a very good thing for business.

The arrival of the bridal party snapped me out of the fashion show that was going on in my head. Karen and Ruthann sidled in together. Miriam arrived a few minutes later, looking like she was being dragged over the threshold by her mother. Josie straggled in last, her dark hair flat and in need of a wash, her mascara smeared under her lower lashes, and dark circles confirming my suspicion that the bride wasn't sleeping well.

As the bridesmaids slipped into their dresses, I pulled her aside, grateful that I could still see her as a bride in my mind, perfectly coiffed and ready to walk down the aisle in the dress I'd made for her. "Are you okay?" I whispered.

She brushed her stringy hair away from her face, her eyes looking a little wild, like a tiger who wanted out of her cage. "Nell left the bead shop to me," she blurted out. "Why would she do that?" She stared at me as if I had a crystal ball that could see right into the past.

"You were friends. Almost family," I said. It was the best I could do, but I also thought it was the truth. Nell had chosen her family, and she'd chosen Josie. It was a small consolation that she'd felt that kinship before she died.

It took a few minutes for Josie to regroup, but she did, throwing her shoulders back, mustering a smile, and stripping out of her clothes behind the changing screen. It took ten minutes for her to wiggle into her Spanx and then, with my help, into her gown, but when she emerged from behind the screen, the room fell silent.

Ruthann, floating like an ethereal faerie in her pale green chiffon, fluttered her hands as she looked at Josie. Karen, looking curvy and feminine, nearly swooned. Even Miriam, whose dress was the simplest design, yet looked supremely elegant on her trim figure, smiled.

It was Lori Kincaid, the soon-to-be mother-in-law, who finally spoke. "Josie," she said, "you look lovely."

And she did. The bride was a vision. The French Diamond ivory silk was perfect against her warm olive skin, the hand-pleated bodice accented her curves in just the right manner, the flowing train made it look as if she walked on clouds, and the painstakingly applied beads caught the light and shimmered like diamonds.

Her eyes glistened as she looked in the oval mirror, her hands lifting to cover her mouth. "Oh, Harlow, you did it! Loretta Mae said you could do it, and you did. It's beautiful." She looked renewed, as if a light suddenly shone from inside her. "I feel like . . . like . . . like anything is possible."

Mama's hand squeezed my shoulder, and Gracie squeezed my hand. My own eyes pricked. From the looks on the bridesmaids' faces, they were experiencing the same thing.

Chapter 46

Several hours later, the fittings were over and all the dresses, with the exception of Miriam's and Holly's, which still needed tailoring, had been pressed and delivered. I still had a long night ahead of me, but I took a break, sipping lemonade with Mama and Nana at Meemaw's kitchen table. "My charm," I announced, my nerves zinging like pinballs through my body. "My charm is my sewing. It's being able to picture just what a person needs—or wants—and making it a reality."

Mama nodded sagely. "I thought as much."

I looked past her at the fluttering curtains above the kitchen sink and smiled. Meemaw. "You did?"

"Loretta Mae dropped enough hints over the years," Nana said. "Saying you were gifted with your hands and that you'd stitch people's dreams together one day. The thing about the charms is that you have to discover them for yourself."

"Looks like all those girls' dreams are coming true, thanks to you," Mama said.

She was right. Karen wanted to sparkle and have her husband notice her. I didn't know for certain that he would, but if he didn't, he was a fool. Ruthann wanted to feel beautiful on the inside, as well as on the outside. The confidence she exuded in the dress told me she did. Miriam wanted peace, I thought, and from the look on her face, she'd get there soon. As soon as I finished her dress.

And Josie . . .

"I thought Josie was going to cry when she walked in

here," Mama said, "but in that dress, she looked like a princess."

The kitchen pipes moaned and it almost sounded as if they were saying the word "happy." Satisfaction and pride filled me. "Happy," I said, confirming Meemaw's message.

"Yes," Mama said. "She looked happy."

"You did good, Harlow," Nana said. "And let me tell you, stitching people's dreams together is a whole lot better a charm than your mama's or mine. Goat-whisperer. Pshaw," she spat out. "That was Butch's joke, if you ask me."

Mama and I laughed. Nana loved her goats more than life itself. She was all piss and vinegar. And I was floating on air. For the first time since I'd been back home in Bliss, I, too, felt like anything was possible.

Chapter 47

By eleven o'clock the day of the wedding, I fully understood an old Texas saying Meemaw used to spout off: I felt older than two trees. It was just three hours until the ceremony. By the time it was over, I was sure I'd feel older than three trees. I'd stayed up late, adapting one of my off-the-rack Maximilian dresses for Holly and it had fit her perfectly. Only Miriam's still wasn't quite done.

I had had plenty of time while I sewed to think about the new information the sheriff had revealed. The father of Nell's baby still seemed the most logical choice as the killer. He probably had the most to lose. But other than Nate, there were no potential daddies who'd been in Buttons & Bows, and the sheriff thought one of the people in my shop that day had stolen cording that had been used to strangle Nell. Problem with that was I still hadn't found hide nor hair of a single piece of cording, braiding, or any other trim that would make that odd pattern on Nell's neck.

I'd been so sure Nate was guilty that I hadn't given much thought to any other possibilities, not really, but now . . . "You can let it go," Will had said when he doctored my cuts a second time.

I'd pushed my glasses to the top of my head and rubbed my eyes. "But what if—"

"No what ifs. It doesn't matter what Nate's up to with the company. He didn't have anything to do with Nell's murder. He's in the clear. You just need to finish the dresses. You didn't promise Josie anything else."

I realized he was right, of course, but sitting on the front porch with a piece of leftover fried chicken, courtesy of Nana, and a glass of ice-cold lemonade, I couldn't stop worrying that Josie was stepping into a hornet's nest and if she wasn't careful, she was going to get stung, but bad.

I looked at my watch. 11:15. Two hours, forty-five minutes. Finally, the gate in the arbor creaked open and Miriam trudged through, the glimpse of peace she'd shown yesterday all but gone. Now she looked as though the weight of the world was on her shoulders. Dark circles and the Dallas Cowboys ball cap on her head spoke loud and clear. She'd gotten less sleep than I had, not a good look for the maid of honor of the biggest social event Hood County had seen in a dozen years.

The latch reengaged with a loud click. "Hey," I called, waving the chicken leg I'd just taken a bite of.

"Hi," she said absently, glancing at the spot amid the bluebonnets where Nell had been found.

"Isn't it hard looking at the yard, knowing someone died right there?" she asked as she came up the porch steps. "Do you think you'll ever be able to look at it the same way?"

I'd asked myself that very question a hundred times since that night. "Hard" didn't even begin to describe the spectrum of emotions I had experienced. "No, I don't think I will," I said, putting the chicken down, my appetite gone.

She needed to get into her dress, anyway. I still had a few things to finish, but until she tried it on, I couldn't wrap it up.

Just as I started to stand up, she sat in the chair next to me. "We should get started," I said, but then I lowered myself back down.

She rocked slowly, to and fro, to and fro, lost in her thoughts. "I used to think death was about the person dying and how they felt," she said after a stretch of silence.

I settled against the back of the chair and fell into rhythm with her. "And now?"

"Now I think it's more about the people left behind. I think if you believe there's something more than what's here, the moment death comes, you'll be at peace. But it's the rest of us, the ones left behind who have to deal with our grief . . . *That's* the hard part. Will I ever be able to forget her?"

What an odd question. I hoped I made a big enough mark on the world and the people in my life that they'd take joy in remembering me. "Do you want to forget her?"

Her only answer for a few seconds was the creaking of her chair. "No."

"The fact that she was in our lives means that she had an impact on us. Even on me, and I barely knew her." Her gaze stayed glued to the thatch of bluebonnets. "I'm going to put a fountain there," I said. "In memory of Nell."

She nodded, fighting the tears glistening in her eyes. "That'll . . . that'll be real nice," she said.

Will had told me to leave it alone, but one thing had been bothering me since meeting with the sheriff. I hadn't been able to get her alone during the final bridesmaid fitting, but now was my chance. "Miriam, when did your dad get back home?"

She wiped away a rogue tear with the back of her hand and considered my question. "Friday."

"That's what I thought, but I heard your mom say no one was allowed to drive his car except him. But didn't y'all come here in the Lincoln?"

She grimaced. "My mother's not allowed to drive his car," she said, "and neither am I. But the boys are."

Ah, the male chauvinist good-ol'-boy thing. "So Nate was—"

"No," she interrupted, shaking her head. "Nate had his own car. He had some meeting to go to. Derek drove us."

She started rocking again. "He and my dad both go back and forth. Home for a month, then back to the Ivory Coast or wherever it is they go. Derek's been home for four or five weeks now—"

He has?

"—and it's been a nightmare. Ever since—" She stopped and gnawed at the corner of her fingernail and snuck a glance at me. "All they do is fight. They can't hardly stand to be in the same room with each other."

I stopped rocking, trying to sort everything out. "Miriam, you just said Derek drove 'us.' Were you there? Did you come into my shop that day?"

"Only for a minute. I waited in the car."

"You know Nate has an alibi. When Nell was killed, he was on a trip somewhere."

She sighed and allowed herself a small smile, the first one I'd seen from her since I'd been back in Bliss. "South Texas. I heard. I . . . I was so afraid maybe he'd done it."

"Why?"

She shook her head. "I can't . . . I just . . . it was a mistake."

I thought about how Miriam had said it was her fault Nell had died, and how Nell had been hiding Josie's ring in a button jar. I stopped rocking again. "Did you tell Nell where Josie's first engagement ring was? Is *that* how she was able to steal it?"

Her eyes popped wide and she gawked at me. "What?"

"The day she was killed, she hid the ring in the shop. I found it—"

Her voice came out in a faint whisper. "Where is it?"

I held my hand up, stopping her. "It's safe." I didn't add it was in Meemaw's safekeeping. I suspected Meemaw hadn't known what Nell was up to, thus the rogue leg and shattered mason jars. But as I'd finished the bulk of Josie's dress, I'd recounted aloud everything about the murder case, hoping she was listening.

"She was hiding it for me," Miriam said. "*I* stole the ring."

I tried not to react, keeping my rocking chair rhythm steady. Whatever I'd expected, it hadn't been Miriam copping to a jewelry theft.

"I gave it to Nell to hold and now she's dead."

"But you're the only one who knew Nell had the ring,

besides Nate, right? And he wasn't in Bliss when Nell was killed—"

She covered her face with her hands. "Oh, God," she moaned. "All I want is to keep Holly safe. If anything happens to her . . ."

I squeezed her hand, willing enough strength into her to get through the wedding. "It won't, Miriam. Just tell me who—"

She looked through me, like she was looking into the past. "It's not Nate. It was never Nate," she said.

Chapter 48

"Diamonds," Miriam said.

"A girl's best friend," I said.

She said, "Nate."

I said, "Innocent."

It felt like we were playing a word-association game. Either that or rewriting the lyrics to that old 1970s song "Undercover Angel." She said, "Derek." I said, "Shiver." I still couldn't believe I'd dated him, even briefly. It was better left forgotten.

She said, "Diamonds" again.

I said, "What about them?"

"This is going to sound crazy, I know, but hear me out." She took a deep breath before saying, "I think Derek is using the family company to illegally import diamonds."

She could have hit me with a wispy yard of organza and sent me flying clear to East Texas. The Kincaids were oil tycoons, for pity's sake. Diversification of a stock portfolio was one thing, but going from black gold to conflict diamonds when you were already billionaires? I almost laughed.

"Why would you think that?" I asked.

She launched into the story. "I was at Nate's office a few weeks ago for a board meeting. Holly had to stay after school, but she'd lost her cell phone and I hadn't replaced it yet. I gave her mine so she could call me at home when she was ready to be picked up. Anyway, I went to Nate's office a little early to talk to him about this idea I had to open a bookstore. I wanted Nate to invest in it."

"Right. I heard your dad talking to Will Flores about it at the party the other night."

"Nate was tied up with his secretary, so I waited in his office. His cell was on the desk and he got a text. I thought it might be Josie, but it was from Derek."

She shook her head like she still couldn't believe it.

"What did it say?"

"It was cryptic, but he basically said that it was too late for them to stop the next shipment and that Nate was an idiot if he thought it was going to be easy to get out."

"And you think he was talking about diamonds?"

She nodded, falling silent as a couple of kids ran past the porch, their parents strolling behind them. "I didn't have much time, but I scanned some of Nate's old texts. He and Derek went back and forth over the size of the first diamond Nate had put into a ring, and then argued about how to get the second diamond. Nate asked when the next shipment was scheduled and where it was coming from. I've been researching how it's done," she continued. "Someone acts as a dealer. That person sells them to another dealer across two countries' borders. Eventually they end up here. Diamonds can be exported from one country to another. A dealer doesn't have to show where they came from, only certification from the country they're leaving at that moment. Nate didn't kill Nell, but he and Derek are in deep."

I couldn't tell her what I was thinking—that Nate was probably scheming to blow the whistle on the operation. The night Nell was killed, that had to be what he'd been working on. "And if Nate didn't kill Nell, you think that—"

"Derek did."

She got up and paced the porch. "They're my brothers. I know you must think it's warped, but how can I turn them in? It'll kill my mother. It'll ruin the family name. And the wedding—" She collapsed into the rocking chair again.

At least now I understood why she'd dropped out of

the wedding party, but it didn't help me figure out how she should handle this.

"Nell always seemed to 'get' my family. I could talk to her and she'd understand. I didn't know what to do, so I asked her. She told me that everything would work out. She said she'd hold on to the ring for me while I figured out what to do."

"And you think Derek found out?"

She nodded. "And if my brother wants something, especially something he thinks is his, he'll do whatever it takes to get it."

A chill crept up my spine. I wondered if doing whatever it took this time included murdering Nell.

Chapter 49

Mama showed up at the shop door and prevented us from any further discussion of the Kincaid family. She back-combed Miriam's hair, giving it just the right amount of Texas volume. Meanwhile I finished the side seams of her dress, helping her into it when her hair and face were done.

She looked in the mirror, and I watched that sense of peace visibly flow through her. "It's beautiful."

The mint green linen, cut with a slight flare at the hem, had turned out exactly as I'd envisioned it. It brought out her Irish heritage, the rusty highlights in her hair vibrant and bold.

I sighed, relieved, knowing that my charm was working its magic with Miriam. She wanted peace. That's what I'd given her. Whatever happened, it would all be okay for her. I hoped.

By the time she left, Mama and I had less than thirty minutes to make ourselves presentable for the wedding. "I'll see you there," she said, hurrying out the door to get herself ready. I took the stairs two at a time, speeding through a shower in record time, pulling my wild hair into a slightly less wild updo, and shimmying into my all-time-favorite shapewear slip.

With no time to deliberate, I chose the first dress I saw in my closet, an off-the-rack navy-and-white number that looked a little like the outfit Debbie Reynolds wore in *Singin' in the Rain*. I grabbed hold of the hanger, but instead of coming off the closet rod, it didn't budge. "What the—" I tried again. Stuck like glue.

It didn't take long to realize why. "Meemaw! I don't have time for this."

Just like before the Kincaid Family Foundation gala, the clothes in my closet suddenly slid back and forth along the rod. It felt like we were on a rocking ship, the clothes sliding to the right as the boat tipped to starboard, crashing to the left as it lurched to port.

I lunged, reaching into the fray, trying to grab hold of a dress. Any dress. The wedding was going to start in twenty minutes! But each time I almost got hold of one, thinking I'd won the battle, the hullabaloo in the closet snowballed and I was forced to stagger back. "Loretta Mae Cassidy," I said, stomping my bare foot on the cool hardwood floor. "Are you *trying* to make me late?"

The chaos in the closet stopped, but of course there was no answer. She made the pipes moan and fluttered curtains when it suited her, not when it suited me. But a chiffon floral print dress, courtesy of a Maximilian surplus sale, slipped off its hanger and fell to the floor.

I was too tired to think, anyway, so I grabbed it and slipped it over my head. It had a five-inch empire waist with black accent trim, a faux halter top where the fabric actually draped down the center of the back and reconnected with the waist, and a full skirt. Large lavender, pink, and cream flowers were complemented by touches of coral, green, and a lot of dark gray for contrast. The instant I zipped up the back, I felt flirty and feminine and wondered why I'd never worn it.

I adhered to Heidi Klum's general philosophy of a garment accentuating either boobs or legs, but not both. I took a quick look in the mirror. The flirty dress hit my legs at midcalf, floating over my hips, long enough to cover the scrapes and cuts still visible on my legs, and while the V neck wasn't deep, it did just enough to accent my 36Bs.

As I slipped on a pair of strappy lavender sandals, my mind processed everything Miriam had told me. It was so much easier to believe Derek could be responsible, but something about it didn't feel right. It felt like part of the story was still missing.

I headed for the stairs, stopping short and bolting back to my dresser. I'd wrapped the little velvet jewelry bag in the stack of napkins I'd taken from Seed-n-Bead and had hidden it in my lingerie drawer the night before, but something in my gut told me I shouldn't let it out of my sight. I grabbed the whole wad, shoved it in my purse, and raced for the hallway. My heels clicked as I hurried down the stairs. I really was late now. Why hadn't I asked Mama to come pick me up? Why hadn't I had the battery replaced in Meemaw's old truck? Without a car, I'd have to walk. I grabbed the doorknob, yanked the door open, and bolted..."*Oof!*"...right into someone's chest.

"Whoa. You've really got to be more careful," a playful male voice said, gripping my shoulders, pushing me back slightly. I caught glimpses of a black jacket and slacks, white dress shirt, and solid, faintly metallic forest green tie. A shiver swept over my skin as I looked into the face of the dashing man darkening my doorstep.

Mercy.

"It's my door," I quipped, shocked at the flirtatious note in my voice.

"That it is. I thought—" Will stopped in midsentence as he got a good look at me, then let loose a low whistle. "Wow. You look...That's a...I mean, wow. You look...stunning."

The heat of his Rhett Butler accent made my heart give a little pitter-patter.

"I thought you might need a ride," he said.

Aha, now I understood the drama in my bedroom. Meemaw had *wanted* to keep me here, though how she'd known Will was coming by was a mystery. The ceremony was set to start in two minutes. I grabbed my clutch and slammed the door behind me. "I'd love a ride."

I tapped my foot impatiently as he got behind the wheel. The Catholic church was only a few blocks away, but it felt like hours. "Where's Gracie?" I asked when I realized we were alone.

"She wanted to be there early to help Holly with the flower girl bit." He bit his lip like he was keeping a secret.

I smiled, the coil of nerves in my stomach untwining a bit. "What?"

"Miriam dropped the sewing machine off after the funeral. Gracie's been staying up late every night working. You've inspired her."

I swelled with pride. "Really? What's she making? Is she using a pattern? Tell me everything!"

"Whoa. I have no idea. She dragged the bins into her room and went to town. As long as she's not working on her own wedding gown, we're good. I want her thinking about graduating from high school and college, not white dresses and veils."

"Good plan."

Not a soul was in sight as we pulled up to the church. No surprise there, since the ceremony was probably already starting. We hurried through the double doors into the vestibule. "There you are! Where have you been? Never mind!" Ruthann grabbed me by the arm, wrenching me away from Will's side. "We need your help. The veil Josie got was supposed to go with her first dress. It doesn't work with this one!"

The veil! We hadn't tried it on with the dress yesterday. I kicked myself at the oversight.

I threw an apologetic look over my shoulder at Will as Ruthann hauled me off. He lifted his hand in a motionless wave. Maybe it was my imagination, but he looked disappointed.

Ruthann dragged me into the bridal room off the side of the vestibule. Karen and her husband stood just outside the doorway. She looked beautiful in her dress, glowing with a confidence I hadn't seen in her up till now. She gave Ted a dreamy smile, which he returned with a kiss. Score one for dreams coming true.

He headed off to the sanctuary and Karen followed me into the room. Talk about bedlam. The room looked like a tornado had spun out of control, destroying everything in its path, except Josie. She stood smack in the center of the room, the skirt of her gown fanned out around her, looking serene amid the chaos.

"She's here!" Ruthann announced.

I tossed my clutch aside as Miriam handed me the veil. We locked eyes for just a minute, silent encouragement passing between us.

Josie's gown, with its silk and pleats and hand beading, was classic and ethereal. The veil was poufy and looked like it belonged with a prairie wedding dress.

I set to work reconstructing it, clearing out a space on the floor and laying it down. "Scissors," I said, like a surgeon requesting a scalpel.

Someone immediately put a pair in my hand. I cut the tulle to elbow length, removing the second layer. I cleaned up the edges and stood. "Bobby pins."

The bridesmaids were like highly trained OR nurses. Bobby pins magically appeared in my hand. I spun Josie around. Her hair was pulled back into a doughnut-sized bun, wispy strands of loose hair framing her face. I pinned the veil underneath the mound of hair on the back of her head, letting it cascade artfully down her back.

"Perfect!" Karen said.

Ruthann squealed.

We turned at the knock on the door. Josie's mom came into the room. She fanned herself with her hand. "You look beautiful, m'ija," she said in her thick Spanish accent.

Josie's smile was as brilliant as the illegal diamonds on her finger. "*Gracias, Mama.*"

"*Lista?*" Mrs. Sandoval asked.

Josie let out an excited sigh. "Ready." Before I left, she gave me a hug. "I put this dress on and every worry just melted away, Harlow." She swung her arm out, gesturing to the bridesmaids. "I don't know how you did it, but it's like you somehow brought out the best in us." She squealed, grinning up at the ceiling. "And in a few minutes, I'm going to be Mrs. Nate Kincaid."

Chapter 50

Lucky for me, I didn't have to choose between sitting with Mama or sitting with Will since they'd somehow managed to sit next to each other, and only five rows from the front of the church. Will stood, letting me pass by so I could take the spot between them. Many of the same people who'd been at Nell's funeral were here to celebrate Josie and Nate's wedding. The senator and Mrs. Zinnia James. Ted Mitchell.

The Kincaids were in the second pew on the right side of the church, while the members of the Sandoval family and their friends sat on the left side. Madelyn Brighton stood at the front of the church toward the left side of the altar. I leaned over to Mama, pointed to Madelyn, and whispered. "What's she doing?"

"Looks like she's taking a picture."

She sure was. Her camera was aimed straight at us. She hadn't mentioned that she was the official photographer of the wedding of the year in Hood County. I caught her eye, lifting my shoulders in a question. She responded with an innocent shrug, notching her chin up and smiling.

Seconds later, the music started with the traditional Canon in D and the processional began with Ruthann gliding down the aisle, followed by a stunning Karen. Madelyn snapped pictures, moving around the church like a ghost, shooting from all angles, like a photographer at a runway show.

Holly was next, looking magical in the dress I'd altered for her. Miriam paused at the end of the aisle before starting down. She gave a cursory smile. I glanced around, confident that I'd been the only one to notice how strained it was.

But Derek's presence, standing next to his brother at the altar, was too much for me to ignore. The suspicions Miriam had shared with me about her brother put a damper on the event and the pride I felt when I looked at the bridal party's dresses. The smug smile he directed at Ruthann as she floated to her place, followed by the surprised arch of his eyebrows as he noticed Karen, made the muscles in my jaw twitch. He passed over his niece, glowering as Miriam glided down the aisle and a wave of indignation crashed over me.

Miriam might not feel able to tell the sheriff what she suspected her brother of doing, but *I* could.

Will leaned over and whispered, "You okay?" just as the first notes of the Bridal March played.

As we stood and turned to face Josie, I grabbed my cell phone from my clutch. "Fine," I whispered back. Josie started down the aisle on her mother's arm and a collective gasp flowed through the church. She was captivating. Her hair, her figure, the dress—the whole nine yards, literally. It was all perfect.

Madelyn was at the end of the aisle snapping pictures. A warm glow surrounded Josie like a protective aura. I wondered if *that* would show up in Madelyn's photographs.

Nate, waiting for her at the altar, somehow managed to look boyish in his black tux. The priest greeted the congregation and we sat. The bride and groom had eyes only for each other, but my gaze roved, taking in every detail.

I saw diamonds everywhere. On my mother's right hand, where she wore the ring Hoss McClaine had given her. On Karen's wedding band. Diamond studs in Miriam's ears. Derek's college ring, a miniature of his father's, flashed with diamond specks. A sparkler glinted from Ruthann's right hand. Mrs. Kincaid was weighted down with glistening stones on her left hand, around her neck, and at her earlobes.

Everywhere I turned, I caught streaks of brilliance.

My own naked hand immediately set to work on the material of my dress as my gaze went back to Derek. I felt like a pressure cooker, Miriam's story bubbling inside me until I thought I was going to explode.

Will cupped his hand on mine. "You sure you're okay?" he whispered.

I stopped the catlike clawing motion of my fingers. "Yeah. Fine."

"Really? Because you're giving Derek a death stare. I wouldn't want to be on the receiving end of that."

I forced my gaze back to the bride and groom. The priest was midway through his greeting, telling the story of how Josie and Nate had met, and I couldn't keep it in a second longer. I leaned close to Mama and whispered, "What's Sheriff McClaine's cell number?"

Her eyes were tearing, but she managed to gape at me. "You're going to call the sheriff now?" she whispered back.

I lifted my cell from my lap. "No, I'm going to *text* him." My index finger was poised over the touch pad. "Mama?"

"What makes you think I have it?"

I had an answer ready. "It's a small town. Don't you have *everyone*'s number?"

She looked at me a beat too long, like she was trying to decide if I knew something I shouldn't, but then she caved. "Tissue, please," she said as she took out her phone and scrolled through her contacts.

I riffled through my clutch. No tissue. Just the napkins wadded around the velvet jewelry bag. Thinking about the ring got me thinking about Nell. From what I knew of her, she seized opportunities. Miriam had gone to her with a problem, and Nell had added two and two together and seen diamond-studded dollar signs in her head.

Mama held her hand out, waiting for the tissue. I pulled the napkin off the bag and started to hand it to her. The logo on the napkin stopped me cold. Gold lettering on a textured red background.

REATA RESTAURANT.
LEGENDARY. TEXAS. CUISINE.

My conversation with Zinnia James came back to me. She said she'd seen Nell at the restaurant. Nell had a stack of napkins from Reata in her bathroom. I could hear Nell's voice as she said she'd never been there. I stared at the napkin. Then where had this come from?

The adrenaline rushing through me turned to ice. Nell had lied, but why?

I handed the napkin to Mama, who promptly dabbed her eyes, then showed me the sheriff's number.

My text to the sheriff went out the next second: *Whistle-blower*, and I held my breath to see if he even had his phone with him.

He shifted in his pew, reached in his jacket pocket, and a few second later, my phone vibrated. *Who is this?*

Harlow! I texted.

And? he messaged back.

I could sense his annoyance through the satellite waves. And, I wrote, grateful he couldn't hear my irritation as my fingers flew across the touch pad. *Derek K— illegal diamonds.*

SEND.

My phone buzzed and I read his message. *More.* He was a man of few words.

I didn't want to send him a thesis, but I didn't want to be so obtuse he wouldn't understand my point. Miriam didn't know Nate was blowing the whistle on Derek. She went to Nell about her smuggling theory, but what if Nell was—

My phone vibrated.

"*Shhh,*" Mama hushed me, her finger to her lips.

I responded by angling toward Will, showing him the texts as I read the sheriff's message. *Miriam K knew . . . told Nell.* Then I added one word: *Blackmail.*

McClaine turned to look at me over his shoulder, giving me a quick nod; then he dropped his phone back in his pocket. Over and out.

If Nell suspected that Derek was dealing in illegal diamonds, would she have tried to blackmail him? If she did, and Derek paid, she would have been able to pay back the money she'd borrowed from Karen and Ted to buy the bead shop.

But what if it was more than that? What if *Derek* had gotten Nell pregnant? It still didn't explain why she'd lied about never having been to Reata, but she had been horribly wrong if she'd gotten it in her head that she and Derek plus baby made a family. From what Will and Mrs. James had both said, the Kincaids wouldn't have welcomed a pregnant Nell into their home, Derek's child or not.

I tried to focus on the wedding ceremony, but Nell's death skulked in and out of my thoughts. I couldn't stop thinking that Nell had risked it all—and lost.

An hour later, the ceremony was over, we'd made our way to the banquet room catty-corner from Bliss's Opera House on one corner of the square, and I was still unraveling the threads of my tangled thoughts.

The room was an organized sea of round tables covered in white linen tablecloths. Triangular folded napkins, silverware, water goblets, and wineglasses sat at each place setting. Instead of vases filled with cut flowers, fresh Easter lilies in pale green ceramic pots, softened with shimmery white organza ribbon, dressed each table.

The room was festive with white, pale olive green, and lavender helium balloons strategically placed at the entrance, next to the deejay's speakers, and at either side of the buffet tables. Twinkling white lights edged the exposed beams of the ceiling and dotted the cascading rose trees on the cake table, the buffet table, and around the room.

It was magical—if only it hadn't been tainted by murder. Josie was effervescent, floating from table to table, Nate by her side. Karen snuggled close to her husband. She'd told me that Nell's will had been read and she was now partners with Josie. I hadn't thought she wanted to own the bead shop, but I'd never seen her look happier. Her husband's adoring gaze probably helped.

Gracie glided up to us wearing a sleeveless dress, a fabric purse slung over one shoulder and cutting a diagonal across her body. "Wasn't that beautiful?" she gushed.

She reminded me of Liesl in *The Sound of Music*, ready to break into song and dance. Looking at her, I suddenly realized why. "Did you make your dress?"

She beamed, nodding.

It was a straightforward pattern without any design lines, but she'd constructed it well. She'd used an inexpensive polyester blend. A cotton blend would have worked better for the simple shift, but for her first attempt at an entire dress, and from what Will had said, made in the wee hours of the night, she'd done an amazing job. I hugged her. "It's fantastic, Gracie."

Her flush deepened. "Thank you," she whispered, fingering the long, braided strap of her purse.

"You make the purse, too?"

She nodded, pulling the rectangular bag from her hip to show me. "Isn't it awesome? It's like a hippie purse from the seventies."

"Minus the fringe," Will said.

Reaching out, I brushed my fingers over the thick weave of the torn fabric braid with its frayed and feathery edges. The pattern was distinct. One of the three strands was significantly wider than the others so the design was lopsided. "Did you weave this yourself?"

She shook her head no. "There was a whole bunch of it in one of the boxes I got from Holly's mom. It's, like, flawed, right? Kind of uneven, but that's why I like it. Cool, huh?"

My breath hitched, half of her words fading to black. "The fabric bins? Miriam gave you those, too?"

Will spoke up. "She said she hasn't used any of it in years. Probably been sitting in a closet in her house. When she dropped them off, I thought she wanted me to take them to the rummage sale, but then she said she wanted Gracie to have fun and just experiment."

Gracie grinned. "So I made a purse."

A thread unwound from the mess of details in my

mind, and an idea began to form. I searched the room until I spotted Madelyn Brighton, and waved my arms over my head to flag her down.

Will and his daughter stared at me. "Darlin', what in the world—"

My wide-eyed look froze the words on his tongue. "Those bins weren't at Miriam's house. They were at her parents' house. Where Derek stays when he's in town," I added slowly. "And he's been in town for almost five weeks."

"Crap," he muttered, whispering, "You really think so?"

"Think what?" Gracie asked, flicking her gaze back and forth between me and her dad.

Before we could answer, Madelyn sidled up to us. "Trying for a position with air traffic control, love?"

"Moonlighting as a wedding photographer?"

She raised her voice slightly to be heard above the cacophony of voices. "The man they'd contracted with canceled at the last minute and since Bill and Nate were schoolmates . . ."

"Ah. Got it."

I took my glasses off and tried to wipe away the smudge, but my fingers trembled with nervous energy. I shoved them back on, looking past the streak. Will laid his hand on my back, infusing me with his calm mojo.

"I've been wanting to come by your shop and have you work your magic." Madelyn gestured up and down her body as if her outfit said it all. "As it is, I was forced to wear the same drab skirt and blouse I always do." She gave a spastic little laugh. "I *will* be by, now that you've finished the bridal dresses, eh?"

"Anytime," I said. I already had ideas on what to make for her. Color to bring out the emerald green of her eyes. Something a little less structured. More flowing to match her magic junkie bent. I took a deep breath and got to the point. "Madelyn, do you still have your camera?"

She patted the purse at her side. "Of course." She set it down on a nearby table.

"Is that a camera bag?" Gracie peeked at the light green interior.

"It's an *Epiphanie*," Madelyn boasted.

"I don't know what that is," Gracie said, "but I love it."

"Only the most stylish camera bag out there. Never would have bought it for myself, but my dear heart does the spectacularly unexpected sometimes." She stroked the faux leather with affection. "He got it for me the day after the party at the Kincaids', in fact."

Gracie peered up at Will with a coquettish smile. "Daddy?"

"Uh, no." He read the one word like a psychic. "First comes a camera, then a bag. Maybe."

She rolled her eyes.

Madelyn had taken her Canon out, removed the lens cap, held the camera up, and focused. "Smile," she directed.

I put my palm out. "Oh, no, not for us," I said. Her finger depressed a button and the camera clicked.

Too late.

"No?" She lowered the camera and shot me a puzzled look. "You don't want your picture taken? But you all look splendid together."

"No—"

Gracie frowned. "We don't?"

"What I mean is—"

"She means yes," Will said.

I stared at him. "I do?"

He pulled Gracie next to him and put his arm around my shoulder. "You do."

Madelyn went into photographer mode. About a hundred pictures later, she finally got one she liked.

Gracie started to wander off, but Will called her back. "Let me hold your purse for you," he said.

"I got it, Dad," she said just as Holly called to her from across the room. She held up a cup of sparkling pineapple punch.

"Harlow wants to take another look," he said. A hasty nod of my head and a wink convinced her. She handed the purse over and, with a wave, hurried over to Holly.

Quick thinker, that Will Flores.

When Gracie was out of earshot, I told Madelyn my theory. "I know patterns and design," I said. "The braid on this purse has the same sort of scheme as the markings found on Nell's throat. The *strangulation* markings," I added.

Her eyebrows shot up in surprise as she took a closer look. "You may be right."

A rush of heat swept through me. I was one hundred percent sure I was right. "Do you still have the pictures of—" I lowered my voice to a whisper and finished, "Of Nell's neck?"

Chapter 51

I tapped my foot impatiently. Will and the sheriff had been gone only five minutes, but already it felt like hours.

"How long will it take to know for sure?" Madelyn asked.

I had no idea. "I guess the sheriff'll have to—I don't know—take it to some forensics lab. In Fort Worth, maybe? Doesn't it take a while to run fiber tests?"

"It doesn't on TV, but—"

"But this is real life." So unless the killer stood up and waved a guilty hand, we'd have to wait for confirmation that the murder weapon was from the same torn fabric braid Gracie used for her purse, and that could take days.

Josie and Nate worked the room, gliding from table to table, greeting, hugging, and chatting with all two hundred of Nate's parents' closest friends. Lori Kincaid had schmoozing down to an art and she was teaching it, on the fly, to Josie. She led the newlyweds, made introductions, said something witty, and stepped back as her son and new daughter-in-law spread their social wings.

She whispered to Josie as they moved to the next cluster of guests. But Josie hung on every word Nate uttered, gazing at him with adoring eyes.

"He really loves her," Madelyn commented.

Nate looked at Josie with equal adoration. "He sure does."

There was still no sign of Derek.

Josie's mother and aunt were already seated. They each had their hands primly folded and resting on the table. The aunt looked like she wished she could be anywhere else, but Mrs. Sandoval's expression was filled with hope. Just like Mrs. Kincaid's dreams for Nate, or any mother for that matter, it was clear that Mrs. Sandoval wanted nothing more than for her daughter to be happy.

If Derek's indiscretions came to light, the Kincaids would be dethroned, forced to relinquish their title as first family of Hood County. I hoped the love Josie and Nate had for each other would be enough to weather the storm Nate was bringing on them, as well as the news that his brother, Derek, was a murderer.

Madelyn touched my shoulder. "My husband beckons," she said, pointing to her own personal professor. "Let me know when Will gets back, will you?"

"Definitely," I said. She headed off in one direction and I made a beeline for Dulce Sandoval to offer a little reassurance that Josie had done good.

But Zinnia James sidelined me. "Sugar, you look spectacular," she gushed. "When word gets out about Josie's gown and the bridesmaids' dresses—and the next Kincaid wedding—you'll be turning customers away at the door . . ."

Her voice slipped to the background as I quickly scanned the room looking for Derek. I didn't see him anywhere, but noticed that Ruthann had found herself a handsome man. With her posture, her dress, and her demeanor, she reminded me of a politician's wife. Or an oil tycoon. That girl needed to get out of Bliss. She seemed destined for bigger things.

"Mark my words, your designs are going to be featured in *D* magazine," Mrs. James was saying. "The festival and pageant this summer, followed by the fashion show in the fall, will put you on the map. I can see it now."

I hoped she was right. "Thank you, Mrs. James," I said, then asked, "Who's that with Ruthann?"

She peered at the table I indicated. "That is George Taylor."

"Ah," I said. "So *that's* what an eligible bachelor looks like." I'd hoped Ruthann would find someone classier than a man who talked about his conquests.

She raised one eyebrow. "If you say so."

I laughed. "Ruthann told me how he's one of the most eligible bachelors in town. Maybe they'll start dating."

"Hmm. Young people don't give it much time, these days, do they?"

"What do you mean, Mrs. James?"

"Oh, it's just that I thought she was involved with someone."

"No, I don't think so."

"Odd. I must have been mistaken, then," she remarked.

"Mrs. James, remember how you told me you'd seen Nell at Reata?"

Her sharp eyes flashed. "Of course."

"I know you said you couldn't tell who she was meeting, but do you think it might have been Derek Kincaid?"

"Until the day that poor girl died, I hadn't laid eyes on Derek Kincaid in more than six months."

Did I hear her right? "You saw him the day Nell died?"

"Twice, actually. He was driving his mother—so thoughtful. He sat in the car while everyone gathered in your shop. I did see him talk to his brother for a few minutes, and Jeanette McDaniels's daughter, Ruthann, over there, she chatted with him for a while. Then I saw him later that night, you know. Very odd."

She started to sashay off, but I stopped her. "Are you sure it was the same day?"

Someone called to her, but she turned, holding a finger up, then said to me, "I specifically remember it was that night because I heard about the murder the next morning."

"Where did you see him?" I asked, hoping it was near the crime scene. He could have taken that braiding from his parents' house, met Nell at Buttons & Bows, taken care of his mistress and blackmailer all at once, and been done with it.

"He was down at the Stockyards."

"In Fort Worth?"

"That's right," she said, and my theory flew out the window. "The senator and I met some friends at Billy Bob's. We walked in as he stumbled out with a group of people."

My hopes sank. Drinking and dancing at the biggest honky-tonk in Texas meant Derek had not been alone, and he'd also been nowhere near the crime scene.

Which meant he couldn't have killed Nell.

After the bombshell dropped by Zinnia James, I needed a cold drink. I sidled up to the portable bar, set my clutch on the stool, keeping my cell phone out in case Will texted about his status, and ordered a red wine. Two men leaned against the counter, ice tinkling in their tumblers. I sneaked a peek . . . Keith Kincaid and a tall scarecrow of a man. Their voices were low, but I edged closer after the bartender handed me my glass of wine.

Once again I put a snippet of Meemaw's advice to practical use: *Be quiet and listen.*

"Didn't think any of 'em would take the plunge," Mr. Kincaid was saying in his John Wayne voice. "Knew right after Derek graduated from high school that *he* wasn't the marrying kind. Strings plenty of 'em along, though, that's my boy! Got one practicing over there."

I couldn't turn around to look behind me, but my heart went out to whoever Derek Kincaid was stringing along.

"Even gave her a ring, the fool," his father said. "I almost did that. Stopped myself just in time, but she wound up with it anyway and, good God, it bit me in the ass."

They guffawed. Then the gangly, ginger-haired man said something, his voice so low I had to strain to hear. Something about betting on how long the Kincaids' marriage would last. "We all lost," he said. "You and Lori have stuck it out."

Mr. Kincaid gave a bitter snort. "It would cost me more to divorce her than just deal with her. No prenup. She'd take me to the cleaners. Hell, she'd sell me up the river. A few too much between us to just call it quits. Now I'm trading a homegrown hellhole for an African one. Damn money. It's an addiction."

He had a lifestyle to maintain. Once you had money, I imagined it was hard to give it up.

The redheaded friend moved right along in the conversation, never missing a beat. "Derek might fall in love someday, and if he does, he may settle down yet."

I sipped my wine. Derek Kincaid wasn't going to any chapel; he was going to jail for his smuggling activities.

"You got Nate out of the nest—"

"Only took thirty-four years," he said with a scoff.

"And Miriam—"

Mr. Kincaid saved his most bitter laugh for his daughter. "Lasted all of, what? Three years? Lori and me, least we know we're stronger together than apart."

Stronger together than apart. If they'd been spoken by someone else, those words would have been poignant and meaningful. As it was, they fell flat and made me feel just a tiny bit sorry for Mr. and Mrs. Kincaid. Whatever was between them didn't sound like love. That was not the type of marriage I wanted to be in . . . if marriage was in my future.

I caught a glimpse of a silver-haired couple. They held hands, and as he leaned over to whisper something in her ear, she giggled and batted his arm.

I smiled to myself. *That* was the kind of marriage I wanted. One that would make me laugh and smile well into my nineties.

Chapter 52

The minutes turned to hours. I'd chatted with Josie's mother and aunt, gotten a second glass of wine, and strolled the perimeter of the hall, listening for any snippets of conversation that might contain a clue that would help me unravel the final threads of Nell's murder.

I had nothing but a bunch of details that didn't seem to add up to any cohesive answer. I checked my cell phone, thinking I'd missed another text from Will. Why was he taking so long?

Josie, Nate, and the wedding party, sheltered from the potential discovery of the murder weapon, laughed and danced to Waylon, Willie, and the boys, easily transitioning a while later to the Macarena.

Mama ambled over to where I sat with Madelyn, who was splitting her time between me and her tweed-jacketed husband, Bill. She plopped a plate of food down next to the Easter lily centerpiece. As we picked at the chunks of fruit and cheese, I filled her in on the torn fabric braid Gracie had used on her purse and how the uneven pattern looked like a match to the odd strangulation marks on Nell's neck. "The thing is," I finished, "if Derek's alibi is true, and Nate's definitely not a suspect, who had access to the bins—and who else would have wanted Nell dead?"

"From what I know, that house is a fortress. Nobody's gettin' in who wasn't invited in," Mama said.

That was right. Josie had told me about the gate and how she hadn't been able to get in to give her mother the glass cleaner. For the briefest second, I entertained the idea that Mrs. Sandoval had killed Nell. She would have had access to the fabric bins with the probable murder weapon, she knew Nell was coming back to my shop that night, and she lived alone, so most likely had no alibi. But I couldn't pin a motive on her. Nell had been good to Josie, even leaving her share in the bead shop to her.

Unless . . .

Could she have somehow known Josie was in Nell's original will and killed her so Josie would inherit the equal partnership?

Karen and Ruthann came up on either side of me, wrapped their arms around me, and squeezed. "We can't thank you enough," Karen cooed. "I don't know what it is, but Ted is a changed man tonight." She stood, twirled, and grinned. "I think it's the dress."

"Definitely," Ruthann said. She pulled her arm from my shoulder, her ring catching on a particularly curly loop of my hair. "Sorry!" She freed her finger and did her own spin, dropping her shawl. "I just made a date with George Taylor," she gushed.

"No!" Karen giggled. "Wait till the wine wears off, Ruthie."

"Maybe you're right," she said. Gathering up her shawl, she grabbed Karen's wrist. "Come on. There's Derek. Now *he's* a catch."

They fluttered their fingers at us and scurried off toward Derek, who'd been watching them, that same smug smile on his lips that he'd had at the church when he'd seen Ruthann glide down the aisle.

My stomach turned watching Ruthann fall against him, as Karen scooted back to Ted. I followed Derek's arm as it snaked around Ruthann's waist. Soon they melted into the crowd.

"Which leaves Mr. or Mrs. Kincaid," I said, picking up where I'd left off.

I glanced at the chair next to me where I'd put my clutch as Mama said, "Or their daughter."

My mind screeched to a halt. "Where's my purse?" I bent down to peer under the table. I searched around my chair, even lifted my napkin up in case it had shrunk and was now a miniature version of its former self. But I didn't see the purse.

It hadn't.

"It's gone?" Mama asked, her accent deepening so that "gone" sounded like *ga-won*. "Is the . . . you-know-what still in it?"

My skin turned instantly clammy, my heart hammering in my chest. I'd set it down on the stool at the bar, right next to Mr. Kincaid, while I was listening to him regale his friend with stories of his affairs.

My conversation with Mrs. James shot into my head. She'd said she hadn't seen Derek at Reata, but that day in Buttons & Bows, she'd said she'd seen Keith Kincaid and his lawyer there plenty of times.

I whirled around, my head spinning. I slapped my hand over my mouth. "It wasn't Derek."

"What wasn't Derek?" Mama asked.

Madelyn's mouth had formed a speechless O.

"Keith Kincaid and Nell. You were right, Mama—it was a married man." And Mrs. Kincaid knew about it, I suddenly realized. That's why she'd so pointedly asked about Reata. They were stronger together than apart because they knew each other's secrets, Mr. Kincaid had said.

I searched the table and chairs one more time, just in case I'd overlooked my purse. It hadn't materialized.

I must have left it on the chair at the bar. *Please let it still be there*, I silently pleaded. I ran back to the bar while Mama and Madelyn looked everywhere else.

The barstool was empty. No purse. And that meant no ring.

Miriam sat at the head table, looking miles better than she had that morning, although it was clear that she was tired. My charm wasn't fully working with her. Curious. With my cell phone as my only comfort, I made a beeline for her and cut to the chase. "Who knows I have the ring?"

She stared at me. "I . . . I . . ."

The deejay's music pounded in my ears. The questions Will and I had talked about pumped through my mind with the same blinding rhythm. "Where did you find the ring, Miriam?"

"It was in my dad's desk. In his study," she added. "I was looking for a paper clip and ... and I saw it. After those texts, I knew it was one of the diamonds ... so I took it."

Like a trigger, I suddenly remembered Ruthann, or maybe it was Karen, saying Nate couldn't return the engagement ring to a store because of the custom diamond and that his dad said he'd take care of it. My fingers carved through my hair. How, how, how could I have forgotten that?

Cold sweat beaded around my hairline. Could Derek have pulled off a diamond-smuggling operation alone? More conversations flooded back to me. He and his dad took turns coming home. *Someone* had told me that, though at the moment I couldn't for the life of me remember who.

Another thought struck me like a bolt of lightning. I left Miriam staring at me, trying to sort out all my disjointed thoughts. The same scenario I'd worked out if Derek had been the father of Nell's baby worked if Keith Kincaid was the father of the baby. Only he hadn't been in the country when Nell was killed. If Nell had tried to blackmail him into staying with her and becoming some kind of a family, he would have relied on the one person he trusted to take care of things.

I was back to Derek.

Only Derek had been at Billy Bob's when Nell was murdered.

So who?

Where were Will and Sheriff McClaine? I couldn't ... I needed fresh air. Or better yet, the ladies' room. Across the hall. Through the entrance. Up the stairs.

I stopped at the door, more pieces falling into place. Mrs. James had said something about another Kincaid wedding, hadn't she? But Miriam wasn't seeing anyone.

Keith Kincaid's chastisement of Derek circled back to me. "Got one practicing over there," he'd said. "Even gave her a ring, the fool."

Mama had put Hoss's ring on her right hand because she wasn't ready to go public, just like . . .

I pushed open the door and stepped in before I realized I wasn't alone. Everything seemed to happen in slow motion. My purse sat on the sink, its contents spilled out on the counter. A blur of olive green chiffon. An acrylic-nailed, French-manicured hand held Josie's first engagement ring.

The scene spun together, becoming a cohesive whole.

The door closed behind me with a quiet *whoosh*. My gaze lifted. And I stared at the face of a killer.

Chapter 53

My mind suddenly conjured up the voices I'd heard outside Buttons & Bows the night Nell died. Mama and I had overheard an argument. Snippets of conversation. One quiet voice we couldn't make out, and another, agitated. It hadn't been lovers.

It had been Nell and Ruthann.

She moved like a gazelle, effortlessly positioning herself between me and the door. "Why?" I asked, but I knew the answer. I'd heard it from Lori Kincaid herself, that first day in Buttons & Bows. *It takes time and effort to maintain an image. It's like a house of cards. One bent corner, and the whole thing comes toppling down.*

"Was it the blackmail or the pregnancy?"

The vein at Ruthann's temple pulsed. "Take your pick. Both? I had to do something. She was going to ruin things for me. The pregnancy was bad enough, but, look, I'm under no illusions. I know Derek really loves me. Men like the Kincaids cheat. And Nell went after him. Mrs. Kincaid learned how to deal with it—"

"Yeah, diamonds are a girl's best friend."

She flashed the rock on her right hand. "This is my engagement ring."

"No, it's your payment for services rendered. He's been working you, Ruthann. He got you to do his dirty work—don't you see that?"

Ruthann let the ring drop into her hand, showing it to me on her palm. "Derek said Nell could keep it. It's worth forty thousand dollars. She could have sold it, raised her kid, and everything would have been fine."

"But she wanted love, not money."

Ruthann had killed Nell to protect the reputation of a family she wasn't even a part of. I didn't have a sliver of doubt that she'd do it again to protect herself.

The only way out of the bathroom was the door I'd come through. And she was blocking it. I asked her another question to keep her talking while I figured out what to do.

"Do Mr. and Mrs. Kincaid know ... what you did to Nell?"

"Derek and I planned it together. It was a game—who could come up with the better plan. When he showed me Miriam's old sewing stuff, I knew it would work. I made sure he went out with friends that night. No one knew about me and him yet." She smiled softly. "He said he wanted me to be his secret for a while longer."

My heart went out to her. She really thought Derek would stand by her, and nothing I could say would change her mind. I looked at my purse. "How did you know I had the—"

"You are so talented, Harlow, but you're not very smart. I watched you at the bar listening to Mr. Kincaid. I'd already put things together. When that shelf at your shop broke and the jars fell, I knew Nell had been trying to hide it, but Karen swept it all up first.

"Then when I saw you grab the jewelry bag from the street after the funeral, I knew you'd figured it out." She looked at her reflection, then shook her head like she still couldn't believe it. "You have such a gift. It's too bad." She methodically packed up my purse, all except the ring and the velvet drawstring bag.

My useless cell phone mocked me. I'd seen Gracie and Holly text without even looking. Me? I was quick when I was focused. Texting blind on a touch pad?

That was when I noticed it. A length of torn fabric braiding hanging from her hand.

She'd had the element of surprise with Nell, but she didn't have that with me. I kept at her. "Miriam found out about the diamonds. This family's coming apart. It's too late, Ruthann."

She swallowed, shaken. "What do you mean?"

"I mean—" I began. I heard someone approaching the restroom door. Blood pounded in my throat, but no one came in. My imagination.

"I mean, she knows that her brother is smuggling diamonds from country to country until he can bring them into the States. She knows that Nell was blackmailing the father of her baby and she was killed because of it. She told me everything," I said, holding my arms out as she took a step toward me, "and I told the sheriff."

Ruthann let out a guttural screech and lunged, but the door *whoosh*ed open, crashing into her. She fell forward, sprawling flat on the ground.

An energized Miriam careened in after her, landing on her back. I grabbed the braided cloth and wound it around Ruthann's wrists just as Hoss McClaine burst through the door.

He took one look at us, made a quick retreat, and sent in the deputy sheriff in his place. "Let's go," she said, hauling Ruthann up. "You have the right to remain silent . . ."

Chapter 54

"You could have died," Mama said after she'd heard what happened in the ladies' room.

Ruthann McDaniels was arrested for murder. Keith and Derek Kincaid were taken into custody by the sheriff until the FBI arrived to haul them both away for smuggling conflict diamonds. Not the happiest ending for Josie and Nate's wedding, but definitely memorable.

"But I didn't. No one was hurt." Except Nell.

The pink-streaked petals of the Easter lily quivered. It sat on the coffee table next to the little tin box.

"Mama," I said with a hiss.

She snapped her gaze to the Easter lily, gave a quick little gasp, and lickety-split, fisted her hands.

Madelyn cocked a curious eyebrow. "What's going on—"

Mama's effort to stop wasn't working. The flower whiffled its petals. I watched helplessly as the lily grew larger before our eyes.

"Oh!" Madelyn covered her mouth with one hand, pointing a giddy finger at the flower with the other. "Oh, look! Am I . . . is that real?" She looked at Mama, who'd cracked one eye to look at what her agitation about my encounter with a murderer was doing to the pretty flower. Madelyn's husband, Bill, was in the kitchen fixing drinks for us. Thankfully. "I knew it!" Madelyn exclaimed.

"Mama, stop!" I ordered.

Her face was fully contorted now. She was no dainty

Samantha Stevens from *Bewitched*, wiggling her pert little nose to put chaos in order. The streak in her hair looked more pronounced the more effort she exerted. Her face turned the color of a radish and she looked ready to blow.

"I think she's trying," Madelyn said, peering at Mama.

A tense minute later, the flower shivered, its petals spasming. Slowly it began shrinking, giving a final shudder as it returned to its normal size.

Mama's face went slack. She slumped back in her chair, exhausted from the effort. "I don't know what's wrong with me. I can't control it."

I snuck a look at Madelyn, the self-proclaimed magic junkie. The only way to describe her expression was electrified. She touched her fingertips to a flower petal. "I've never seen something so beautiful."

My phone buzzed and a text from Will came through. *On my way.*

Finally.

I read it to them, relieved to see the feverish thrill pulsing through Madelyn begin to simmer down.

"Is Hoss—er, the sheriff—fixin' to come back, too?" Mama asked when she'd regained the power of speech.

"I don't know." I wanted to tell her not to keep the sheriff a secret like Derek had kept Ruthann a secret, but I realized I was hiding Meemaw, keeping her to myself, so I kept my mouth shut.

A rogue thought struck me. Ever since I'd been back in Bliss, Mama had been struggling with her charm. There was nothing to warrant this change . . . except that she was in love. Was Butch's charm also a curse? Fall in love and the charm goes haywire? Was that why Nana's goats were always escaping? Was that why Loretta Mae had remained single after my great-great-granddaddy passed?

My temples throbbed as the next thought bounded into my mind. *What would happen to my newfound charm if I fell in love?*

I had no more time to think about it. Bill returned, carrying a tray of novelty glasses he'd dug out of my cupboard. He set the tray on the coffee table just as the bells hanging from the front door jingled. The door opened and, as if triggering an electrical surge, the lights flickered. A puff of air seemed to come from underneath the coffee table, fluttering the lily's petals and forcing the fabric swatches in the little box up into the air, like tossed confetti.

They danced in midair for a split second too long, landing just as they'd been—in the box.

Meemaw.

The flickering stopped as Gracie walked in, followed by Will. Hoss McClaine came in last, closing the door behind him. Everyone talked at once, but I felt the weight of someone's stare. Looking up, I realized it was really the weight of two people staring. Hoss McClaine and Will Flores both looked at me with undivided attention.

"Can you believe it?" I asked, trying to make light of what had been an intense afternoon. "We caught a murderer today."

"We couldn't have done it without you, Harlow," the sheriff said at the same moment Will said, "You almost got yourself killed, Cassidy, and that is *not* what Loretta Mae would have wanted."

Both of them had valid points. I'd done my civic duty, but now I'd do what Meemaw wanted, which was living, safe and sound, discovering family history, and forging new friendships.

I focused on Hoss McClaine. "I was lucky."

"Some people have a knack for crime solving," he said.

Will perched on the arm of the sofa. "You have a knack for dressmaking," he said. "You should stick to that."

I had a *charm* when it came to dressmaking, in fact. "I certainly will," I said.

"Luckily Bliss doesn't have a lot of murders," Mama said, "so you'll be able to stay out of danger, let the sheriff do his job, and do what you do best."

"Perfect," I said. "So we all agree. No more murder

and lots of sewing. Mrs. James will be keeping me plenty busy. I won't have time for much else anytime soon."

I felt a tickle on my foot. Reaching down, I grabbed hold of one of the little fabric swatches I'd discovered in the pile Nell had gone through. It was the one I hadn't recognized. The one that was plaid. The one I'd thought didn't belong.

I'd been wrong. A crystal clear picture of a plaid shirt suddenly danced in my mind, and I knew without a shadow of a doubt, that it was meant for Will. I smiled. I'd stick to dressmaking, just like he wanted, but I knew I'd have to make the time for a special project.

I looked at my mother and Hoss McClaine. Meemaw had brought me home to them. I looked at Madelyn Brighton and her husband, and at Gracie and Will. We sat together in my perfect little dressmaking shop on Mockingbird Lane. She'd brought them all into my life. Loretta Mae had gotten what she'd wanted, true, but I smiled, suddenly enveloped in warmth. I'd gotten what I wanted, too. I was home.

DRESSMAKING TIPS TO MAKE YOUR
SEWING MAGICAL

1. Always press the fabric at each step of your sewing project. A hot iron ensures a professionally finished garment.
2. Using elastic in a waistband: before inserting your measured elastic, mark it with stitching at the center front, center back, and right and left sides. This way, you can balance the gathers of the waist between the four quarters of the elastic.
3. Fittings aren't only for professionals! Fit your garment three to four times during construction. Try the garment on both right side out and wrong side out. Mark corrections on the wrong side, but remember to transfer the markings to the opposite side (because you'll be turning the garment right side out). Not everyone measures the same on both sides, so this is an important step.
4. Fill three bobbins with the correct thread before you start any project. This way you won't have to stop to rethread when your bobbin runs out.
5. Before you begin any hand stitching, thread several needles with the correct thread. This will allow you to keep sewing, rather than breaking your momentum by having to stop and rethread.
6. One of the most important tips is to enjoy the process. You slip into your creative zone, especially when doing handwork. Sewing can be meditative, and you should enjoy each step of any dressmaking project!

Read on for a sneak peek at the next book
in the Magical Dresskmaking series,

A FITTING END

Available from Obsidian in February 2012.

June in North Texas is no picnic. It was only seven forty-five in the morning, but the heat index was already at the extreme-caution level. The humidity didn't help the index . . . or the way I felt. The second I walked outside, the moisture clung to my skin. My curly hair, pulled up into an artfully messy ponytail, instantly frizzed. And I was one hundred percent positive that I was melting from the inside out.

There was nothing to do but grin and bear it. I knew it took a season for a body to acclimate to a region's weather patterns and I'd only been back in Bliss for a few months. I grabbed a bottle of water before climbing into my ancient pickup truck, formerly owned by my great-grandmother and recently brought back to working order by Bubba of Bubba Murphy's Repair Shop. The one thing Bubba didn't fix was the air conditioner, which meant I'd look like a drowned rat by the time I got where I was going. Far from swanky country club material, but I'd been summoned by Mrs. James. Enough said.

I opened the window as I drove, but only hot air blew over me. By the time I made the thirteen-mile drive to the Bliss Country Club, the blond streak in my hair, a trait all the Cassidy women shared, had broken free from its restraints and hung limply down the side of my face. I did my best to tuck it back into place.

The parking lot was bursting, but only a handful of golfers was on the course. Maybe they'd all woken up with the roosters and were already on the back nine. But the second I stepped inside the air-conditioned lobby of the club and heard the hushed and agitated undertones of the people milling around, I knew the back nine wasn't seeing all the action; every golfer in town seemed to be right here. Seeking refuge from the heat and humidity? Possibly, but the knot in my gut was telling me that something else was going on.

The whispering seemed to stop as I pushed through the throng of people toward the ballroom. Was it my imagination, or was everyone looking at me, and not in a *Look, it's the dressmaker, Harlow Cassidy, and isn't she an icon of fashion?* way, but in a *Let's give her a wide berth like you'd give one of the Salem witches* kind of way.

Like day-old pea soup, the crowd thickened at the doorway to the ballroom. "Excuse me," I repeated over and over, finally bursting through the choked entrance. The room, complete with the monstrous catwalk, looked just like it had when I'd been here with Josie. Except that the runway lights blazed, which was odd since it was so early.

I'd worn slacks this morning—not my usual clothing choice, but the club had a dress code and I didn't want a run-in with the country club clothing police. In and out, that was my goal. I wanted to get back to the shop, work on Libby's dress, fit Gracie for hers, and ponder the ripped gown from Meemaw's old armoire.

Mrs. James was nowhere in sight. Everything looked just as it had when I'd been here with Josie the other day. Peering at the stage, I spotted my sewing bag, just where I'd set it down and forgotten it. It had been knocked over, the contents spilled out onto the stage. When no one was looking, I climbed onto the catwalk and was just ready to scurry down it when a voice called from behind.

"Ms. Cassidy."

I spun around. Everyone seemed to be staring at me, but I couldn't see who'd actually called me. A thread of anxiety slithered through my veins. From the moment I'd walked into the club, I'd felt like something strange was definitely going on, but now I was beginning to think it had something to do with me.

Paranoia? Being a Cassidy meant people had always

looked at me as if I was one second away from casting some sort of spell on them, but this . . . this felt different. Less cautious suspicion and more morbid curiosity.

I started down the runway, stopping short when I heard my name again. "Harlow Cassidy?"

This time when I turned around, the runway lights were like a spotlight and Rebecca Quiñones, reporter for channel 8 news, looked up at me from the end of the catwalk. She held a microphone at her side, her navy skirt and cream-colored blouse were crisp and unwrinkled, and her slick black hair was a ribbon of silk flowing down her back. I patted my own limp hair and wondered how she withstood the brutality of the weather. "I'd like to ask you a few questions," she said.

I put my palm to my chest. "Me?"

She flicked a look at the man who stood off to her side. He nodded, flipped a switch on the bulky black television camera perched on his shoulder, and suddenly I knew we were rolling.

"You *are* Harlow Cassidy?" Rebecca Quiñones asked.

I opened my mouth to respond, but before I could answer, she went on.

"The same Harlow Cassidy who owns Buttons and Bows? You're a custom dressmaker and fashion designer—is that right?"

"That's right," I said, the coil of nerves that wound through me tightening their hold. How did she know who I was, and why would she care?

"What's your relationship with Macon Vance?"

My mind raced. I closed my eyes for a moment to think. Behind my eyelids, streaks of color and memories smeared. "Macon who?" I said. If it was someone from my childhood here in Bliss, I couldn't remember. "I think you have the wrong person."

"Macon Vance, Ms. Cassidy. The golf pro for the country club."

"I don't know him," I said as I turned around. I needed to find Mrs. James, do what I had to do to get Gracie on the schedule for the pageant, and get home to work.

I heard the dull thump of rushing footsteps and suddenly Rebecca Quiñones was in step with me, albeit on the ground next to the catwalk instead of on the platform itself. "Isn't that your sewing bag?" she asked, pointing to the end of the stage.

Suddenly I saw that Sheriff Hoss McClaine had crouched next to my Dena Rooney-Berg nanny bag, which I used for my travel sewing kit.

"Y-yes." Red flags shot up in my mind and my mouth grew dry.

"And what do you keep in your sewing bag, Ms. Cassidy? Needles? Scissors? Tape measure?"

The same items that could be found in any dressmaker's sewing bag. Criminy, the woman was persistent. I pushed my nerves aside, gathered up my gumption, stopped walking, and turned to face her. "Why do you ask, Ms. Quiñones? Do you have a rip in your skirt that needs mending?"

She gave a smile, and I wondered if the effort would crack her makeup. It didn't. But it did show me that even her teeth were perfect. Straight and pearly white, the perfect contrast to her olive skin. "No, Ms. Cassidy. My skirt's fine, but thanks. Actually," she said, growing serious again, "I'm wondering if you had a personal relationship with Mr. Vance, and if so—"

"I don't know any Mr. Vance," I said, cutting her off.

"Macon Vance? The golf pro here at the club," she repeated.

I shrugged. "I'm not a member here."

"That's right. You're here . . ." She paused and tilted her head to the side. "Why *are* you here?"

"I'm a dressmaker," I said. "I'm making a gown for one of the Margarets." Or three if you counted the one I'd finished and Gracie's, even if she wasn't officially a debutante. Yet. "If you'll excuse me, I'm looking for someone."

As I approached, the sheriff suddenly stood, his voice raised. "Dust it," he said to one of his lackeys. Rebecca Quiñones watched me. Behind her, the cameraman was still rolling. "I wouldn't be surprised if the sheriff wants to take a closer look at your sewing supplies, Ms. Cassidy," she said. There was a snarky little edge to her tone that made me think she knew something I didn't.

"Why?" I said, hesitating. Why was the sheriff here, anyway, and what needed dusting?

Rebecca Quiñones stared at me. "You mean you haven't heard?"

I looked around, noting the odd mix of somber voices and bustling activity. Suddenly, I felt like I'd been transported back to the porch of 2112 Mockingbird Lane, watching a crime scene unfold in front of me. The same feeling I'd had then—one of helpless shock—came over me. It couldn't happen twice, could it? Not another . . . *murder*? "Heard what?" I said, my voice as somber as the newscaster's expression.

"The golf pro, Macon Vance." She pointed a perfectly manicured acrylic nail in the direction of stage left. "He was found murdered and I believe the sheriff was just about to take your bag, and everything in it, into evidence."

The breath suddenly left my lungs, heat spread to my cheeks, and a wave of dizziness slipped over me. "Murdered?" I looked back toward my bag of supplies, and noticed something I hadn't seen a minute ago. My inexpensive orange-handled Fiskars were on the ground, a good couple of feet from my bag, like they'd been dropped in a hurry. I started, a lump catching in my throat. They didn't look right. The blades were open and stained with something dark. "How?" I asked, barely choking the words out.

Rebecca Quiñones had followed my gaze. From the corner of my eye, I saw her wave her microphone. The cameraman moved in closer, getting a tight shot of me. I tried to turn my back, but Rebecca said, "Stabbed," and I froze. Because I suddenly knew what the dark substance on the shiny blades of my sewing shears was.

Blood.

Amanda Lee

The Embroidery Mysteries

The Quick and the Thread

When Marcy Singer opens an embroidery specialty shop in quaint Tallulah Falls, Oregon, everyone in town seems willing to raise a glass—or a needle—to support the newly-opened Seven Year Stitch.

Then Marcy finds the shop's previous tenant dead in the storeroom, a message scratched with a tapestry needle on the wall beside him. Now Marcy's shop has become a crime scene, and she's the prime suspect. She'll have to find the killer before someone puts a final stitch in her.

Stitch Me Deadly

Trouble strikes when an elderly woman brings an antique piece of embroidery into the shop—and promptly dies of unnatural causes. Now Marcy has to stitch together clues to catch a crafty killer.

**Available wherever books are sold or at
penguin.com**

OM0046

Sofie Kelly

Curiosity Thrilled the Cat
A Magical Cats Mystery

When librarian Kathleen Paulson moved to
Mayville Heights, Minnesota, she had no idea that
two strays would nuzzle their way into her life.
Owen is a tabby with a catnip addiction and
Hercules is a stocky tuxedo cat who shares
Kathleen's fondness for Barry Manilow. But beyond
all the fur and purrs, there's something more to
these felines.

When murder interrupts Mayville's Music Festival,
Kathleen finds herself the prime suspect. More
stunning is her realization that Owen and Hercules
are magical—and she's relying on their skills to solve
a purr-fect murder.

**Available wherever books are sold or at
penguin.com**

Also Available

Leann Sweeney

The Cat, the Quilt and the Corpse
A Cats in Trouble Mystery

Jill's quiet life is shattered when her house is broken into and her Abyssinian, Syrah, goes missing. Jill's convinced her kitty's been catnapped. But when her cat-crime-solving leads her to a dead body, suddenly all paws are pointing to Jill.

Soon, Jill discovers that Syrah isn't the only purebred who's been stolen. Now she has to find these furry felines before they all become the prey of a cold-blooded killer—and she gets nabbed for a crime she didn't commit.

"A welcome new voice in mystery fiction." —Jeff Abbott, bestselling author of *Collision*

Available wherever books are sold or at penguin.com

OM0009